Boyd Anderson has one previous novel, *Children of the Dust*, written in collaboration with Rory McCourt. *Errol, Fidel and the Cuban Rebel Girls* is his first solo flight. He lives in Sydney, but goes to Penang to eat.

ERROL, FIDEL and the Cuban REBEL GIRLS

a novel

BOYD ANDERSON

UQP

First published 2010 by University of Queensland Press
PO Box 6042, St Lucia, Queensland 4067 Australia

www.uqp.com.au

© Boyd Anderson 2010

This book is copyright. Except for private study, research,
criticism or reviews, as permitted under the Copyright Act,
no part of this book may be reproduced, stored in a retrieval system,
or transmitted in any form or by any means without prior
written permission. Enquiries should be made to the publisher.

Typeset in 12.5/16 pt Bembo by Post Pre-press Group, Brisbane
Printed in Australia by McPherson's Printing Group

The University of Queensland Press uses papers that are natural,
renewable and recyclable products made from wood grown in sustainable
forests. The logging and manufacturing processes conform to the
environmental regulations of the country of origin.

Cataloguing-in-Publication Data
National Library of Australia

Anderson, Boyd.
Errol, Fidel and the Cuban rebel girls / Boyd Anderson.
9780702238567 (pbk)
9780702238253 (pdf)
Castro, Fidel, 1926 – Fiction.
Flynn, Errol, 1909–1959 – Fiction.
Cuba – Fiction.
A823.4

For Oola, my small companion.

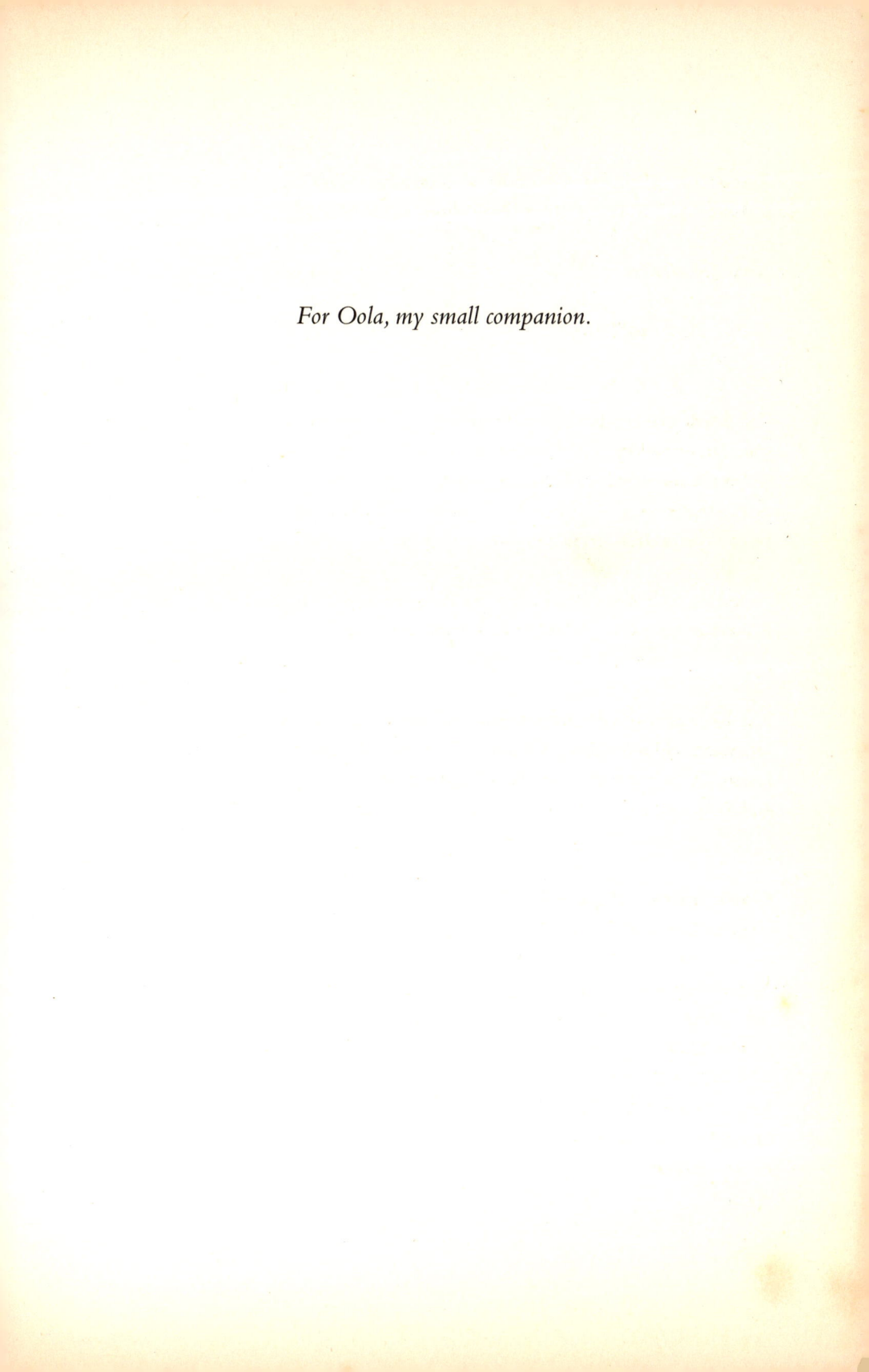

'You once liked the blissful mobility, but then you wonder, who's the real you? And who's the chap on the screen? You know, I catch myself acting out my life like a goddamn script.'

– Errol Flynn

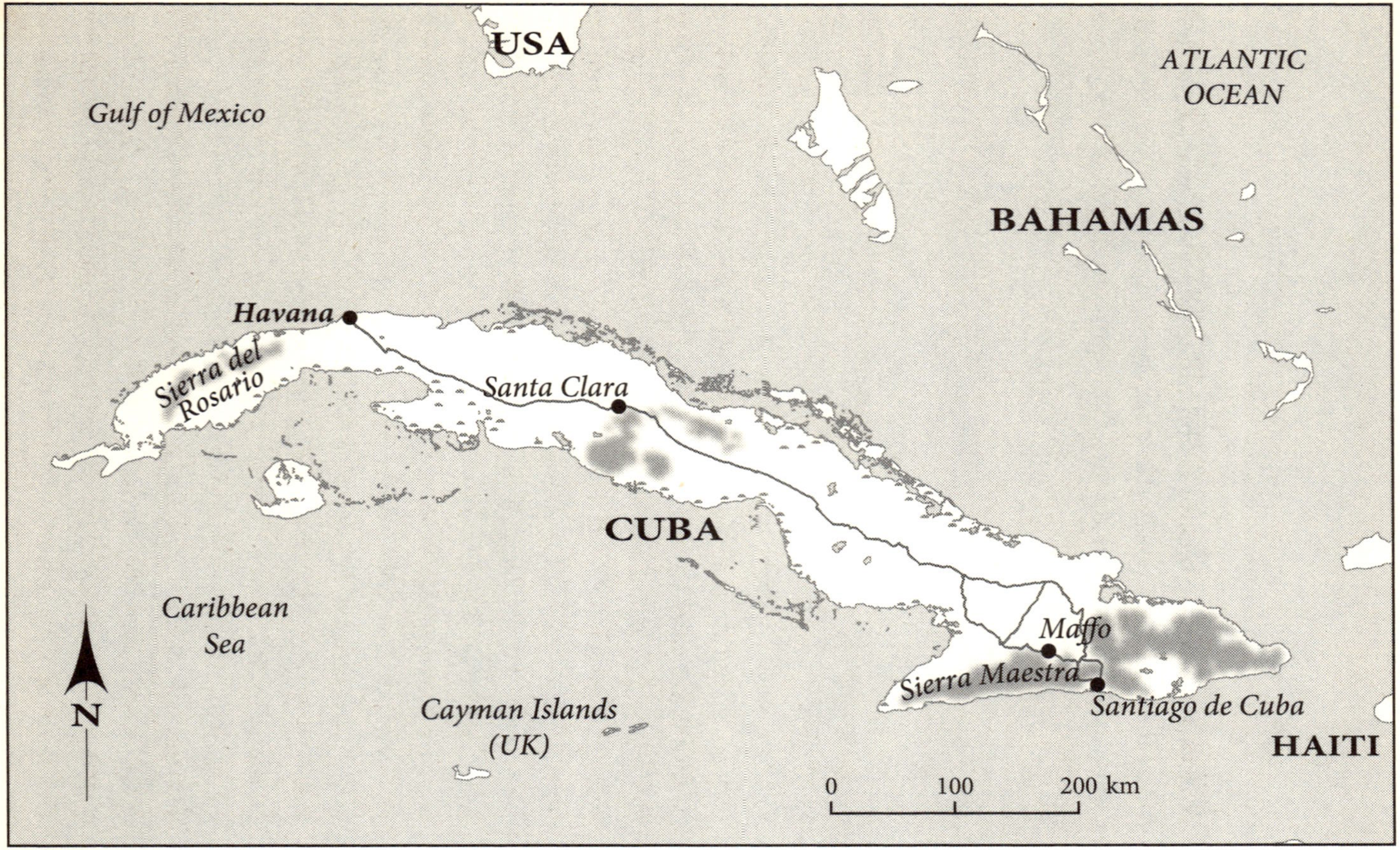
USA
ATLANTIC
OCEAN
Gulf of Mexico
BAHAMAS
Havana
Sierra del
Rosario
Santa Clara
CUBA
Caribbean
Sea
N
Maffo
Sierra Maestra
Santiago de Cuba
Cayman Islands
(UK)
HAITI
0
100
200 km

Havana, 15 October 1959

Fidel did not care for the tango, but what to do? The record was a gift, and Che was such a good friend, such a famous companero. *The Argentine rhythms played softly on the German hi-fi in the corner of the suite, a* bandoneon *squeezing out a bordello mood above searing strings. The mood he didn't mind. He liked to have the lights on when he was in bed, pink lights under pink lampshades, and the windows open and the curtains pulled back. There was a cool breeze off the harbour at this time of night and the windows on the twenty-third floor caught it nicely. Who needed air conditioning? Who needed power? Who needed* yanqui *engineers? Who would dare, even if they could, look through these windows? He lay there letting the breeze play across his bare chest. He could feel it tickle his* pinga. *The girl on the left, the dark one, was too close, the sweaty skin of her buttocks sticking to his. He blew cigar smoke across her face. She didn't stir. He raised his leg and kicked her onto the floor, all legs and hair and wobbling* tetas. *She squealed and woke the girl on the other side, the fair one with the creamy skin, who grunted and sighed and stretched a hand blindly to stroke his cheek. He let her long nails get caught in his beard and then blew smoke in her face, too. She opened her eyes and smiled and took the cigar from his mouth, lay back and drew on* it heavily, like a man. He liked that about this one. The other one crawled back up onto the bed.

There was a tentative knock on the door. 'What?' said Fidel. Nothing happened. 'What?' he said, louder this time. The door opened slowly, just a crack.

'Pardon, companero,' said a disembodied voice. 'I have news.'

'Well, come in,' Fidel said impatiently.

Chico took one step into the room, his eyes lowered, fixed on the olive green rebel cap in his hands.

'Well . . .?'

Chico quickly looked up. All he could see of his prime minister were the dirty soles of his feet, his pinga flopped across his thigh, and his cigar sticking up into the air like a submarine's periscope. 'Word has come, companero. It is Senor Flynn. He is dead.'

Fidel raised his head from the pillow to look at him. 'You did this, pistolita?'

'No, companero. His heart did it, they say.'

Fidel snatched his cigar out of the woman's mouth and considered it, rolling it between finger and thumb, this symbol of the revolution, watching the smoke rise in a funnel and then dispersing in intriguing patterns into the humid atmosphere of the room. This was the symbol. Not H Upmann. H Upmann was not a symbol of anything but corruption. This was a Romeo y Julieta, a true revolutionary cigar. H Upmann was dead, gone the way of el heroe sintetico. Gone the way of Don Juan.

'This is good news,' he said. 'He was a son of a bitch.'

'Yes, companero,' Chico said. He turned to leave.

'Tell Raul,' Fidel said. 'We will forget him now.'

'Yes, companero.'

'We will never speak of him.'

'No, companero.' Chico disappeared.

Fidel stuck the cigar between his teeth and patted the fair one's closest teta, marvelling at how the shiver played across it and then settled, and *patted it again, fluttering his fingers over the nipple until it hardened and sat up for him. He took it between his lips and flicked it with his tongue and spat it out. He turned to the dark one, raised his leg again and planted his foot into her rump, sending her tumbling once more to the floor. He stepped over her and crossed the room. He flicked the arm of the record player, sending it screeching across the grooves, and turned on the radio. He twisted the dial through the Miami stations that played Cuban rumbas, persisting until eventually hearing a sad* guajira. *That was what he wanted to hear. A lament for* el heroe sintetico. *Every man deserved a lament, even that one. But he knew it wasn't really for the Don Juan at all. It was for himself. How he missed the uncomplicated times in the Sierra Maestra. He looked out the window over the harbour under moonlight and blew smoke into the breeze, closing his eyes and opening his nostrils to it as it drifted back into his face.*

'Revolution *is in the air, Don Juan,*' *he said in English.* 'You *son of a bitch.*'

1
People don't get killed in movies.

Port Antonio, 9 August 1958

Okay, I was dead. Me, that son of a bitch. I had finally fulfilled the predictions of countless doctors, studio heads, gossip columnists and women of my acquaintance and given up my faithless ghost. And it's typical of that damned Fidel that he should try to upstage me at such a significant point in my life's drama. To get his entrance in first, as he has just done. I suppose I shouldn't really blame him . . . I've done both to him on occasion, as you will see. But what he has also done by getting in first is to rearrange history, another knack of his. The fact is this story doesn't start with him on the twenty-third floor of the Hilton. It doesn't start in Havana at all. You could say it should really start in Tasmania, after all it's where I was born, but that's far too long ago and way too far away. Fidel never wanted it to be told, which is the main reason why you haven't heard it until now. But it was never his story to tell. History is written by its winners, which means this story is mine, and so I'll choose where to start it. Jamaica.

Port Antonio, to be exact. A quiet little neck of the Caribbean woods, 500 miles from Havana as the crow flies, or two hours as the plane flew in those days. I had just written in the first draft of my memoirs that I considered myself barely halfway through my life's span and was now considering my prospects for the second half. You might say I was deluding myself: how to top the first fifty years of what many good judges (me included, I'm not too shy to admit) said was one of the century's most bizarre lives? If I had known that in fact I had just one more year left in me it might have caused my toes to curl up right there and then. But I was happy enough in my delusion and had no idea such a fate awaited, in spite of countless warnings. There and then I was actually consumed with the consideration of two pressing problems, and it is with these that the story should begin because they were the reason our paths crossed, mine and Fidel's. Mine at the end of everything, and his at his beginning.

I had recently returned to Jamaica, which was now 'home' as much as anywhere in the world, from six months on a draining location shoot in French Equatorial Africa. *The Roots of Heaven*, that one was called. More like the roots of hell. I'd had to contend with 130-degree heat, wild animals, relentless insects, exotic illnesses, sick and dying crew, John Huston, Orson Welles and recurring bouts of malaria. You can take your pick which was the most difficult to endure, although my own pick would be Orson, The Boy Wonder. There's only so much bombast and bitterness I can take, so many old hat magic tricks, so many hours spent waiting while he argues the toss with the director about how to shoot a scene. I agree with Rita Hayworth when she divorced him: I couldn't take his genius anymore.

The exertion had taken its toll on my body in an unusual way. Oh yes, I had been given two years to live, but that was fifteen years before. Now I seemed to have lost the ability to (not to put too fine a point on it) enjoy what I enjoyed most, and was most famous for enjoying, and what was living without that? My second problem was not nearly so novel – I was broke.

I was in no doubt that the years ahead were going to be difficult and the memoirs, even if they sold a million, would still leave me high and dry. They would leave me high and dry because the last few years had drained every last drop. Not of vodka, of course, there was still plenty of that, and as I lay there deep in thought I took a decent swig to remind me of the fact. But just about everything else had been drained from me, bled from me by the vampire. Lili Damita, past wife, present bloodsucker. Like a Salamaua leech. *In Like Me*, that's what I was going to call my memoirs, and at least that was shaping up to be something I was happy with. *In Like Me*. Clever, huh? And I thought it would show the bastards of the press and the bastards of Hollywood who could take a joke. Wait till they get a load of it, I thought. All those twittering vaginas and all those Hollywood has-beens who needed a publicity department to make their lives sound interesting. All I ever needed a publicity department for was to keep a lid on mine. Now they could read all about it for themselves, and then they'll see that 'in like Flynn' is no laughing matter. If that's what you think of me, boys, I'll really give you something to think about. Lili can think about it, too. Lili the leech. There's still plenty left in the bucket to tip a good load on her. She's got everything, she can have the bucket, too. Feed the load to her latest girlfriend. Let the bitch wallow in it, Lili, then lick it off. You were good at that. Are you still good at that, you twittering vagina? Still good with the tongue, are you Lili? I'll bet you are. Man or woman, no fucking problem.

'A penny for your thoughts, Cap'n.'

The sweet bird of youth interrupted my bitter musings. 'They'll need to be worth a lot more than that if we're to save this sinking ship, my sweet.'

'How's your drink?'

My free hand instinctively hunted around under the sun-lounge for the Zubrowka. 'Still got half a bottle.'

'You're slowing up.'

'Slowing up or slowing down, it's age, you know. It gets harder when you're ...'

Christ! What did I say *that* for? Was it some sort of Freudian slip?

'Go on,' she said, like she hadn't even noticed.

'Well, let's just say that some things get harder, others don't. Come and sit beside me. Help me finish this stubborn bottle.'

'Don't be so tough on yourself,' she said as she lowered herself onto the sunlounge. 'It'll come back.'

'Of course you would think that,' I said. 'At fifteen you can afford to wait. What am I talking about? At fifteen it just doesn't happen in the first place.'

'Forget it. Think about something else. What are you doing out here, anyway?'

'What am I ever doing out here? I'm lazing under my favourite almond tree with the glorious green Caribbean at my feet, the most marvellous view in the world, and the most singular libation in my hand, and the smallest companion a man ever had at his beck and call. What more could a fellow want?'

'Is that what I am? Your small companion? You make me sound like a dog.'

'Ah, Woodsie, you don't know how a man longs for a small companion. It's the kindest thing anyone has probably ever said to you.'

'I don't know about that.'

'No, and neither do I, because I have no idea what anyone else has ever said to you. But I can't imagine anything kinder. Or more heartfelt. Come here.'

I reached out between the lounges, taking care not to spill my drink, and she took my hand. I pulled her over, pulled her right on top of me, the coconut oil on my chest making her slip all over it. 'Someone will see,' she said, although not convincingly.

I adjusted to the extra weight, taking the pressure off an old 'war wound', which was my wishful thinking for a couple of fractured vertebrae sustained by Captain Blood in a battle with a Spanish galleon on a Hollywood backlot. 'Who's to see? Earl's gone. There's no one in the house, and we're too high.'

'When did Earl go?'

'Didn't he say goodbye to you?'

'Doesn't matter,' she shrugged. 'I'm glad he's gone. I didn't like the way he talked to me. Like I was some schoolgirl or something.'

'Oh, honey, maybe if you hadn't called him a doorstop. He's just a bit old-fashioned.'

'Why do you need him, anyway? You can write yourself. Why do you need him?'

'Well, sometimes you just need someone else to put a bit of discipline into what you write. You know me. Discipline's not my strong suit. But that's what a ghost writer can do.'

'Yeah . . . Earl the ghost.'

'Well he won't be haunting you anymore,' I said before draining my glass. She refilled it and took a sip for herself. I watched her swill it from cheek to cheek as she closed one eye to consider. 'Drinking at your age. You'll get me arrested.'

'Drinking is the least of the ways you've led me astray, Cap'n,' she warbled through vodka, a trickle running down her chin. She swallowed, considered some more, and then nodded. 'That one's okay.'

'Thank you, loyal taster.'

'A pleasure to be of service, your swordship.'

I stopped wriggling against her chest. Another Freudian slip or not, that remark was uncalled for. I was having such a good time with her on top of me like that and she had to spoil it. I took an irritable swig and sat up. She slipped right off me and onto the grass. 'Hey . . .' she said.

'Sorry,' I lied. 'I have to get back to work.'

'Work? What work? Earl's gone, hasn't he? I thought you were finished.'

'Thinking is work. Thinking is the most profitable work of all, believe me. And right now, if I don't think how to make some profit, then it's goodbye to all that.'

'All what?'

'All that,' I said, waving my arm in the general direction of the house behind. 'It's a literary reference. Oh, I forgot. You don't read, do you?'

She jumped to her feet and stood there defiantly. 'That's not fair. I read.'

'Fan magazines don't count. Be a honey and leave me alone to think for a bit, will you.'

She stalked off across the lawn. 'Get your own goddamn drink . . . honey.'

I allowed myself a quiet chuckle. Well, there'll be no honey tonight. At least that was something I didn't have to think about for the rest of the afternoon. A night without fear of failure, one night's reprieve. How had it come to this? This was one thing I didn't spill to Earl the ghost. In like . . . in like Rin-Tin-Tin. Who was I kidding? Bet it never happened to the damn dog.

I took a deep breath and a slow sip and watched a ketch round the rocky headland, pointing high into the wind. Home at last. Perhaps it was time to bring the *Zaca* home, too. I could get a crew to sail it to Jamaica, wouldn't have to go to Majorca to get it. I hadn't been sailing for weeks, working all the damn time, and I missed it. Sailing . . . the only pursuit worthy of the quester. Swimming, diving, they're all very well. Larking about in a speedboat has its place. But I really missed the salt on my face and the solid teak deck under my feet. The slap of two masts filled with wet sail. The slap of bare arse below decks. I hadn't heard that in ... I looked at the ketch and imagined the slap of its own canvas. It looked about a 50-footer. Not even half the size of the *Zaca*. They'd have to sail it straight from Majorca, not stop anywhere in the US or it would get seized. What Lili didn't have, the IRS wanted. Jamaica, the *Zaca*, that was just about all that was left, and unless America invaded Jamaica and Majorca, they wouldn't get them. They'd seize me too if I turned up in the States. An exile from my own country. The land of my choosing. So much tax had I spilled into their coffers over the years, I told them I was willing to forget it if they were, but they wanted blood. Blood from a stone. That's what I was, a Flynn-stone. I thought about getting Jamaican citizenship. What would that be, British? I could get British. I had enough British relatives to swing it. Not so many on mother's side. In fact, with the old *Bounty* mutineer on mother's side, maybe it wouldn't be so easy. They tend to hold a grudge, the Brits. On father's side they were mostly Irish, if you went back far enough. But Ireland was Ireland now, not part of the union. I sighed and wondered if I could get my old Australian citizenship back. It had been nearly twenty years since I'd given it up, longer since I'd been anywhere near the place. Christ, that would really be admitting it's all over. Hello, folks, I'm back. Things have all turned to shit for me, so I'm back.

I rolled my hips to relieve the pressure on my back. It felt like more than just the back this time. Could be the kidneys. They'd warned me about my kidneys. And my liver, for that matter. A Swiss doctor told me once I had a couple of days to live because of the state of my liver. Smiled when he said it, too. I guess it was his idea of breaking the news gently. I swigged down some vodka to make the pain go away and stuck an imaginary finger in the air at Dr Smiley. How much did I owe the goddamn IRS anyway? It seemed like it was a different figure every time I asked anyone. Barry was my manager, why couldn't he give me a straight answer? Who was I kidding? Barry, my manager? Barry Mahon couldn't manage a brothel on a barracks square. But that wasn't fair. Barry didn't want the job. It was forced on him. If he wasn't such a damned good pal to have around, a good drinker with a good sense of humour, I could have let him go when I no longer had any need for a pilot. Any need? Ha! Any use, was the truth of the matter. When the plane gets taken from you what's the point of having a pilot? Anyway, that wasn't fair, the crack about the brothel and the barracks. Should really take that back. Barry had always done a damn fine job of organising the parties on the *Zaca*, and that was as close as you'd care to get to a brothel on a barracks square.

What would the *Zaca* be worth these days? Half a million ten years ago, so what now? X plus renovation, plus inflation, plus reputation, minus depreciation. Barry, just put figures to all that and report back, there's a good chap. Would it get more in Spain or in the States or somewhere else? Spain? Who was I kidding? Who had the kind of money I needed in Spain? Franco's the only one with the money, and I'd be damned if I would sell the *Zaca* to that butcher. He wouldn't know what to do with it anyway. Can't take it to the States, even to sell it. Could sell it in Jamaica. A buyer wouldn't mind coming down to Jamaica to give it the once over. Better still, Cuba. All those high rollers. Gangsters and film stars. Damn the film stars. Not selling the *Zaca* to any of those cocksuckers. The gangsters were almost as bad. Cocksuckers with guns. But a lot of money passed through Havana. A hundred and twenty feet of schooner parked in the harbour could get some drunken bum excited, some Texas oilman or Chicago meatpacker with a fat wallet and a thin grasp on reality. A few of the old parties on board would get the whole damn town excited. A roll of the dice in the casino at the Seville followed by a roll in the hammock on the most beautiful damn schooner in the world. The best damn schooner in the world . . .

No. I was not going to sell the *Zaca* to a Texas oilman. She was all I had left from the good old days, and even if I had nothing else in the world, the *Zaca* would be enough. I'd go back to living on her. I'd spent years doing just that, I could do it again. Roaming the seven seas in an alcoholic fog. Floating over the surface of life. The unimaginable below, the unreachable above and the next drink shimmering on the horizon. Yes, wouldn't mind doing that again. Call out the riot squad, sir, and lock up your daughters, madam, Flynn's back in. Mr Taxman, get off your assets and take a running jump off a high liability, you're not getting the *Zaca*.

But what else? I couldn't avoid the States forever. If I wanted to make another comeback, that's the only place to do it. Where else, England, Italy? Waste of time. Tried it. Nothing in it. No point. Hollywood or bust. Zanuck had given me a couple of chances and there would be someone else to give me another. But only in Hollywood. They were even talking about Academy Awards just a year ago, after *The Sun Also Rises* and then the Barrymore part. The sun rose then, and it would rise again. I'd heard there was a new play about Barrymore in the works. I was now the definitive Barrymore, knew the man better than anyone in the last years of his glorious existence. I could play him as a tribute and no one could give him a better tribute than I. That would mean Broadway, of course, not Hollywood. New York was fine. But it was still in the States, and unless I got the IRS off my back . . .

Didn't they understand I had a lifestyle to support? King Farouk, Ali Khan, Prince Rainier . . . pals like that didn't come cheap. I had to find money. There was always the Alhambra. I only had a half share, but it had to be worth something. Why did I ever let Victor Malenkoff talk me into that deal? 'Fleen, eet's Havana, we can't meess.' Yeah, sure, Maestro. It's a goddamn movie house, not a casino. What's not to miss with a goddamn movie house? A half share in a casino, now that'd be worth something. George Raft knew what he was doing when he got into the Capri. George Raft used to take advice from Bugsy Siegel, and who did I have to give me advice? Al Blum. Al fucking Blum. Shouldn't speak ill of the dead. Christ, Al Blum was always dead from the heart down. Skimmed the coffers, cooked the books, and fell off the twig when the taxman came calling. Thanks again, Al. I'll take Barry Mahon any day. Trust beats experience every time.

I wondered if my bridges were irretrievably burned with Jack Warner. I drank a lot on the set doing the Barrymore job, but hey, that was the character, wasn't it? Some would just call it method acting. No, Cyclops wouldn't have me within a mile of his precious lot. After twenty-five years, too many burnt bridges, too much water passed under them. Jack was an arsehole, but he knew about money. What did he always say? Flynn, I can forgive you most things, but this . . . No, that wasn't it. Well, he said that often enough, but it was something he always said about money. That was the only time he ever said anything worth listening to. When the wolf's at the door, toss it a write-off. That was it. Or something like that, anyway. A tax write-off, that was what old Cyclops swore by. Swore it got him out of all sorts of scrapes. And what's the best tax write-off? A movie. A smash flop. Another Warner Brothers classic, coming to a theatre near you. But be quick. For a limited time only, short run anticipated.

I thought about my *Adventures of William Tell* project. More disaster than adventure, but what a tax write-off. Just enough in the can for a 30-minute short. About an hour and a half short, as a matter of fact. Trouble was, I wrote the cheques and my dear Italian partners got the write-off. I could do it again. This time I didn't want it to succeed. This time it had to bomb, and that shouldn't be hard. Errol Flynn played William Tell at Grauman's Chinese Theatre last night. William Tell lost.

Victor was in Havana. He had been involved in some bigger bombs even than William Tell. And made them all over the place, too. I finished my drink and took myself into the house to make the call. Victor was just the kind of producer I needed.

'Holaaaa!' Two syllables were enough to tell me Victor was on the other end of the line. Two syllables of his terrible, affected, Russian-inflected Spanish.

'Hullo Maestro,' I said. 'How's my partner in crime . . . ah, I mean in Havana? Greased any good palms lately, passed any bad cheques?'

'Fleen! And you? Sucked any good cocks?' It never failed to jolt me when Victor cursed. After all, except for his dark hair, he looked and sounded a lot like old Cuddles Sakall, everybody's favourite character actor uncle who played Bogie's headwaiter in *Casablanca* and, less famously, my comic relief sidekick in *Montana*. He was just as corpulent and had at least as many chins as Sakall, but there was little that was cuddly about Victor.

'How's it going up there, chum?' I said. 'Still too much sugar in the mojitos?'

'Always too much sugar in the mojitos, Fleen. What can you do? It is the national industry. But it is Saturday. You know how it goes on Saturday. It goes like the Chinese curse. We live in interesting times.'

Victor's adjectives were like a barometer. Things were never simply good or bad, he was never just well or unwell. 'Interesting, huh. Is that good?'

'It is only interesting. I won't know if it is good until . . . a little while yet, I think. Are you calling because you've heard the news? Concerned for your little investment?'

'What news?'

'The news from the east, from the mountains.'

'I don't know what you're talking about.'

'You what? Where are you?'

He knew where I was. I had heard the person-to-person operator tell him. 'Jamaica.'

'So . . . still playing the Captain Blood. They don't have newspapers in Jamaica?'

'Somewhere. Haven't seen one for a while.'

'Get one. Learn about our interesting times. You have a vested interest.'

'Not much of a one. You wanna buy it? You wanna be the sole proprietor of the Alhambra fleapit?'

Victor was proud of the Alhambra. I could feel his irritation crackling down the line. 'Fleen, you are talking about Havana's only art deco picture palace.'

'Okay, you wanna be the sole proprietor of the illustrious Alhambra art deco picture palace?'

'You joke, of course.'

'No joke. Interested?'

It wasn't the first time I had put such a proposition to Victor. The business of the movies had always fascinated him, from putting together a freelance deal right through to exhibiting a finished product. No interest in the creative side, of course. His dream was to produce a film that he could show in his own theatre, and I always suspected that getting me involved with him in the Alhambra late one night when my judgment had been compromised was part of the plan. But he was yet to enjoy success at either end of the business.

'Interested perhaps,' he said. 'But not until things here settle. We have not been bombed yet, but it is hard to know which way the wind will blow tomorrow.' There was always some excuse to keep the partnership alive.

'That's easy, *viejo*,' I said. 'It's August, it's Havana. East-northeast. Steady at this time of day. Maybe eight knots.'

'Fleen, you talk gibberish.'

Enough of the gibberish. Victor had a short attention span, one of the reasons for his lack of success in the movie business, and I knew I was already testing its limits. Here was his opportunity to get himself in on the kind of film he'd always wanted, a film with Errol Flynn. 'You interested in a project, then?' I said. 'Maybe shoot it in Spain.'

'Spain? You cannot make movies in Spain. Believe me, I have tried. You will lose your shirt.'

'Well, that's the general idea. I want to lose a shirt and say I lost the whole wardrobe.'

There was just the briefest of pauses as his mind latched onto the concept. 'Oh . . . I understand. You wish to write off. But first somebody has to pay, no?'

'You have to prime a pump, don't you, *viejo*? You've got good accountants. You can make it work.'

'Not in Spain, old friend. Too . . . how should I say, dangerous? What is your project?'

He'd wanted in on the William Tell deal before and was most upset when my Italian partners vetoed it. I thought he would still be interested. 'William Tell.'

'Oh Fleen, you must take me for . . .'

'It doesn't matter what it is. It could be anything. The Flaming Flamenco Dancing Zombies, for all I care. With Spanish guitars.'

'Fleen . . . comedy was never easy for you, was it?'

'I'm not joking.'

'Maybe so. But no, not just now. Later maybe. When I know how things here go. This Batista, he worries me.'

'He hasn't worried you in the past. Been most accommodating.'

'Yes . . . his accommodations may have a termination date. We must wait and see. Maybe not too long. Goodbye, Fleen.'

Batista worried him? The only time Batista worried anyone like Victor was when they were late with el Presidente's cut of the take. And what was all that about the wind? There had to be something to it for Victor to turn me down flat.

I braved the heat and the dirt of the town, the scabby dogs and wretched goats, the rum shops and calypso bands, to pick up a copy of the *Herald Tribune*. Arthur Miller had been cleared of contempt of Congress. Marilyn would be happy. God, were those two ever happy? I flicked through the pages and found why Victor was living in interesting times.

BATISTA RETREATS FROM MOUNTAINS

Cuba's President Fulgencio Batista has pulled his government troops out of the Sierra Maestra mountains in the east of the island nation leaving the highest ground in Cuba to rebels. Operation Verano had been expected to crush all anti-government resistance, but after two months the regime's 10,000 strong force has failed to defeat what is generally thought to be just a 300-man guerrilla army.

Those numbers were familiar, they had a classical ring to them. I drove back to the house and looked it up. Ten thousand men resisted by three hundred. I was right. Ten thousand Persians and three hundred Spartans. The Battle of Thermopylae. I looked up those mountains. The Sierra Maestra. The Battle of Sierra Maestra. What did Maestra mean? Maestra, maestro, master. Masterful Mountains. God, Victor, you missed your chance. Too late now, Maestro. Barry's turn now. Trust beats experience every time. Forget about Spain. Forget about William Tell. The Battle of Sierra Maestra. What a story. What a write-off.

Los Angeles was three hours behind. I phoned Barry that night to tell him I had a job for him.

'You're not in another jam down there, are you chief?' he asked quite reasonably. 'I don't gotta come all the way from LA to clean up another mess, do I?'

'Nothing like that. I've been a good boy.'

'Oh yeah? What's the matter, running low on alligators?'

The same old joke. Wasn't anyone ever going to forget about the damn alligator? 'I want you to put your producer's hat on again.'

'Oh Jesus. You know what happened last time I did that.'

'Let's just put the whole William Tell thing down to experience, eh. Now's our chance to profit from it.'

'Profit would be a fine thing. Just not with me trying to produce it.'

'Listen . . . it's a great opportunity, great idea. You've heard about what's happening in Cuba?'

'What's happening? No, don't tell me . . . Extra! Extra! Read all about it! Mob opens another casino!'

I was pleased to learn I wasn't the only one ignorant of developments in our old stamping ground. 'No, it's the rebels. Three hundred rebels have just beaten Batista's ten-thousand-man army.'

'So . . .?' I could see the incredulous look on his face. All the way from LA I could see that look that said anything that happened outside of LA was pointless.

'So . . . don't you think that's a story? It's Sparta all over again.'

'Spartacus, you mean? Listen, Kirk Douglas has already . . .'

'Not Spartacus. Sparta. It's like a legend come to life.'

'What legend would that be? Robin Hood, Custer? No, don't tell me, Captain Blood.'

Like I just said – anything that happened outside of LA was pointless. 'Don't be an arsehole, Barry. This is real. And we could get it.'

'We could get burned, that's what we could get.'

He was right, of course. And that was the whole point. But I knew I wouldn't sell this bill of goods by telling him the truth. There was no challenge for him in the truth, and if there was one thing Barry loved to buy, it was a challenge. 'Bullshit,' I said. 'It'll be a smash. And I want you to produce *and* direct.'

'Jesus, I was bad enough at just *one* of those jobs.'

'Directing is a piece of cake. Just common sense. I'll help you out.'

'And what are you doing at other times in this epic? When you're not helping me direct, that is. *Objective Cuba* starring Errol Flynn, is that about the size of it?'

'Maybe.' My thoughts hadn't extended that far, but why not? Trade off one of my old film titles, that wasn't a bad idea. Barry was smarter at this than he was prepared to admit.

'You wouldn't want to trust what's left of your reputation to me, buddy. You need a better swansong than that.'

'Who said anything about swansongs? This is comeback material. And you'll be the director. Make a name for yourself.'

'Errol, all I'll make is a fool of both of us. I can't direct. Never could, never would.'

'Barry, if that arsehole Mike Curtiz can do it, believe me so can you. I've watched him bluff his way through enough times. And Raoul Walsh, he did it with one eye closed.'

'Funny man. And you're talking about the guys who made you a star.'

'And now you can do it again. Christ, you flew Spitfires over Europe, you were a goddamn ace. You're a fighting fucking sonofabitch, Barry. You can do anything. What was that place you escaped from? Stalag something?'

'Stalag Luft Three.'

Stalag Luft Three. As if I didn't know it was the legendary Stalag Luft Three. As if I didn't know it was the greatest escape in the history of warfare. As if I didn't know Barry was a genuine war hero. They'll make a movie about you one day, I'd said to him dozens of times. In the wee small hours, a skinful in each of us, and I'd say, they'll make a movie about you one day, and the only problem with that is I'll be too old to play you. And they did make a movie about him, and not only was I too old, I was too dead. They had to get some new guy. Some guy called Steve McQueen.

'Stalag Luft Three,' I said. 'Do you know what I wouldn't give to be you? Robin Hood, Captain Blood, they only exist in movies. You're the genuine article. How many did you get out?'

'Seventy-six. I didn't get them out. I was just one of them.'

'Don't be modest, Barry. What did they call you, the tunnel king? Wasn't that it?'

'I got caught, remember? And a lot of good men got killed. People don't get killed in movies.'

'Only caught on the Swiss border. How far was that? And that was just one time. How many escapes did you make? They'll make a movie about you one day, chum.'

'Yeah,' he said wearily. 'So you say.'

'They'll pin a great big medal on you, mark my words.'

'Yeah . . . well . . .'

Genuine heroes can never resist a challenge. I could feel him weakening. 'Come on Barry. It'll be great. An adventure. And nobody'll get killed.'

'Where you wanna make this turkey?'

Right then, I knew I had him. 'Cuba, where else?'

'A turkey shoot in Cuba.'

'Just think of it, swaying palms, fragrant flowers and willing wenches. I'll tell Sloppy Joe's you're on your way, get them to line up the daiquiris and mojitos. Tell you what, I'll even cover the war for the newspapers while we're there. Get us good publicity. I did it in Spain, remember.'

Spain. My one attempt to really test myself in a genuine war, not some celluloid romp. At least that was the idea. The execution left everything to be desired. I'd talked old man Hearst into backing me as a correspondent for his yellow rags. How naïve was I about Spain? How naïve was I about Hearst?

'You won't be covering it for Hearst, though, this time,' Barry said, like I had to be reminded.

'Fuck Hearst. He's a bastard. Anyway he's dead. Gone to bastard heaven. Or bastard hell in his case. Plenty of others will be interested. Flynn's made enough news for them over the years. Now they can return the favour.'

'Yeah . . . well . . . writing for the newspapers is one thing, but who's going to write your script?'

Something else I hadn't yet thought about. What the hell . . . 'I am.'

'You?'

'Why not? I've written books. Two of them. Writing another one right now. How hard can a screenplay be? I've read so many I could write one in my sleep.'

Later that night I was sitting over my typewriter with a fresh Zubrowka in my hand. I liked to pass it under my nose and take in its herby aroma of bison grass and alcohol. I knew it was bison grass because the label told me so. There was even a long blade of it in the bottle. Beverly had gone to bed alone, as I'd planned. She was asleep, now I was going to write in mine. By convincing Barry, I had convinced myself. What a salesman! Missed my calling. This didn't have to lose money, this could *make* money. This could take me all the way back to Hollywood. Fuck you, Jack fucking Cyclops Warner. You'll be dead before I am, you bastard.

Battle of Sierra Maestra, I typed. It didn't look good. Too close to John Huston's *Treasure of Sierra Madre*. They'd just say it was stolen from a pal. Not stolen, a tribute. Like when Huston named a boat in one of his Bogart romps after a favourite old yacht of mine. No, Huston wouldn't buy it. Especially not after all our rows in Africa. A name on a prop is one thing, a name on the title page is something else. I tore the sheet from the roller, screwed it up and threw it across the room. The Battle of Masterful Mountain, I typed. Screenplay by Errol Flynn. Now *that* was a title page.

2
A higher high concept than boy meets girl.

Port Antonio, 15 August 1958

I brushed my teeth and rinsed with vodka, spitting white pasty foam down the plughole. Some would say a waste of good Zubrowka. Perhaps rum was more appropriate for this particular task. I stared at the plughole as the last of my spit slid into the netherworld. Slid into the desolate black hole that led into the sewer that led into oblivion. I had hardly left the house in days. I wondered if people could tell I had a problem. I'd lost my looks, could they tell what else I had lost. Would they see it in my eyes? I refused to look in the mirror. There was one right there above the basin, but I refused to look at it. I'd always avoided mirrors. Didn't look even when there was someone good-looking looking back. Hated seeing myself. No one ever understood that about me. All those inflated egos checking their profiles, their best angles, the fall of their hair, a mirror in front, a mirror behind, one over here, another over there, looking, checking, preening. And I did none of it. They couldn't stand it. The most beautiful face in Hollywood, by popular agreement, and I couldn't give a damn. Drove them mad. I thought about Bette Davis and laughed out loud. My dark victory over old Bette bug eyes. Beauty was everything in Hollywood, and that was the trouble. It was this face that got me into trouble, got me into Hollywood, got me into my life of shallow distraction.

I knew what I'd see if I looked now. Didn't need to be told, not even by a smug Bette Davis. That was one of the many good things about being here, so far from Hollywood: no Bette Davis in Jamaica. No Michael Curtiz, no Jack Warner ... no point going on. I didn't need to be told that my face had hardened, my neck thickened, my complexion mottled, lined, creased. Worst of all, the eyes. They had once sparkled and flashed, I had seen it for myself on the screen, under jaunty forest green or US Cavalry blue. I glistened, I know I did. Even in black and white I shone like a star, and Bette Davis hated me for it. Fuck Bette Davis. No, one has to draw the line somewhere. Oh Errol, you poor dear, look at those eyes, all puffy and hollow. I could hear the old drama queen saying it. I could say it myself, with just the right ridiculous attempt at an English accent, that affected intonation. No one plays the virgin queen better than you, Bette. She hated me saying that. *No one plays the virgin queen better than you, Bette!* And so what about the eyes? I'd never cared about my looks before, I was not starting now. What did it matter? My face was my fortune *and* my cross. *Beautesse oblige.* What could I have done with my life if I hadn't fallen for the easy path my looks offered? My face was my fortune and now both were gone. I still had my name. My name could get me another fortune. It could get any woman into bed. Not that there was much point at the moment. All I needed was marketing. That's what I always said to Jack Warner. Anyway, better to have puffed-up eyes than puffed-up ego, Bette. So nice to be in Jamaica while she was in Hollywood. One of the many and varied attractions of Jamaica. Bette Davis wasn't there. Or Michael Curtiz, or Jack Warner, or ... what was the term? Et al. Yes, et al to all of them.

'Et al to all that,' I said to the plughole that led to oblivion.

I hauled myself into the bedroom. Jack Warner was right about one thing – there used to be a spring in my step, and now my heels dragged like anchors across the floor. I sat on the bed and fixed another Lucky into the holder, clenched it between my teeth and fired it up. That old sparkle, that Lucky Strike, that lucky streak. Six days and nothing to show for it. Six days on page one. Seventeen pages, but every one of them a page one, so that doesn't count. Where was Earl the ghost when I needed him? Write it in my sleep? How true was that? How many times had I woken up with my face pressed into the keys? I wasn't an Orson Welles, I had to admit. Not that Orson would ever hear it from me. What was it he used to say? A screenplay is all about an angle, a pitch, a high concept. What the hell was a high concept? Easy for Orson. Get one *Citizen Kane* under your belt and you're a goddamn genius. Get one *Citizen Kane* under your belt and you can even get away with a stinker like *The Lady from Shanghai*. So what was the high concept for *Citizen Kane*, Orson? How does boy meets girl, boy loses girl, boy gets girl back, fit into that?

Here's one for you, Orson: Boy Wonder meets Dolores del Rio, Boy Wonder loses Dolores del Rio, Boy Wonder settles for Rita Hayworth.

Or how about this: Rebel meets girl, rebel loses girl, rebel gets girl back?

Christ!

I lay on the bed and blew smoke at the ceiling. Discipline! I needed discipline. Start with the classics. Yes, Thermopylae in the Caribbean. Rebel meets girl, Rebel goes off to fight at Thermopylae, Rebel gets victory, and the girl back. A narrow mountain pass was the whole point of Thermopylae. That was how three hundred Spartans beat ten thousand Persians. How did three hundred Cubans do it? Was Batista so hopelessly corrupt that juicy odds of 33 to 1 weren't enough for him? House odds at roulette, and not enough for that fat bastard, Batista. He was the house and still he got done, at 33 to 1. A house of cards, that's Cuba. Victor had good reason to be worried about which way the wind was blowing.

A shadow crossed the ceiling and I became aware of Beverly standing in the doorway. Without even looking I knew she was giving me one of her bored-teenager looks. 'Are you going to bed early or are you just lying there?' she said, just like a bored teenager.

'I'm thinking,' I said.

'Oh, that again. Making a profit yet?'

'I'm thinking about opening a casino in Havana. That would make a tidy profit, wouldn't it? The House of Cards. How about that?'

She shuffled up to the bed beside me. Now there was something to get interested in. 'I like it,' she said.

'You would. You've never even been into a casino. No, I'm not thinking about Havana, I'm thinking about Jamaica. What's so good about Jamaica?'

'It's where the writers of the Bible got their description of Paradise.'

'Christ, you sound like a vulgar travelogue.'

'Well, that's what you said to Earl, isn't it? Don't you remember?'

Remember? I could barely remember Earl. Half the time I spent telling him my life story was in a boozy haze, which I suppose was appropriate as a boozy haze was half my life story. 'Did I? Remind me to have a word with the editor. No, I'm thinking it's not so much what *is* here that's good, but what's *not* here. People, mostly.'

'Hmm. I'll tell you something else that's not here, and it's *not* why I like Jamaica, because I don't like this thing not being here.'

'I see. I don't spy with my little eye something beginning with . . .?'

'T.'

'T. Ummm . . . tail. There's not much tail here, is there?'

There had not been much tail for far too long. I had always had this irrational dread of castration and had never been able to figure out where it came from. My mother, said the amateur shrinks so free with their opinions. But the same amateur shrinks said it was irrational. What the hell did they know? They were women. What could they possibly know about castration? Or the futility, the desolation, the *decrepitude* of incapability? What could they know except the understanding smile and the hollow absolution?

'TV,' she said. 'There's no TV.'

'Spoken like a true adolescent. You miss your Leave it to Beaver, don't you. Something beginning with B. Beaver. Not much of that here, either. Anyway, you've got that one wrong. I *like* Jamaica because there's no TV. No TV in Paradise. No Captain Blood reruns, no Robin Hood, no squirming through the fucking Sea Hawk. No reminders, no rear-view mirrors, no reason to . . .'

'Go on.'

I didn't want to go on. I just wanted to stare at the ceiling. 'What do you thirst for, Woodsie?' I said, staring at the ceiling.

'You want another drink?'

'No, I mean thirst . . . yearn for. Your heart's desire, your holy grail?'

'Holy grail?'

'Yes, your life's great quest. Ah, forget it . . . you're fifteen. You don't have a life yet.'

She flopped into a chair, frowning and pouting at me. 'I have a life. How can you say I don't have a life?'

'If you don't thirst for something . . . you don't have a life. I'm nearly fifty. Do I have a life? Do I have . . .'

She looked at me. I just blew smoke out of the corner of my mouth in a long sigh. What was the point of having this discussion with her? 'Why are you looking at me like that?' I said. 'There'll be no talk of suicide tonight, my pretty. I've got a future in front of me now. I just need a high concept to make it all fall into place.'

'What's a high concept?'

'Aha! That's the sixty-four-dollar question, isn't it.'

'Sixty-four *thousand* dollar question, and if you ever watched TV you'd get it right.'

'What's a thousand between friends?' I said. 'Or even sixty-four thousand? Or to be precise, between my own inadequate high concept of the question and yours is 63,936 dollars. Now, that ain't hay, my dear. Frankly, my dear, I *do* give a damn about 63,936 dollars these days. Maybe I should be aiming higher, like you. A higher high concept than boy meets girl. Washed up old has-been meets girl. That's a concept. Not a particularly high one, though.'

'You still haven't told me what it is.'

'If I knew, Woodsie, I wouldn't be lying here staring at the ceiling. Somewhere else to start . . . a story must have a hero, says my friend Orson, who studied the Greeks. Or if you really want to stretch yourself, an anti-hero. Like Charles Foster Kane.'

'Who's he?'

'Before your time. No, I'm complicating things. Stick with the hero. A good story must have a hero.'

'Like what? Robin Hood?'

'Don't remind me.'

'Why? I love Robin Hood.'

'He's twenty years younger than me.'

'Don't be so hard on yourself.'

'Oh, we're not going to do that again tonight, are we?'

'I'm sorry, I didn't mean anything.'

I knew she didn't. That's the thing with young girls – they have yet to hone their cynicism. That's one of the many things. 'Never mind,' I said.

'A good story needs romance,' she said. 'You should know, of all people.'

'Romance in the jungle? A bit damn uncomfortable. Believe me, I've just been to deepest darkest Africa, remember?'

'Oh? So what sort of romance did you get up to there?'

'Just a figure of speech, Woodsie. Anyway, with all the poxes in the water over there . . .' I stopped again for another vacant sigh. I had to keep reminding myself that there was no point.

'What?'

'Ah . . . nothing.'

'It's not Africa, I told you.'

'Yeah . . . so you say.' But it had to be Africa. I knew it. What else could it be?

'So . . . in Cuba . . . do they have women rebels?'

'Who knows? Anything's possible. It's Hollywood. Or an approximation thereof. Anyway, it's not women we need. No parts for Ava Gardner or Rita Hayworth in this rebel jungle romance epic adventure. No tired old broads. It's girls we want, rebel girls . . . like Lita.'

'Who's Lita? One of your old conquests? One of your, what do you call them? Glittering . . . ?'

Another thing young girls have yet to hone – jealousy. Yeah, sure, they get green-eyed in an ingenuous kind of way. They pout and throw tantrums, too, just like their mothers. But their tantrums don't extend to throwing kitchen knives or taking you for everything you've got. Beverly knew she was onto a good thing with me, and I suppose she knew I wouldn't be around forever, in spite of my bravado. I could be a good springboard for Beverly, and that was fine by me.

'No, Woodsie,' I said. 'Lita was a genuine rebel girl. A rebel girl in Spain they cut in half. A courier, not a fighter. They never gave her a chance to be a . . .' It came to me suddenly. I sat up on the bed and the holder was bouncing between my clenched teeth, ash dropping all over my shirt. 'I've got it, Woodsie!' I grabbed the holder from my mouth and pointed it at her. 'Attack of the Rebel Girl. Girl meets rebel boy, girl loses rebel boy, girl becomes rebel girl to get rebel boy back. Now *that's* what a high concept is.'

'Where are you going to find a rebel girl?'

'I've got one right here. Attack . . . no, too outer space . . . *Assault* of the Rebel Girl. Hang on, why stop at one? Assault of the Rebel *Girls*. Starring Errol Flynn and Woodsie. I beg your pardon, Woodsie . . . starring Errol Flynn and Beverly Aadland. Stick that in your pipe and smoke it, Orson!'

A rebel girl. I could see she liked that. She crawled across the floor to the foot of the bed, took hold of my feet and pulled herself up, slithering up my legs, across my stomach, my chest, purring until I gave her that pleased-with-myself look, and growling until she saw the eagerness was coming back. She got to my chin and bit the stubble gently. 'That's a great idea, Cap'n. So that's a high concept, is it?'

'A high in the sky fucking apple pie till you die concept,' I murmured.

'Ooh, what's that?' she said. 'What's that I feel?'

'Aiming higher, Woodsie. I'm just aiming my concept higher. Big boy meets sweet girl.'

'Tell me that story, Cap'n. Make it romantic.'

She was fast asleep, breathing steadily, a gentle rasp coming from somewhere deep in her throat. I stubbed the cigarette in the ashtray, sending half a dozen butts tumbling to the floor, fixed another to the holder and lit it. Lucky Strike. Every time I saw the words a picture of men scurrying around like termites on a New Guinea mountain flashed before my eyes, men so desperate to find those two words they were willing to trade their health for the rest of their short lives. And sailing a schooner up the Sepik and blackbirding and shooting Birds-of-Paradise out of the sky and dodging poisoned spears and smuggling diamonds and rigging cockfights and stealing diamonds and buying dusky virgins . . . I could summon up a picture of every crazy adventure from those days. Did I still have an interest in two claims 8,000 feet up that mountain, or had I lost them? Or had I dreamed them? Oh, yes, 1,500 pounds I made on that deal. More than I could have dug up in ten years on that godforsaken miserable mountain. Fifteen hundred pounds . . . and blew it all on a boat. A boat and a poker game. That's my story and I'm sticking to it. A boat that sailed me right up the coast of Australia. How many men had done all that before they turned twenty-one and then rescued Olivia de Havilland from distress at least a dozen times as well? Rescued her a dozen times and bedded her not once. Best not to, I'd have broken her, cut her in half. Seen one woman cut in half, didn't ever want to see another. What I was going through now was simply natural. To every thing there is a season, and my body needed a rest. I'd been told that enough times. How I believed it now. And I'd been told every other organ in my body was starting to fail, so it stood to reason that one would too. The poor bloody thing had permanganate of potash shoved up it so many times, not to mention Christ-remembers-what-else, that it was a damn miracle it *ever* worked properly.

I looked at the little face of an angel half buried into the pillow. Woodsie, my wood nymph, my Sandra Dee doll, my Lolita. When would they be making the film of Lolita? Would they really dare? I knew they wanted me. I'd played a lush or two recently, got good reviews, now they wanted me for Humbert Humbert. Who better? Like the reviewers said, just playing myself. But if they wanted me then they had to have my wood nymph, too. That was the deal. What better way to thumb my nose at the world? Young girls, they'd been whispering for years behind the backs of their hands. Where there was smoke there had to be fire, and there was no bigger fire than my farce of a trial in the early years of the war. So big it knocked Hitler, the Japs, the whole damn war off the front pages day after day. How terrible, they whispered. Such young girls. Like I was the only man who had ever behaved in such a manner. Didn't anyone read history anymore? Didn't they know about all those kings, even 'respectable' English ones? And emperors, especially Chinese ones. Didn't anyone travel anymore? Hadn't they been among the Africans, the Arabs, the Islanders . . . the Mormons, for Christ's sake? Didn't they go to museums? When they gushed over Paul Gauguin's use of bold colour and stark contrast, did they whisper, 'Yes, but have you heard about his thirteen-year-old wife?'

Lolita. I was really looking forward to that.

My own Lolita was my opportunity for bold colour and stark contrast. She was my blank canvas, primed for use, carrying no taint. I could mould her, shape her, fill her head with my views on life and her mind with ideas. And in return, she wouldn't use me, try to corral me and then take everything I had when she found she couldn't. Older women always wanted more than I was prepared to give. This one observation I was ready to concede to the amateur shrinks – my issues with older women started with the very first. My mother. And my modus operandi for dealing with them, too. I simply ran away.

I nudged my Lolita with my elbow. Nothing. I nudged again, harder. She grunted. I shook her shoulder.

'What . . . ?'

'Did I ever tell you about the time my boat capsized and I had to swim across the Sepik River with my Kanaka boys, and the District Officer was on my tail?' I waited.

Her face was in her hands. She blinked into the bedside lamp, hair plastered into the creases of a frown right across her forehead. 'What . . .?'

'Yulu got taken. Crocodiles everywhere. He screamed. It was terrible. I felt one brush my leg, but we made it across. All except Yulu. I don't mind telling you, I shook for days after that.'

Her hands crawled up her face again. 'You told me . . . you told Earl . . . you read it to me . . .'

'Did I? I forget. Ever felt stark terror? You can't be afraid of death after that.'

'Why'd you wake me up?'

'It's all right. Go back to sleep.'

She grunted and threw herself onto her other side, pulling the sheet up over her head. I took a sip of vodka. A false dawn. No epic romance again tonight, not even a one-reel wonder. I said it was Africa, she said it was all in my head, and if I was honest with myself, I knew she was right – big boy meets sweet girl, big boy lets sweet girl down, sweet girl goes to sleep, big boy escapes from crocodile . . . again. It was all in my head. That's where everything was these days.

I climbed out of bed and stood up straight beside it. I bent to touch my toes, pain shot up my spine and I got no closer than a foot from them. There was a time when I could touch the floor, palms down. I pushed my hands lower, willing them closer, bending my back and ignoring the pain with stabs at my feet, stretching the hamstrings that wouldn't be stretched, ignoring the pain behind the knees as well and got an inch closer, and then an inch-and-a-half. I straightened up and felt the blood rushing into my heavy legs. A surge of new life. I did it again, spreading my feet a little to get another half-inch, and another. A little weight in the saddlebags would help. I bent again holding a bottle of vodka by the neck in each hand and got another half-inch, and then I was touching my toes with the bottles. I straightened and felt a tingle in the back of my thighs, all the way from knees to buttocks. A tingle that even seemed to remedy the pain. I strode around the room in a circle. Yes, I was striding. I would do this every day, and one day there would be a spring in my step. Or was it all in my head?

3
Every New York hoodlum, his dick is in Cuba.

Havana, 30 August 1958

Flashbulbs popped, people stared, a girl squealed. There was always a girl to squeal. The crowd at the airport parted like the Red Sea, parted as if I were the great Charlton Heston and not just the once-great swashbuckler striding across the concourse, cigarette holder pointed jauntily in the air, blonde on the arm, trolley piled high with bags trailing in my wake.

'Fleen! Always such a disturbance when you arrive.'

'It's called a scene, Maestro, an entrance. Entrance is everything, old man. One of the three golden rules. How are you?'

'You must tell me one day the other two.'

I raised my head. People said it was my stock-in-trade, the baronial air, but what I was really doing was fancying myself as a lion sniffing the breeze. 'Aah, smell that, Woodsie. That's Cuba. The air rich with cigars.'

'And rum,' said Victor.

'How's Havana, Maestro? Has it missed me?'

'Eh,' Victor shrugged. 'You know Havana. Same old poverty in the back streets, same old gangsters in the front. Who is your little friend?'

'Woodsie, meet the Maestro. Victor meet Woodsie.'

'And so many bags,' Victor said. 'It can't all be tennis racquets. How long do you plan to stay?'

'Open ended, chum. Got my survival kit right here.' I showed him my small leather briefcase with FLYNN ENTERPRISES blocked in gold. 'A few necessary medications and a Bible. All a man really needs. Woodsie, on the other hand, well, you know how kids are. Had to bring the whole toy box, didn't you, honey?'

Beverly scowled at me and pointedly turned her attention to a display of postcards outside a shop. I strode up to the counter and bought myself a tin of a hundred Egyptian Dimitrinos and threw my pack of Luckies into the trash. I tucked the tin under the arm with the briefcase, clutched the wooden case of the portable typewriter in the other, and we marched through the terminal, causing turned heads and delighted whispers as we went, a procession of three and a trolley of matching luggage. Already I could feel that spring returning. Gaiety and romance, that was what the travelogues promised you'd find in Havana and they were right, as far as that goes. I'd had some wonderful winters in this town and just the thought of them, as hazy as they were, was enough to almost revive the spring. The Dimitrinos helped. Dimitrinos always reminded me of winter in Havana. And the typewriter – I was returning as a writer, not a playboy. I could look bloody Hemingway in the eye.

Victor struggled to keep up, heaving his bulk from side to side with each step and patting sweat from his brow. Keeping up with me had always been a struggle for Victor. Beverly sashayed. I knew that's what she would call it, because she had seen them do it on the Steve Allen Show, the dancers, when they walked they walked like ballerinas moving with confident poise to their positions. Sashay, she called it, because she'd heard that word and said it suited those dancers and their walk. So she was sashaying through the terminal on the arm of Errol Flynn. *Get a load of this, you all.* I thought I knew Beverly pretty well.

'Where have you put us up?' I asked Victor. 'Nothing too new, I trust.'

'The Nacional, of course,' Victor said. 'They are looking forward to seeing you. Everything is forgotten.'

'You'll love the Nacional, Woodsie. Elegant, right by the seafront. The games aren't even rigged. My favourite hotel in Havana.'

'He is in good company there,' Victor said to Beverly. 'It was Al Capone's favourite, too.'

'It's got a fabulous swimming pool,' I said to her. 'About thirty strokes, end to end, and a cabana club, very popular. You can be a water baby all day long. I spent months at the Nacional once, making a film, a couple of years back.'

'Everyone remembers,' Victor said.

'You just told me they'd forgotten,' I said.

'Merely an expression. Perhaps all they remember are the good parts.'

'Maestro, they were all good parts.'

'Not in that film,' Victor said.

I stopped to size up my partner in Havana in his crumpled Panama suit with short pants and open-toed sandals. 'Cuddles, when will you ever listen to me? Your wardrobe desperately needs attention. And you can't wear white. Fat bastards like you should steer clear of white.' Victor hated me calling him Cuddles, so I used it sparingly to boost its effect.

'It is what one wears in the tropics,' he sniffed.

'So, in St Petersburg, did you dress like a Cossack?'

'You know nothing about Russia, Fleen.'

'I know they don't speak with affected Spanish accents, *viejo*.'

We were followed in our limousine by a taxi for our luggage.

There was a bottle in the little bar in the back of the seat and I twisted it around to read the label. 'Where's the good stuff, chum?'

'It is Cuba,' Victor said.

I poured myself a Bacardi, lit a cigarette and stretched out. 'We'll have to get ourselves a better class of limo service.'

'This one *is* the better class. All the best gangsters use it.'

I swigged a mouthful of rum and spied a sunroof. I drained my glass, opened the roof and stood straight up, holding imaginary reins and whipping imaginary horses into a gallop. 'Hi-ho Silver!' I cried. The wind blew the cigarette out of my holder. I considered the emptiness of it, and sat down.

'You are a child, Fleen,' Victor said wearily, fanning himself with his Panama hat.

I fixed myself another cigarette. 'There was a time, Maestro, when they said that every boy in America would have traded his best baseball bat and glove to be me.'

'There has been a war since that time,' Victor said. 'The boys have grown up.'

I lit my cigarette and said to Beverly, 'One thing you'll learn about Victor, Woodsie, he has no sense of humour. Life ceased to be funny when a plane he was supposed to be on crashed into the Mediterranean without him. He's not supposed to be here, you see, and it concerns him.'

'You did not even know me then,' Victor said. 'And you do not understand the concept of destiny.'

'A Comet, wasn't it, Maestro? Never trust British aeronautical engineering, my friend. The British do ships, not planes, and destiny's got nothing to do with it. You were simply too late, and it wasn't the first or the last time you've got it wrong, only that time you got it wrong and it happened to be right. I live in hope the same will prove to be the case with our association.' I stuck the holder back between my teeth and peered through the window at dazzling light, vivid paint and cheerful *habaneros*. As far as I knew, ever since the Spanish had been kicked out, daytime in Havana had always been dazzling light, vivid paint and cheerful *habaneros*. 'There doesn't seem to be much excitement on the streets. All looks the same to me. I thought the citizens would be on edge, getting barricades together, preparing to repel the barbarians at the gate.'

'The barbarians are one thousand kilometres away in the mountains. When they get to the gates I will tell you. This is something I will endeavour to get right.'

'So many Cadillacs,' said Beverly. 'I swear, you don't see so many Caddies even in LA.'

'You will see many cars here you don't see in LA,' Victor said. 'Cars with machine guns, especially. Look for the green ones that have no shine.'

'No need to scare the girl, Maestro,' I said. 'She's a temperamental film star. Might storm off home. Where would we be then?' He crossed his legs in the seat opposite us, his hairy skin exposed between shorts and sandals. 'Your legs have probably scared her enough already.'

Beverly smiled and watched the passing Cadillacs for a glimpse of a machine gun.

'This film,' Victor said, 'does it have a title? Or are you still working on that?'

'It's got a title.'

'A pity. I had a suggestion. *Fleen's Folly*. Or perhaps *Son of Fleen's Folly*, as William Tell already had *Fleen's Folly* for a subtitle, no?'

'*Assault of the Rebel Girls*,' I said.

Victor raised his eyebrows. '*Mi dios*,' he said softly. 'You wrote this script, is that what you said?'

'A few chums cleaned it up for me.'

'Don't tell me . . . Robert Rich. No doubt, as you wrote it, there is a juicy part for Fleen. No character role this time. A hero role again, no?'

'A hero role again, no. Supporting role only. I play an American correspondent covering the war for the Hearst people.'

'Hearst? You have put that in your script?'

'A touch of irony leavens the mix,' I said.

'And what name is your American correspondent? Would it be Ed? Ed something? Something close to Murrow?'

'The part has no name. Just the American Correspondent.'

'Errol Fleen playing anonymous character roles. How the world has turned.'

The world had certainly turned. Havana's dazzling light was misleading – even I knew the sun was no longer shining on its cheerful inhabitants the way it had before the troubles began. No doubt Victor would say there had always been troubles in Cuba, but not in Havana. The same old Havana? Not with all the stories of rebel bombs exploding in government buildings and gunfights in the narrow streets. The mob may be used to such high jinks, but normal people, normal people like Hollywood movie stars, tended to be put off. I wondered just who was going to be around to play with this winter. 'Is Pedro in town?'

'I am sure Pedro, when he finds out that you are in town, he will also be in town.'

'You'll like Pedro,' I said to Beverly. 'Makes one thousand dollars a day from sugar and knows how to spend it. What's not to like with someone like that?' I turned back to Victor. 'And speaking of making money every day, what's the latest with your friend, Senor Batista?'

Victor patted his brow and turned to confirm that the driver was only driving. 'I think later.'

'Oh, look at that big place,' Beverly said, pointing excitedly through the window. 'Is that our hotel? I didn't know they had American hotels here.'

'They're all American,' I said. 'Italian-American, Jewish-American, Irish-American . . .'

'That one is the Riviera,' Victor said. 'It is gauche. Meyer Lansky's folly.'

'Jewish-American,' I said.

'An even bigger folly than Fleen's,' he continued. 'But at least it gave the Nacional something to think about. Which is why they decide to forget. These days they can't afford to remember.'

'Hey, Cap'n, what was that movie anyway, the one you did here? How come you never talk about that one?'

'I never talk about any of my films once I'm finished with them,' I said.

'Sure,' Beverly said with a weary nod. 'What was it, anyway?'

'*The Big Boodle*.'

'*The Big Boodle*? What's a boodle?'

'You've heard of *The Big Sleep*, haven't you? It's another one of those.'

'A sleep, you mean? What, like a nap . . . a siesta or something?'

'I take it back what I said about your film,' Victor said. 'It will have to be the *Return of the Son of Fleen's Folly*.'

'Humour has never been easy for you, has it, Cuddles?'

'Jesus Christ, Fleen, how old is this girl?'

'Woodsie? She's old enough.'

'When you say that, I worry for you.'

'What's to worry about? This is Cuba, not the States. Anyone can have a young girl here. It's the national sport, chum.'

'And in Jamaica?'

'Nobody cares. Look, it's what the public expects of me, isn't it? A decent chap shouldn't let down his public.'

Victor threw himself back in his chair and flung his arms in the air with a loud groan. 'I give up with you!'

In a quiet room he would have attracted all eyes, but in this one, a room devoted to so many of the national sports, no one saw, no one heard, no one noticed the large dark man with hairy legs. The radio blared loud rumbas from Miami; bottles clunked, glasses clinked and ice clattered over the bar; men, women and young girls negotiated loudly before fibreglass mermaids swimming in fibreglass walls, and I said, 'Don't give up, old sport. And don't worry.'

'Someone has to worry for you.'

A waiter came to our table. 'What do you want?' Victor said. 'How long since you enjoyed a good mojito?'

'No such thing,' I said.

'Oh, be charitable, *compay*. A daiquiri then, or *cuba libre*. Christen your visit with an appropriate holy water. Support local industry.'

'Vodka,' I said to the waiter. 'Zubrowka if you have it, Smirnoff if you don't. Straight. A little ice. And no sugar.'

Victor shrugged. 'A good choice. The same for me.'

'So which way is the wind blowing today?' I said after the waiter left.

'Let me see,' Victor said. He stuck his finger in his mouth and then thrust it high above his head. He looked around the room. And then he leaned close over the table and beckoned me to join him there. 'From the east,' he whispered. 'From the mountains, as always. There will be two Cubas one day. One for the rebels, one for us. So long as Havana is in our half, it doesn't matter. So long as there are no rebels in our hotel swimming pools, eh *compay*.'

'If you're on that side, why are you whispering?' I whispered.

'You never know who is on the other side.'

'And el Presidente, will he be in Havana?'

'Oh, that mulatto thug. He is a bigger gangster than Meyer Lansky. So many gangsters makes it difficult for an honest shyster to make money.' I had to laugh and sat up in my chair. Victor beckoned me back. 'Batista, he is thick with all of them,' he said. 'Lansky, Luciano, Costello, Trafficante. Thick as thieves. You take your pick who runs the country, Batista or the *yanqui* triumvirate. You know who I mean? Lansky, the US ambassador and that crooked telephone company.'

'Now Victor . . .' I began with a sceptical shake of the head, but Victor ploughed on.

'Luciano, the US deport him, no? To Italy, yes? He flies in here, no problem, any time he wants. Sometimes he stays right here in this hotel. Sometimes he stays in Lansky's hotel. Sometimes, I think, he stays in the Presidential Palace. As long as he has Cuba, he will never need America. There are more casinos here, and no questions asked who owns them. Luciano, he can teach Batista about the brains for business. Batista already knows about every other organ, how to cut it out and splatter it in a gutter.'

'You're not exactly talking current affairs, Maestro. You're just giving me a history lesson. Ancient history. It's been going on here since before you or I ever set foot in the place.'

'But now it is worse. Now every New York hoodlum, his dick is in Cuba. You don't know . . . the people, they hate Batista more every day and Batista he gives them more to hate. Look around. This bar is empty.'

I looked around. The bar was far from empty, although it was not exactly a typical Havana shoulder-to-shoulder Saturday night. 'Empty?' I queried.

'The tourists they stop coming when too many bombs blow up in the streets. Today, there are more blackouts in Havana than blackjack. And now, since this summer, in the mountains, these rebels in the east . . . *aiy!*'

So even Victor had to admit that it wasn't the same old Havana after all. For the first time I began to consider whether my plan was going to actually get off the ground. I hadn't really weighed up the danger of our enterprise, too much else to think about, but then the riskier the venture the bigger the rewards. I was sure he was just exaggerating. Cubans liked to exaggerate a situation, play it for more drama, and Victor liked to fancy himself a Cubano. 'Batista comes from the east himself, doesn't he?'

'Trouble has always come from the east,' he said. 'In Cuba, for one hundred years, trouble grows in those mountains. It likes the cold air. In America there was the wild west, in Cuba it is the wild east. The devil's playground it is out there. This time maybe, the devil he is a communist.'

The waiter returned with our drinks and we waited for him to leave.

'Something I can't figure out,' I said, 'how did he lose that battle? He had so many men.'

'Pft.' Victor waved his hand dismissively. 'It doesn't matter how many he has. And it wasn't just one battle, it was a campaign. Two, three months. But what can you expect? Those *casquitos* of his, they are not soldiers. He has purged all his officers, closed the officer school, the university. His army is a rabble, a chicken without a head.' Suddenly he burst out laughing. 'What did I say? Chicken? And you say I can't be funny. Fleen, you know nothing about humour.'

'Okay, I'll tell you what I know,' I said. 'I look around here, this bar, and I don't see worried faces. I see people having a good time. The only people I see whispering are us.'

'Of course. This is Havana, no? Saturday night, no? Good time capital of the world, eh *compay*? Anything you want, twenty-four hours, your place or ours, as long as you pay, no problem. One day the wind it will blow it all away, not soon, a few years maybe.

And then we will have to deal with a new dictator, new rules, same thing. Same same. This dictator, Batista, maybe he won't be around to see this. Every day someone is shooting at his palace, breaking his windows, stoning his walls. He cannot shoot everyone. One day, maybe not so long now, one of the officers he purged will have enough backbone for another coup, another sergeants' revolt maybe, and then we have a new dictator who maybe can resist the wind for a few more years. One day, I think, no one will resist. Meantime, Batista is the thug in the Presidential Palace. He is *our* thug. We get what we want. No one will succeed to shoot him through his window, blow up his car. While people get what they want he is safe from that. It is the one in the mountains we should get. This communist in the mountains. He has no window, we can't shoot him through it. He has no car, we can't blow it up. But he is the one the thugs must kill. One day, maybe, Lucky Luciano will have his own army and send it into the mountains. Then this Castro fellow, he will have a real fight on his hands.'

4

Introducing the American Correspondent.

Havana, 17 September 1958

'Stop fidgeting,' I said. 'Can't you sit still for five minutes?'

'I've never been in one of these before,' she said, twisting and turning to cast her eye over every square inch of leather.

'Well, it's your birthday. Everyone should try something new on their birthday.'

'What is it? It's a Coupe de Ville, isn't it?'

'I don't know. It's a Cadillac. You wanted a Cadillac. Now sit still.'

'Where do they keep the machine guns in this?'

More than two weeks we had been in Havana, and every day, whenever we went out, the same joke. I hoped it was a joke. Victor had no idea what he had started. She was as brown as a nut, her hair so sun-bleached it was almost white. That's what two weeks by the pool does to a Sandra Dee doll.

'When do I get to open my present?' she said.

I nudged the box away from her with my foot. 'Good girls know how to wait.'

'I've never been able to wait.'

'That's because you've never been good. How's your headache?'

She pressed her forehead with the heel of her hand. 'It'll go away. I told you, all it needs is some Bufferin.'

I was gazing out the window. It was only a short run up the hill to the Capri, short enough to walk. But it wasn't how you travelled to a hotel in Havana, it was how you arrived that mattered.

'When can we stop for Bufferin?' she said.

I wasn't even listening. Victor said he was bringing one of his associates, and I was never sure what to expect when my Russian friend used the word 'associate'.

'Bufferin,' she said again. 'When can I get the Bufferin?'

'Bufferin?'

'Yeah, you know, the one on TV with the anvils in the head. You said we would stop. Why can't . . . ?'

'I told you, vodka's the only thing for pain.'

'Not everyone's like you, you know. Not everyone can . . .'

'Oh Christ, all right.' She'd been on about it for an hour, and why she couldn't have just taken herself down to the hotel drug store . . .

Anyway, 20 feet of chrome, fins and white sheet metal pulled up at the kerb. I clambered out behind the driver and slammed the great door after me. The girl behind the counter could have been Dolores del Rio, a *young* Dolores del Rio – raven hair, caramel skin, succulent lips and those flashing green almond eyes. *Ojos verdes*, I remembered. *Ojos verdes tentadora*. She reminded me of the first time I went down to Tijuana with Tony Quinn, but I was struggling to remember what I was here for now, and with the Spanish to get it.

'Senorita, quiero . . . ah . . .'

'Si, senor?'

When the first green-eyed waitress in Tijuana asked me what I wanted, *'Dos tequila, por favor'* was all I could say, but I wished I knew the Spanish for what I really wanted. And now I had the same kind of feeling.

'*Por favor . . . quiero un paquete . . . um . . .*'

'*Que?*'

Dolores del Rio. She was always too old for me. A pity. Not too old for Orson. Not too old for The Intellectual Giant. What was that damn thing she wanted? Aspirin, yes, but the one with the what? The anvils? My Spanish still wasn't up to explaining the one with the anvils. '*Ah, perdone, ah, quiero comprar . . . ummm . . .*'

Her green eyes twinkled. '*Ah, si comprendo.*' She bent down behind the counter, found the *paquete* she was looking for and slid it furtively across the glass under the cover of her hand. '*Es esto lo que quiere usted, senor?*' she said with a smile.

'Is this a joke?' Beverly said, opening the paper bag as the car pulled away.

'I couldn't remember what you wanted,' I said, still laughing.

'But you remembered these?' she said, holding the packet up.

'No . . . it was just . . . can't you see the funny side?'

'You want me to take Trojans for my headache, is that supposed to be the funny side?'

I couldn't answer, rocking back in the seat with my arms holding my chest together and my shoulders shuddering uncontrollably.

She wound down the window and threw the packet into the street. 'We've got no use for those anyway,' she said, and that made the funny side disappear instantly. Sometimes even girls can be as cruel as women.

Victor, thankfully in long pants for a change, was waiting on the steps of the casino at the Hotel Capri with a swarthy man half his size in a Bermuda jacket and smelling of California Poppy. The casual wardrobe was a bad match for the slick hair and failed to dispel an impression that he would have been more comfortable in an Italian suit, the kind that was cut generously under the arms. I looked for the bulge, but it was difficult to hide a gun under an off-the-rack summerweight jacket, and I was pleased to see Victor's associate was unarmed. It was fair to expect a night without too much trouble. The two girls on their arms were young, flashily dressed and paid for. Victor said George Raft had sent his apologies, called back to Hollywood at short notice, but he'd arranged for the VIP treatment for the Errol Flynn party. I knew what the short notice must be as George had just finished a movie with Marilyn Monroe. 'You do a movie with Marilyn Monroe,' I said, 'you have to expect to get recalls at short notice.' Which was true. I wasn't just name-dropping, although I thought Mr Bermuda jacket might have raised one eyebrow when I said it.

Mobsters and movie stars went together in Havana like tommy guns and violin cases, but it was a relationship that always made me uneasy. Of course, I availed myself of their services as much as the next man – more than most, in fact, as you couldn't have much fun at all in Havana without tipping into their coffers – but I preferred to keep them at arm's length if I could help it. I liked to get into a bit of trouble every now and then, scrap a little, roustabout, and that sort of thing was dangerous with those guys. They had no sense of humour and they carried guns. Not everyone in Hollywood had the same sensitivities. Havana may not have been as fashionable as Monte Carlo, but it was certainly closer. The glamour was a bit glitzy, but Hollywood had always appreciated glitz, and the private planes kept the airport hopping around the clock in the good old days. Everyone I knew in Hollywood used to come to Havana then. There was no law to worry about, no gossip columnists hanging around the bar, and you could lose a fortune without feeling like you were locked up in some basement speakeasy.

We made our entrance at the casino and played roulette and blackjack, had the best seats for the sequins and feathers show with acrobats and long-limbed dancing girls balancing chandeliers on their heads, and then back to the tables for more roulette and blackjack, throwing money around my wallet could ill afford and knocking back daiquiris my ill body could afford even less. The stars in Beverly's eyes were better for her headache than any anvils in her head. I tipped extravagantly enough to be noticed, but not so extravagantly I'd be talked about, and then we had a supper of lobster drowned in more daiquiris, followed by baked alaska, and Victor organised a guitar trio to sing Happy Birthday to Beverly, which did not embarrass her in the slightest. The cake came to the table with applauding waiters and sparklers planted in its frosting. No candles, because Victor didn't know how many to put on it and was afraid to ask. The cake was cut and a slice placed before each of us, and those three girls, you wouldn't believe they had just polished off a whole lobster each. The appetites of youth, I thought, and gave them my slice. Enough sugar in the daiquiris for anyone, I said, and ordered a vodka, straight, a little ice.

I could feel Victor's associate sizing me up the whole night. Eventually he said, 'They say you're doing it tough. You don't act like you're doing it tough.'

'Never underestimate the element of surprise, Al,' I said.

'It's Sal.'

'You see, I have a small problem . . . reconciling my gross habits with my net income. But I'm working on it, Al. Besides, there's nowhere like Havana to coax money out of a man, is there? If there's blood in the stone, Havana will find it. Al, I've won and lost all around the world. Cockfighting in Manila, the ponies in Hong Kong, fantan in Shanghai, poker in New Guinea . . . I won my first boat on one hand of cards in Sydney. But nowhere gets the pulse racing like Havana.'

'Is that so,' Sal said lazily as his gaze took in the room.

'Have you heard from Barry?' Victor asked.

'Spoke to him just today,' I said.

'Progress?'

'Of sorts.'

'Are you sure he is the man for this?'

'There's no point putting in a bid now, sport. I gave you your chance.'

'Oh Fleen, how many poisoned chalices must I take? And your script, progress also?'

'Still polishing. Just a little.'

Victor turned to Sal. 'Just a little, he says. I know his littles. Fleen, he has no littles.'

'So I've heard,' Sal said.

'Well, Fleen, I look forward to be dazzled by your polish.'

The headwaiter showed two men to the next table where two girls were waiting. They exchanged familiar nods with Sal as they sat down.

'Some of Raft's old buddies,' I said. 'Greaseguns for hire, wouldn't you say, Maestro? Oh, sorry Al. No offence.'

'It's Sal,' said Sal. 'No offence taken. And how about Errol? Who gave you a moniker like that, Warner Brothers?'

'No, Al, my good parents, God bless 'em. When I arrived in Hollywood I came as the genuine article, the complete package, batteries included, no assembly required. All I had to do was turn up.'

'Yeah? What article? A horse's ass?' Sal laughed and looked at the Cuban girls, who knew what was required of them and giggled like children.

'They don't make 'em like me, you see,' I said, straightening myself up and puffing my chest out melodramatically. 'Someone like me has to come along naturally. I don't expect you'd know this, Ed, but since you asked, would you care to learn the etymology of Errol?'

'Sure . . . why not,' Sal said, shrugging and craning his neck to see what was going on now at the next table.

'You know what I mean when I say etymology, don't you? But what am I saying, you must be from somewhere in the Mediterranean. Sicily, if I'm not mistaken. Greek would be a second, or even third language for someone polished like you.'

'I ain't Polish, pal, or from the Mediterranean. I'm from Jersey.'

'But Errol, being Irish, well . . . it means hero who comes from the west,' I said with a good flourish of arms. 'Warners couldn't top that, could they? When I arrived in Hollywood they didn't have to do a goddamn thing except show me where to stand. Who told you where to stand, Al? Who gave you your standing orders when you were starting out in . . . Jersey?'

'Dutch Schultz, if you have to know. Ever heard of him?'

'Who hasn't? He was almost as big a ruthless bastard as Jack Warner. Of course, Jack's still a ruthless bastard because he's still alive, but otherwise . . . Dutch Schultz, eh. A boy has never wept nor dashed a thousand kim.'

'What's that supposed to mean?'

'The last words of your old boss. Or some of them. Raved for hours like a madman, they say. Or a poet, according to others. Pleaded for his mama and asked them to take his shoes off. That's what happens to ruthless bastards when they know they're going to die, Al. They plead for their mamas and ask for their shoes to be taken off. Why do you think they do that?'

Sal nodded slowly, his eyes narrowing. 'So what do heroes from the west say when they know they're gonna die?' I took a drag of my cigarette, exhaled the smoke in a bored sigh and said nothing. Without their guns, I could still handle guys like Sal. 'What's west of LA, anyhow?' he said. 'You from fucking Hawaii or something? You one of them hula dancing babes? Is that what you are . . . Errol?' He laughed again, and again gave the Cuban girls their cue.

I'd had enough of him. There wasn't much happening, anyway. The night needed some spicing up. 'I'm from the fucking ocean depths, Ed. I'm from the . . .'

'We are having a good night, Fleen,' Victor said, apparently disagreeing with my own assessment of proceedings. 'You are not going to spoil it, are you?' He looked at each of the girls in turn. 'We are having a good night, no?'

Beverly slurped her daiquiri and said, 'A good night, a happy night, happy birthday to me.'

The Cuban girls looked at one another and whispered behind their hands. *'Ah, perdone,'* Victor said to them. *'Esto es una noche buena, si?'* The girls nodded and giggled. 'You see, Fleen. It is unanimous. Don't spoil your friend's birthday. She has had so few.'

'I'm a simple man, Maestro,' I said. 'Peace loving, home loving, law abiding. Why, I have the heart of a child.' I offered an inane grin and flicked my cigarette holder up and down between my teeth.

'That explains the girlfriend,' said Sal.

'I'll forget you said that, Al.'

'Don't concern me one way or the other.'

I started to get up from my seat when Victor put his heavy hand on my shoulder. 'So Fleen,' he quickly said, 'finishing your script, phone calls to Los Angeles . . . these are not keeping you busy, surely. How have you been spending your days? I know better than to ask about your nights.'

'Oh, you know,' I said, settling back down. 'Passing time at the country club. It's surprising how many faces I remember.'

'Most surprising,' Victor said. 'In the country club you always had difficulty focusing.' He turned to Beverly. 'It never ceased to amaze me how he could do such things on a horse as he did in such a condition. And play tennis also.'

'Play and win,' I said. 'Don't leave out the best part.'

'Are you still winning, Fleen? Can you still hold your own with Donnie Budge?' Victor turned to Sal, who was giving a good impression of not giving a damn. 'There was a time Fleen could do that, you know, Sal. Of course, that was in the old days. Yes, they were certainly old days.'

'Could hold his own then, could he?' Sal said indifferently. 'I'll bet he could still do that. He looks to me like someone who holds his own.'

So he had a sense of humour after all. A rather primitive one, but at least it was a start. 'I pace myself these days, ah . . . friend,' I said. 'Only do what I have to, toning up, a little exercise, just enough to get in shape for my picture. But you'd know all about that, wouldn't you? You know about everything else.'

'Getting in shape?' Victor chortled. 'To do what? To play the American Correspondent? Surely you only need exercise your elbow for such a role, and that is one part you always keep in shape.'

I threw back the last of my latest vodka and slammed the empty glass on the table. 'Fuck you, *viejo*,' I said, and climbed up onto my chair. I steadied myself, and every head in the room turned. I looked down at Sal, who had jumped to his feet and stepped back. 'You wanna see a hula, Al?' I knew it was going to hurt, but I did it anyway. I leapt from the chair to the middle of the table, sending cake and glasses flying, and began swaying my hips in the closest manner to a hula that my damaged back could handle. And then I threw my arms triumphantly in the air. 'Introducing the American Correspondent,' I roared. 'Coming soon to a theatre near you.' And the table collapsed underneath me.

When we were finally standing on the front steps waiting for our drivers, Sal breasted the American Correspondent and looked up into my eyes. 'You sure like to have people talk about you, hero.'

'Al . . . it's not what they say, it's what they whisper.'

In the Coupe de Ville I gave Beverly her birthday present.

She tore the paper off slowly, concentrating and doing her best to stay focused. She opened the box and raised her eyebrows. 'What . . . what is it?'

'What the hell does it look like, Woodsie? It's a fucking naked broad.'

In fact what it was, was a gold-plated statue of a reclining nude, just eighteen inches long.

'But . . .'

'Oh, look at the kisser. It's you, sweetheart. A genuine gold-plated Woodsie. An original Joe Dubronyi. A fucking masterpiece.'

She looked at the face and had to blink to force eyes and brain to grasp what she was holding in her hands. Its features were a perfect two-inch miniature of her own. 'Who's Joe Du . . . Du . . .?'

'Dubronyi. The fellow who did it. And be careful. Don't drop it. I haven't paid him for it yet.'

'How'd he do it?'

'I gave him your photo.'

'You gave him a photo of me like this? When did . . .'

'No, just your face. A photo of your face. I described the rest from memory. I know it's been a while, but . . . Anyway, he has a regular supply of delightful nymphets willing to supply their bodies for the sake of art. It's your head on someone else's body. You'll notice the breasts are not quite as generous as your own.'

She studied every angle all the way back to the hotel, holding it up to the light, turning it one way and the next, marvelling at its golden glow and trying hard not to drop it on the floor. 'This is the best ever, Cap'n,' she said. 'Better'n the earrings, the charm . . . you know . . . best present I ever . . .'

Later that night, when Beverly was asleep, her 18-inch look-alike reclining on the bedside table next to her head, I took a taxi to the Riviera Hotel and an elevator to the eleventh floor. It was said that Meyer Lansky kept rooms on the eleventh floor, but no one could really know that because Meyer Lansky, although he had his suite on the twentieth, was inclined to sleep in a different room of his choosing every night. The Dolores del Rio of the Drug Store was waiting. She wasn't Sandra Dee, she wasn't a gold-plated nymphet. She was the solid gold article, and five-feet-five.

I had earned a name all around the world for what I was doing there on the eleventh floor of a hotel that didn't even have my real name in its register. In fact, I had many names. In the States I was a heel or a skunk. In England it was rotter or cad. In Europe, roué or libertine. *Confidential* magazine, of course, was considerably more colourful. They called me whatever they thought they could get away with, and what they couldn't they said between the lines. But the fact is, I never went after a woman simply to put a notch on my gun. It was the contest that I found irresistible. The thrill of the scrap, the cut and thrust. It was the same as my reputation for being a roustabout – I didn't get into a brawl in a bar to get another victory. Again, the contest was the thing. The scrap – that was when I felt truly alive.

Sometimes I wished it were different. When Carole Lombard was killed in a plane crash I saw what it did to Clark Gable, and I don't think he ever got over the fact he would never see her again. It doesn't matter how many women I knew, or how many *Confidential* said I knew, I never knew one like he did then. I envied Clark more than he ever understood.

That night, the contest with Dolores del Rio of the Drug Store was to be the answer to my restlessness, my impatience for change. Nothing personal, but I had been dancing a fruitless teenage jive with Beverly for too long and ached for a progressive dance. A mambo, a rumba, a cha-cha-cha with raven hair, caramel skin and *ojos verdes tentadora*. But in the end it made no difference. Damaged vertebrae, I said to her. And Africa. Terrible what poxes in the water can do to a man.

5
The importance of being Ernesto.

Havana, 25 October 1958

En Habana se permite todo. In Havana anything goes. The municipal anthem. For weeks I played myself morning, noon and night. Keeping up appearances. Living up to expectations. The Chinese have a saying for it: When you are at your lowest is the time to live your highest. Mornings at the cabana I played the poolside celebrity, afternoons at the country club the courtside raconteur, and evenings at the casino the big wheel at the roulette table.

Flynn had a saying for it: When you're down and out, go to the best spots. I played the sportsman at the Oriental Park races, the seaman at the yacht club and at the Sports Palace I played Gentleman Jim once again at ringside. I even played the *habanero*, dancing painful cha-cha-chas with a dozen women a night at the Montmartre, the Nacional, the Capri. I kept Beverly happy one of the few ways I now could, with trips to the department store so alluring they called it The Enchantment, and to O'Reilly Street in the old town where I bought her Spanish lace shawls and tortoiseshell combs, and wished I could buy her the green almond eyes to go with them. In between times I played scriptwriter.

Look Hemingway in the eye – that was a laugh. A few chums had cleaned it up for me – that was a lie. Shoot in Cuba? You must be loco. That was the best advice those particular chums offered. There were no more drug store girls, hatcheck girls, cigarette girls, no any sort of girl, except Beverly. Beverly could be trusted with my secret. If word got around ... it's not what they say, it's what they whisper. I gave them plenty to whisper about at the Zombie Club, Sloppy Joe's, the Sans Souci, where I did my best to shine brilliantly in the casino under the stars. There were *cabaret espectacular* nights under the crystal arch of the Tropicana and voodoo shows on the roof of the Hotel Seville. I laid on one of my famous suckling pig parties. The Nacional wouldn't be in it this time but Ernie Hemingway was keen to have it at his place. Mary Hemingway put an end to that. She'd heard about the one in Jamaica when the pig found its way into the swimming pool with an alligator right behind it. Everyone had heard about that one. Mary thought Ava Gardner's skinny dip had been quite enough foreign bodies in her pool for one season. She didn't seem to appreciate that Ava was more dangerous than any alligator, so if her pool had survived Ava then it could handle anything I could throw in it, but the party was held at Pedro Rodriguez's place. Even at Pedro's, the man who made 1,000 dollars a day from sugar, the Hemingways didn't turn up. A fair sprinkling of the Miami mob did, which put a dampener on proceedings even before everyone ended up in the pool.

There were only so many suckling pig parties and nightclub nights to use as an excuse to avoid what was necessary. Barry was close to finalising arrangements in LA and he'd soon be arriving with the company and the expectation that the script would be waiting for him. Writing at night was impossible. After a day of drinking and an evening of even more, I just stared at the keys, wondering what wonderful combination of words they held if only I could hit them in the right order and woke up with my face pressed into them yet again. I dreamt, I drank, I hallucinated. I thought of Thomas De Quincey and how he had used opium to produce his own wonderful combination of words. I went to my survival kit and took a syrette of vitamin M to cleanse those dusty doors of perception. In the morning I found I had perceived nothing – the words I had typed made no sense and I was now exhausted of words completely.

Where was the discipline? Did De Quincey have any discipline beyond a regular tug on the opium pipe? But what was I thinking? Why was I looking for inspiration from one hundred years ago when Papa Hemingway was right here in Havana? Hadn't Hem told me once that he only worked in the morning? Got to see the sunrise, he said. That made more sense than sticking your stomach with morphine and filling your head with gibberish. I didn't take a drink until midday for a week. That was better discipline than Hemingway himself could manage, but all it did was give me a headache. Hem said he wrote five hundred words a day, every day. It was important to get up early, shake off the hangover and write. Just write. And don't stop until two pages are full of words. I gave it a try. The first morning I dragged myself out of bed when sun came streaming through the curtains I'd left open the night before. I retched into the sink, hawked, coughed, tried to take a piss, but avoided taking a drink. I eased myself into the chair and fixed on the typewriter through barely open eyes. The little portable loomed large but offered nothing but the purity of its white enamel. Seton Miller had given me that typewriter to encourage me to write the story of my life. Seton Miller, who had put the words in my mouth when I was Robin Hood, the Sea Hawk, Captain Courtney. Someone who's been a devil all their life, he said to me, needs a white typewriter to find the words of angels. But he didn't tell me anything about discipline.

I stood under the shower and let it pound onto my aching head for ten minutes. I dried myself and looked at the typewriter again. The angels were not seeing fit to visit. Five hundred words a day. It was a screenplay I was writing, not a goddamn *Farewell to Arms*.

But even a screenplay needed to be a hundred pages, and I had maybe twenty I was happy with so far and a rough outline on the rest with a scant few ideas from the Hollywood chums. Eighty pages at two pages a day was nearly six weeks, if all went well, and Barry would be in Havana long before that. If I had a fair chunk of it done, I reasoned, say fifty or sixty pages, they could make a start and I could finish it during production. I had been on enough shoots where that had happened. Making it up as you go along, I think, was the technical term. If I finished all the location scenes first and let them run around the jungle for a month I could concentrate on the interiors. They were the thing really, because they carried the dialogue. The dialogue was the tricky bit. People just never understand how hard dialogue can be. Actors never understand. I had to forget I was an actor. Fifty or sixty pages was an hour of screen time. It would take them a month to shoot that, giving me that month to finish it. Making it up as I went along. But that was if all went well. Tapping away at a typewriter under a hurricane lamp in a tent on a mountainside with bullets whizzing around may be all right for a genuine American correspondent, but it was not a definition of all going well. And if all went well in pre-production, that was just where I would be.

Just write, Hem would say, that's the important thing, so I did. The first time I finished five hundred words in a morning I was so delighted I ripped the paper from the typewriter and hurried it down to the cabana to read to Beverly. But I'd only got half way through my recital when I recognised it to be a regurgitation of a passage in one of the books I'd written twenty years before. Another time I found myself writing a scene at a river, and my rebels were swimming across it when one got taken by a crocodile, and I wrote 'Yulu lets out a frightening scream and goes under,' and I realised I was dreaming with my eyes open. I took a drink.

Hem once said he did his best writing standing up, shifting weight from foot to foot to relieve the strain on the legs. Nietzsche's dance, he called it. More vitality on your feet, according to the wise old kraut. I tried it, touching my toes every now and then to relieve my own particular strain. It got me nowhere. Hadn't Flaubert said it was hopeless to try thinking or writing except when seated? I took another drink and decided to consult the Great Man himself. It was past 10 in the morning, so I knew where to find him – perched on his stool at the end of a massive mahogany bar like a bear in an angel suit with his white hair, white beard, white linen. *His* stool because he was deaf and blind to his left, and there no one could sit anywhere but to his right. *His* stool because he had marked out the territory as if he'd cocked his leg all around it, and after he won the Nobel Prize they put his bust in bronze up on the wall above it to make everything official. Now no one was permitted to sit on stool number one at the Floridita but him. The importance of being Ernesto.

All the stools are high in that place and they give you a good view of the busy bartenders, the tables, the cigar stand, the photos of Hemingway and friends on the walls. More importantly, from those stools, with our Hemingway special daiquiris in our hands – double Bacardi, lime, grapefruit, thick with shaved ice, and the only sugar from a little maraschino – you could see every joker who came into the place. I told him he owed me for that quip and he looked at me warily over the rim of his cocktail glass.

'Let me see if I can get this right,' I said. 'Any picture with Errol Flynn as its best actor is its own worst enemy.'

He winced. 'That got back to you, eh. Listen, it's a compliment. They massacred my goddamn book, like they always do. You were the only good thing in it.'

'That's a back-hander of a compliment, chief. A back-hander worthy of Rocky Marciano.'

'Hey, at least I didn't say what I thought they should call it. *The Bum Also Rises*,' he said dramatically, sweeping his hand across an imaginary marquee. 'See Errol Flynn playing Errol Flynn in his long-awaited comeback.'

I forced myself to bite my lip. I was always biting my lip around Ernesto.

'So what's your story?' he said. 'Sure you know what you're doing?'

'It's only writing, Hem. Anyone can write.'

'No, Colonel, you don't understand. You have to be hurt to write anything worth a damn. Have to have nightmares. And you, you gotta stop being so happy, gotta get yourself hurt.'

'Well, I get the nightmares all right. Does that qualify me?' I could see in his face that nothing would qualify me as far as he was concerned. 'It's about the rebels in the east. A kind of a cinema verite look at . . .'

'Cinema verite?' He looked around anxiously. 'Did you hear that?'

'What?'

'My shit detector just went off. Since when have you guys been interested in truth?'

I picked up my glass by the stem and cocked my little finger. I knew the man's weak points well enough. 'How's that little runabout of yours going? Pillbox, isn't that what you called it? How big is it again?'

'Pilar, you ignoramus,' he said, wrapping his own fat fingers around his glass. 'And it's thirty-eight feet. I suppose you can tie a knot in yours. And you're about sixty years too late. The important Cuban rebels are all dead.'

'There seems to be a new edition, though, doesn't there.'

He straightened up on his stool and surveyed his domain. It was still early and there was more action at the cigar stand. 'Yeah. A few months back three of them ended up in the gutter outside my front gate. Enough lead in them to start a scrap metal yard.'

'And to think I was told there were no barbarians at the gate yet.'

'The bastards killed my dog, too.'

'The rebels?'

'No, Batista. Not personally. His goons. Rousted us in the middle of the night looking for guns. Poor old Black Dog. He barked, they clubbed him to death. He's half a Chino, you know. That's what they say. The Little Sergeant is half Oriental. That'd be the inscrutable half, the half that's impossible to pin down. Like why in this day and age there's a president happy to have a country full of people who can't write their own name. And the diseases they die of . . . there's no excuse for pestilences from the Dark Ages killing so many people in the twentieth century. Is that in your story?'

'It's not the stuff of movies, Hem. Gunfights, chases and feats of derring-do, that's what movies are made of.'

He looked at me and shook his head. 'Didn't I hear you say truth just a minute ago?'

'Hem . . . we live, we die, and always sooner than we'd planned. That's the only truth. And anyway, I said verite. Sometimes, some words just defy translation.'

'Tell you what I'll do,' he said, 'if you still say I owe you one.'

'I still say you owe me one.'

'Okay, I'll pass you something. Not my line of work, really, but I like it and thought I may . . .' He shrugged and eyed his empty glass. 'Hell, other writers have been pinching my stuff for years. This one I'll donate. It's from Ray Chandler originally, so you can thank him. He kept writing it into movies and you Hollywood geniuses kept giving it the red pencil.'

'All right, chum, you've got me hooked.'

He leant in close and spoke softly behind a covering hand. 'A secret note written in lipstick.'

'A secret note written in... what's that got to do with anything?'

'Leave that up to you. All Ray's movies were black and white. I guess red lipstick on white paper loses its effect in black and white. Yours'll be colour, I suppose, big star like you.'

I'd heard stories about him starting to lose his grip. Maybe they were true. 'This is how you repay me, eh? With a joke.'

'It's no joke, boy. Gunfights, car chases and notes written in lipstick. Sounds like a smash. But they say it's a stalemate down there in those mountains, you know. All that fighting last summer, they've run out of juice. Are movies made about stalemates?'

'Well, I'll just have to see if I can stir the pot a little,' I said.

'What about this Castro guy, he kind of interests me. You know how some people do. You just like the way they wear a hat, or the strange ways their lips move. There's something about him. One day he just might march into Havana. That'd make a decent climax for a movie, wouldn't it? I was there for the liberation of Paris in '44. Nothing like it. You know when Sinatra has a room full of people collapsing at his feet? Have you ever looked in his eyes when an audience does that? I know what it's like. When I rode into Paris with all those tanks and good-looking GIs in their good-looking uniforms, I felt just what he feels. Fucking intoxicating.' He chuckled as he drank, swirling it around between his cheeks.

'So was that before or after you liberated the Ritz?'

'Been trying to get that feeling back ever since.' He slapped me on the back, a little too hard. 'You should try it some time, chief.'

'You're right. Next time they liberate Paris I'll make sure I'm on the spot.'

'You do that. The cinema verite of intoxication.'

He was a good drinker, Hem. Could hold both his liquor and his temper well in a bar. He always fancied himself as a 'hard' drinker, but let's face it – daiquiris and mojitos? I ask you. I never saw him with a black eye or a busted knuckle. He was like every writer I had ever known – he could *talk* a hard game. Maybe that's why I never went far as a writer. Nothing to do with happiness at all.

'If you manage to meet him,' he said, 'it'll be some kind of miracle. Herb Matthews tracked him down last year. You remember Herb from Spain?'

'Don't think I was there long enough to meet the gent.'

'No? But you must have seen his Castro story in the *New York Times*. They put him on the front page, pictures and everything. All black beard and rumpled fatigues. The pirate rebel. A nice contrast to Batista and his flunkies in their starched uniforms and jangling medals.'

'Can't say I saw it.'

'Don't you read the papers when you're not in them, Colonel? Herb told me he went down to Santiago and just waited. Put the word around he wanted to interview *el Gigante*. That's what they call him. Like trawling with a long line for a big fish. I never believed him, has to be more to it than that, but who knows with all this cloak and dagger FBI malarkey? Apparently Castro likes his picture in the paper. You want a hero for your movie? He was born for the role, old ego *Gigante*.'

'That kind of hero, huh?'

'Is there any other kind?' Hem grinned and began humming a marching tune. '*Adelante Cubanos . . .*' he sang quietly. 'Don't know the rest. Something about cruel and insatiable tyrants, I'm told.'

'Probably a good thing. Probably not healthy to go around singing songs of revolution within earshot of the cruel and insatiable tyrant. When I feel the urge myself, I always prefer the Marsellaise. That revolution's old enough to avoid creating excitement in the palace.'

'The Marsellaise? I didn't picture you as the bloodthirsty type.'

'Haven't you seen *Casablanca*? That scene in Rick's when Henreid leads the whole bar in a patriotic chorus. Stirring stuff, Hem. Makes the hair on my arms stand up, even now.'

'Even now? I'm surprised the hair on your arms can even *sit* up these days. That's what people don't understand about you, isn't it, Colonel. They think you're just a low shit, but really you're a rank sentimentalist. Rocky Marciano signing off. Salud!'

6
I could feel it on the back of my neck.

Havana, 2 November 1958

I marvelled at how inspiration could come from the most unlikely places. Certainly I had gone looking for it at the Floridita, hoping it might drop from the bar into my lap like a wayward peanut. But it wasn't what I'd heard from the master about writing, and it wasn't the battle of wits. It was when the guy slapped me on the back with his fake bonhomie that what I wanted fell into my lap. Just after he told me about Frank Sinatra.

 Hemingway didn't have much of a nose, but he always managed to look down it to look at actors. He looked down it and called me Colonel. Colonel Custer, one of so many make-believe heroes I've been. He had seen intoxication in Sinatra's eyes when the crowd was at the singer's feet, and it was a thrill the most important writer of his generation had only experienced once himself and then dreamed about for the next fifteen years. That was my inspiration. You should try it some time, the Great Man said, looking down his nose, like it would be something new, something I too could only dream about. But the writer's dream is the film star's reality. I'd had countless audiences at my feet, even in my bed. The first time I ever set foot in Havana, Hemingway's hometown, I had a convent full of schoolgirls, even their nuns, chanting my name in the street, pleading for my appearance on a balcony. And where was that balcony? On a whorehouse! The world at my feet, nuns and schoolgirls baying at my window. For Cap-i-tan Blerd! For Errrrol! A goddamn house of special integrity. Riding into Paris indeed. Hemingway could not even dream about such a thing as that. That's when the self-doubt evaporated in a shimmer of belief. A priceless shot of confidence with a vodka chaser. And the writing came easily. Who needed ghost writers? *The Bum Also Writes!*

I wrote in the secret lipstick note on the third page of the script, looking down my nose as I tapped at the keys. In a week I had the first fifty pages. Who said nothing good came from happiness? I was as happy as Larry Olivier, and then it was Sunday. Another of Hem's rules for writing – never do it on Sunday. Bad luck to write on Sunday, says Ernesto.

The morning started like any other – I got up, retched, hawked, coughed, tried to take a piss, had a drink. I took myself down to the Terrace for a proper breakfast, just for once. I listened to the church bells as I drank a double bloody mary and pushed scrambled eggs around a plate. I lit a cigarette and gazed out through the garden to the Caribbean. A 20-knot wind was gusting from the northeast, a good sailing wind. The yacht club would be the place to be this afternoon. But before then, a walk. Nietzsche said that only thoughts reached by walking had value. I fitted my custom-made John Barrymore false nose under sunglasses and a Panama hat and took to the streets under the royal palms of Vedado, anonymously joining the Sunday promenaders in their white linen suits, avoiding the eye contact that *habaneros* customarily took to be an invitation for an exchange of views.

Havana was like two towns – the congested bustle of the decaying old Spanish colony and, next to it, the wide boulevards of the grand new city of the republic. The old town, where there was barely room to move, was fine for writers and other low life, but we movie stars liked the new one with all its hotels and casinos. The new one was made for parades. I paraded past the ostentatious sugar mansions with their wedding cake frosting and their bougainvillea walls, tried my Spanish on some frayed old domino players in the shade of Indian laurels, and cocked my ear to the rumbas and congas and mambos throbbing from the outdoor cafes. Along the graceful curve of the Malecon I watched a white cruise ship sailing on the tide, Americans gathered along its rails to catch their last glimpse of Havana disappearing before their eyes. Waves crashed into the seawall, leaving the pavement sparkling beneath my feet and the spray filling my nostrils with salty air. Like the first vodka of the day it went straight to my head and made me forget the pain in my back. The great phallus of the lighthouse mocked me from Morro Castle, but at that time of day the *jineteras* were still recovering from a hard night's work and their contemptuous hissing calls of *'Una chica, senor?'* would not be taking the spring from my step.

I strolled up La Rampa past the clubs, past my shared cinema, locked up tight until the afternoon, to the new Hilton. Not exactly Nietzschean, the thought I had was to take a look at the prize that cost Albert Anastasia his life, gunned down in a Manhattan barber shop for trying to muscle in on Havana by way of this new jewel in the Batista crown. It was bigger even than the Riviera and Meyer Lansky probably couldn't stand that. It was the biggest Hilton in the world, so they said. I wandered into the vast soaring lobby to see what the future held for Cuba, and found Las Vegas.

I picked up a *Herald Tribune* and sat down with a vodka in the lobby bar. I had finished it by the time I noticed the story about the plane. A Cubana Viscount en route from Miami to Havana had crashed into the sea off the east coast of the island. Miami to Havana was only a couple of hundred kilometres, and the crash was three times that distance in the opposite direction. It didn't make sense until I saw the word 'Hijack'. Rebel sympathisers had hijacked the plane to run the blockade and deliver weapons to the guerrillas in the mountains. Hijack an aircraft! Who ever heard of such a thing? Where did they think they were going to land it? How did they ever think they were going to get away with it? What sort of crazy devotion to a cause did that take?

Victor said the wind was coming. One day, not soon, there would be two Cubas. Hemingway said the situation was in stalemate. Hijack an aircraft to run guns! That didn't sound like a stalemate. That didn't sound like there would be two Cubas. A storm was on the horizon and I could feel it on the back of my neck, whipping up the sea, flicking white horses across my bow. Time to shorten the sail, Barry, time to rig for a big blow. Time for Captain Blood to get all hands on deck. I hurried back down to the hotel to call Los Angeles.

7
Not the way to make a movie.

Santa Clara, 12 November 1958

When Barry and the company arrived in Havana I wondered what had taken him so long. Two months to put together what certainly looked to be the youngest cast and oldest crew I had ever seen? It wasn't the cast and crew that was the problem, Barry said, it was convincing anyone that it was a serious project. There had been an outline but no script, and Errol Flynn's name only went so far these days, even with the small bankroll we needed. Barry's cast of actors included a Johnny, a Jackie, a Marie and Barry's wife, Chloe, none of whom had ever been in a movie before. It seemed to me that wasn't surprising when, apart from Chloe, they all looked like where they were before was at school. Barry shrugged and said that he used Beverly as a yardstick, and I had to admit he had a point.

According to my script, the American Correspondent would make contact with the rebels through the Havana underground. I would be furtively slipped the note written in lipstick, hop a plane down to Santiago and then make my way into the mountains. Simple as that. And that was as much planning as we had for making the actual connection. Victor asked if we intended to make a comedy. The underground make contact with Errol Flynn? A note written in lipstick? Havana was crawling with secret police in their machine gun cars, he said. Every police station was rumoured to be equipped with a torture chamber and if we went stumbling around looking for the underground we were likely to find out if the rumour was true.

I told him how I heard that Herb Matthews and the *New York Times* had simply gone down to Santiago and put the word around. Trawling with a long line, as Hemingway put it. Barry said the *New York Times* didn't go fishing. They would have had a better plan than that, and besides, Herb Matthews may have had the *New York Times* behind him, but he didn't have a cast and crew in tow. Sitting around and twiddling so many thumbs until a guy with a beard and a gun saw fit to come down from his mountain to see who was putting his name about was not the way to make a movie. Victor said the man with the gun wouldn't come down from his mountain for anyone. We would have to find our way to him. He said Batista boasted of a 'ring of steel' around those mountains, although he'd had to admit that claim was looking a little suspect after other reporters from America had followed Matthews. But we shouldn't have to put the word about very far, he said. A dozen *yanquis* with a camera in Santiago? Everyone would soon know what we were there for, including Batista.

Barry shot the Havana scenes of tough police chasing young girls over the weathered rooftops of the old town. Beverly herself was happy to have some company her own age and swapped the mojitos for granizados to be sociable. I left them to their fruit punch and took Barry, Chloe and the 'experienced' film crew for a night at the Tropicana with Victor. If the tourists had stopped coming it didn't show. We rubbed shoulders with eight hundred people, not including a couple of hundred dancers on the stage, among the tables and up among the palm trees, and when Victor introduced us to more of his associates – a Lefty, a Jimmy Blue Eyes and someone called Bill who he later said was really known as the Fat Butcher – we thought it was time to get on the road.

It was 1,000 kilometres to the Sierra Maestra, the mountains in the east where the rebels were biding their time, and they were not only remote, but high and covered with thick forest. Just finding the rebels was going to be difficult. Batista had already found it *too* difficult.

Our caravan took to the Central Highway in a couple of old Plymouth wood-sided station wagons that Barry had laid his hands on. I labelled them Woodsie 2 and 3 – Return of Woodsie and Woodsie Rides Again. The original Woodsie ignored me and tried to learn her lines. We stopped overnight at Santa Clara, less than half way down the highway, and at dinner on the square I made sure 'the kids' got extra minty, extra sugary mojitos and soon everyone was happy.

Chloe asked what our plan was once we got to Santiago. I shrugged and said we would just put the word around in the right places. Someone would come forward. 'How will you know that someone is not one of Batista's agents out to trap you?' Chloe asked.

'The rebels have beards and armbands,' I said. 'The armbands say 26 JULIO. It means the twenty-sixth of July, the date they attacked their first barracks down in Santiago.'

'Tell me you're joking,' Chloe said.

'No, seriously. They attacked a barracks and got caught. Well, most of them got killed actually, but Castro only had to spend a couple of years in prison.'

'Tell me you're joking about expecting to find men with armbands in Santiago,' Chloe said.

'No, honey, I'm not serious,' I said, keeping a straight face.

'Thank God for that.'

'I expect them to put their armbands in their pockets in Santiago. We'll be able to spot them with the beards.'

Barry laughed and Chloe shook her head. Chloe never did appreciate my sense of humour, but she was only a woman, after all. As much as Barry was my buddy, I had always had difficulty with his wife, perhaps because he *was* my buddy. Older women can even get jealous of men, and I'd had three wives who, the older they got, the more they proved the point. Beyond that, Chloe and I just seemed to rub each other the wrong way. I don't know what it was with her, but as for me, she reminded me too much of my mother. It wasn't especially rational. She didn't look like her, sound like her, smell like her. Neither did Bette Davis, and yet it was the same thing there. Perhaps it was just that they were always suspicious of me, meeting head-on my instinctive attempts to lay on the charm. What's so wrong with a little charm between friends, I ask? Or between mother and son?

'I'm sorry, Chloe,' I said. 'You know me. Pluto in the dog house, that's my problem, isn't it?'

She pulled a face and clicked her tongue. 'Jupiter in the fifth house.'

'That's right . . . Jupiter in the fifth house. I'll try to remember it. I'm terrible at that astronomy racket of yours, the mound of Venus and all that.'

'Astrology,' she sighed, 'as you well know. And perhaps you are referring to the *transit* of Venus, which can be either astronomy or astrology.'

'Am I?' I said. 'Yes, I suppose I am. Transiting the mound of Venus, now that's a racket I understand.'

She sighed again and turned her back to me. 'Have I told you I've been getting into shape?' I said to Barry.

'What for?' he asked.

'You never know. Watch.' I quickly got to my feet.

'You're not going to do your new party trick, are you?' he said.
I was puzzled at that. 'Which party trick?'
'The table leaping one.'
'Ah. You heard about that.'
'Everyone's heard about it,' said Chloe.
'One version I heard had you leaping over gangsters with their guns drawn,' said Barry. 'Tell me that's not true.'
'An exaggeration, sport. Watch.' I touched my toes three times in quick succession, straightened up, stuck my hands on my hips and grinned as though my back wasn't on fire.
'Impressive,' said Barry. 'How's the swordplay coming along?'
'I'll be leaping from balconies again before you know it.'
'Isn't it time you grew up?' Chloe said wearily.
'Why honey . . . I'm still growing,' I said, bending my aching back to kiss her hand.
'I can see that,' she said with a nod to my waistline. No sense of humour, that woman.
I pulled my chair from the table and placed it between Chloe and her husband, forcing them to make room as I sat down and leant close to her. 'I intend to live the first half of my life,' I said, fixing her with my eyes and my holder with another cigarette. 'The rest will take care of itself.'
'You intend to live to a hundred then, do you?' Chloe said.
'Of course. Doesn't everyone? No doubt you can see it in my stars.'
'It could simply mean you intend to live only half a life.'
I had just opened my mouth to respond when, from across the square, somewhere on the edge of town, the unmistakable rapid pop of automatic gunfire stopped all conversation.
'That doesn't sound like fireworks,' Barry said.
The war hero in him must have surfaced, because he crossed the street to the square. Ride to the sound of the guns, I thought

as I watched him, a line from one of my more memorable movies. A waiter ran after him and suggested he return to the table. We decided it was time to retreat to the safety of our hotel rooms. On a pillar outside the hotel Barry pointed out a graphic poster. *Wanted – Ernesto Guevara*. Next to a sketchy image of a man with a beard was a hammer and sickle.

Later that night I stood on the balcony to our room. I could feel the malaria coming on again, hot one minute, cold the next. I opened my survival kit and took out the phial, the bottle and a glass. I poured a measure of quinine, washed it down with Zubrowka and cocked my ear to the sporadic gunfire. Victor had said they were 1,000 kilometres from Havana, these people. Today we had come no more than three hundred. It looked like the barbarians would be at the gate before Victor knew it.

8
A dozen *yanquis* with a camera in Santiago.

Santiago de Cuba, 19 November 1958

The shivering and shaking lasted a day, all the way down the highway to Santiago. They laid me out in the back of Woodsie 2, clutching my survival kit, sweating buckets and hallucinating rivers filled with crocodiles, jungles filled with cannibals, bars filled with brawlers. The quinine helped to make them go away, the vodka helped me survive. They say my condition made the roadblocks easier for them to negotiate – nobody wanted a raving *yanqui* on their hands.

In Santiago, Barry busied himself with shooting street scenes during the day and putting the word about at night, quietly looking for some sort of underground connection in the bars and coffee houses. Although Victor had said that a dozen *yanquis* with a camera would be noticed in Santiago, it was obvious he hadn't been to Santiago himself. There were plenty of *yanquis*, even a US naval base just along the coast. In a town that took American sailors in its stride, the activities of our little group tripped little interest. Santiago was a thousand kilometres and a world away from Havana. One was just across the water from the United States, the other deep in the heart of the Caribbean.

Santiago was closer to Jamaica and Haiti than Havana and casinos, nightclubs and lobster restaurants were an even more foreign country. Years of revolt against the regime, of bloody suppression, of young men stealing away into the mountains to join the rebels, of their mothers and sisters marching in the streets, had created an atmosphere of open hostility toward the belligerent government *casquitos* hanging around every corner.

Barry had heard that there was a kind of password among the underground. To make contact you simply asked after 'Senor Cohen'. I said that if he had heard that, what made him think that Batista's police hadn't heard the same thing? You're asking the wrong questions, I said. You don't sidle up to a stranger in a bar and ask anonymously after a Jewish gentleman and expect to get an answer. Spectacle was the way to attract attention and open doors, and if there was one thing I knew, it was how to make a spectacle of myself.

I lived up to my legend in front of a new audience, throwing the production bankroll around a couple of well-chosen bars and houses of special integrity, paying a raggedy street charanga band to follow me about during the day, getting into scraps at night, dancing on more tables, and riding a horse around another plaza, disturbing the dignity of the town hall by galloping under its colonnade as an after-dinner entertainment. After twenty-five years of movie training I could make it look spontaneous, but I also made sure no one could see the corset under my shirt holding my back together. I was considering a plan to drive one of our Woodsies into the country club's swimming pool when Barry told me he had made a connection with the mysterious Senor Cohen, which was fortunate for all of us. The police had treated my equestrian antics with indulgence, but the country club was not to be fooled with.

★

'Senor Cohen' lived in Vista Alegre, said to be the Beverly Hills of Santiago, and if this was the rebellious Jewish Quarter then the rebellious Jews were doing very well in this far-flung part of Cuba. The Beverly Hills analogy appeared quite appropriate when Barry and I arrived late that night. The palm trees towered over expensive houses and the hoi polloi was nowhere to be seen. In the dark, Senor Cohen's house was about the grandest we could make out. On the stone gatepost was a bronze plaque: 'El Encanto'. It appeared it was named after Havana's most enchanting shop. Beyond wrought iron gates and a sweeping gravel drive stood a small castle with a door twice as high as a man. I said that it was obviously a bum steer, that Barry had been sold a line. He had been told that this particular Senor Cohen was connected to the Bacardi family, and people like the Bacardis, people who lived in such houses, had no sympathy for rebels, no interest in disturbing the status quo. Slowly, the door swung open. A toffee-nosed manservant showed the way to an oak-panelled reception hall and then left us to be impressed by a wall of fading tapestries and another of gilt-edged portraits of conceited men in Spanish uniform and ornamental women in lace mantillas. I was inspecting a large oil painting above the moulded fireplace, a colonial Goya-inspired landscape of a sugar estate surrounded by orderly rows of palms, when a chimpanzee in red Chinese silk waddled up with a tray of champagne.

'Senor Cohen, I presume,' I said. He held the tray under our noses until we took a glass and bared his teeth at each of us in turn before leaving again. We looked at one another and shook our heads. Barry seemed nervous. 'What kind of revolution do we have here, sport?' I said.

'I don't know,' he said. 'But the pay must be peanuts.' He wasn't as nervous as he appeared.

Another door opened for the manservant who invited us into the next room. It was a study, lined with books and smelling of cigars and leather. An attractive young woman in a plain cotton dress stood demurely by a desk with one low-heel before the other and hands delicately clasped in front, a picture of Catholic school deportment. I strode across the room to her, as Essex in the presence of his Queen, and bowed. 'Good evening, senorita, I am . . .'

'I know who you are, Mr Flynn,' she said with a sobriety to match her wardrobe. 'How could I not know? Everyone in Santiago seems to be talking about the great Captain Blood.'

Now I had to put on my best self-conscious Essex. 'You embarrass me, senorita.' I kissed her hand.

'I doubt that, Mr Flynn. And if you are kissing my hand to determine my marital status and my availability, I assure I am not married, and so your gesture is impolite, is it not?'

This required a complete reassessment. 'Indeed you are correct . . . senorita.'

She smiled, and then laughed, and then reached again for my hand. 'I am sorry,' she said as she shook it gently. 'I am just playing. Please call me Alicia.'

We sat down on the same side of the desk and the chimpanzee returned with more champagne. Alicia offered no explanation and we ventured no questions. We sipped champagne and steadied the nerves with small talk until Alicia suddenly came to the point. 'What interest does a movie star have in this part of Cuba?' she said. 'We are the poor part. Even President Batista has little interest in us.'

'Our interest is strictly commercial,' Barry said. 'We believe we can help you publicise your cause, and you can help us make a popular movie.'

'My cause?'

'The revolutionary cause,' Barry said.

'Your cause, Alicia,' I said. 'Shouldn't we lay our cards on the table? I think I recognise commitment when I see it.'

'Oh, I see,' she said with eyebrows raised. 'Your experience as Robin Hood, of course.' It was the first time I noticed the glint in her eye.

'Errol,' Barry said, 'Senorita Frias has MIT for her alma mater. Chemical engineering, wasn't it, senorita? Don't think you can just . . .'

'Oh, not at all,' I said. 'It's just that one doesn't easily associate a political struggle with someone with the looks of Lupe Velez.'

Alicia grinned indulgently and smoothed the dress over her thighs. 'I suspect to you, we Latin types all look alike.'

'No, no, no. Lupe wasn't at all like Dolores del Rio. And of course, Carmen Miranda . . . *well*. But Lupe . . . Lupe had fire.'

'Lupe Velez,' said Alicia. 'Didn't she die with her head in a toilet?'

'Oh, an old wives tale,' I said, although I knew it wasn't.

'I will remind you of that one day. You grouped me with the old wives.'

I was good at covering embarrassment with a hearty laugh and a slap of the thigh, something Mike Curtiz drilled into me while I was still young. 'So tell me, Alicia. Cuba's had rebels for one hundred years. What makes these different?'

'You tell me something first. In Havana, did you hear this . . . there will be no rebels in our swimming pools?'

'You know,' I said, 'I do believe I did hear something like that.'

'Then that is your answer.'

That was a conundrum worthy of MIT, and I told her so. 'But might it not be that this time they are *communista*? This time they are not alone in the world?'

'Not *communista*, Errol. *Fidelista*. This time the mountains are heaving with *candeladas*, moths at the flame, as we say.'

'And what role might a lady such as yourself fill among these bearded moths?'

'My *barbudos*, senor?' She leaned forward and lowered her voice. 'Can I trust you?'

I did the same. 'No one here but us monkeys. You can trust Robin Hood.'

'But can I trust Don Juan?'

I slid forward onto my knees, taking her hand in mine. 'Upon my father's sword, senorita.'

She sighed and got to her feet. Without another word she left the room.

'That's gonna wipe the fuck-you grin off your dial,' Barry said. 'Now you've gone too far.'

I sat back, crossed my legs and lit a cigarette. 'Barry, old chap, you just don't know women. In this house, nothing is too far.'

We sipped our champagne in a silence broken only by the ticking of a grandfather clock in the corner. After a minute or two it chimed for midnight, causing both of us to jump from our chairs just as the door opened again.

'No need to get up,' the young man said. 'My name is Julio.' He was dressed casually in blue slacks and white shirt and could have been anyone we'd seen on the streets of Santiago.

Alicia followed him into the room. 'Julio has been in the mountains to the north with Raul,' she said. 'He will soon be on his way to the Sierra Maestra, so you are lucky to catch him.'

'You are joining up with Castro?' I asked.

'With Fidel, *si*, eventually,' Julio said. 'Senorita Frias tells me you, also. That is your wish?'

'Well, not to join up,' Barry said. 'Merely to follow. We would like to follow you with our camera. Use our actors among your men. Film any skirmishes that may occur.'

'I see,' said Julio. 'And interviews? You seek the interview, of course.'

We looked at one another. 'Of course,' I said.

'I see,' said Julio again. He nodded his head and looked at his shoes. 'You support the struggle, no?'

'Our interest is a professional one,' Barry said.

'You do not intend to take up arms?'

'Only cameras, I assure you.'

Julio continued nodding. 'This regime, this Batista. You know he took the office with violence. Only with violence can he be removed. You understand?'

'Oh, of course,' Barry said. 'What you do is what you have to do. We are here to do a job. A job for both of us.'

Julio nodded and turned to me. 'And you, senor. You have taken up arms in the past, no?'

'Well . . . many of my roles . . .'

'No, in Spain. You have taken up arms in Spain.'

'Oh, I wouldn't say . . .'

'They say you killed a man.'

It sounded to me like 'they' had been reading too much *Great Gatsby*. 'I'm afraid that too many things are said about me.'

'So it is not true?'

'I think you will appreciate, senor, in my position, I can't afford to confirm any such rumours.'

Julio and Alicia exchanged quick glances. 'You must be aware, senor,' Julio said. 'Fidel, he has killed many. If there is anything to your mission that is not as you say, he will not hesitate to kill you.'

As the gates closed behind us, Barry couldn't wait. 'Are you still sure about this? This Fidel character sounds like murder incorporated.'

'It's just a bluff,' I said, lighting myself a relaxing Dimitrino. 'Kill me? What do you think that would do to his cause? No, they're just testing our credentials. I think Herb Matthews got out with his life.'

83

'Oh yeah? And interviews? Why the fuck did you say that? We don't even have sound. This guy who's killed so many, what's he gonna do when he works out we're just jerking him around?'

'Don't worry,' I said. 'I can fake it if we have to.'

Barry looked at me like it was the first time he'd ever heard me say something absurd. 'Christ ... you think you can just flim-flam these guys? You're not in Hollywood now, Errol. They carry guns here.'

I slipped a reassuring arm around his shoulder. 'Barry ... do you really think Jack Warner doesn't carry a gun?'

We walked along the dark street with just the sound of our footsteps for company until a mambo rhythm carried softly on the breeze from town. 'Do you think he was anyone?' Barry said. 'High up, I mean.'

'Senor Cohen, you mean? Without a beard? He's a flunky. Steals into town to deliver messages and fuck his rich mistress. How old would you say she is?'

'I dunno. Late twenties maybe. Wait a minute ...' Barry stopped and took hold of my arm. 'You're not planning anything. That Lupe Velez routine ...'

'Don't worry, old sport. She's too old for me. Too old for him, too. But if she is connected to the Bacardis, that could be useful.'

'For what?'

'Why, cheap rum, of course.'

'Christ, no wonder he didn't trust you. You do know that, don't you? He didn't trust you.'

'No, not at first,' I said. 'But he came around. I can be an acquired taste.'

9
A part with something to say.
Santiago de Cuba, 22 November 1958

When news of Tyrone Power's sudden death reached Santiago de Cuba it sent me into a feverish tropical spin – a cocktail of melancholy shaken over malaria that laid me low in my room at the Casa Granda for two days. Beverly played nurse, plying me with quinine and hiding from me the vodka, applying cold towels to my forehead and neck one minute, thick blankets over my chest the next, bathing away the perspiration and listening to my raving laments for Ty, for Bogie, for Barrymore, Freddie McEvoy, Alan Hale, Walter Huston, Lupe Velez . . . all the dead departed. She wrote some of it down, intrigued by its random scatological poetry, I suppose, and when I emerged from the hell my body put me through and my mind created for me, she told me that she learned more about her 'big companion' than she had gleaned in all the previous months we had been together.

I said, you want to know why this news has knocked me about? Let me tell you about Ty Power. Before the war he was the resident swashbuckler at Fox, the pirate with a glint in his eye and a knife between his teeth, the crusader with a sword in his hand. Swashbuckler! Was there ever an uglier word in the English language?

He said he was sick of all the knight-in-shining-armour roles. He wanted a part with something to say. Demanded it. I know all about that. Everyone wants to be beautiful, everyone's jealous of it. Let me tell you, be careful what you wish for. They let him do *The Razor's Edge* to shut him up for a while. Then it was back to the swordplay and the damsels in distress. And that's how he died. In a goddamn swordfight with George Sanders. Collapsed from a heart attack at 44. At least he had a decent swansong – *Witness for the Prosecution*. He was good in that at least. And who does all that sound like? Swap his *Razor's Edge* for my *Forsyte Woman*, swap Fox for Warners, swap *Witness* for *Too Much Too Soon*, and who do you get?

Jack Warner used to call us the Fabulous Five – Flynn, Power, Gable, Cooper and Bogart. The names in lights that meant money in the bank. Bogie's gone, now Ty. Who's it going to be next?

'He had a line in *The Sun Also Rises*,' I said over a consoling vodka. 'Everyone behaves badly given the chance. Nice line, huh? Hemingway wrote it, Power delivered it, but it's Flynn who lives it. You know what else he said? The secret of charm is bullshit. That's a Ty Power original, that one. The . . . secret . . . of . . . charm . . . is . . . bullshit. And it's one we've both lived. You know why I can't wait to get into those mountains, Woodsie? I just may be lucky enough to catch a bullet. The hell with it all.'

'You don't really want that,' she said.

'The hell I don't. Catch a bullet and let some corner of a foreign field be forever . . . what am I, anyway? Be forever whatever I am. You think I give a damn about this shit of a film we may or may not make? A bullet . . . that's why I went to Spain. I didn't care about sides, not even about adventure. The only struggle I cared about was the one in my head. I'll tell you something else. I've only ever told one person about this, but I'll tell you now. What the hell, you'll read it in my book one day anyway. There was a week once when I couldn't stand any more what I'd become, what they'd made me. A phallic symbol. A shallow, philandering fool. Every night that week, when I came home from the studio I stuck a gun in my mouth and tried to work up the courage to pull the trigger. Every night! For a week! Maybe more. I can still taste that barrel and that oil. That's when I really started to drink. That's when I started trying to drink myself to death. But booze never gave me the guts to pull the trigger. And booze doesn't take away that taste. You know who that other person was I told? Ty Power. In the dust out the back of a rat-infested cantina in some godforsaken nowheresville in boondocks Mexico. He'd been along the same dark alley. That's what he called it, the dark alley. When do you come out of that alley, Woodsie? When you work up the courage to pull the trigger, or when the drink finally takes you away? Or when you just drop dead in the middle of a swordfight with George Sanders? Is that where salvation waits for me, too? I'd rather it be up in the mountains, in a gunfight, with Batista, or Castro, or whoever's up there waiting for me. Ty Power went right through the war, fought in the Pacific, and comes home to die on a fucking soundstage or a backlot or a godforsaken nowheresville in Mexico. They wouldn't even let me go to war. Every other bastard went, but not me, no. Not fit, they said. 4F. General Custer one minute, four-fucking-F the next. When Ty Power was plugging Japs I was shooting blanks at make-believe Indians, or fighting make-believe fights with a make-believe John L Sullivan. Up in the mountains, I can die with my boots on up there, all right. Not in a fucking movie. Not in a fucking Hollywood nowheresville. Not in a fucking dark alley, a blind alley. The mountains . . . that's for me, Woodsie . . . that's for me . . .'

'You're drunk,' she said.

But I was already asleep.

10
If anyone can make us famous, it is you.

Sierra Maestra, 25 November 1958

Before sun-up we *yanquis* squeezed into our Woodsie wagons with the camera and left Santiago, heading north. Barry had given strict instructions – one small bag per person, and shared words with me when I appeared with Beverly and half a dozen bags. Out of her earshot, I blamed it on Beverly: She's the star, old man, what can you say?

We met our escorts at first light in Palma Soriano, 50 kilometres up the highway. They were truck drivers – sullen, heavy set, bearded – and in our crowded wagons we followed their belching diesel lorry for another 50 kilometres around the northern edge of the mountains to the outskirts of Jiguani, where we were told to wait. Barry had a short discussion with one by the side of the road, and when he returned he said we would not be required to venture deep into the mountains after all. The rebels were on the offensive, Barry said, and their new camp was nearby. We were led to a sugarcane farm at the foot of the hills where we left our vehicles. Our gear was transferred onto pack mules, and once again we followed our two guides through the canefields and onto the low slopes of the cloud forest. Eventually, we reached a coffee farm with what our guides called a *bohio*, a palm-thatched shack under the twisted red limbs of an almacigo tree, where we unpacked.

Mist held the peaks and hid the sun as we sat around on the smooth dirt floor. The only furniture was a tired rocking chair, which none of us was willing to trust. A stone fireplace supported the entire structure, and our guides cleaned it out to make a fire. They cooked up a pot of beans and rice before changing into military fatigues, slinging rifles over their shoulders and slipping 26 JULIO armbands on their sleeves. Then they left us to the mosquitoes and disappeared into the forest. After dark, barking dogs heralded the arrival of a third bearded rebel. He was older than the guides and had the same brooding look about him, but was more sociable. He introduced himself as *companero* Chico. He spoke only Spanish, but we managed to grasp that he had been sent by *companero* Julio to stay with us until *companero* Fidel could see us. We asked when that might be. *Companero* Chico just smiled and shrugged.

We practised our fractured Spanish for the next hour or two, and while Chico was happy to talk about Santiago, the weather, coffee and the small bottle of home-made rum he shared around, he had nothing to say about himself and clearly had no understanding of who his *yanqui* guests were or what we were doing there. Around midnight a low whistle came from the forest, which set the dogs off again. Chico followed it and five minutes later returned among a column of heavily armed 26 JULIO *rebelde*, a dozen bearded young men. Most of them packed into the small room that was the farmhouse, sitting on the hard-packed floor around the walls, and looked sullenly enough in my direction to make me feel decidedly uncomfortable.

The one sitting next to Chico produced a cigar and offered it to me. 'You bring food?' he asked in a voice only slightly above a hoarse whisper.

'We have canned food,' Barry said. 'Do you want some?'

The rebel turned his tranquil gaze to Barry and then offered him a cigar as well. 'No, we have food. Food for you to eat, I mean to say. There is vegetable garden here. You can eat from it. There is chicken, you can eat egg. You must always leave one egg or chicken he will not lay. Chicken is not for you to eat. Pigs also, not for you to eat. We leave some sausage for you in the can and some milk. With sausage you make soup to eat. Water for soup from stream down this hill. You make no fire in the day, only fire at the night to cook. One meal a day only. You make the fire already today, but no more.' He turned again to me as I lit up my cigar. 'Julio, he say to me you wish to make us famous.'

'Julio?'

'*Si*, Julio. He say if anyone can make us famous, it is you. Is that so?'

There were about twenty pairs of eyes on me now as I sucked on the cigar to fire it up. 'Julio, yes, we met Julio in Santiago a few days ago. Julio and Alicia. Delightful couple. He said he was coming to join up with you.'

'Join with us? He is already join with us. Julio he has been with Raul, my brother. You wish to make interview, no?'

I hadn't expected my bluff to return to me so quickly. 'Well, yes . . .'

'Already I have interview. I have been on front page of the *New York Times*, do you know? The famous Herbert Matthews, he interview me. He is famous, no? Only pictures he take with the box camera. They look okay. Now I think television. Only television matters now in America. Huntley and Brinkley, Ed Murrow, these men matter. Do you know these men?'

The softly-spoken voice, the trusting eyes, the naïve appeal, they had conspired to deceive me. This was ego Gigante? I don't suppose it was his intention, it was just that I had been presented

90

to kings and queens, dined with presidents and prime ministers, traded blows with studio moguls and hotshot lawyers and thought I had their measure, and I simply expected the leader of the revolution to carry himself in a similar self-important manner. 'You . . . you are Fidel?'

'*Si, por supuesto*. And you are Errol Flynn. I have seen some movies with you. You look different. I like your *Don Juan*. But tell me, why no Spanish in *Don Juan*? Everyone in English, with stupid accent. No one in Hollywood can speak Spanish? Do you know Marlon Brando? Can he speak Spanish? His Mexican picture, *Zapata*. *Mierda!* Speak in the English like *chilito*. And they make him look like Chinaman, like the village fool. He win Oscar for being the village fool? You know who is writing that picture? John Steinbeck. He is a great writer, no? Why is he writing Zapata to be the village fool? And Zapata, why they make the picture about him? Why not Jose Marti, father of Cuba *libre*? Zapata was not *rebelde*, he was *bandido*. The land is all he want for the people. The land is good. But what of the worker? What of the health? What of the education? What good is the land when you are sick, when your son he cannot go to school? These are the things I want to say to Ed Murrow. These are the things I want American people to know. Also how their gangsters destroy my country. All their drugs, they come through Cuba. How can that be? Your people must know this. We win our freedom from Spain, and America take it away from us. We have no freedom. This time we will have our revolution, we will have our freedom. American people must know this. I like Americans. I like you. I do not like your gangsters and your *bandidos* who steal our sugar, our fruit, everything we have. Such things must not go on. America owns America, Cuba must own Cuba. That is fair, no? Ed Murrow, he will have the interest in this, no? He will have the interest in what I say.'

'Oh, I'm sure he ...'

'I say too much, no? Always I say too much. We talk such things tomorrow. I stay for tomorrow. Tonight you talk. Tonight I listen. We all listen.'

And they did. For hours in the cold mountain air the business of revolution was put aside. Over enamel mugs of warming homemade rum they listened to my stories and Fidel's translations. Hollywood stories, the kind that *Confidential* magazine overheard in a bar and then fashioned into a boozy scandal. Why should *Confidential* be the only fabricator of truth? There was an audience at my feet and I certainly didn't want to disappoint them, so I told them stories of Bogart and Gable, Barrymore and Rooney, the adventures of the Bundy Drive Boys and with my leading ladies, although not of any conquests that weren't already in the public domain, which still gave me hours of ammunition. In Lupe Velez there was particular interest, and when I told them how she could rotate her breasts in opposite directions at the same time, acting out her performance in the middle of the room, they applauded. I told them of Charlie Chaplin's nose powder parties, Abbott and Costello's stag film nights, George Raft's ... Fidel wasn't interested in hearing anything about George Raft, however juicy. I told them of how much King Farouk could eat, Ali Khan could gamble and Diego Rivera could go through the loco weed. I told them who had been seen through the two-way mirror above my bed, and how I had swung from chandeliers at parties like I had swung from the rigging in *Captain Blood*. I told them how, when making *Captain Blood*, I once crashed to the deck when malaria struck. I lay on the earthen floor of the *bohio*, shivering and shaking and wielding an imaginary cutlass, and they laughed.

Under this deluge of tired old tales, the other *yanquis* drifted off one by one and the other *barbudos* drifted outside. Fidel and I were the last men standing on legs made a little unsteady by the homemade rum. Fidel said he loved the movies. When he was growing up in Santiago he went every Sunday. He said he loved the westerns best, the ones where the cowboys' guns never ran out of bullets. We talked of America. He chewed his cigar and said how he had always admired Roosevelt. The New Deal, he said, this was what he wanted to give to Cuba. To overthrow Batista and give Cuba a New Deal, like Roosevelt's. I told him about my dinners in the White House with the Roosevelt family. Fidel looked at me with astonishment and said, you know Roosevelt? Not any more, I said. I asked him how he had done it, how he had beaten ten thousand men with just three hundred, just like the Battle of Thermopylae. He lifted his head like a proud beast and said yes, he had three hundred soldiers, but also six million Cubans on his side.

We talked of writers, of our parallel experiences of solitary confinement, Fidel in prison on the Isle of Pines and me on a remote copra plantation in New Guinea, and how we had both filled our desolate nights and exercised our impressionable young minds by devouring the classics. Fidel argued for the French humanists, I for the German philosophers. I claimed victory by weight of numbers, Fidel laughed. We compared notes on Karl Marx. I said he was a crashing bore, Fidel said he had a fine time reading him, enjoyed every page. How could you contend with that? So I changed the subject ... to music. Never met a Cuban who didn't love music. Oudrid's *Siege of Zaragoza*, said Fidel, had inspired his revolution.

I didn't know much about Oudrid, but I could dance to anything. I hummed Guantanamera and danced a cha-cha-cha. Anna Pavlova, I told him, was the first woman I fell in love with. He didn't know much about Pavlova. I had been taught by Hollywood masters, Fidel couldn't dance a step. You must be the only man in Cuba, I said. Fidel supplied lyrics to my humming, the

Versos Sencillos of Jose Marti for Guantanamera. He was off-key but those verses were moving to any Cuban, any time. You cannot tell a Cuban about music, he said to me.

Fidel asked me about Spain. Wasn't I with the Loyalists, on the Republican side? I said I had to be careful about taking sides. Hearst had threatened to brand me a communist in all his newspapers, destroy my career for putting a Republican slant to my reports and Jack Warner had put a muzzle on my response. In a conflict one must choose a side, Fidel said, the middle ground is the dangerous ground. That sounds familiar, I said. You said it when you were Don Juan, said Fidel. And we laughed.

Fidel said that everyone who stands up to *bandidos* like Hearst gets called a communist. Well, you'd better prepare yourself, I said. Hearst destroyed Cuba, said Fidel. Made so much noise about the sinking of the *Maine* that America had to go to war against Spain. Cuba was America's prize, he said. Cuban sugar was Hershey's prize. When the Spanish surrendered, it was the American flag that was raised, not the Cuban. Cubanos were not even invited to the ceremony.

When we ran out of rum I opened up my survival kit and poured two large vodkas. Fidel grabbed the leather bag from me and pulled out the Bible. You read this? Faith, hope and love, I explained, and the greatest of these is love. The gospel of Don Juan, said Fidel. And we laughed.

We swapped stories of our conquests. Don Fidel's were from his days as the student prince at university in Havana. Don Errol had plenty of stories about Havana himself . . . and Sydney, and New Guinea, and Manila, and Hong Kong, and Macao, and Saigon, and Calcutta, and Marrakesh. I didn't even get started on Europe and America. But Fidel was still young, I said. Plenty of time to catch up, plenty of women to go around. I told him about the sort of future he had to look forward to, about the Russian princess I met who liked providing the S and expected the M from me. You have been to Russia, asked Fidel. No, that was in New York, the first night I was ever there. Fidel said he had spent his honeymoon in New York. I said the Russian princess had the most beautiful slender ankles. Slender ankles were what to look for in a woman. Breasts, said Fidel. *Tetas* were the best aphrodisiac. The women in Mexico, he said with his hands cupped before his chest. He had spent much time in Mexico. Ah, Mexico, I sighed. Don't get me started on Mexico. A woman there had put cocaine on the tip of my penis once. That was an aphrodisiac, I said. I'd tried aphrodisiacs all around the world – India, Spain, France, China – from oysters to Spanish fly, rhino horn to tiger testicles to all kinds of roots, leaves and barks – none of them work like the touch of a beautiful woman, I said.

I asked him if he was still married. Divorced, said Fidel. I said I had been married three times myself, legally that is, although never truly married at all. It might be legal, I said, but it's not natural and Fidel agreed that must be true. The vodka was talking now, and I said women think they are more profound than us, they think men are superficial, only after one thing. It's true. We are. And so are they. They are after our houses. I told him how I had once bugged the ladies room at a party. What I heard taught me more about women, and more about myself, than a year with a shrink. Don't think a woman's mind is any nobler than a man's, I said. They swore like sailors. But a woman friend is the best friend you can have, I said. Just so long as it's platonic. They're good, honest. They stick by you, stand up for you, tell you what you need to know. The trick is keeping it platonic. That's always the hard part. In me, the vodka would not shut up.

In Fidel, it had gone silent, or he had simply run out of things to say. He was still young, after all. I said that in every woman is a touch of man, and in every man a touch of woman. Women know this, women understand us better than we understand them. You want to know the best aphrodisiac? Reach for the woman in you and you will reach the woman in front of you.

I wasn't sure if Fidel's English was up to an appreciation of that, and perhaps it was a bit trite anyway. It was the drink that was making me trite, and the drink was making the Cuban maudlin, even uneasy with the discussion. I lightened the mood with some jokes, about the organ grinder's monkey, about the world's last limerick contest, about the cross-eyed plough horse. When light crept into the farmhouse we were still laughing, still drinking. I could drink around the clock. I told Fidel about *Assault of the Rebel Girls*. He loved the idea. He said he had the real thing fighting for him already, a platoon of women he called the 'Marianas', and he didn't even want to see a script. He shook Chico awake. *Pistolita*, he said, Senor Flynn should have anything he wants, Senor Flynn would make the revolution famous. And then he asked me about what he had heard, that I had killed one of Franco's Nationalists in Spain. I ummed and ah'd and Fidel said, you have conquered so many women, but I think not so many men. He woke the rest of his rebels and led them back across the field and into the forest. It seemed important that he at least had the last word.

I woke Barry. Was that Fidel Castro I was talking to, I said, or Li'l Abner? If he's Mr Murder Incorporated then he disguises it well. Whoever he is, he's been away from civilisation far too long. Maybe it's jungle fever. I don't know what they'll do if they win this revolution. The State Department or the CIA or the FBI or whoever handles these things . . . they'll eat this poor sucker for lunch.

As long as we get our picture before lunch, Barry said. As long as we get our picture.

11
Such a man is *el commandante*.

Sierra Maestra, 5 December 1958

I never met a Hollywood film star who didn't love being a Hollywood film star. And why wouldn't they? Living the Hollywood dream, as the columnists were fond of saying. Even Orson Welles, as much as he claimed to be above such trivial pursuits, lapped it up. The only time I saw a film star who felt differently was on those occasions when I had to look at myself in the make-up mirror. My dream was never to be a film star. An actor, yes, for a time, but that wore off. A writer, an academic, a scientist like my father – all these had appeal. A sailor, definitely. Unlike most Hollywood hopefuls I didn't pay my dues waiting tables, jerking sodas or getting down on my hands and knees under the desk of some big shot producer. In fact, I wasn't a Hollywood hopeful at all. I didn't arrive in town with stars in my eyes and nothing in my pocket. I was sent for. I stepped off the boat with Lili Damita in my pocket. No, I simply took the easy option. My looks, my athleticism and (let's face it) my charm gave me an easy in with Hollywood. Being a writer, an academic, a scientist, these take work.

I always thought I could walk away from it at any time and pursue one of my dreams, but a job like that is a honey trap. The fame, the money, the adulation — the easy women — they tie you down, and fasten a ball and chain around your leg that takes more strength of character than I possessed to remove. Honey became one of my many addictions. Does an academic get mobbed at the airport? Does a scientist get his choice of overnight companions wherever he goes? And writers — if the best of them all dreams of just once more tasting the thrill of a bit of anonymous adulation, how could that life ever measure up after the bright lights of Hollywood have illuminated your cerebral cortex?

No, it was never real work. And that's why I tried to make it so. To treat my days at the studio like a day at the office or the factory — turn up on time, do my job, clown around a bit, go home. Just like a regular guy. I didn't mind those days. Eight hours, ten hours, sixteen hours at the studio and the rest in the company of books or my pals or someone of the other type who simply would not be denied. What I really didn't like was the location shooting. My reputation doesn't allow for the fact that I was always something of a homebody, and I know such a misconception was of my own making. But I was never happier than when I was home in the hills on Mulholland Drive or by the sea at Port Antonio. Even my yachts when I was cruising the oceans, they were my home. On location there was nowhere to retreat to, no castle where the drawbridge could be drawn up and I could forget about betraying the promise of my youth.

On location I was often unreasonably angry and to relieve such a state I played pranks to amuse myself. I'd make an entrance for a scene in my birthday suit, causing the less robust of my leading ladies to fall in a heap. I'd put dead snakes in underwear, spiders in props and, yes, drive the odd automobile into a swimming pool if the situation really needed a shot in the arm. A shot in the arm often made location shooting bearable.

I only played my tricks on people I liked. They were tests, I suppose, to see how much I actually liked them. What was the point of playing a prank on someone I didn't like? That was a waste of a good prank. There were other ways to get at the people I didn't like.

Our Cuba location shoot was probably the most unusual of my career, such as it was by that stage of my life. We were a small company, and there was no studio at the end of a line of supply, no comforts laid on. Our resources were strictly our own. I was too old to be angry by then. Dreams and promise are the privilege of young men. I was a tired Hollywood film star and I had learned to accept my lot. Raging against the dying of the light, this was something I fancied beyond me now. It took the trials of those months to shake me up.

I watched Barry standing ankle deep in mud on the bank of the stream as he raised the megaphone to his lips. 'Everyone except Errol and Beverly, remember . . . backs to camera. I don't want to see your mouths. First positions everyone.'

Chloe moved the horse between me and the camera and ducked down with the reins out of shot. Barry squinted through the lens. 'And Errol and Beverly, you two remember . . . speak distinctly, move your lips. This is a tight two-shot over the saddle and I can't tell you often enough we have to dub all this dialogue, so give us something to work with. If you fluff your lines, just keep going, don't stop. Okay everybody . . . camera!'

'Rolling.'

'And . . . action!'

'Haven't I seen you some place before, on TV or somewhere?' Beverly said to me clearly.

'Could be,' I said. 'But what's a pretty girl like you doing down here?'

'I'm looking for a man.'

I gave her my best double-take. 'A what?'

'A man.'

'A worthy pursuit, I must admit,' I said, and threw in just a suggestion of my sly grin.

'Cut! Check the gate. That's a print.' Barry had been reading too many film books. 'How was that for camera?'

'Maybe once more,' the cameraman said. 'The horse is standing there like it's stuffed. Maybe Chloe could just get him to move his head, or something. So we know he's alive.'

'It'll be fine,' Barry said. 'Moving on. Set up for the wide.' But probably not the right film books. He turned to me. 'How was it for you?'

'Stuffed, just like the horse. Shouldn't we introduce ourselves? I mean, this is the first time we meet. Shouldn't we at least swap names?'

'I thought we agreed not to use names,' Barry said. 'American Correspondent and Rebel Girl, that's what it's always been.'

'I know . . . but Johnny's Johnny, Jackie's Jackie. I was thinking . . .'

'Go on,' said Barry. 'I knew I shouldn't have brought the writer on location.'

'Well, what about calling Beverly's character Peggy?'

'Why Peggy? Why not go the whole hog? Why not Peggy-Sue?'

'It's my little joke. You remember my trial? That was my complainant's name. Maybe the LA Attorney's office will see this. I'd like that.'

'Oh, I know. Look out the porthole, Peggy. That was the famous line, wasn't it?'

The famous line, second only to 'In like Flynn', that was still following me around, fifteen years after the trial. 'Yeah, another great moment in fiction. How about it?'

'How about this – you flip the bird to the LA Attorney some other time. We're on to the wide.'

The camera was repositioned to cover the edge of the cane-field with the stream in the background. We actors all arranged ourselves into a single file with the horse.

'Okay, no dialogue with this one,' Barry hailed. 'Just fix those happy-to-have-found-you looks to your dials and let's get this in one. Errol and Beverly, don't forget to exchange glances at second position.' He strode up to a patch of mud near the edge of the cane. 'That's here, okay? This mud near your mark.'

'That's not mud,' said a voice among the crew. 'That's mule shit.'

'Hard to tell the mule shit from the horse shit in this one,' I said.

Barry preferred not to hear me. 'Okay everybody . . . camera!'

'Rolling.'

'And . . . action!'

We passed in front of the camera and up the track. Beverly and I shared an awkward look, as directed, when we reached the manure.

'Who the fuck is that?' Barry said. He was glaring down the track where a group of riders was approaching from the opposite direction. 'Cut! Cut! Are those people in shot?'

'Right across top of frame,' the cameraman said.

'Christ! Who the fuck are they?' Barry zoomed in on the newcomers through his viewfinder. 'Well waddaya know . . . it's our friend Chico.'

'At last,' I said. 'A dispatch from the front line. It's been so long I thought old Fidel had forgotten about us.'

There were five riders, Chico and a woman on horses and three men on mules. The woman had a rifle over the shoulder of her fatigues and *bandoleras* crossing her chest. The other three men looked like peasant farmers, with battered straw hats and ragged pants. 'I am Lucia,' the woman said. '*Companero* Fidel sent me to be translator. He says no one here can speak Spanish.'

'Perhaps not very well,' Barry conceded.

'Also he send *Trio Rebelde*,' she said, pointing at the three farmers. 'He say you need music. They make good music.'

She barked at the farmers in Spanish. They quickly jumped from their mules, unhitched guitars and congas, and without stopping to draw breath, burst into a folksy mambo.

'What music?' Barry shouted above the din.

'Movies have music, no?' the woman said. '*Trio Rebelde*, they make good music for your movie.'

Barry looked at me, and I stopped laughing long enough to shrug at my director.

'They can do for you Guantanamera,' the woman said. 'But *companero* Fidel, he say no cha-cha-cha. He say this movie it should have no cha-cha-cha.'

I liked the look of Lucia, sitting up high and proud on her old nag, looking down her nose at us *yanquis* and our frivolous pursuits. I thought she was probably pushing forty, so it would be difficult to find a role for her among our rebel girls, but the *bandoleros* and the grenades pinned to her chest, these were interesting props. Later I asked her to send Chico off to the arsenal and bring back a supply of each. Lucia looked at me with disdain. Arsenal? They were a mobile force, they had no such thing. Fidel was laying siege to Maffo, a well-armed Batista garrison. They couldn't afford to give us *bandoleros* and grenades. All right, I said, but what about the armbands, the 26 JULIO armbands? I asked her just to put it to Chico and let him see what he could do. Fidel said whatever we want, I said.

I still liked the look of the woman. After Chico was on his way I discussed an addition to the script with Barry — a scene with

Lucia playing a den mother to the girls. I had no idea where the scene would fit, but we would find a place for it somewhere.

The light was going as we all helped to quickly set up a rebel campfire scene, with hammocks strung between trees and ammunition boxes for seats. The camera was positioned behind Lucia's shoulder, ready to pan over the faces of the girls hanging on her every word. 'What should I say?' she asked.

'It doesn't matter,' I said. 'We're not shooting for sound and we can't see your mouth. Say whatever you want.'

'Action!' called Barry.

'Guantanamera . . . guajira Guantanamera . . .'

'Cut! Cut! What's with the goddamn mariachi boys?'

'Music, old chap,' I said. 'Movies have music, no?'

Barry took the band aside and gave them cigarettes and told them they wouldn't be needed for a while. The leader removed his hat and politely objected, pointing to me, and Barry explored the limits of his Spanish to explain the situation. He then took me aside. 'We're losing the light. Can we save the pranks for another time?'

Again the camera rolled. '*Companero* Fidel,' Lucia said to the girls, 'he is a great warrior. No one can fight like Fidel. No one can be smarter. And we women who know him . . .' She turned around to me standing by the camera.

'Don't look at us!' Barry said. 'Look at them!'

Lucia turned back to the girls. 'We women who follow him, how can we not love him? Such a man . . .' And again she turned her face to me. 'Such a man is *el commandante*.'

'Cut!' Barry screamed. 'You can't look at the damn camera!' he threw his hands in the air and heaved an exasperated sigh. 'Set up for the reverse,' he said to the cameraman.

He knelt in front of Lucia. 'This time, sweetie,' he said, 'don't say anything. Just smile and look at the girls. And don't, whatever you do, don't look at the camera.' He turned to Beverly. 'In this shot I want you to ask Lucia a question.'

'What question?' said Beverly.

'It doesn't matter. This time we can't see *your* face.'

'Well, where's my script?'

'There is no goddamn script for this, honey,' Barry said. 'We're just picking it up.'

'You mean making it up,' Beverly said.

'Look,' Barry said impatiently, 'just ask her a question. And use your hands and move your head a bit. So we can see that it's you talking.'

'What am I saying?'

'Ferchrissake! Action!'

Beverly looked at Lucia, looked at the sky, looked at Barry.

'Don't look at me! Look at her! Ask her a question!'

'Ummm . . . Hey! When do we get to shoot the enemy?'

Lucia frowned at her. 'Are all you Americans so bloodthirsty?'

'Cut! Jesus, Lucia. Just smile. Don't say anything.'

'But . . . she asked me a question.'

I whispered into Barry's ear. 'I don't think we really need this shot, sport.'

'That's a wrap,' said Barry. 'We've lost the light.'

I signalled the band.

'*Guantanamera . . . guajira Guantanamera . . .*'

'Are all you Americans so bloodthirsty?' I said to Barry. 'I like that. Let's use it somewhere.'

12
And now you expect me to buy a ticket.

Sierra Maestra, 6 December 1958

The American Correspondent and the Rebel Girl sat in the shade of a guaguasi tree by a mule track that led deep into the cloud forest of the Sierra Maestra as the camera rolled. The American Correspondent loosened the laces on his boots and asked the Rebel Girl why she was here in these foreign mountains, why she wasn't back in New York painting nails in her beauty parlour. Enunciating clearly so that her lips formed visible vowels for the camera, she said, 'Why, I think it's every young American's duty to show the world what freedom means.'

That was enough for me. I took my survival kit to the edge of the clearing while the camera was set up for the next shot, a bold charge by the entire cast into the canefield, weapons at the ready. The charge of the light relief brigade. So many nights curled into a hammock were playing havoc with my vertebrae. Turning my troublesome back to the crew I took a quick shot of vodka. I reached up for a low hanging branch and could just touch it with my fingertips. I jumped up the few inches it took to take a grip on the branch. Hanging there like that for a minute, for as long as my arms could manage it, stretched my spine and helped with the pain.

'When will you make the interview with *companero* Fidel, senor?'

I released my grip and dropped to the ground gently. Lucia was not an unattractive woman, in fact had probably once been a bit of a looker, but it was terrible what a few years of hard living in a mountainous jungle could do to the complexion. The shapeless fatigues certainly didn't help. Beverly still had the figure to fill them out, but Lucia just seemed to be poured into hers like potatoes in a sack. 'I haven't even seen *companero* Fidel for two weeks,' I said to her.

'But you see, he is *el commandante*. He is pressing for the victory.'

I lit up one of my Egyptian cigarettes and offered her one. 'I appreciate that, Lucia, but it's difficult to do it without him. The sound of one hand clapping, if you see what I mean.'

'*Companero* Fidel he has already defeated many towns,' she said, ignoring the pack of cigarettes. 'The revolution it sweeps over Cuba. Soon he will defeat Maffo. Already the plans for Santiago we have. Santiago will be a glorious battle, a long battle. Santiago is the heart and the soul of Cuba. Soon it will be as an island in Fidel's sea.'

I undid the red bandana from around my neck and wiped the sweat from my forehead as I took a good look at this rebel woman. 'Mm, stirring stuff. Can I get you a soapbox?'

'A . . . soapbox?'

'Look, how about you take us to Maffo. It's not far, is it? Those planes that have been buzzing over us, that's where they're going, isn't it? Sometimes we can even hear the bombs, or the artillery, or whatever it is. We've been stuck here in the wilderness for two weeks trying to make our own little war for the camera. What we need to see is the real war. We need to film gun battles, fighting, some of the revolution you say is sweeping the country. We want to show that to the world. To show the world your struggle. How about you ask *companero* Fidel if we can move a little closer to the action?'

'You will make the interview then?'

'Well, if the *companero* can't come to the mountain . . .' I eased myself onto the ground, my back against the tree trunk. 'Why are you all so fixed on this interview, anyway? What makes you think the world is so interested in what a bunch of rebels in faraway Cuba have to say? Give me some gun battles and I'll get you on the CBS news. Talking . . .? It's just talk.'

'When we win, they will be interested.'

'That may be so, when you win, but . . .'

'But you don't understand. We *are* winning. Soon we *will* win. Fidel, he wants everyone to understand, when we win he will make the equality for all Cubans. He will make Cubans equal like Americans.'

'Yes, well . . . some, no doubt, will be more equal than others.'

Lucia squatted on her haunches next to me. 'What do you mean?'

'I don't think, in the new social paradise,' I said, wagging my finger in the direction of the canefield at the bottom of the track, 'that we'll see *companero* Fidel down there bending his back with the masses, cutting cane.'

'But you are wrong, senor. This he has already done. Fidel and *companero* Che they cut the cane together many times.'

'*Companero* who?'

'Che.'

'What sort of name is Che? It sounds like a sneeze.'

Lucia sighed and looked down the track at the company – the cast stretched out, smoking and chatting; the crew less than flat out setting up for the shot. 'You think you are funny,' she said, her face turned away. 'You don't understand.'

Revolution – it was such a serious business. Not to me, of course, because I was yet to see a dead body in this one. 'Well, Lucia, I'm trying. But stuck out here in the middle of nowhere, it's difficult. When all you see of the revolution is a few bearded men every now and then checking up on us . . . and an attractive woman, of course . . . Why all those beards? Is it because Fidel wears one? What's he got to hide, a double chin? Is it some kind of Samson fixation?'

'Senor, this is what I say, you don't understand. We have no time to live like others. To shave the face, it takes time every day, no? Put on the make-up, wash the clothes, cut the hair . . . all these, not important.'

I preened my moustache and stroked the stubble on my chin. 'I suppose I could try it.'

'You talk of Samson and you think I do not understand. It is you who does not understand. I know of Samson. I went to the convent school, I know of such stories. You laugh and talk of Samson. But Fidel is not such a story. Fidel . . . I worship the ground where he walks.'

'That's a bit melodramatic, isn't it, old girl?'

'You don't understand, a man like you.'

'You keep saying that. And what do you mean, a man like me?'

'A man like you, senor, a man who rape the young girls.'

I was only aware that my jaw had dropped when the cigarette holder tumbled into my lap. I grabbed it, brushed the smouldering ash from my shirt and made a point of grinding the butt into the dust. 'What you are talking about is nonsense,' I said.

'I see it in the newspaper,' Lucia said coldly. 'Even in Havana I see it in the newspaper.'

'If you are talking about that farce of a trial, you would have also seen that the case was dismissed. Thrown out. And you would have seen the word *statutory*. It was not rape, it was *statutory* rape, an entirely different thing to what you are thinking. It was a long time ago, senora, and it was a charade. A trumped up circus created to advance a few political careers, and I'll not have . . .'

'Senorita.'

'What?'

'Senorita, not senora.'

'As you wish . . . senorita.'

'And not *old girl*. You prefer senoritas, no? You prefer young girls, no? Is it so that real women they frighten you? Fidel, he is a man of real women.'

She was no longer looking at me, but gazing around the clearing again with considered nonchalance and a distinctly smug air. I gathered myself. I had lost my temper, and when you lose your temper, you've already lost, as I seem to remember from one of my old dialogue lines. I fixed another cigarette and smiled deliberately at the rebel woman.

'I like my whisky old and my women young. What's so wrong with that? You're kind of the whisky type yourself.'

Her smugness slowly evaporated. 'What do you mean, whisky?'

'You don't understand,' I said, lighting up and drawing with satisfaction.

'You could never have me,' Lucia said. 'Never.'

I stretched out against the tree and put my hands behind my head. Suddenly I found myself thinking about Bette Davis again. 'Tell me,' I said. 'Did Fidel put you up to this?'

'Put you up? What is put you up?'

'Put it this way, Bette . . .'

'Lucia.'

'Lucia . . . when I was a boy we kept ducks. And you know what I discovered about ducks? I discovered that if you feed a duck a piece of fatty pork he can't digest it. It just passes right through him within a minute. That was quite a thing to observe, beak to bum in one minute flat. Now, that got me thinking. I tied a length of string to a piece of pork and fed it to a duck. And then, when it came out the other end, I fed it to another duck.

Pretty soon I had half a dozen ducks all joined together by my string. Arsehole to breakfast time, as we used to say in Australia. Then I tied the ends of the string together and sold tickets. Roll up, roll up! The world's first living bracelet! I made a pretty penny out of that discovery. Who says science doesn't pay?'

'Why do you tell me this, about your cruelty?'

'Well, it's kind of like a parable. Like those stories you heard at that convent of yours. Samson and so on. You see, you're kind of like one of those ducks. You've been fed a line and now you expect me to buy a ticket.'

'I do not understand.'

'Don't you? So we're not really so different after all.'

13
Here is your war.
Maffo, 12 December 1958

I estimated that it was probably less than ten miles to the front line at Maffo, but it took us the best part of a day to get there, with Lucia riding a horse in the lead and Chico driving the mules. We negotiated a network of mountain tracks, seeming at one stage or another to turn in every direction of the compass, not merely the necessary due east. It was late in the afternoon when we joined the rebel lines in a position overlooking a town.

The only reason we knew it was the front line was because Lucia told us so. In fact, one of many front lines in Cuba, she said. Otherwise, what it appeared to be was a camp, not unlike a New Guinea mountain village. It was more orderly than a New Guinea mountain village, but not so much that it could be picked out from above. Bush-thatch huts of varying sizes from small sleeping lean-tos to larger assembly shelters offered little in the way of privacy for the grim bearded men milling around, armed to the teeth with grenades, machetes and sticks of dynamite, as well as the customary rifles and submachine guns. Chico and Lucia engaged in an animated conversation, and from their looks and their gestures, it was obviously about the gringos now in their midst. All conversation stopped when a twin-engine plane flew low overhead. *'Veinti-seis,'* Lucia snarled, refusing to flinch. The American-built B-26 dropped a single bomb right into the middle of the little town.

'That, I assume, is Maffo,' I said. Black smoke was rising in two separate columns, and now a third began to climb into the soup suspended in the grey sky.

'Maffo,' said Lucia, nodding first, and then slowly shaking her head.

'If we're up here, who's doing the bombing down there?' Barry asked. 'Have you guys got your hands on some aircraft?'

'You think America it gives Fidel planes?' Lucia said. 'No. Only Batista has planes.' She turned to Chico and they spoke quietly in Spanish.

'Why is he bombing the town?' Barry said.

'Our men are down there,' Lucia said. 'We have men all around. Batista, he does not know where we are, so he bombs everywhere. He is an animal.' She pointed to a lump of a building in the middle of the town. 'That is where the tyrant keeps his *casquitos*. That warehouse. We have them surrounded. You want to film this? Here is your war.'

A second plane flew over, shedding crates on parachutes apparently destined for the warehouse. We watched them float down as only one out of the three landed on target. Suddenly the whole town seemed to erupt in a storm of gunfire carried up into the hills on the wind. Barry and I looked around to assess what we had – a scattering of rebels and a smoking village. It didn't look promising, to the naked eye or the camera.

'Well, sport,' I said, 'what do you want to do with this? Not very exciting, is it?'

Barry scratched his head. 'I guess . . . well, the domestic life of a rebel. Maybe a shot of the town, when a plane does another run.'

'Where is Fidel?' I asked. 'Is he around here?'

'I cannot say,' Lucia said.

'Cannot say, or will not say?'

'He knows you are here.' She turned to a group of men who had gathered to stare at the *yanqui* arrivals. 'He gives these men to you for your film. Today they are for you.'

'And tomorrow?'

'Tomorrow maybe.'

Until we lost the light we filmed our troop of rebels on their way to war. We shot them advancing through trees, hacking through scrub, marching along tracks, singing their revolutionary refrain. Beverly and Johnny and the rest of the cast of *yanqui* rebels joined them, but there was no war to be filmed. Shooting guns or exploding grenades was out – ammunition was expensive and, until they eventually captured the warehouse in the town, in short supply; and too much activity in the forest would only give the aircraft something to shoot at.

There were no planes at night, so after dark we set up a light and shot some night scenes. We found an interesting ruin with a low wall and a romantic backdrop, although in the dark it was invisible to the camera, which rather defeated the point. Johnny was positioned by the wall, looking like a real *rebelde* – beard, fatigues, cigar, rifle. The Rebel Girl had at last found her Rebel. Beverly rushed to his side and they embraced. 'Oh, Johnny,' she said dreamily as he wrapped the rifle around her waist.

'You little idiot,' Johnny said, grinning with his just-kissed lips and shaking his head. 'What are you doing here?'

'I had to see you.'

'Well, you sure picked a fine place to do it.'

A genuine rebel moved into shot, lips obscured to camera as directed, and rattled off a line in urgent Spanish. 'All right,' said Johnny, which was an eloquent reply since he didn't speak a word of Spanish. He took Beverly in his arms and kissed her again. 'Sorry, honey,' he said. 'But we both have a job to do. I'll see you later.' He marched resolutely out of shot, leaving Beverly to gaze after him with a theatrical long face.

'Cut!' said Barry. 'Okay everyone, we'll set up for Beverly and Marie with the radio.'

Barry sat against the wall and went over his script with a flashlight. I eased myself down next to him. 'How much more of this?' I asked.

'You mean tonight?' Barry said.

'I mean the whole damn thing. I mean we've been up here for three weeks and all we've got to show for the war we're supposed to be in the middle of is some smoke at the end of a long lens. To top it off, sport, I've almost run out of vodka. Have to save what I've got for medicinal purposes only.'

'I thought it was all for medicinal purposes.'

'Yes, well you may think that. But this is serious, chum. My beverage of choice is down to homemade jungle juice.' I straightened my legs flat along the ground and stretched my arms above my head. 'Hammocks and my back were not made for each other. I don't need to mention the diet. Except to warn you that if I see one more can of Carnation milk the only dialogue you'll get out of me is a *moo*. We haven't got one frame of real action. Unless we can get the camera in amongst the fighting, we're . . . well, it's supposed to be an action flick, isn't it?'

'I guess it's up to Fidel,' Barry said. 'So where do you think he is? Way behind the lines being a general, I suppose. Maybe that's why she's so coy about telling us.'

'Somehow, I don't think he's the retiring type,' I said. 'He's crazy enough to be right in the middle of things.'

'You mean down there?' he said, nodding into the darkness, but more or less in the general direction of Maffo. 'That's more than crazy. He'd have to be plum loco. If he gets whacked the whole revolution will probably just burn itself out.'

'Maybe. And what makes you think he's not loco? What about the interiors? We can get them anywhere, can't we? Havana, LA for that matter.'

'Sure. We might get some action here in . . . what's this place?'

'Maffo,' I said, and I was a little beyond masking my contempt by this stage.

'Yeah, Maffo. It'd be nice to get a climax on film. Like a march into town, people cheering.'

Ah, the euphoria of the victory march again. 'Who have you been listening to now, Ernie Hemingway? We could wait months for that. They don't look like they're in a hurry. They look like they're squeezing those bastards to death down there in that warehouse. Or starving them to death, anyway. And how do you know there'll be any cheering? That town's being blasted to hell. What's to cheer about?'

'It can be arranged,' Barry said, rubbing thumb and forefinger together.

'Maybe so. But it's not Paris, is it. Not even Havana. It's a pisspot *pueblo* in the middle of nowhere. If we have to wait for little Miss 36-24-35 to get us close to the action we might die waiting.'

'You obviously see more in *companera* Lucia than meets the eye.'

'Wishful thinking, chum. Or maybe I've just been in the middle of nowhere too long. I'll tell you what, you stick around for the glorious victory of Maffo. I'll do my fake interview with the intrepid leader so he doesn't get pissed and put the lot of us up against a wall, and then I'll beat a tactical retreat to Havana and get Victor to organise some interior locations. Does that sound like a plan?'

'Don't be too hasty. Batista's goons are sure to know we're here now. Just because you're Errol Flynn don't think they're above giving you a taste of the torture chamber.'

'They wouldn't dare.'

'So you keep saying. Don't count on it, buddy. Anyway, chief, it's not like you to leave before the party gets started.'

'Barry, old chap, this is one party that may never get started. Somehow, I don't think I'll be missing much.'

14
You can't teach a Cuban about music.

Contramaestre, 15 December 1958

I was soon told to have other ideas about escaping back to civilisation. No interview, no escape. In any event, there were no planes now, no trains and the road between Santiago and Havana had been cut in several places by rebel columns.

For two days we shot scene after scene around the camp, and then finally Chico returned in a jeep. At last the interview was to be done and he had orders to bring Barry and me to the field headquarters. We loaded up the camera and a small tape recorder we found amongst the gear, and took off along the dusty tracks between forest and canefield.

Soon the road ahead was filled with black smoke, and Barry used his best broken Spanish to ask if we were being transported into the middle of a battle. '*Quemamos la cana,*' said Chico. We burn the cane. Without another word, he looked into the sky, skidded the jeep to a stop and killed the engine. The drone of another engine quickly filled the sudden silence. Above us we could see a single-engine light plane hovering like a hawk. Chico scowled and cursed and restarted the engine, hurrying the jeep toward the burning cane. Through the dust I watched the little plane following us down the track. As it zoomed overhead I saw bursts of flame spurt from the side of the fuselage. We sped into the smoke and again skidded to a stop. The plane buzzed above the smoke a couple of times before heading off to find an easier target. Chico put his feet up on the dash and nonchalantly lit himself a stub of a cigarette. 'Well, old chap,' I said to Barry, 'here is our war.'

I offered a brand new Egyptian cigarette to Chico, and the three of us sat for twenty minutes inhaling both kinds of smoke until Chico was satisfied it was safe to continue. Eventually we drove out from our smoke screen and arrived at a rusty old corrugated iron factory surrounded by green cane, like an over-long but well-kept lawn. It was not dark and sinister and belching smoke, but sprawling over these verdant fields it appeared no less a satanic mill than any to be found in Yorkshire or Lancashire. Great idle chimney stacks rose above the brown iron – more mocking phalluses – and shambolic trucks covered with improvised armour were haphazardly parked in their shade. Among them was a lone Sherman tank with the markings of the Cuban army whitewashed over, and through a gaping iron door could be seen mortars and machine guns stacked around the slack jaws of a monstrous cane crusher.

We were taken inside the peeling clapboard of the mill's office to finally lay eyes on the elusive *commandante*. He was sitting behind a well-worn desk in a glass-partitioned room, chomping on a cigar and working over papers. Half a dozen of his *barbudos* sat around the walls on the floor and Chico had them make space on the lino for the two *yanquis*. Fidel, the king on his borrowed throne, did not look up and said nothing. 'Now, here is *your* war,' Barry whispered to me.

After a few minutes Fidel stacked his papers, thrust them at the nearest of his *barbudos*, and gazed down at his new arrivals. 'So . . . you are here,' he said. 'My interview now.'

Barry looked around the dim office with its flaking varnish

and mildewed paint. The only light came through a grimy window. He stood up and flicked the wall switch without effect. 'Too dark in here,' he said.

'Too dreary as well,' I said. 'You don't want to look like some pencil-pushing manager from United Fruit, do you? How about in the mill, among all those wonderful weapons?'

'Not enough light there either,' Barry said.

'Does that really matter?' I said to him. A charade could be taken too far.

'We move the weapons,' Fidel said with a dismissive wave of his hand. 'We interview under the sun.'

'Under the sun?' Barry said with some alarm. 'Under the planes, too. We'll make nice targets out there in the open.'

Fidel leaned back in his chair and dismissed us again. 'No bombs here,' he said. 'This mill it is American. They will not dare to bomb American property. Come.' He jumped to his feet and strode out the door, *barbudos* scurrying in his wake.

Barry did his best with what he had. He set up two ammunition boxes in the shade of a tree before a background of war equipment. He gave me the tape recorder and set up the camera. Interviewer and interviewee took their seats, and Fidel passed his cigar to one of his *barbudos* to hold. He took a moment to gather himself, slowly conjuring up a boyish grin and appealing eyes. Barry simulated a clapperboard with his fingers in front of the lens, and said, 'Fidel Castro interview, take one, mark.'

'So Mr Castro . . .' I began.

'No,' Fidel said. '*Companero* Fidel.'

'Very well, *companero* Fidel. Why have you taken up arms against the government?'

Fidel frowned first at me, then at Barry. 'What is this question?'

'Cut!' Barry called spontaneously, and quickly remembered to finger the switch on the camera.

'This is Cuba,' Fidel said, now jabbing his finger at my chest. 'This is not your congress, your house of common. There is no vote here to change government. The victory can only be won on the battlefield. This is the way in Cuba.'

'Okay, that's good,' I said. 'Now can you say it again while the camera's rolling?' I winked at Barry who went through the motions of marking a second take.

'*Companero* Fidel, why have you taken up arms against the government?'

'I already answer that,' Fidel said.

I sighed and shrugged. What else do you do with a guy like that? 'I'll start again,' I said to Barry, and snapped my fingers to the camera for a makeshift slate. '*Companero* Fidel, what do you hope to achieve with your struggle?'

It was like he flicked a switch in himself. Suddenly he was the likeable, naïve rebel just down from the mountain, the one that we met in the tobacco farmer's shack with the engagingly hoarse murmur and the open camaraderie. 'Why, we wish to restore the 1940 constitution of Cuba,' he said in the courteous tone of voice he had in reserve. 'We wish for land reform, to restore the land right. We wish for the worker to share in the company profit in all Cuban industry. We wish to banish from Cuba the men who steal from the Cuban worker, who make deceit on the Cuban people. These men, they will lose the property they steal. These are the things we wish for, we struggle for. These are our revolution.'

I bit my lip and took a moment to think. 'Um, yes ... and what would those reforms mean for the Cuban people?'

'Freedom for Cuban people. Freedom from tyrants. Freedom for Cubans to own Cuba, not American sugar companies. Freedom for Cubans to live with health, not die with disease. Freedom for Cubans to learn, not be slaves.'

'Slaves to ...?'

'To sugar. Cuba it is America's sweet tooth. Americans they will give up their precious liberty before they give up their sweet tooth. I hear candy sales they went up when your Senator McCarthy he blacklist everyone. I am America's dentist. One day Americans they will thank me. I will stop them to get so fat.'

It was a cute little metaphor. I wondered how many times he had used it already. I had to agree with Hemingway: there was something about this fellow. He had an undeniable magnetism when he was like this. My first impression had been that he was a Li'l Abner, and that was partly right. He may have been smart enough to trot out witty remarks for the camera, but he did a good line in innocence as well, vulnerability even. How could they possibly say he had killed many men? I began to get a feeling for why Lucia was so protective of him.

'So, sugar,' I said, 'this is why you are revolting?'

'Sugar is the symbol. One thing only, but important thing. Without sugar, they say, there is no Cuba. How can that be? Sugar is not natural for Cuba. Columbus he bring it. Colonialism, sugar, slavery . . . this is Cuba's story. So much sugar, no place for any other thing. We cannot even feed our own mouths for the sugar.'

'So what you are saying is that sugar . . .'

Fidel's face hardened. 'Enough of sugar,' he said abruptly with a wave of his hand. 'Ask something else.'

The old switcheroo – vulnerability had suddenly been dismissed. I cleared my throat and changed tack. 'Very well. Let's discuss what everyone in the outside world would really like to know about you and your movement. Are you a communist?'

'The only person who say I am communist is Batista.' And just like that the charm switch was on again. 'He say I am communist so he can get the guns and the planes from America.'

'So you are not communist?'

'No. I do not agree with communism.'

'You prefer Fidelismo?'

'What do you mean?'

'Oh, it's something I heard one of your followers say.'

Fidel smiled at me like a cat eyeing cream. 'Which one?'

A good reporter always protects his sources. 'I can't remember,' I said. 'Might have been in Havana. So, you don't agree with communism?'

'No.'

'Don't get me wrong, I understand. You're young. Everyone should be a communist when they're young. It's the only time you can afford the luxury.'

'I am not communist. I say that already.' He looked up to Barry. 'How much of the film now?' he said tersely. 'You need new film now?'

Barry fingered the switch again. 'Change rolls, you mean? No, we've got special rolls for this. We can shoot at very low speed to save film. Sometimes it's hard to even tell if the camera's turning over.'

'You know, I noticed that,' I said.

'I think is enough for now,' Fidel said. 'More later.'

Barry looked up at the sky. 'Yeah, we're losing the light for today, anyway. Tomorrow?'

'Maybe more tomorrow,' Fidel said, and he snatched his cigar back and strode into the office with his attendant *barbudos* in his trail.

I lit up a cigarette and helped Barry pack away the gear. 'How well do you think America's dentist understands English?' he said to me quietly.

'Which one?' I said. 'The friendly one or the scary cigar-chewing one?'

'Either.'

'He's not bad. Better than my Spanish, that's for sure.'

'Yeah. I was just thinking ... maybe you should go easy on calling him sugar and saying he's revolting.'

'You think he caught that one, sport? He didn't appear to.'

'Look at it this way ... he's got more guns than I've ever seen in one place before, and I get the impression he likes being in charge. It's a volatile combination.'

'But Barry,' I said with mock contrition, 'you weren't sitting close to him like I was. He's been in the jungle a long time. I guess you could say I called it the way I smelt it.'

'Maybe . . .' Barry said slowly, 'for the rest of our time as guests of the *companeros*, we follow our sense rather than our senses.'

'Good advice, old chum. See . . . I told you you had the head for this production lark.'

We carried the gear into the office building and found Fidel waiting for us inside the front door, a bundle of nervous energy. He took me by the elbow and steered me into a musty broom closet, closing the door behind us. While my eyes slowly adjusted, all I could see of him was the red glow of his cigar as he wagged it at me in the narrow neutral territory between our noses. 'These questions, communism,' he said, 'I do not want these questions. I could not be communist.' He pointed at the cap on his head. 'You see the red star here?'

'No,' I said. I still couldn't see much at all, but I knew the cap was completely plain.

'Communists are heathen. When a boy, I went to the boarding school of the Jesuit. I want the independence from the *yanqui*, not the communism. America it will understand, no? We make the declaration of independence, so America it will understand.'

I felt around for a switch. I had to see just what kind of expression was on his face. If I was going to tell him he had about as much hope of being understood by the powers-that-be in America as I had, I had to see his face. I couldn't find a switch so just avoided the question. 'Oh, I know all about boarding schools,' I said. 'I've been expelled from some of the best.'

'Expelled?'

'They asked me to leave, threw me out.'

'So it means rebel, no? I also, I rebelled.'

It's not what I expected to hear from a leader. Expelled from school? But then I supposed that he had probably taken up this rebel business early. I supposed it had given him time to develop all the different Fidels he had at his disposal, because out of sight of his *barbudos* there was a third. Even in the dark I could sense him shedding the autocratic bluster like an uncomfortable skin. I decided to take this bull by the horns, to stop avoiding his charges and make some thrusts of my own. 'All right,' I said, 'but if you don't mind a little advice . . . you don't mind a little advice, do you?' He shrugged but said nothing. 'Then might I say that you shouldn't talk about America the way you just did?'

'What is the way I just did?'

'About Cubans being slaves to American sugar companies, and about America arming your enemy.'

'Why not? It is the truth. I must show the *yanqui* I have the *cojones*. You know *cojones*?'

'Even I know that much Spanish. Look, it may be true, but statements like that . . .' I considered the aptness of what I was about to say. It was certainly apt. '. . . are red rags to the bulls in America.'

'What does this mean?'

Fortunately, the door was warped and a little light could sneak its way in. At last I could make him out, and the expression on his face was one of genuine concern. 'Americans will think you're a communist,' I said. 'All that you said about workers sharing in profits, confiscating property . . . Americans won't understand that. That sounds like communism to them. That's why I asked you. It gave you the opportunity to deny it. Believe me, if you want to get on the CBS news, if you want sympathy among the American people, don't say anything that makes you sound like a communist. The other day you talked to me about healing the sick, teaching the children. These are the kinds of things you should be talking about to Americans. It makes you sound like some sort of messiah, especially with that beard of yours, and the wardrobe. Unless I've lost my touch, I'd say that American women will love you, and that's half the audience won over already. All that you said about workers sharing profits and so on, that makes you sound like comrade Lenin. Leave comrade Lenin for your own people. For Americans, try being the Cuban messiah. You're just clearing the temple, aren't you?' I gave him my most charming Errol Flynn grin.

Fidel looked at his boots. 'It is true, I have to learn much in English. We know we will not win without the newspapers. Can it be, when you are here, we can talk about this?'

'Well, I'm no teacher. I'm just a tired old actor, one who . . .'

'Yes, but you have much experience.'

It takes a charmer to recognise a charmer. How could I not warm to this character? 'Probably not the kind of experience you need, old sport, but I'll do my best. So tell me, when you take over the palace, what makes you so sure the people will go along with you? If you want my experience, I'll tell you that Havana will be a hard nut to crack, and people only follow along when there's something in it for them. Batista gives Havana what it wants, by and large. And anyway, what makes you think there won't be another generation of rebels waiting in the wings?'

'Senor,' Fidel said with a trace of a sneer on his lips, 'the shepherd may change, but sheep, they remain sheep.'

Another switcheroo. It was hard to keep up. 'Phew . . . don't say that on camera tomorrow.'

Fidel shrugged. 'Maybe no time tomorrow. Maybe some other day. Today I ask army *commandante* in Maffo to lay down weapons, come to our side, join us. He say no. Tomorrow we begin to make him pay.'

Such an amenable young man, I thought. How did he ever come to be expelled? 'You know, I might be able to help you a little after all. Let me tell you something about negotiating. Erich Korngold told me once . . . he was the fellow who wrote the music for my best pictures. A brilliant musician and a wise old head. He told me once that it doesn't matter what people say, it's how they say it. He says if you listen for when their voice drifts into the minor key, that's when you know the hammer's about to fall, and you have to get in first. That was how I handled Jack Warner for twenty years, and it always worked. He never knew how I did it. Of course, you have to have an ear for music. But as you told me before, you can't teach a Cuban about music, can you?'

Fidel blinked at me and chomped on his cigar. 'No,' he said after a moment's consideration. He opened the door and as light flooded our little closet, I lost him in the glare. 'You cannot teach a Cuban about music.'

Even if I had not been trapped in these remote mountains, escape to civilisation had begun to lose its attraction. Hemingway seemed to understand more about this Fidel character than I had been prepared to concede. The way someone wears a hat, the way their lips move, he said, rather curiously I thought at the time. Fidel's cap without a red star, his lips always wrapped around a cigar, maybe a writer's powers of observation had allowed old Ernesto to see something in the guy that I was just beginning to appreciate now I had spent time with him. Now I had spent time with him I could add to the observations: the way he holds meetings in pitch-black broom closets. I was looking forward to hanging around.

That night Barry and I were invited to join Fidel and his inner circle for a meal in the mill office. The circle included Lucia, Chico and two *barbudos* that we didn't think we had seen before, but with all those beards it was difficult to tell. Fidel introduced them, starting with Lucia. 'She is one of the first members of our movement,' he said. 'She has been in battles many times. She is the true rebel girl, no?'

I waited for her to object, to insist that she was a woman, not a girl, but coming from Fidel's lips it didn't seem to concern her. *El commandante* moved on to his *barbudos*. 'This is Carlos. He is *la voz*, our voice to the people and to the world. Carlos he is in charge of our radio, Radio *Rebelde*. Carlos is *mi critico*, my critic.'

He moved to the second new face. He was old for a *rebelde*, with flecks of grey in the mandatory beard. 'Huber is one of my *commandantes*. Huber is our worrier. About everything, Huber worries. He is *mi conciencia*, my conscience.'

And finally to Chico. 'You know Chico. He is *mi pistolita*, my little gunman. That is my joke because Chico, he is not so little. He is from Spain. Like you, he was in that war. He is a very good gunman.' He patted his *pistolita* on the shoulder and smiled. 'Be careful of my Chico, eh.'

We all laughed and sat down at the table. Chico seemed to be a calm and collected soul, but I always got the feeling he was capable of anything Fidel asked of him, no matter what Fidel asked. There was a time when I might have chanced my left arm with him, although that time was long past.

Plates of beans and rice suddenly appeared, a jug of water was passed around. 'This is what we eat,' Fidel said. 'No *hamburguesa* for the gringo here. *Moros y cristianos*. Moors and Christians, black and white. It is the symbol, no? Like sugar.'

'Yes, just like sugar,' I said, scooping up a modest spoonful, reluctantly I have to say. 'Only different.'

'Lucia she doesn't believe me when I say you have married many times.'

I took a look at Lucia at the other end of the table, but she was head down over her plate. 'Oh, not so many,' I said. 'Just three times. That's modest in Hollywood terms. But you see, Lucia, women won't let me stay single, and I won't let me stay married.'

'Maybe if you married a woman,' Lucia said without looking up.

'I assure you each of my wives was a woman. No men. And no *perros, caballos, cabros* or *burros*, either. I made sure of that.'

Everyone suddenly stopped to look at me. Fidel began to laugh, and all except Lucia joined in. *'Burros?'* he said.

'No dogs, horses, goats or mules,' I said. 'Did I say something wrong?'

'*Mulos*, you mean, not *burros*,' Fidel said. 'Or you say your wife she is stupid.'

I laughed my best Robin Hood laugh. 'Well, perhaps that's what I meant to say.'

'This film you make,' Huber said, 'you must make some of the poverty of Cuba. Take your camera into our villages, see what Batista does to our people.'

'We will certainly do that,' Barry said. 'Once we get some good battle footage, we'd like to get some of that.'

'You know of Nasser in Egypt?' Fidel asked. 'He makes the agrarian reform. That is what I will do for Cuba. Agrarian reform,' he repeated carefully. He had learned the words well.

'I understand,' Barry said. 'And do you think we can get some battle footage?'

'Battle footage? You mean you wish to film the battle?'

'Why . . . yes. If it's convenient.'

'It makes a better movie than agrarian reform,' I said.

Fidel ignored my comment and shrugged. 'Maybe one day.'

Barry pushed his plate away. He'd hardly touched it. 'You

know, *companero* Fidel, I've heard you were scouted by one of our ball teams. A pitcher. Is that true?'

Fidel shrugged the other shoulder. 'In school, at university, I play the games. Baseball, basketball, these I enjoy.'

'And diving,' Barry said. 'You're a diver, right?'

'Cuba is good for the diving. Caribbean, so of course. But for me, not for many years.'

'Errol's a diver, too. You should do some together one day. He's been down past a hundred feet. He's good at all that water stuff. I saw him beat Johnny Weissmuller in a race once.'

'Yes, well,' I interrupted, 'Johnny was old and fat by then.'

'Johnny Weissmuller's never been old and fat,' Barry said. 'And you were drunk.'

'Well, there you are,' I said. 'That explains it. I had the assistance of rocket fuel.'

'Who is this Johnny Weissmuller?' Fidel asked.

'Tarzan,' Barry said.

'Or perhaps he's more famous for being the husband of Lupe Velez,' I said. 'Johnny's had about six wives, I think, Lucia. Of course, apart from Lupe, I can't personally guarantee the others were actually women.'

Everyone had finished eating, but no one seemed to want to make a move before *el Gigante*. Fidel swallowed a mug of water and tapped the table. He thought for a moment, and then fixed his gaze on me. 'Carlos, he has our radio. Maybe one day you also help him. Carlos, show him our radio.'

Carlos led me into another room. Against one wall was a tall rack of boxes, dials and glowing valves. 'This is the mobile transmitter,' he said. 'It goes where *companero* Fidel goes. We send his speeches to the people on the short wave. Also news of the battle, two times every day. Also the music and literature, we send.' He leaned close to my ear. 'He talks to you, senor,' he said quietly. 'He will not talk to us.'

'Who? Fidel?'

'*Si*. You we all see he talks to. Even Raul, even Che, some time he say nothing to them.'

'Well, I wouldn't know about that, sport. Can you get any music on this thing?'

'Our broadcast, it is not until nine o'clock.'

'Yes, but does this contraption receive, or does it only send?'

Carlos flicked a couple of switches. The valves brightened as he twiddled with a dial until he found a Miami station. I recognised the Latin rhythm of Tea for Two. 'Sounds like a cha-cha-cha,' I said. 'Turn it up. Your boss simply adores the cha-cha-cha.'

I went back into the other room and bowed elaborately to Lucia. 'Senorita, may I have the pleasure of dancing with the most beautiful woman in the room?'

Lucia didn't know where to look. 'She is the only woman,' said a glowering Fidel.

'That has no bearing on her beauty,' I said. I took her hand and gently elevated her from her seat, wrapped my arm around her waist and guided her across the floor. I pushed her away, pulled her back, threw in side steps and turns, swaying my ageing hips and shuffling my feet, grazing the floor on the cha-cha-cha beats, never taking my eyes off her. I grabbed her and held her close. 'You know,' I whispered into her ear, 'you dance as well as any girl.' Lucia blushed, but held on tight.

Suddenly the music stopped. Fidel was standing in the doorway to the transmitter room with his hands on his hips. 'We have no time for this . . . this . . .'

'Famous Cuban music,' I said. 'It's what you're fighting for, isn't it? A symbol of . . .'

Fidel threw his cap on the floor. 'This is not Cuban music! This is gringo music!'

'Really? Well, it's all the rage in the States. I thought it was

Cuban.' And I really did. It was a damn cha-cha-cha, after all. Lucia broke away and hurried from the room. 'That was short and sweet,' I said. 'Say . . . any chance of a drink?'

Fidel strode over to his seat and stood behind it, leaving his cap on the floor. 'We do not drink,' he said, which was also news to me, having already spent a night getting drunk with him.

I picked up the cap, dusted it off and handed it back to him. If I had to bet, I would lay money on the fact that no one had been this provocative to him since he got out of Batista's prison. I was enjoying this stoush. 'No,' I said. 'Of course not. There's a war on. Tell you what . . . if you're going to be busy tomorrow, how about we take this opportunity for that little talk you wanted. You know, about my experience.'

Again Fidel glowered at me, drumming all ten fingers on the back of the chair. 'I have broadcast to make,' he said eventually.

I looked at my watch. 'Oh, yes. At nine o'clock, isn't it? How about after that? I talk better at night anyway.'

Fidel held his glare for what seemed like minutes. Finally he tugged the cap down over his forehead and marched into the transmitter room, brushing past Carlos. *'Cierre la puerta,'* he snapped, and Carlos closed the door.

I turned to Huber, sitting at the table with his chin resting on his hands and a wry smile on his lips. 'How long does he speak for?' I asked him.

'El Gigante,' Huber said, 'he can speak for hours when he is angry. He can speak for hours however he feel.'

El Gigante spoke for three hours. The others left to attend to the business of war, or the eventual filming of it in Barry's case, leaving just me at the table, listening to the faint drone of the endless speech in the other room, and preparing two cigars from the necessary medications carried in my survival kit. It was midnight when Fidel emerged from the transmitter room to find me waiting for him. He had to understand: I didn't give up easily.

The two cigars lay side by side on the table. I picked one up and offered it to him. 'Smokum peace pipe, eh?' I said with a friendly grin. 'How did your speech go?'

Fidel did not look at the cigar. He paced back and forth wringing his hands. Finally he drew close to speak into my ear, as though confiding in me. 'I explain the end, it justify the means. Machiavelli, no? Ed Murrow, Huntley and Brinkley, do they know this Machiavelli?'

The pattern was clear now. In the company of his flunky *barbudos* he was all thrust with me, but when we were on our own he was more than prepared to parry. I lit both cigars. 'Well if they don't, I'm not sure they'd be willing to give you three hours to explain it.'

Fidel looked curiously at his cigar. He waited until I had drawn on my own and then reached across and swapped them over. 'Which one you think best?' he said casually.

'They're both the same,' I said, sucking vigorously on the other cigar. 'Flynn specials, custom made. Try it. Draw the smoke into your lungs. Taste the difference.'

'No, I mean Ed Murrow or Huntley and Brinkley. Matthews, he say Murrow. You agree?'

'Ed Murrow? Ed Murrow's a legend, a pioneer. But his time was radio. For television, if that's what you want, perhaps Huntley and Brinkley. Mind you, I'm no expert, no PR consultant. What you need, when the time comes, is a good PR company.'

Fidel drew on his cigar and nodded. 'PR . . . it means propaganda, no?'

I had to laugh at that. 'You know more than you're letting on.

Actually it means public relations. Every good leader needs some PR sometime.'

Fidel looked at his cigar again. 'What cigar is this? Where do you get it?'

'Custom made by yours truly,' I said. 'Loaded with vitamin M. Tastes different, huh?'

'So . . . public relation,' Fidel said. 'What is this?'

'They're the professionals who can do what you want me to do for you. Advise you on how to get your face on the news, on the cover of magazines. How to convince Americans you're not a communist, not a threat. That's going to be your issue, you know. Convincing America you're not a threat.'

Fidel was blinking slowly as he puffed on his cigar. 'What threat? I do not threat. Only Batista and his dogs do I threat.' He studied the cigar again. 'This smoke . . . it is blue.'

'The natural colour of the doors of perception,' I said, the effects now gradually descending. 'It's good for you . . . prepare you for battle . . . clear your head . . .'

Fidel's eyelids began to droop. Slowly he climbed up onto the table and lay flat on his back. He drew on the cigar a few more times, and then it fell from his mouth in a little shower of sparks. I picked it up and stubbed it out on the floor, being careful not to damage it. I drew a couple of times on my own and stubbed it out in the same way. I climbed up onto the table next to the leader of the revolution and drifted into beautiful sleep.

15
In the *revolucion,* everything changes.

Contramaestre, 16 December 1958

I was clawing at the water with windmill strokes, getting more desperate with each wild swing, struggling against the river's angry current, faster even than Johnny Weissmuller. Johnny Weissmuller never had a croc on his tail. Except in movies. This was no movie. Johnny Weissmuller never had to swim the goddamn Sepik. Swim the goddamn Sepik with the law on his tail. Yulu got taken. He screamed as his head disappeared under brown water. Crocs were everywhere. I pounded out the strokes. And then I felt my feet clamped in the jaws. Desperately I looked around. 'You are *yanqui,*' the bearded rebel said to me. 'You die on the battlefield. This is the end.' *Barbudos* were everywhere. I tried to grab handfuls of water, but it was no use. Under I went, deep into the brown abyss, my lungs bursting. 'The end . . . it justify the means.'

'Errol!'

I sat bolt upright. The hammock tipped me out and I fell heavily to the floor, sucking gulps of air into my lungs.

'Jesus, Errol, are you okay?'

I looked up, blinking into Barry's face. I knew the face, now I had to remember where I was.

'You were shaking like a goddamn jackhammer,' he said.

I climbed slowly to my feet, shook my head and looked around at a vast industrial hall filled with rust and grime and caked fibre. Molasses filled my nose and I remembered where I was. 'Shaking . . .?' I shivered. 'That's the fucking least of it.' I stretched my back and grunted with pain. 'I haven't had a fucking drink in . . . you know, I can't remember how long. All I need now is the fucking fever to hit me. Got any water?'

Barry fetched me a water bottle and watched as I drained it dry, dribbling it down my chin and neck and soaking my shirt. 'I haven't seen you drink like that since . . . maybe I should qualify that. I haven't seen you drink *water* like that since . . .'

'Since the last time I passed out on the Chinese molasses, probably.'

'Well, I ain't seen you do that in a while, buddy. I was going to say since the last time you drove a Buick into a swimming pool and forgot to close your mouth.'

I found a smile somewhere and coughed and held my back. 'What time is it, anyway?'

'Eight,' he said. 'In the morning, in case you're wondering. Listen . . . I'm going back to the camp. No point me hanging around here. I've got an idea for a nude bathing scene.'

'Nude bathing?'

'Yeah. In that stream. I'll get all the girls in there with a bar of soap.'

'Sounds absolutely delightful,' I said. I rubbed the grin from my face vigorously with the palms of my hands, blubbering like a hound dog. 'Oh, Christ. I feel fucking terrible.'

'You look how you feel.'

'Thanks. A nude bathing scene, eh. Just what I need. A bit of firewater even better. When do we leave? I'm feeling better already. Hey . . . wait a minute. The goddamn interview. Chief *barbudo* won't appreciate us lamming out on him.'

135

'Forget about chief *barbudo* for a while,' Barry said. 'Chief *barbudo* said *vamos muchachos* this morning and lit out. Gone up the road somewhere for a pow-wow with the other big chiefs.'

I eased myself down onto the hammock and steadied it. 'Well, that's good news. I've had enough sparring for a while.'

'Good news for me, but not for you,' Barry said. 'If you want a drink you'll have to raid your medicinal stock. Chief *barbudo* wants you to stay here and help Carlos with his radio . . . whatever that means.'

'Help Carlos? Do what?'

'Don't ask me. You're the goddamn hero. You must have said something last night. What was that you said about being an acquired taste?'

Barry made his escape, hitching a ride with a column leaving for the re-engagement of hostilities at Maffo. I took as much time as there was to put the river and the crocs and poor Yulu back where they belonged – in the distant but not dim enough past – and duly presented myself to Carlos. I asked how I could be of assistance to Radio . . . ?

'Radio *Rebelde*,' said Carlos. 'Che he give it the name. Che, it is his idea.'

'Che? Who is this mysterious fellow with half a name?'

'Che he lead the struggle at Santa Clara, senor, the Las Villas front.'

'So . . . what is it you want from me on the radio front?'

'This idea, it is Fidel's.'

'You mean me? I'm Fidel's idea?'

'Fidel he see the opportunity with you. Fidel he always make the opportunity.' Carlos shrugged and turned his attention to the transmitter. 'Now we have thirty transmitters, all over Cuba, Havana even. Our people, they can hear us all over the Caribbean, Mexico, South America. All this we do in eight months.'

I nodded at the black box of switches and dials and didn't know what to say. Obviously I was supposed to be impressed. 'Eight months, how about that,' I said, shaking my head and clicking my tongue. 'Radio . . . what?'

'Radio *Rebelde*.'

'Radio *Rebelde*. All over Cuba, eh?'

'Can I say something to you, senor?'

I stopped shaking my head. 'Of course.'

'You are like Fidel, I think.'

'I like Fidel?'

'No . . . you are like him. You say things to someone just to find out what he really think.'

'Do I? When did I do that?'

'You say he is communist. You must not say this.'

'I didn't say he was communist. I asked him if he was.'

'It is the same, senor.'

'You know, I get the impression it's a touchy subject with him.'

'*Si*,' Carlos said. 'Fidel is not communist. I, I was once communist. No more. Communists, they are here in Cuba, but they go with the wind. You know what I mean when I say that?'

'Sure, opportunists. Doesn't sound like the communists, but it sounds like what you said about Fidel.'

'No, senor. I mean they go with Batista. The leader of the communists, yesterday he was the Batista minister, today he wish to go with Fidel. It is . . . what can I say . . . ?'

'A tricky situation,' I said. 'So you, before you were a Fidelista, you were a *communista*.'

'Please, senor, if you have the question about this, you speak to Raul. Raul, he knows about this.'

'No, I was just curious. If Fidel is a communist or not is none of my concern. I'm just here to make a movie. How I got caught up in this . . . this debate, I don't know.'

'You are reporter, no? I understand. I, too, I am reporter. Fidel, he told me you were reporter in Spain.'

'Look, I don't know how . . .' I sighed and sat myself down. 'What do you want from me, sport? What's this idea that Fidel has?'

'Fidel he want from you to make a speech for him.'

'He wants me to write a speech for him?'

'Write a speech for you. For Radio *Rebelde*.'

'You mean speak over your radio?'

'*Si*. You are famous everywhere. People will listen.'

'Jesus, you're kidding, aren't you? I'm in enough trouble back in the States as it is. If you're being heard in Mexico, you can bet you're being heard in Washington. That's all I need. The IRS *and* the FBI on my case.'

'You do not agree to make a speech?'

I opened my mouth, but quickly shut it again. Carlos appeared mild-mannered enough, had innocence in his eyes, but so did one of the Fidels I had met. How many Carloses were there? What did these *barbudos* conceal underneath their beards? I was on my own in a rebel outpost, surrounded by guns, and a thousand kilometres from Havana. It would be easier to escape to Port Antonio, and to escape to Port Antonio I would probably have to swim. 'Don't get me wrong,' I said. 'I'd like to help. But my Spanish is hopeless. If I spoke in Spanish, even reading from a script, no one would understand me. And if I spoke in English, well, what would be the point?'

'Senor, in your movie, you were Zorro, no? You were Don Juan? Your Spanish, people understand then, no?'

'No, I wasn't Zorro. Ty Power was Zorro. And Don Juan, it was in English. In America we speak English. In movies we speak English.'

'*Si*, senor, I understand. I have lived in Miami. I can help you.'

The river was back. I could feel the brown water rising again over my head, could feel myself being dragged again into its dark abyss.

'I speak English okay, do you think?' Carlos said.

'No problem with your English,' I said. 'Big problem with my Spanish.'

'Maybe we just try a little. You try this . . . *Aqui Radio Rebelde, la voz de la Sierra Maestra, transmitiendo para toda Cuba.*' He looked at me expectantly.

'*Aqui Radio Rebelde . . . la voz . . .* what was the rest?'

'*La voz de la Sierra Maestra,*' Carlos said slowly, rounding every syllable, '*transmitiendo para toda Cuba.*'

'*La voz de la Sierra Maestra, trans . . .* what was it?'

'*Transmitiendo.* It means transmit, through the radio. Transmit, *transmitiendo*, same, no?'

'Yeah, same. Look, I was never good at learning my lines.'

'*Transmitiendo . . .*'

I had to take some deep breaths as a new wave of nausea flooded over me. At first I thought it was the malaria, but it wasn't something physical, it was all in my head. Déjà vu. It was a quarter of a century ago. Mike Curtiz grilling me on my lines, my delivery, my character, my Captain Blood. It was Mike Curtiz all over again, and the nausea filled my head.

'*Transmitiendo,*' I managed. 'What was the rest?'

'*Para toda Cuba.* For all Cuba.'

'*Para toda Cuba.*'

'Good. You can do.'

Mike Curtiz all over again. 'Now, just a minute. If every sentence takes this long I'll miss the whole goddamn revolution.'

'So we try. You write speech in English, I translate to Spanish. Tonight you read.'

I put my face in my hands and looked into the abyss. I filled my lungs with air, driving out the nausea, and opened my eyes.

'All right. I'll write something. But you understand I can't take sides. As an American citizen I am forbidden to take sides in a foreign war. That's our law.'

'In Spain, senor, you do not take sides?'

'No, I was a reporter. And I wasn't an American citizen then.'

Carlos shrugged. 'I am reporter, no?'

'Yes, but you are Cuban. This is your war.'

'Your American government, it take sides, no? It take sides with Batista. It take sides all over South America. That is against your law, no?'

'That's different, that's politics.'

'Different? In your country your government can break the law, but not the people, they cannot. This is also the way of Batista in Cuba. He break the law all the time. So America it is same as Cuba, no?'

I leaned back in the chair and groaned with exasperation. 'Carlos ... my friend ... please. I am not responsible for what my government does. I can only be responsible for what *I* do. A humble citizen, a single citizen.'

'Please, senor, I make the joke with you, now you make the joke with me. You are not a humble citizen, you are the famous movie star.'

'I ...'

'Your government, it is there because you vote, no? It is there because you say so. Everyone in America say so.'

'Not everyone.'

'No ... but more than say no.'

'And I don't vote. We are a free country. We are free to decide not to vote for any of the bastards.'

'So ... free not to take the responsibility.'

'That's right. And because I didn't take the responsibility then, I'm not responsible for whatever the US government is doing with Batista now, or Castro, or anyone in these parts. I am here to make a movie. That's all. Can I go make my movie now?'

'Your speech. You must write your speech.'

Carlos was stopped by the sound of raised Spanish voices coming from the other room. He opened the door to reveal Huber standing toe to toe with a rare species of rebel – a beardless one. When they saw me they stopped arguing and stepped away. Huber turned his back. The beardless one barked at Carlos in Spanish. He spoke so fast I couldn't understand a word of it, but the way he jabbed a finger in my direction, I was in no doubt who was the subject of this one-sided conversation. He then approached me. His boyish face gave nothing away. His voice had been full of anger but his face was a blank.

'The interview, it is done?' he said quietly.

Huber stomped from the room and slammed the door behind him.

'Is it something I said?' I asked.

'The interview?'

'Not finished yet. We got interrupted.'

'Fidel has gone. You must be gone.'

'Oh, that's fine with me. Carlos has other ideas, though.'

'No matter Carlos. Fidel has gone, you must be gone. You must not be here.'

He turned on his heel and followed Huber. The raised voices resumed again as soon as he closed the door.

I turned to Carlos. 'Who was that?'

'He is Raul.'

'You mean Raul Castro?'

'*Si*. He goes to meet with Fidel.'

'He doesn't look anything like his brother,' I said. Carlos shrugged. 'And he hasn't got a beard.'

Now he nodded. '*Si*. Raul, he is secret agent.' The corners of his mouth turned up just a fraction, just enough for me to realise that Carlos was one rebel I probably did not have to fear. 'I will take you back, senor,' he said.

'What about my speech?'

'Maybe it is different now. It changes, you know. In the *revolucion*, everything changes, no? *Revolucion*, that is what it means, no?' This time the grin spread wide and white teeth gleamed. He slapped me on the back.

'Yes,' I said. 'It certainly does.'

Carlos drove me back himself, ducking and weaving the jeep along dusty tracks between the canefields. 'Are you going to burn all the cane in Cuba?' I shouted above the rushing wind.

'Maybe,' Carlos smiled at me. 'Without sugar, there is no Batista.'

'But that'll put half of Cuba out of work. Or is that a case of the end justifying the means?'

'Fidel is angry with you, senor. It is not good for Fidel to have anger for you.'

'Why is he angry with me? Because I asked him if he was communist? He's going to get that a lot, you know. He might as well prepare for it.'

Carlos shrugged. If an Englishman raises one eyebrow, if a Frenchman purses his lips, it seems to me that the characteristic national expression of the Cubano is a shrug. 'Maybe when you dance,' he said. 'Maybe your dance, it is not what we do, senor.'

'Seems to me, Carlos, if you don't mind me saying so, there's a lot of angry people in your revolution.'

Carlos looked at me and again offered his characteristic national expression. 'Maybe so. When you make change, this happens, no? You were in Spain. You saw this happen.'

'I don't know where all this Spain business is coming from,' I shouted. 'I was only there for two months. Madrid and Barcelona and the road between, that's about what I saw.'

'You can see much in two months, no?'

'I was only a journalist-observer. I was there for the Hearst newspapers. What I saw was a very dirty war. So dirty Mr Hearst wouldn't even print my stories. You know what I had to do to get my stories printed? I had to go to the wife of the President of the United States.' Carlos gave me a disbelieving frown. 'Yes, Mrs Roosevelt. Senora Eleanor herself. But look ... that war was different. That was two big armies backed by a lot of foreign help. That was the first act of a world war. This is not like that. Franco, he's still there. More than twenty years and he's still there. Do you think, if you ever win this revolution, do you think Castro will still be there in twenty years? I don't think so. This is not like Spain.'

'But senor, it is like that. America, it helps Batista. Maybe we should go to Russia to help, no?'

I shook my head slowly. 'You don't want to be the meat in that particular sandwich, chum. You're likely to end up hamburger mince.'

We drove in silence for a few minutes. I watched the sun set over the hills, the unburnt cane glowing gold, and over the road the burnt cane spiking up out of the black earth, dark and sinister.

'You know where I first got the idea for a movie about rebel girls?' I said, and didn't wait for a response. 'In Spain. There was a girl there, fighting on the Loyalist side. A city fighter. A partisan. She wore just a plain dress, never a uniform. She could slip from one side to the other. She kept a gun down the front of her dress.' I rubbed my chest beneath my shirt. 'A big revolver, forty-four or something, right between her breasts. Right between her *tetas*. Luckily for her she had big *tetas*.'

'We have women like her,' Carlos said. 'In the city we have women like her.'

'Do you have women like this? She was caught. She was raped, tortured and murdered. They almost cut her in half. I saw her body and it made me sick. Do you have women like that?'

'*Si*, senor. We have women like that. We have the dirty war also.'

'Sweet Jesus. Well, I hope I never see that again. Lita, that was her name.'

'Something like that . . . it makes you take up the gun yourself, no?'

'It makes you want to take up the gun, yes. But only once did I do it. I was ordered to. Had no choice.'

'So . . . you have taken sides then.'

When we arrived at the camp it was dark. I asked Carlos to wait while I got something from the hut. I retrieved the small wooden case, opened it up for him and shone a flashlight on the lustrous white enamel of my Olympic portable typewriter. 'Will you give this to Fidel for me?' I said. 'A peace offering . . . but don't say that. Just say . . . just say that with this he can write the words of the angels.'

'*Las palabras de los angeles,*' Carlos said. 'That is Hollywood, no?'

I was beginning to like Carlos.

Two days in Fidel's headquarters meant two days without a drink. I didn't know I could go two days without a drink. I thought my hands would be shaking, that I'd be racked, but that night, when I took my first drink of the local firewater, it burnt my gullet and settled in my stomach like hot coals, and that was when my hands shook. Two days to make up. But I didn't. I had just two drinks and set the bottle aside. We had rigged a groundsheet as a curtain to our hut for some privacy. I said to Beverly that I wasn't going to sleep in a hammock anymore. I needed a solid bed for my back. I spread a bedroll on the dirt floor, and she joined me there. She must have sensed there was a change.

How many months had it been since I had taken her in my arms and followed up with all that taking a woman in your arms was meant to be? Had always been. Before the days of false dawns, of understanding looks, of self-inflicted ridicule. To every thing there is a season, and suddenly I was in season again. Ripe. Six months of fallow ground for a bed, of being hard on myself and soft on her. The epic romance returned in a sweeping tide. The sword again tasted blood. In like Flynn. At last.

I woke before dawn. The hard ground was no better than the hammock. I went outside and walked around in circles, holding my back and feeling pleased with myself. I was challenged by a guard who shone a flashlight and stuck the muzzle of a carbine in my kisser before ignoring me. I went back into the hut and poured myself a small glass of rum. I put it to my lips ... but I found I didn't feel like drinking it. I put the glass down and picked up my notebook and pen and started to write.

> To seek
> To yearn
> To strive
> Perhaps to reach
> Not yet
> One day
> No promise

> To crawl the desert of a life
> To cross the plain of mediocrity
> To the well on the horizon
> To thirst for it
> To see it
> Perhaps to reach
> Not yet
> One day
> No promise

Faith of the faithless
Love of the loather
Urge of the wretched
Work of the shirker
Cause of the blithe
Addiction of the clean
Envy of the sated
Perhaps to reach
One day
Show promise

Beverly stirred and blinked into the lamplight. 'You okay, Cap'n?'

'Never better,' I said.

'You should lay off the booze more often.'

There she was, telling me what I needed to know, like a good friend. A woman is the best friend you can have, I said to Fidel only a few weeks ago. Just so long as it's platonic. How many had I known like that? Too few, a precious few, I had to admit. But Beverly was one. I hadn't planned on the platonic part. It had simply been unavoidable.

She lifted herself up onto one elbow. 'Watcha doing?'

'Oh . . . just writing about our adventure.'

'A diary, you mean? I didn't know you kept a diary.'

'Not a diary, a . . . a story.'

'Is this for the papers?'

'No . . . just for me.'

'What's it called?'

'I don't have a title yet.'

'I know what it should be.'

'What's that?'

'How I got my mojo back.'

I had no idea what she said and told her so, but I knew exactly what she meant. 'Maybe I'll call it *The Grail*.'

'You said that before. What is a grail, anyway?'

'It's the cup that holds what you thirst for.'

'You mean the glass.'

'Yes . . . perhaps I mean the glass.'

She lay her head down again and went straight back to sleep. I looked at the glass of rum still sitting there, undrunk. I picked it up and passed it under my nose. Firewater irritated my nostrils. I pulled my survival kit from a bag and took out the bottle of Zubrowka. The blade of bison grass was standing in the last inch of vodka, the last inch I had. I tipped the rum from the glass, rinsed it with a little water, and poured my last inch of vodka. I passed it under my nose. Sweet, sweet grass. I drank it. One sweet, sweet glass. I opened my notebook and at the top of my adventure story I wrote the title:

The Thirst.

16
I guess there's more to this war stuff than I thought.
Palma Soriano, 20 December 1958

Lucia brought us the news that *companero* Fidel had moved his headquarters to a bigger sugar mill, a few miles closer to Santiago and more comfortable. There had been quite a struggle to take it and he wanted the battle in the movie. Taking an American sugar mill, she said, was better for the movie than taking a Cuban town, which was all very well, but now it seemed we were to film a battle that had already been fought.

Fidel had put another two dozen men at our disposal. As more towns were taken more *casquitos* decided to stop shaving and join the revolution. The whole country was beginning to see which way the wind was blowing, and it was blowing off the Sierra Maestra.

While we awaited the *commandante*'s pleasure we shot a small gunfight at a railroad crossing in the canefields. With Batista's makeshift air force still making a nuisance of itself, we had to film at night, lighting a steam locomotive and cane train with all the portables we had. Johnny and his rebels took the train right up to a truckload of *casquitos* and killed every last one of them with blanks.

While the lights were being packed up and the train fired up for its return to the mill, Barry took Beverly and Marie and a small crew into a canefield and sat them down with a handie-talkie radio. 'This is the scene before the battle,' he told them. 'Duck down on action, and when you come up look camera right, that's where the bad guys are disappearing down the road. Okay . . . camera.'

'Rolling.'

'And . . . action!'

Beverly put the radio to her ear. 'Hullo command, this is outpost one. The truck just passed us. Eleven men. No automatic weapons. Over.' She turned eagerly to Marie. 'Come on, let's go down to the railroad crossing.'

'I'm afraid we have to stay here until somebody relieves us,' Marie said methodically.

'Relieves us?' protested Beverly. 'We'll miss all the fighting.'

Marie put on her best schoolmistress manner. 'Our job is important here. Suppose somebody else came down that road.'

Beverly nodded with widening eyes as she handed over the radio. 'I guess there's more to this war stuff than I thought.'

'Cut!'

'Jesus Christ.' I said. 'This war stuff? That's not in my script.'

'Improvised dialogue,' Barry said.

'Oh, really? Where'd you pick it up, the corner malt shop?'

'Don't worry. We can change it anyway you want . . . once we're in LA. We'll burn the cane now. That's what you wanted, isn't it? You said you liked the cane burning idea.'

I took an irritable tug on my cigarette. 'I don't know why I care. It doesn't matter.'

'That's right. It doesn't matter. Just remember what we're here for. It's just a movie. A fucking B movie.'

'Barry, old chum, there aren't enough letters in the alphabet for this one. Tell me this . . . how was Woodsie supposed to see, in the dark, with the truck speeding down the road to the battle, that none of those men she was supposedly spying on was carrying an automatic weapon?'

'Christ, Errol, we just agreed it doesn't matter.'

'Hey, Cap'n,' Beverly said, wrapping her arm around mine, 'don't get so upset.'

'What . . . are you and Barry a tag team now?'

She led me out of the light. 'You've been taking it easy, haven't you? Keep taking it easy. It'll come back again if you just take it easy. It's only been a few days this time.'

I concentrated on fixing a cigarette to my holder. 'Taking it easy is not the problem,' I said. 'I don't know what the problem is, but . . .'

She pulled my arm and spoke softly into my ear. 'The booze. You said it was firewater, anyhow. Maybe it's poisoning you.'

This was too much. Friend or not, this was life advice from a girl younger than my own son. I glared at her and shook my arm free. 'Woodsie, the problem right now is not firewater. The problem is my name will be on this calamity and I'm starting to worry about that.'

'Your name's been on lots of movies.'

'Yeah . . . but not immediately preceding the word *presents*. That's new for me. So far all we've got is a dozen rolls of hokum. Not one decent battle.'

'What about tonight, the train one?'

'I said decent. And nothing of Fidel.'

'You did your interview last week.'

'No we didn't. We just pretended to. We need some good *generalissimo* stuff . . . Christ! Now listen to me, I sound like Barry's writing my lines. We need to see *el Gigante* directing his troops. Can't pin him down. He's a slippery bastard. Tells you one thing, does something else. Unless you're actually standing there in front of him, you can't tell what's going to happen next.'

Beverly just shrugged. 'That's war, I guess.'

This made me cough on my cigarette. 'You're not on camera now. You don't have to feed me Barry's Oscar-winning dialogue.'

'No, I mean . . . you know . . .'

'Yeah, I know. In the *revolucion* everything changes.'

'Yeah . . .' she said. 'It does, doesn't it.'

'Action!' Barry yelled, and the rebels moved into the cane with torches burning. It quickly took, and soon flames were leaping into the night sky, silhouetting the *barbudos* like black ghosts in an infernal Dante-esque tableau. 'Look at that, buddy! Look at that! There's more to this war stuff than you thought, eh?'

17
El bailarin, el heroe.
Palma Soriano, 24 December 1958

Carlos squeezed the four of us into his jeep – Beverly, Barry, Chloe and me. Fidel had just paid a visit to the family farm, he said, for the Noche Buena feast. It was the first time he had seen his mother in years. Tonight he would be in a good mood for us.

It was a much larger mill he had moved into, with solid brick and stone buildings, tiled roofs with three smoke stacks and two water towers rising above them to the stars. Carlos drove up an avenue of palm trees, pulled into a wide portico and then led us into a hall filled with people. An improvised sign was stretched across the far wall – *Feliz Navidad*. In the centre of the room, surrounded by his *barbudos* and their rebel women, was Fidel, and not far away I recognised his merry men: Raul, Huber, Lucia and Chico. Fidel saw us arrive and greeted us warmly, one by one. He then steered a matronly older woman over to us. Apart from us gringos, she was the only person in the room not in olive green. She was small and dark, with a weathered complexion and sad eyes behind heavy black-rimmed glasses.

'*Mi madre*,' Fidel said proudly, his hands gripping the woman's shoulders.

'Your mother?' I said. I took her hand. 'You must be very proud of your son, senora.' I kissed it, and she shyly put the other one to her mouth.

'*Mi madre* she has no English,' Fidel said.

'Ah-hah.' I tried out my Spanish. '*Usted mucho . . .*' I turned to Fidel for help. 'What is proud?'

'*Orgulloso.*'

'*Usted mucho orgulloso de su hijo, senora.*' She giggled behind her hand like a girl. 'Did I say the right thing?' I asked Fidel, still holding her other hand.

He smiled. Carlos was right about his mood. 'Near enough.'

I shook my head and clicked my tongue. '*Senora, usted . . . ah, no parece suficiente viejo.*' Again she giggled and shook her head.

'That one pretty good,' Fidel said. '*Mi madre*, she have me young.'

He wheeled her away, but she kept turning back over her shoulder. I smiled and waved.

'What did you say to her?' Beverly asked me.

'Oh, I just said she looked too young to have a son Fidel's age. At least, I hope that's what I said.'

'You need glasses,' Beverly said. 'She looks like she's had half a dozen Fidels.'

'Woodsie, she probably has.'

A grinning Fidel returned. 'She has seen you in movies. I bring her all this way to meet you.'

'Always nice to meet my fans,' I said.

'So . . . you film battle here at mill tomorrow, no?'

'Yes, tomorrow,' said Barry. 'The Christmas Day massacre.'

'You have what you want?'

'Thank you, yes,' Barry nodded. 'We've got jeeps, trucks, tractors . . . we've got a cast of thousands, and all the right uniforms.'

Fidel frowned. 'You have thousands?'

'Just a figure of speech, old chap,' I said. 'We have more than enough. I'm surprised you can spare it all.'

Fidel shrugged and adjusted his belt, repositioning the holster on his hip. 'We capture much equipment, much men. The men, if they are not criminals to our people, they can join us. We give their uniform to you. It is the Christmas present, no? Any more you need, you tell Chico. Maffo, soon it will be ours. Maybe then we give you thousands, eh?'

Cheers erupted from the end of the room as a roast pig was carried in, high above the heads. 'I'm surprised you celebrate Christmas,' I said.

'For *mi madre*,' Fidel said. 'Raul and me, we have not seen her two years now. Tonight we even have drink after we eat. We all enjoy.'

A scruffy old man and young girl were led into the room and helped up onto a table. The man pushed the battered straw hat back from his forehead and began picking a Cuban folk melody on a twelve-string laud guitar with the girl keeping time clapping the claves. As the pig was stripped of its meat and passed around, the girl wailed a lively *guajira son* in a high-pitched voice and the *barbudos* nodded their heads to its beat and shuffled their feet. Men and women stood around the musicians, eating, swaying and restraining themselves.

I leaned into Barry's ear. 'If they're not careful, the revolution will break into a dance.'

I saw Fidel's mother watching the musicians, a grin from ear to ear, nodding to the beat. I made my way to her side. '*Por favor, senora,*' I said, bowing deeply and then struggling to find the words. '*Ah . . . dance . . . danzon . . . usted conmigo?*'

She laughed and allowed herself to be led onto the floor. *Barbudos* made room for us and cheered. '*Bailar, senor,*' she said. '*Bailar . . . no danzon.*'

'*Bailar*,' I said. 'Yes, let's *bailar*!' I caught the attention of the old man on the table and circled my hand quickly. 'Up tempo, old chum . . . mucho the tempo.'

She obviously expected to meet the swashbuckler, and I tried to give her more than she expected, sweeping my newest fan off her feet, dancing her around the room to the applause of my audience.

Every Cuban knows how to dance, and she was no exception. After a few minutes of swirling and laughing she broke free and fanned her flushed cheeks. '*No, no, senor . . . no mas, por favor, no mas . . .*'

I bowed again, as elaborately as I could, and joined in the applause. Over her shoulder I saw Lucia grinning and clapping enthusiastically, and I caught her eye. I quickly took her by the hand and whisked her onto the floor. The cheering and applause soon faded. Above the strumming guitar and the girl's singing, a deeper voice boomed across the room.

'*El bailarin!*'

Fidel strutted into the middle of the floor with a slow and deliberate handclap. '*El bailarin, companeros . . . el bailarin . . .*'

I swung Lucia around the rebel leader, stepping boldly with my rediscovered spring, clutching her waist tightly and ignoring the obvious concern now showing on her face. But she moved lightly, spontaneously, responding to my moves with natural grace. And then I felt her heavy in my arms. Her head drooped into my elbow. I took all her weight when I realised she had fainted.

Fidel wordlessly ordered Chico to cut in on me. Quickly the *pistolita* stepped onto the floor and wrapped his arms around Lucia and carried her away. I rushed after them. 'Give her some air!'

Chico jostled her in his arms and the drooping head lifted, the eyes opened. She blinked and looked around. Her hands went to her face. She wriggled herself free and ran from the room.

Fidel signalled for the music to cease. He began his slow hand-clap again, and the tide of people receded, leaving me standing now alone in the middle of the floor. *'El bailarin,'* said Fidel. *'El heroe . . .'*

Every face in the room was turned my way. It could be said that the audience was at my feet. Or was it to be the bullet I had expected? If it was, I found it didn't fill me with alarm. It was me against the revolution and I was charged with adrenalin. Custer at the Little Big Horn again, Robin Hood in the castle of the Sheriff.

'That's the second time she's run out on me,' I said to my audience. And then I broke into an exaggerated smile and gave my best Lord Essex bow to each corner of the room in turn. Only the other *yanquis* applauded, nervously. Fidel stopped clapping and sauntered up to me, his hand casually resting on the holster on his hip. '*El bailarin*, perhaps,' I said to him. '*El heroe*, no.'

'No,' Fidel said. 'Your fight, it is in the bar room. In Spain against the fascists, in the world war, no fight from you. In Cuba we fight in the battle. This it is the reality. For you it is too late for the reality.'

But this *was* the reality. Here I was, in danger, in genuine danger, and not a camera to be seen anywhere. 'Fighting is a lot like dancing,' I said. 'You lead with your left. They're both competitive, you see. Just different objectives. Didn't you say we'd have a drink? Is it time yet?'

Fidel glared at me. Without moving his eyes, or his hand from the holster, he snapped his other fingers at the old man, and they picked up with another folk song. 'We can drink,' he said to me. 'Yes, we can drink. We can drink because it is the celebration. You will drink for another thing. You will drink to be someone else.'

As Fidel turned away, Barry, Chloe and Beverly were quickly at my side. 'I think it's time to go, buddy,' Barry said.

Carlos joined us. 'Senor . . . maybe you and Fidel, you are too alike.'

'That's the second time you've accused me of that particular sin,' I said to him. 'I thought you said you were a journalist.'

'*Si.*'

'Well you don't seem very observant for a journalist.'

'Perhaps more observant than you,' Chloe said.

'I don't know about that,' I said. 'Did you give him that typewriter?'

'*Si,*' said Carlos.

'Did he like it?'

'*Si.* I think so.'

'Well . . . I'll try another peace offering.'

I took a cigar from my pocket and pushed through the *barbudos* to Fidel. 'How about a drink *and* a smoke?' I said.

Fidel did not even look at me. He took the cigar, dropped it to the floor, and stepped on it with his boot. 'That is all Cuba is to you. Good time, gamble, have our women.' He turned his back.

'You're right,' I said to Barry. 'I think it's time to go.'

Carlos led us from the room. I saw Fidel's mother. I asked him what her name was. Lina, he said. I made my way over to her and kissed her hand again. '*Buenas nochas, Senora Lina. Es un placer.*'

On our way to the door I saw Lucia. 'One day, Senorita Lucia, I hope to finish a dance with you.' I blew her a kiss, and she smiled. Just briefly, until she saw that everyone was looking at her, and quickly wiped it from her lips.

I felt like I had just been saved from the Little Big Horn by the arrival of the cavalry in a jeep, and it was an exhilarating feeling. As we sped along the dark track I asked Carlos what he meant when he said that I was like his *commandante*. Carlos exhaled slowly and shook his head. 'Oh . . . senor . . . maybe you are right. I am not good to observe.'

'If I was like him,' I said, 'I might understand what just happened. It was just a cigar. A good Cuban cigar.'

'You know, Errol,' Chloe said, 'for someone as smart as you, you can be mighty slow sometimes. You take the guy's stage and all you offer in return is a lousy cigar.'

I thought it was a strange thing to say. 'I wasn't trying to upstage him,' I protested.

'The hell you weren't,' Barry said. 'You can't help yourself. And next time you do it, don't offer him a cigar. He's Cuban. The cigars are his.'

I stretched my arms, put my hands behind my head and grinned. 'Maybe you're right,' I said. 'The cigars are his. But tonight the mojo might be mine.'

'The what?' said Chloe.

'Just something between me and Woodsie,' I said. 'Just me and Woodsie.'

18
The Christmas Day massacre.
Palma Soriano, 25 December 1958

We filmed our version of the rebel attack on the sugar mill on Christmas Day, ignoring what had actually occurred a week earlier for what Barry called 'choreography for the camera'. I asked him where he had heard that one, and if he had been hanging around with Orson Welles lately, and he ignored me as well.

A boiler was fired up to make smoke for one of the chimneys in a long shot, and then the morning was filled with gun battles. Rebels stormed the mill buildings, leaving prostrate guards in their wake. They dashed down alleys and through doorways and over walls, and guards scrambled from their barracks. Barry insisted on shooting close-up sequences of running feet. 'Action art,' he called it. He showed his guards how to stack rifles into tee-pees, rehearsing it over and over until they could grab their weapons without causing a collapse. After his early takes I offered that we should perhaps re-title our movie 'Assault of the Keystone Kops', and Barry continued to ignore me. When they had perfected it, Barry liked the action so much he shot it again and again. By this time I was certain about Orson.

The outnumbered rebels were forced into retreat late in the morning, sneaking away in the shadows and the mouldy whitewash of the satanic mill. According to script, Johnny was hit by a sniper and left where he lay.

Beverly and Marie were captured and manhandled from a jeep by guards. 'Get your lousy hands offa me, ya big lug!' said Beverly colourfully, but it didn't matter, our budget extended to neither sound nor colour.

Barry called a break and I retreated to a quiet spot in the shade of a tractor. Beverly found me as I was peeling my orange. 'Don't you want some water?' she said, offering me her bottle.

'Water is for swimming,' I said. 'This is far more invigorating. But then I haven't been running around all morning in the heat, playing Captain America. Might I say on that point, your running itself is looking more to me like *Miss* America. You have to pump your arms to look convincing, not swing them about like a girl.'

'I *am* a girl,' she said.

'You're a rebel girl. Rebel girls have to know how to run.'

'Maybe you'll have to teach me,' she said, swigging from her bottle. 'You're good at that.'

'I used to be. Not any more. Couldn't run to save my life these days.'

'I mean you're good at teaching me.'

'Yes, I know what you mean.' I patted the ground next to me. 'Take a seat. If I know Barry he'll have you on your feet again soon enough.' She sat down and leaned her back against the big tyre of the tractor. 'I used to love running. I loved the sound of the wind in my ears. I had someone follow me in a car once along Mulholland Drive. I found that the windrush started at fifteen miles an hour, and at twenty miles an hour it sounded like one of those jet engines. I tell you, running like that, free as a bird in the sky, it was like a drug.'

'So ... now you can't run like that, is that why you take, I dunno ... less strenuous drugs.'

'Perhaps so, Woodsie. Speaking of which, are you sure you don't want some of my Christmas cheer?' I held out a wedge of my orange.

'No, I'm fine. I can still run. Like a girl, maybe, but I can still run.'

I held it up to her mouth. It was dripping juice through my fingers. 'Come on, don't let all this goodness go to waste. They say it's full of vitamin C. Miss America has to keep her strength up.'

She snatched it and bit the flesh from the skin. She coughed and spat juice. 'What is this?'

'Did I say vitamin C? I meant vitamin R, of course. R for rum, from the orchards of Flynn Enterprises. Unfortunately not V for vodka. And rebel rum at that. Orange makes it palatable, don't you think? Less poisonous. It's a little trick I learned at Warners. Jack didn't like his slaves taking a tipple on the set. I call it my Clark Kent orange.'

Beverly was still coughing. 'Okay ... why ...?'

'Because it's a screwdriver in mild-mannered disguise.' I slurped at the torn orange and licked the juice from my fingers.

'You sure know some crazy stuff.'

I ran my tongue over my lips and watched her as she stripped the last of her wedge from its skin. She had such a sensuous mouth. I knew women who would have spent a fortune on surgery to get a mouth like hers. 'Woodsie,' I said, 'you're one in a million.'

She stopped gnawing and looked at me blankly for a second before chortling merrily. 'Yeah, and don't I know it.'

Now she had me chortling. 'What's it like being sixteen?' I said.

'What do you mean?'

'It's so long ago for me I've forgotten. When I was sixteen the world was still in jerky black and white.'

'Now what do you mean?'

'You've seen a Charlie Chaplin movie haven't you? That's how the world was then ... no colour, and everyone walking around with quick jerky movements. It was very tiring to live in those days. You had to be very fit. It wasn't until I did Robin Hood that colour came along and everything changed.'

She gave me the blank stare again and sighed. 'You expect me to swallow that load of baloney?'

'No, you're right. I never saw the world in black and white. Not even when I was sixteen. Not sure I saw much at all. I grew up pretty fast. Let's see ... 1925, yes it might've been one of the years I missed.'

'What were you doing at sixteen?' she said with an indulgent nod of the head. 'I bet you were your mother's darling.'

'Now, my mother is something I'm sure I saw in colour from the time I was born. I must have been a difficult birth because it's been difficult ever since. Yes, a colourful character indeed, my mother. But I don't think I saw her at all when I was sixteen. I was in boarding school in Sydney and she was in another country altogether. Shore School. Sounds Irish, doesn't it? To be sure, to be sure,' I said, affecting my best Barry Fitzgerald. 'I got expelled for a dalliance with Elsie the laundry maid, which I'm sure will not come as a surprise to you, not to mention my many critics. Or my mother, for that matter. But what may surprise you is that she was twice my age.'

'Twice your age? Lucky for you you're not still like that. I'd be going on for a hundred.'

'Lucky for both of us, Woodsie. Mind you, Elsie wasn't the first domestic to teach me a detail or two about the facts of life. Before her there was Carrie, when I was only twelve. She made me pay good pocket money for that lesson. I've been paying ever since, it seems, one way or another.'

'Twelve, huh. You know what, Cap'n. Sometimes I think you're trying to live your life backwards. Like you missed out on your childhood and now you're making up for it.'

Unfortunately, I didn't even hear her. My mind was in 1925. 'After all that I got a job licking stamps in an office. That was my first employment. Not showing much promise then, eh? I noticed that they counted the envelopes, not the stamps. I made a pretty penny from blank envelopes. Raided the postage tin and blew it all at the races.'

'So that was when you started showing promise.'

'Living down to my mother's expectations.'

'What did she expect?'

'Not too much. But she *wanted* me to be a genius.'

'A genius? Like Einstein, you mean?'

'Why not? Like my father, not like Einstein. He's a genius, kind of, in his own way. Knows more about strange amphibious creatures than anyone alive, so I guess that's a kind of genius. No ... if I have a genius it's a genius for living.'

'You wrote that already, for your book. I read it. Remember? You said it was your philosophy. Any more Clark Kent there?'

I held the orange above my mouth and split off a wedge, allowing the juice to drip onto my tongue. 'All my lines can't be original. What am I saying? I'm an actor. None of my lines are original. And as for a philosophy ... did I really say that?'

'Sure did. You don't remember? You can ask Earl.'

I handed her the wedge and watched with satisfaction as she sucked the juice from it. 'Must have been the booze talking. On the whole, Woodsie, I enjoy life too much to be a philosopher. You have to be a depressed sonofabitch for that racket.'

'You get depressed,' she gargled. 'I've seen you when you're depressed. You just do something silly to get over it.'

'Is that so?' I said. 'Sounds to me like you've been spending too much time with Chloe. You want to be careful around Chloe. Next thing you know she'll be telling you Uranus is in the outhouse and that's why you're too rash and reckless.'

She was too busy inspecting the drained wedge to take any notice of me. 'How'd you get this stuff in here, anyway?' she said.

'Just a syringe. You have to be prepared if you want to survive. Have to be a boy scout.'

'I can't see you as a boy scout,' she grinned.

I finished the last of the orange and threw away the skin. 'It's been a roller coaster ride, hasn't it, our little adventure? Maybe you're right. Before coming here I was down. Then in Havana I was up. I'm always up in Havana, despite our recent difficulties. And then when we started shooting this lousy movie I was down again. And then we meet Fidel and his people, and up I go again. Life's full of excitement, isn't it?'

'Yeah, full of excitement,' she repeated. 'I notice the most excitement comes after you lock horns with that Fidel.'

I wiped my mouth with my bandana and frowned at her. 'What do you mean?'

'You know what I mean.'

'Ah . . . your mysterious mojo again.'

Beverly's doors of perception required no artificial cleanser. She was right. Booze may have been slowly withering every other organ in my body, but not that one. The months of its inactivity had been caused by my own months of inactivity. Before coming to Cuba I had spent so much time going over old adventures with Earl I had none for new ones. Restlessness for the far horizon, curiosity for the closed door, no time for any of that. I was always fascinated how Monet could spend half his life just painting water lilies. Hundreds and hundreds of damned water lilies. I admired his pursuit of perfection, but marvelled at the monotony. Monotony, not firewater, had been poisoning me.

Fidel was a damned fine door to kick open, and it appeared to be just the tonic I needed.

'Some roller coaster,' Beverly said. 'Are you famous for that as well as all the other things?'

'All the other things . . .' She was right about that, as well. I was famous for many things, and none that I set out to achieve. 'You know what? Fame and fortune aren't all they're cracked up to be. You can have money, be an international character and have your face known all around the world, and what does it get you? I mean, really get you. You can have all that, and still wonder whether some guy who just has faith in something is better off.'

'You mean Fidel, don't you?'

'I'll wager he's no disappointment to his mother. Did you see how happy she was?'

Beverly looked at me and slowly shook her head. 'Did you see how happy she was when she met *you*?'

'Strictly temporary, Woodsie. People are happy around me, sure. But not for long. You'll find out. I'm famous for it.'

'So Fidel's not a disappointment to his mom, so what? It's only a matter of time.'

Yes, a matter of time. 'I wonder what Elsie the laundry maid is doing these days,' I said. 'I wonder if she ever thinks about me.'

'You made her happy for a while, did you?'

'While I've gone on to fame and fortune, she might have found something to believe in. Probably doesn't even remember me.'

'Are you kidding? I bet she tells everyone she meets she knew Errol Flynn when he was sixteen.'

'What that must be like . . . something to really believe in.' Fame, fortune and faith – I made a mental note to call Earl and get it into the book.

'She'd be an old lady now,' Beverly said. 'I bet she's sitting on the porch in her rocking chair right now thinking about you.'

'My mother wanted me to be a genius, what then? She's never had any respect for my father's genius.'

'And you say you only make people happy for a while. That Elsie, she's been happy thinking about you for half her life, I bet.'

'She has her affairs and doesn't even care who knows. Like mother, like son.'

'Half her life. That's not a short time.'

'We've spent our whole lives together falling out, one scrap after another. All my life I've been running away from her. All my life I've been trying to find her.'

'You make me happy. You'll *always* make me happy.'

'One of my many thirsts.'

'Beverly, you're wanted,' Jackie called.

'Time to go,' I said. I climbed to my feet and offered her my hand. Just as I took her weight my foot slipped on a piece of orange peel and down I went in an awkward fall, cracking my knee on a sharp edge of the tractor. I sat up and held my ripped pants.

'Oh, it's your knee,' Beverly said.

'Brilliant observation, Holmes,' I said. 'You must be that rebel girl I've been hearing so much about.'

We filmed the second attack on the sugar mill. A tractor hauled a long cane trailer into the yard. Hidden rebels leapt from it and took the guards by surprise. Soon the battle was over, the mill out of *yanqui* hands and safe for the revolution. As the sun sank toward the horizon we filmed the raising of the flag, *barbudos* and rebel girls saluting and cheering happily. Our Iwo Jima shot, Barry proudly called it.

Last scene of the day was Beverly being led into a warehouse to see Marie, taken captive in a previous scene, hanging upside down by the feet. 'Those dirty Batista butchers,' she said with as much gravitas as she had at her command. Everyone agreed it was time to call a wrap.

I quietly asked Barry how he expected to cut all this together. No one seemed to be keeping an eye on continuity. Men were dead on the ground one minute, shooting it out the next. Barry shrugged and said that one Cuban soldier looks like another. 'Stop worrying,' he said. 'It'll be great.'

19
Dying is easy.
Maffo, 30 December 1958

The real battle for Maffo was a war of attrition with the rebels occupying the shops and houses of the otherwise abandoned town, and Batista's desperate *casquitos* defending their warehouse bastion in the middle. It was Hemingway's stalemate in bloody microcosm, and it was not the stuff of movies. The rebels attacked with bullets and the defenders replied with mortar shells. There were negotiated ceasefires when the rebel anthem and calls for surrender blared from a loudspeaker truck driven right up to the walls, but at an appointed hour the truck retreated and the shooting restarted.

Barry was still desperate for action footage. The cut to my knee had become infected, restricting my movements and, quite reasonably, the camera crew refused to put themselves in harm's way, so Barry took the camera himself and followed columns of rebels into a few isolated skirmishes. Filming a large-scale engagement in a guerrilla war though, proved to be an impossible assignment.

Eventually, during one of the ceasefires the rebels broadcast that they were preparing to flood the warehouse with gasoline and put everyone in it to the torch, and the capitulation finally came. Barry and I were taken into the town and told we were to film the surrender. There was no triumphant march and no cheering crowds. The inhabitants had long ago fled into the canefields and beyond, and the rebels were already in occupation of all but the fortified warehouse.

From a bullet-riddled drugstore that had been the rebel forward command post, all we had to film was the herding of two hundred *casquitos* into a square surrounded by submachine guns. Anyone could see what was about to happen. 'They're gonna massacre them,' I whispered, and Barry tried vainly to keep his hands steady on the camera.

Raul Castro stepped forward and delivered the last rites, haranguing the hapless prisoners against the setting sun. He spoke for three full minutes in his shrill staccato. Barry panned over the drooping heads at the end of his long lens and waited for the inevitable. 'Turn it off,' I whispered in disgust. 'We can't use it.'

'They want it,' Barry said, squinting into the eyepiece, 'the bastard's are fucking getting it.'

I couldn't watch. I limped to the back of the shop and slumped onto a broken chair. The triumph of victory was about to become a slaughter and I did not intend to be a witness.

'*Adelante Cubanos . . .*' All around me the voices rang out with the rebel anthem, like the drum roll at the guillotine to drown out the protests and the screams. They would never drown out the gunfire – but there was none. He's torturing these poor bastards, I thought. Raul with the innocent beardless face. The anthem was repeated, and still there was no gunfire. I pushed my way through the *barbudos* to the front of the store again just in time to see the last of the defeated *casquitos* filing back into the warehouse between their crowing guards. Barry had stopped filming. 'What's going on?' I asked him.

'They're handing them over to the Red Cross,' he said.

'Who told you that?'

Barry nodded his head at a rebel standing next to him. 'The young *capitano* here. Ask him yourself.'

'It is true,' the young *capitano* said. '*Companero* Raul he tell the prisoner join us. Who say no, tomorrow we give to the Red Cross.'

'But . . . you'll just have to fight them all over again.'

The *capitano* shrugged. 'Maybe so, maybe not so. Most when he see the difference of Batista and Fidel, he will not fight.'

Barry raised his eyebrows to me. 'A revolution in revolutions,' he said. He turned back to the square. 'I'll get some of *el Gigante* while I'm here.'

Fidel and Raul were standing in a jeep surrounded by cheering *barbudos*. Barry took his camera outside, and I hobbled along behind. We circled the throng to get the last of the sun behind our backs and the chief *companeros* in its golden light. Fidel shaded his eyes and stared in our direction. He jumped down from the jeep and the waters parted for the messiah.

Barry saw him first. 'Oh Christ, he's seen you.'

Fidel strode up to us, removing his cigar to display a broad grin. 'So . . . *el heroe*. You join us for the victory.'

I found myself in involuntary retreat, limping backwards, away from the frontal assault. Fidel stopped and looked at my leg. 'You are wounded?'

'Just a scratch, as they say.'

'You are wounded.' He planted the cigar back between his teeth and wrapped his arms around me in an enthusiastic bear hug. 'Casualty of the revolution.' He stepped back. 'You see what happen here, the prisoners?'

'Yes, we saw.'

He glanced at the camera in Barry's hands. 'You film for us, no? You tell the world we release the prisoners. Two hundred and forty-two, senor. You remember that.'

'How could we forget?' I said.

He gripped both my shoulders. 'We take care of you. Come.'

He led us back to the drugstore and barked a series of orders, sending *barbudos* scurrying in all directions. 'We send you to the hospital. It is not good for you to die for us, not even for the revolution.'

'I'm nowhere near dying, I just . . .'

'We make sure. We save *el heroe* from dying.'

'Dying is easy,' I said. 'It's comedy that's hard.'

Barry winced and Fidel frowned. 'What does this mean?'

'Oh, just something Bud Abbott used to say to Lou Costello.'

Fidel slowly nodded his head. '*El heroe* . . . one day you must know where legend it end, and where life it begin. Soon you must know this.'

'Perhaps not as soon as you, *el commandante*.'

Fidel took the cigar from his mouth and blew smoke into the air as he considered. 'Today we win two important battles. Maffo and Yaguajay. *Companero* Che he take Yaguajay. Soon he take Santa Clara and I take Santiago. Soon we have the complete victory. You must be healthy to see this. You will tell the world. So go now, we take you to the hospital.'

The 'hospital' was a corrugated iron farm shed in an orange orchard outside the village. The floor was muddy with spilt blood and a row of kerosene lamps hung over half a dozen grimy beds and a wooden table. A smaller table next to it held a collection of enamel basins and mugs and a roll of surgical instruments. A woman doctor in bloodied white hospital gown tied over her fatigues moved between the beds, all of which supported men whose bodies were in a far worse state of repair than my leg. I was told to lie on the table and wait. When she got to me, the doctor unceremoniously ripped my torn pants apart and prodded at my painful red and yellow scab with the blunt end of a scalpel that seemed to be a fixture in her hand. Satisfied that it hurt, she grunted and returned to the bloodied rebel in the next bed.

Eventually my cut was properly cleaned and dressed with some antibiotic cream and a bandage. The doctor gave me a penicillin pill. Just one pill? She shrugged and said that an injury like this should not cause such problems. She said my body must be in a sorry state. One more in a long line of doctors to tell me that. I limped from the shed and looked around for my transport. A row of bodies was laid out on the ground with candles flickering at their feet. Cleaning the wound seemed to have inflamed it. I fashioned a walking stick from a broken branch and began limping towards the lights of Maffo, my pants leg flapping wildly. Before Fidel's treatment I was inconvenienced, now I felt like one of the wretched confederates in *Gone With the Wind* limping home after the war.

When I emerged from the orchard I realised the lights I was heading for were not Maffo at all. The night was dark and blackness spread before me with one brightly lit building like an island in the void. I hobbled towards it, unsure if I was going to encounter land or water, and fell into a pit of sand. It was a trap. A small red flag hung limply nearby. I was on the edge of a green, in the middle of a golf course.

Now I could make out the bright lights to be the clubhouse. The place was deserted except for an old caretaker asleep in a cane chair on the terrace, and he stirred as I shuffled my way among the tables. He leapt to his feet with an agility that belied his age, and grabbed a shotgun. I froze as the old man took a fix on me down the length of the barrel.

'You are member, senor?'

'*Si*,' I said with an authoritative nod. 'Of course.'

The old man lowered the gun. '*Perdone*, senor.'

'Now, be a good chap and open up will you,' I said, pointing my rustic walking stick at the door. 'I rather fancy a drink.'

'*Si*, senor.' The old man hurried to the door, opened it, and stood back at attention, the gun held stiffly at his side.

'A guard of honour,' I said with approval. 'I must be the first customer.'

Both of us ignored the fact that I was hobbling, that my pants were ragged, that my face was unshaven, my hair unkempt. I was a *yanqui* and in the golf club that was all that mattered. I made my way to the bar and inspected the display of bottles. Zubrowka was too much to expect, but there was Smirnoff. There was whisky, brandy, gin, tequila and a plentiful stock of Bacardi. 'No ice, senor,' said the old man apologetically.

I poured myself a vodka and drained the glass. 'Ambrosia,' I sighed at him, feeling younger already. 'Even without ice.' I poured another and looked around the room – tables, chairs, a dance floor, a bandstand. I downed the second glass and pushed open a door to reveal a kitchen. Everything was spotless, like a Westchester oasis in a boondock's sea.

The old man put a small pad on the bar in front of me. Two vodka, it said, and there was carbon paper between the pages. I had no money, and was about to confess the problem, when the caretaker offered me a pen. I autographed the chit and added a scrawled membership number in the space provided. The caretaker tore off the top copy and gave it to me. 'Keep it,' I said. 'It's worth more than the drinks.'

'Trust you to find the only booze for one hundred miles.'

Barry was standing in the doorway, hands on hips. 'Barry, old chum,' I said. 'Isn't this a find? Come, let me buy you a drink.'

'Yeah. A real treasure.'

I held up my empty glass. 'I tell you . . . the Tropicana never tasted so good. Even without ice.'

'Can I suggest,' Barry said, sauntering up to the bar, hands still firmly planted, 'the next time we meet *el Gigante*, if there is a next time, you don't try seeing how far you can push his buttons?'

'Why Barry, I don't know what you mean.'

'Sure you don't. Look, he was in a good mood today. One of these times, and it's not the first time I've asked you this, you're gonna push him too far.'

'Maybe it's the Australian in my character,' I said. 'We never did have much time for authority, you know. Anyway, what's he gonna do, shoot me?'

'Yeah, probably.'

'Come on, sport. All those stories about him are just stories. He doesn't even shoot his prisoners.'

'Prisoners know better than to push his buttons.'

I found another glass and poured a drink for each of us, emptying the last of the bottle. 'If that's where my long-awaited bullet's coming from, I can't think of a better person to deliver it. Beats the heck out of George Sanders. Cheers.'

'But it won't be him, will it? It'll be his nice *pistolita*. Cheers yourself.'

We drank our vodkas. 'How about this place?' I said, wiping my mouth with the back of my hand. 'You know what tomorrow is?'

'Dunno . . . Wednesday?'

'New Year's Eve.'

'Oh,' said Barry, underwhelmed.

'What do you mean, *oh*? New Year's Eve. Two big victories and New Year's Eve. *Ano Nuevo!* It's an occasion.'

'Not our victories.'

'So . . .? So we'll invite our good friends and allies, the *rebelde*.'

'To what?'

'A party, chum. A good old New Year's Eve shindig.'

'It may have escaped your attention, Errol, but there's a goddamn war on, and we're in the middle of it.'

'Not anymore. It's moved down the road.' I hobbled out onto the dance floor, waving my stick in the air. 'Peace has broken out all around us here. Good guys are on their way to Santiago, bad guys to the Red Cross.' With no bodies other than our own to absorb it, my voice echoed around the room.

Slowly realisation dawned on Barry. 'Wait a minute . . . here? What do you mean, here?'

'Here,' I said, spreading my arms wide. 'Where better for a shindig.'

Barry shook his head. 'Thank goodness for us there's no time to pull it together.'

I slapped my good leg. 'Of course there's time.'

Barry pointed at my ripped pants. 'Pity you don't have a change of wardrobe. You'd look mighty silly twirling your bad leg around the floor in rags. Or are you going to join up, wear the uniform?'

I clumped my way over to my partner. Suddenly the leg wasn't hurting so much. 'Chum . . . that's where you're wrong. What do you think is in all that luggage I've been hauling around?'

I grabbed another bottle of Smirnoff from behind the bar and quickly limped toward the door. The caretaker held it open for me with one hand, and the chit pad out in the other. 'Pay the man,' I called over my shoulder.

'With what?' said Barry.

'I don't know. You're the producer.'

20
I catch myself acting out my life like a goddamn script.
Maffo, 31 December 1958

'So what is this, a rumba or a mambo?' Beverly said impatiently above the music. 'I can't tell the difference anyway.'

'Neither can I,' I said. My head was swaying to the rhythm and my eyes were closed, but I knew if I opened them I would find a frown on her face. 'Who cares? They're all marvellous. I'm told this one's a bolero. Although I don't think Senor Ravel had anything to do with it.'

We had fashioned a stage for Trio *Rebelde* by moving one of the makeshift tables from an assembly hut into the middle of the camp, but it did nothing for their stage presence. They had little to offer in the way of performance to enliven their material, their faces expressionless and their bodies stock-still. Two guitars and maracas, that was all they had, but the music they produced from such modest means was achingly beautiful and eminently danceable. Just the thing for the golf club.

I sat with Beverly on a log with a few of the remaining rebels left in camp and allowed the harmonies to wash over me. Such music, in the middle of a war, in the middle of the wild sierra – only in Cuba, I thought. Beverly was less impressed.

'What's the matter, not your style?' I said. 'How about it?'

Beverly shrugged. 'It's boring. If you want an opinion, ask Barry. It's more his age.'

More Barry's age. Music for old men. She was only sixteen. I had known her since she had just turned fifteen, and she was growing up quickly. Some of it was my bold colour and stark contrast, some of it self-portrayed. 'Yes, I keep forgetting how young you really are,' I said. 'Barry's busy. Listen . . . you might get to like it. Listen to those harmonies. You don't get voices like that in your rock and roll.'

'No . . . you don't.'

'They tell me it's like the blues, all sorrow and heartache, only up tempo. Poetry in music, and I don't even understand what they're saying.'

'Then how do you know it's poetry?'

'Listen. Don't you find it romantic? You're supposed to be the romantic one.'

'Haven't you heard enough? They'll be okay.'

'They'll have to be,' I said. 'They're all we've got. I'll have to get them to do a cha-cha-cha.'

'What . . . now?'

'No, tonight. Nothing like a good cha-cha-cha to get the juices flowing, the dander up.'

The trio came to the end of their bolero and the rebels and I applauded enthusiastically. 'Remember,' I said, 'you go with them tonight, make sure they get there. I'll be along later.'

'You told me,' she said. 'Why are you going to be late, anyway?'

'Just something I have to do first.'

She folded her arms and looked around. 'So what do I do for the next three hours, boss?'

I got to my feet, stretching and carefully straightening my

bandaged leg. 'Once more into the hut, fair maid, once more, and fill yon heads with our empty thoughts.'

'What's that, more poetry?'

'To sleep, perchance to dream. Alas, the night will soon be upon us.'

'You're crazy.'

'You're right. Anyone who mangles Shakespeare like that . . . we've got a big night coming up, a big year to farewell. Better take a load off.'

'Oh, no,' Beverly said, slowly shaking her head. 'I know what you mean by take a load off. Not in daylight, Cap'n. Anyone can see.'

'Anyone?' I said, looking around the all but deserted camp. 'Anyone's on the road to Santiago. And I've a lot of lost time to make up.'

'Save it for next year,' she said. 'It's not long now. And it'll give you a reason not to get too drunk.'

I put my arm around her shoulders and steered her towards our shelter. 'Next year, eh. Next year I'll be fifty. How about that? There were times, I have to say, when I didn't think I'd make it to ten in the morning, let alone fifty. I don't feel fifty. In fact, I feel better than I've felt in months.'

'I feel like I'm . . . let's see . . . twenty-three. Yes, I feel like I'm twenty-three. A good year. The year I changed my life. The year I fancied I was Ulysses and took myself off to conquer the big wide world. And look where I am.' I swept an arm over the forest, the camp.

'So this is the big wide world, huh?' she said with a smirk.

'One thing Ulysses *has* found in the big wide world, honey, is that there will always be a place for irony. I'm told the Cubans appreciate it. If only I could speak enough Spanish to find out.'

We stooped under the thatched roof of our little hut. Beverly could just stand up, but I had to bend almost double. I winced and grabbed my back. 'I won't be sorry to see the end of this place.' I lowered myself carefully onto my bedroll. 'Rather looking forward to a decent bed for the first time in . . . God, I can't remember how long we've been out here in never-never land. My mind must be going, too. Seems like we've been here half my life. My mind and my body aren't up to this business anymore.'

'You've gotta stop worrying about growing old,' she said.

I fixed a cigarette into my holder. Booze may have been in short supply, but at least the Dimitrinos reserves were holding up. 'It's not growing old that worries me, Woodsie, it's the growing up that goes with it.'

'So is that where I come in? That's what Chloe says.'

'Chloe does, does she? Well, Chloe would know.'

Beverly found her make-up case and busied herself with her face. I watched her fingers tracing the line of her eyebrow in the mirror, preening her lashes, pinching her cheeks. She was totally unselfconscious, as comfortable with me as if I were her husband. She was growing up quickly. And I was her old man. 'Do you think it's true what they say, Woodsie, that old age creeps up on you?'

'I wouldn't know, would I?' she said, flicking the point of a finger into the corners of her gaping mouth.

'They say that one day you look in the mirror and see your father looking back. Do you think that's true?'

She fossicked around in the case and came up with a pencil. 'I haven't seen my father in years, so I hope it's not true.' She arched her eyebrows and touched them up.

I reached over and turned the case around, looking at myself in the mirror under its lid.

'Hey . . .!'

'Christ, is that me?' I said. 'Well, at least it's not my father. He's never looked like this.'

'It's got a curve in it,' she said. 'You know, to make you look bigger, closer.'

'Scarier,' I said, and turned it back to her in disgust. 'Thank God Bette Davis is not here.'

She straightened up the mirror and returned to her eyebrows. 'You know, if you shaved more often and took care of your hair . . .'

'C S Lewis said we read to know we're not alone. Do you agree with that?'

'What . . .?'

'That's not why I read. I read to satisfy my curiosity, simple as that. I'm not curious about whether I'm alone. You'd have to be a hopeless egocentric to think that you were alone, wouldn't you? An ego *gigante*. If I'm alone, then where does that put every other living creature on the planet? Are they all a figment of my imagination? My ego's not big enough to think that's the case, so I'm not curious about it. Does that make sense?'

'No,' she said, and I got the distinct impression she had not even heard me.

'*Cogito ergo sum*, how about that?'

'What?'

'Ah, well.' I lay back on my bedroll. Raindrops were beginning to fall on the roof. 'To know I'm not alone I fornicate.'

'So is that you not being a philosopher again? Who's this Sears Lewis, anyway? Have I met him?'

'Not that I'm aware. He's a writer, an English writer.'

She put the pencil down and looked at me. 'You know, that's the first time you've ever talked to me about a writer. You never talk to me about writers or thinkers or painters or any of those guys. You do that with other folks. Even that Fidel, the first time you met you guys were talking about writers and all that all night. Why don't you ever talk to me about that stuff?'

'That . . . stuff . . .' I repeated slowly. 'That's why. You're sixteen.'

'Yeah, I thought so. That's why you like to have someone my age around, isn't it? You never get any real arguments, you can say what you want and nobody argues, that's why, isn't it?'

She had not taken her eyes from the mirror, just tossed it off like a crumb of empty gossip among the girls in the beauty parlour. 'I never heard anything so preposterous,' I said, affecting my best high dudgeon, but even before the words had finished escaping my lips I was wondering if it were true. 'You're arguing right now, aren't you? It's just . . .' I decided to deal with the simple argument in her question and ignore the real challenge. 'At sixteen you can't be expected to carry one side of a conversation about . . .'

'So teach me,' she interrupted. 'I'm a good learner. I've learned all my lines pretty well, haven't I?'

'Aah, Woodsie,' I sighed. 'How can I explain?' I considered for a moment and came up with a way. 'There was a film a few years ago. It was English, so I doubt you saw it. *Captain's Paradise*, it was called, about a ship's captain who sailed between some port in Europe and another in North Africa. In the European port he had a respectable European wife, the prim and proper kind, who cooked and kept house and brought him his pipe and slippers and kept his feet on the ground. In the African port he had another wife, a wild and hot-blooded Latin type. With her he went to nightclubs and dances and kicked up his heels. And in between, on his voyages, he had his captain's table at dinner every night, where only men were invited, and they discussed philosophy and science and politics.' I sighed again. 'Paradise.'

'So . . . which one am I?'

'I'm not a captain, am I? You're all I've got.'

'Sure . . . that'll be the day,' she said, and then slowly and deliberately turned to face me before adding, 'Cap'n.'

'Tomorrow's 1959, Woodsie. For you it's another year closer to the top of the hill. For me it's another year closer to the bottom.'

'Do you always get like this on New Year's Eve?'

'It's the relativity of time, isn't it? The perspective is different depending on which side of the hill you find yourself. It seems like yesterday I was twenty-three. That's a quarter of a century ago. In another quarter century I'll be nearly eighty. In no time it'll be 1989 and I'll be eighty.'

'Why don't you forget about the new year and think about the party. It's gonna be great. We're gonna have ourselves a fabulous night.' She returned to the study of her unblemished young image.

'Flynn's theory of relativity,' I said. 'When I'm eighty you'll still be only half my age.'

'Yeah . . . and you'll only have eyes for my daughter, if I ever have one. Do you really believe all that stuff?'

'Not all of it,' I said. The rain started to fall heavily. I turned on to my side, stubbed my cigarette into the dirt and congratulated myself for getting away with it, for managing to find an exit before the danger had become inescapable. Another question, another challenge, and she might have forced me to tell the real truth, the one that had quickly worked its way to the surface of my mind even while I was rationalising my way through phoney captain's paradises and fairy-tale theories. The one that said she was right – that I didn't like arguing with women because they argued on a different level to men. They rearranged the field of battle from the head to the heart, forced a man to dig deep, to go where he didn't want to go, where he was uncomfortable going, where he was ill-equipped to win. *Diligo ergo sum.* A man thinks, a woman loves. A man might have to concede and then he'd have to change. The spoils of war for a woman were the changes she forced a man to make. Perhaps Beverly deserved to hear that. It was valuable information for a woman to learn while she was young. Perhaps I owed it to her. If she challenged me again perhaps I would tell her. One day she would leave me and become just another of those twittering vaginas of my bygone days, and then it would be too late. 'Wake me when you've finished painting your face,' I said. 'Should just about be time for you to leave me by then.'

Beverly left with the trio when the rain stopped. I knew precisely where to find what I wanted and went straight to the bag at the bottom of our heaped luggage in the corner of the hut. I took out the long feather and ran my fingers over its length to straighten it. I blocked the cap into shape and fixed the feather to its side. I shook out the suede vest and unrolled the tights. At the bottom were the boots and leggings and the brass-buckled belt and props department dagger. I laid it all out on my bedroll and allowed the familiar tingle to run the length of my body to the top of my head.

'I can strike a line through scrub or pine,' I recited to myself as I massaged my knuckles, 'or play a hand of poker, or ride a hack or hump a black with any other joker. For scrapping is my special gift, my chiefest sole delight, just ask a wild duck can it swim, a wildcat can it fight.'

I was sure we were headed for disaster, another casualty of the revolution, and I would be found dead in a ditch in the morning. The road to the golf club twisted and turned through unruly citrus orchards, and around each twist and turn was another obstacle, too often a small band of rebels who had lost their way to Santiago. It was a moonless night and with the jeep's headlights off and the driver speeding recklessly in an attempt to prove he had a cat's eyes, I took my mind off our imminent fate by imagining the reception that awaited me, should I be fortunate enough to survive the journey. Beverly would already be doing her best to dance to the Trio *Rebelde*, but their complex rhythms would make rock and roll difficult and she didn't know anything else. She would be dancing with Johnny, shuffling and swaying around him as best she could.

As we lurched around a corner on what felt like two wheels, my feathered cap nearly took flight. I grabbed the driver's arm so I wouldn't be thrown out, but he shrugged me off. There was no telling him to slow down, in any language. Right about now, I thought, they would be wondering where I was. Chloe would be telling anyone who would listen that I was out hunting up a pig, and Barry would be grateful the club had no swimming pool. The same old jokes.

Fidel wouldn't make an appearance until late, I was sure about that. I got the driver to stop short of the club and we waited by the side of the road for the *commandante*'s entourage to arrive. There was no point doing what I was about to do unless the *commandante* was there. I could see the party through binoculars. The room was strung with coloured paper and a white tablecloth hanging on the wall wished everyone *Feliz Ano Nuevo*. The good citizens of Maffo were still making themselves scarce until certain that the rebellion had moved on, but Barry had managed to round up a squad of rebels to swell our numbers. I could see they were unwilling to join the *yanquis* on the dance floor, sitting around at the tables listening to the music and refusing a drink.

It was an hour before midnight when he showed up. I watched him strut into the club at the head of his troops and saw Barry rush to greet him. I gave that a few minutes and then nudged my driver. '*Adelante Cubano*,' I said.

The roar of the engine made everyone's head turn to the terrace doors. The driver nosed the jeep between empty tables, its tyres squealing on the ceramic tiles, and stopped just short of entering the room. I was already standing to my full six-foot-two, one suede boot firmly planted on the collapsed windscreen. I saw Barry's hands go to his face, and I knew what he was saying under his breath: 'Another one of his fucking entrances.' The music, the dancing, the drinking all stopped.

'Usually at this point,' I proclaimed with my hands on hips, 'I welcome you all to . . . well, wherever we happen to be. Sherwood, perhaps. But tonight it would be most presumptuous of me to welcome the conquering hero . . .' I bowed with a flourish of my feathered cap toward Fidel, '. . . to his conquered land.'

I jumped up onto the hood of the jeep, ignoring the pain in my knee. 'Suffice for me to say,' I said, pulling the cap back down at the precise angle over my forehead, 'that you are all welcome to enjoy our food and beverage.' I stepped to the front of the hood and made as if preparing to take a leap through the doors, but stopped. 'Only kidding,' I winked. 'I may have had this let out a little, but not so much that it can't burst at the seams.' I climbed down and swaggered onto the dance floor, thumbs hooked into belt. I swept my arm at the bandstand. 'Maestro, music if you please. Oh, *perdone. Musica por favor.*'

The trio picked up again, the dancing only hesitantly. I approached Barry and Beverly standing by the group that surrounded Fidel. 'Didn't I tell you tonight was fancy dress?' I said to them innocently.

'Impressive,' said Fidel through the corner of his mouth.

'Entrance, *commandante*,' I said with a jaunty toss of the head. 'One of the three golden rules.'

'It is the Robin Hood, no?'

'Indeed it is.'

'So . . . no Don Juan for us tonight?'

I threw my head back and laughed the hearty laugh of the outlaw of Sherwood. 'I had three good entrances in Robin Hood. That's a lot for one film, you know. My personal favourite is the one where I knock the castle guards cold with the antlers of a dead stag. You'd certainly find that impressive. We are honoured to have you as our guest, *commandante*.'

'I thought it was the other way,' Fidel said. 'I will stay only short time. We march to Santiago.'

'Can we film that battle?' Barry said.

Fidel grunted and shrugged and said, 'Maybe no battle to film. I ask the colonel in Santiago to lay down the arms, join the revolution, march with us to Havana. Maybe he will. Now I make the speech.'

He stopped the music and stepped up to the bandstand. He spoke for only a couple of minutes in Spanish, a record for Fidel's public addresses, and then cheers erupted and the rebel anthem began to ring out, accompanied by two guitars and maracas. As near as we could make out there had been another victory. *Companero* Che had taken Santa Clara. After a couple of rousing choruses of the anthem, Fidel said that everyone should have a good time, and suddenly the dance floor was swaying with rebel green.

Barry asked him again about the battle for Santiago, if he thought there would be one or not. 'There is confusion,' Fidel said. 'Always when the battle there is confusion. But the colonel he say he order the helicopter for me. Maybe I fly over Santiago on Sunday for the victory.'

'I've never been in a helicopter,' Beverly said. All eyes turned in her direction. Her own just sparkled with innocence.

'Then you must come,' Fidel said.

'A helicopter?' I said. I knew Beverly enjoyed a bit of adventure, I wouldn't have had her around for a year if she didn't, but

I didn't think she could be serious about this one. 'I wish I'd known about that. I could have made an entrance you'd never forget with one of those.'

'But won't it be dangerous?' Beverly said.

'No, no, no. Nobody will shoot me. Many times they try to kill me. Always they fail . . . always.'

For a moment there was one of those awkward silences and it should have been my job to fill it, but Barry took it upon himself. 'I wonder what Senor Batista is doing tonight?' he said. Fidel looked at him blankly, as though the thought had never before occurred to him, and said nothing. 'Big night in Havana tonight, I reckon,' Barry said.

I was curious to see how far Fidel was prepared to go to back his invitation. 'You should take the helicopter ride, Woodsie,' I said. 'When is it?'

'Maybe Sunday,' Fidel said. 'She must come now.'

'You love new experiences, don't you, Woodsie?'

'Come,' said Fidel, and he marched across the middle of the dance floor, his men following in his footsteps.

The driver of my jeep saw him coming and quickly reversed, crashing into tables and chairs as he went and clearing a wide path for the *commandante's* exit. I grabbed Beverly by the arm and hurried her to his side. Now we would see just who was bluffing.

'The three golden rules of stagecraft, *commandante*,' I said. 'Your entrance, your position, the audience's eyes. A man in your position would do well to know them. You said before you were keen to take advice, didn't you?'

Fidel stopped, causing the conga line of men behind to concertina into one another. 'What advice? How to wear the costume and be the fool?'

'This?' I said. 'Oh, it's just something I wear for fancy dress nights. Keeps my fans amused. But you already understand about costume, don't you? I don't have to advise you on that.' Fidel frowned, but it appeared to be more out of curiosity than annoyance. 'I think you're wearing a pretty good one now,' I said.

Slowly the frown relaxed into a grin. 'Robin Hood . . . he steal from the rich and give to the poor, no?'

'That's what he did, all right. That's the legend.'

Fidel chewed his cigar and nodded. 'I also, eh.'

'Yes, my comment is not without irony.'

Fidel continued nodding. 'For me there is no costume, *el heroe.*' He patted my shoulder like an indulgent uncle. *'El heroe sintetico.'*

He led his men out through the door, across the terrace, and to a small convoy of jeeps and trucks waiting for them in the drive. Beverly was right behind him, an escort at each elbow.

Barry stood at my side as we watched them drive away. 'You continue to explore the limits of his English, don't you,' he said.

'As does he with my Spanish.'

'Does *sintetico* mean what I think it does?'

'If you think it means phoney, sport, then I think you're right,' I said.

'Why'd you let her go?'

'Did I have a choice? Love's labour's lost.'

'And hopefully all's well that ends well,' Barry said. 'We need that girl.'

'Listen to us . . . we sound like all the world really is a stage.'

'And you continue to act like it.'

'But it is a stage, isn't it. And as the Bard said, we players have our entrances and our exits. Don't you ever find yourself wondering? You once liked the blissful mobility, but then you wonder, who's the real you? And who's the chap on the screen? You know, I catch myself acting out my life like a goddamn script.'

'So what part did you play tonight?' he said. 'The bandit of Sherwood Forest or the pimp of Sunset Strip?'

I put my arm around him and steered him back into the club-house. 'Another New Year's Eve, chum. There were times this year when I was certain I wouldn't see another one. I think we'd better make it one to remember.'

21
But we are men of good faith.

Santiago de Cuba, 1 January 1959

To anyone entering my hut no doubt I appeared to be sleeping off a big night, lying on my side in a foetal position, knees tucked up under my chin. Yet behind the closed eyelids I was wide awake. In fact I had not slept a moment since beating the rising sun into the Maffo camp by barely an hour. Now I could add insomnia to my list of ills. I was inclined to put it down to sleeping alone, but I knew I would only be fooling myself if I did. I had slept soundly alone more times in my life than my reputation allowed, even on this extended camping trip. Fear of crocodiles, desperate screams, heads disappearing under brown water, these were my metaphysical causations of yet another disease. Dis-ease. The nightmares were coming too regularly now for comfort, too vividly for ease. To avoid the brown river I followed a stream of consciousness, going with its flow from the events of the night to the consequences that would no doubt follow. It was the patronising hand on the shoulder that spoiled the party. Even my father had never done that. Even Jack Warner. Even Ernie Hemingway. Now even bearded young men, green young men, were moved to patronise me. Bearded green young men with cigars to impress their manhood on the world could call my bluff.

El heroe sintetico,' I mumbled through clenched teeth. It was my own fault. I had brought it on myself, had given the fellow the opportunity and he took it with relish. I may as well have been Bozo the clown as Robin Hood. Irony? Who was I kidding? Pearls before swine. Slapstick was the level of comment for these people. A pie in the face, a fall on the arse, they would understand that all right. I had the Custer outfit in the bag, should have worn that. Should have brought the Don Juan. But who remembers Don Juan? Of all the roles I had played, who would pick that one? Barrymore, he was Don Juan, and the only Don Juan. The Robin Hood outfit was probably ruined now, anyway. Diving into a swimming pool is one thing, but diving into the murk of a rain-flooded sand trap was not a good idea. Having to be hauled out only compounded the folly. Chloe was right – Jupiter in the fifth house, too rash and too reckless. I was glad Beverly had not been there to see it. She had seen enough of my folly. What kind of folly was she seeing now from the other Robin Hood? I didn't want to think about that.

Another hand was placed on my shoulder at precisely the right time to allow me to avoid thinking about that. Not a patronising hand; this time a rousing one. I opened my eyes to Barry again. Good old reliable Barry who may not be much of a business manager, but was rising to the challenges of his producer's hat. Good old reliable Barry was leaning over me with concern on his face. 'Are you okay, buddy?' Barry was never patronising.

I took a long and deep breath and rolled onto my back. 'I'll live, if that's what you mean.' I flinched as the damaged vertebrae crunched underneath me.

'Batista's gone.'

I rubbed my face with both hands and rolled my hips a little. 'Who's Batista?'

'*El presidente* . . . the big chief . . . top banana.'

I raised my head. 'Batista?'

'Yeah. Flown the coop. Done a moonlight flit.'

I propped myself up on one elbow. 'What . . . he's gone?'

'How many ways do you need to hear it? Yes, he's gone, left the country. He's not the first president of Cuba to pack it up in the middle of the night, is he? Our buddy Fidel might be the new president already.'

I sat up and shook the sleepless fuzz from behind my eyes. 'No . . . there's gotta be a whole army of generals standing in line before Castro.'

'Well, Lansky's gone too, they say.'

'Christ . . . Lansky? This is serious.'

'I'm taking the crew down to Santiago, shoot the battle. You up to coming?'

'There won't be a battle now, will there?'

'We're going anyway. There'll be something to shoot. Fidel in his helicopter, maybe.'

'You're forgetting,' I said. 'No one will shoot him in that.'

Barry chuckled. 'They say there was a real battle up at Santa Clara. It must have been the final straw. This Che feller derailed a whole troop train. We shoulda been following him.'

'Che . . .' The word aggravated my throat and I coughed, which led to another, and soon I was doubled up, hacking into my chest.

'Jesus, you sound healthy.'

'At my age,' I managed between coughs, 'the only health I can look forward to is a healthy appetite.'

'You mean thirst.'

'Yeah . . .' I took some deep breaths and reached for my survival kit. 'Good thing I restocked.'

'There's a truck waiting to take us,' Barry said. 'You've got five minutes for health care.'

The road to Santiago was in chaos. I must have been the last joker in Cuba to hear about Batista. Trucks and jeeps crawled their way between columns of rebels mingling with cheering people who flocked to hug them, kiss them, touch their fabled beards. It was dark before we reached the city. A mass of people filled the central square, spilling through the maze of alleys and narrow streets that surrounded it. We were given a guard of *barbudos*, by order of *commandante* Fidel we were told, and they pushed us through to the rear of the Casa Granda hotel where just weeks before we had been staying in relative peace and quiet. Now the square erupted in cheering every few moments, applause for a speaker whose soft voice was now raised with exhilaration and amplified to echo off the grand Spanish colonial facades.

We were led through the hotel, shoulder to shoulder with *barbudos*, to the square. Fidel was on a balcony of the town hall, directly above the colonnade through which I had recently performed my conspicuous horse gallop. We were delivered to Carlos, standing on a chair and hanging on to a column and cheering with as much passion as any. He jumped down when he saw me, gripped both my shoulders and fixed me with eyes as wide as Sinatra with an audience collapsing at his feet, as Hemingway riding into Paris on a tank. A cheer erupted behind him that nearly blew him into my arms. His mouth opened and all it offered was an intoxicated sigh. Then he saw Barry and his crew with their camera.

'Hurry! You must go up to the roof! You must film the speech!' He burrowed through people and collected a guard to take them upstairs through the hotel.

'It's useless,' Barry said to me as he was swept away with the tide. 'We haven't got the light.'

'Just do what you can,' I called out to his disappearing back. 'You might have the only camera here.'

Fists shook at the sky, red and black flags and banners waved, rebels had cigars fixed in grins that spread from ear to ear. 'How much have we missed?' I said to Carlos.

'Fidel, he speak for two hours already,' Carlos said. 'Fidel he can speak all night.'

'What's he said?'

Carlos shook his head, his eyes still wide with wonder. 'Oh ... he say so much, senor.'

'So the revolution's over, is it?'

'No, no. The revolution he say now it begins. He say Santiago it is now the capital. We have the new president.'

'Boy, he doesn't waste time, does he? Made himself president already.'

'No. Dr Urrutia, he is the president. Fidel he is too young to be the president. He say he does not want the political office. He say he has not the desire for the power.'

I leaned up against a column and let the energy wash over me. I fixed a cigarette into my holder and grinned. Carlos cheered. *Si! Si! Si!* I let the purity wash over me. It was the purity, not the energy, that was the difference between this crowd and another at any good football game, cheering for their team, waving their flags. How pleasant it would be, to live in a world where purity was also the truth.

Fidel was up on the balcony banging his fist into his palm. Then he pointed to a line of military officers below and the cheers erupted again. 'What's he saying now?' I asked Carlos, who was applauding wildly.

'They are the army and the navy. They have joined the revolution.'

Another cheer even louder than the last. The *barbudos* around us snatched the cigars from their mouths and waved their guns above their heads and shouted, *'Adelante la Habana! Adelante la Habana!'*

'He say now we march, with the army and the navy and the helicopters, the planes, the boats, to Havana. *Adelante la Habana! Adelante la Habana!*'

I looked up to the roof to see if Barry was managing to get any of this. There was barely enough light for the eye, let alone the camera. What a loss if this moment of victory was captured only in the memories of the people. Millions would say they were there this night. Fidel would be ten feet tall, the sky filled with stars, the brightest of all directly above the messiah's balcony. A camera could reveal the truth – Fidel a shadowy figure in the distance, the sky black and overcast. But it would be the truth, and more powerful because of it. Cinema verite, I thought. What a pity we had the only camera. It had all happened too fast, the world couldn't keep up with the pace of Fidel and his revolution.

And then I was seized with the realisation of just what that meant. It *had* happened too fast. Reporters were no doubt on their way right that moment to cover the biggest story in the world, but they weren't there yet. No one was in Santiago de Cuba. Who would ever have thought that the first big news story of 1959 would take place in Santiago, new capital of the Republic of Cuba? I, Errol Flynn, the American Correspondent, was the only reporter on the spot. Being there, I'd heard the real correspondents say, that was the trick. Getting the story was easy. Being there to get it was the hard part. And here I was in the eye of the storm.

'Carlos! Tell me what he says.'

'Senor, there is too much. We record everything. You can hear it tomorrow.'

'Tomorrow? In English?'

'In English? How? We translate for foreign press next week, maybe. We see.'

Next week. Every foreign correspondent in the world would be in Cuba next week. 'Give me something,' I said. 'I can get you in the foreign press tomorrow. Just the main points.'

'He say there will be no more of the bloodshed. He say freedom of the press, of the human rights, the trade union, the worker.'

I scribbled quickly. As soon as I wrote 'trade union' and 'worker' I crossed the words out. 'Anything specific? I need detail?'

'He say he will build the school like a city for twenty thousand children. He say every citizen we will ask for the bag of cement and the trowel.'

'Okay, that's good. No more bloodshed, you say. What about Batista and his henchmen?'

'Oh, senor, Batista he steal the hundreds and millions of pesos. He is the war criminal.'

'So you'll chase after him. Bring him back.'

'Fidel he say no. Others will be punished.'

'What does that mean?'

'I am not *commandante*, eh.'

'I'm asking what you think.'

'Fidel he say no hatred, no revenge.'

The square echoed with another cheer. 'What did he just say?'

Carlos pumped the air with his fist. 'He say the road ahead it has many of the obstacles, but we are men of good faith.'

I had hardly finished scribbling when the biggest cheer of the night went up. 'What was that?'

Carlos looked at me, breathing heavily, fists clenched to his chest. 'He say ...' He squeezed his eyes shut. When they opened there were tears. 'He say four centuries since Cuba it began ... now, this day, for the first time we are really free.'

Carlos wrapped his arms around me, his chest heaving. I looked up over his head. Cubans from wall to wall were embracing. I was a cynical old Hollywood has-been, but just for a moment I allowed myself to believe that it *was* the truth. Just for a moment there was purity. And just for a moment I was Cuban and shed a tear along with the rest of them.

First light found hundreds of people lingering in the square, talking excitedly in groups, breaking into spontaneous shouts of emotion or songs of rebellion, addicted to its fleeting intoxication. Carlos commandeered a small room in the hotel for me to write my story, one with a single bed, the first bed I would get to sleep in since the last time I slept in the same hotel. Half a lifetime ago. I had not slept for nearly two days, so fixed myself a stiff vodka and got down to work.

There was no ice for my drink and no typewriter for my story. I wrote in longhand and, after three room-temperature vodkas, had five hundred words. It wasn't the correspondent's responsibility to write a headline, but I could not resist. I wanted the tenor of the piece to be clear, and after so long without sleep found it difficult to determine for myself whether the five hundred words did the job. Across the top of the first page I wrote:

'MEN OF GOOD FAITH' TAKE CONTROL OF CUBA

That was the clarity of opinion I wanted. I finished the last of my drink. The pillow was very tempting and I knew if I put my head on it I would not lift it for hours. I went downstairs and out onto the square. It was still an intoxicating place to be. I hurried off to the US consulate to talk them into filing my story for me, and for the first time since arriving in Santiago, wondered where Beverly was.

22
Audacia, that's what it is in Spanish.
Santiago de Cuba, 3 January 1959

Two days, and the heady atmosphere in Santiago showed no sign of abating. Barry allowed the cast and crew to join the party until reining them in for Marie's funeral scene. The shoot was way behind schedule, but how was a producer to prepare for filming in the middle of the chaos of a great victory? The funeral scene was to be as per my brilliant script – Marie, who had been done in by the 'dirty Batista butchers', was to be laid out in a chapel Barry had scouted, shrouded in a Cuban flag. But he needed the entire cast for the mourners, including Beverly who was to be featured in grieving close-up. As I was responsible for her absence it was my job to retrieve her.

Through Carlos I was granted an audience with Fidel, who had taken over the entire hotel for the seat of the power he said he didn't want. I was lucky to get a face-to-face, Carlos said. Reporters were arriving from everywhere and already there was a queue for interviews. I said that it sounded like Fidel, whether he wanted the power or not, was going to have it thrust upon him. Carlos shrugged and said, 'Of course.'

The room that was the inner sanctum of the revolution had

a table, a collection of chairs, and two people. In a dark corner sat Chico, the faithfully attending *pistolita*, and behind the table strewn with so many papers that not a square inch of timber was to be seen, was *el Gigante*, his shirt pockets stuffed with yet more papers. When I was ushered in he stood up and walked right around the table to greet me. He opened his arms and hugged me like a long-lost friend. 'Your story,' he said, 'you take our victory to the world.'

I had heard nothing since wiring my report. I had not even counted on it surviving censorship at the consulate.

'Men of good faith,' Fidel said. 'This is very good. You listen to what I say, eh.' With his arm around my shoulders he led me to a chair, sat me down and pulled up another for himself, so close our knees were touching. 'You have the lunch with me, we talk,' he said confidentially.

He turned to Chico and issued a series of orders, going into detail, using his hands to describe precisely what he wanted. When the *pistolita* departed he said, 'We have the *jamon*. You like the *serrano*?'

'The *serrano*?' I said. 'You mean ham?'

'*Si*, the ham. We have the special ham. We have *la pata negra*. It come from the black pig made fat on the *bellota*. You know ...' He cupped his fingers. 'From the oak.'

'Acorns?'

'*Si*, the acorns. I send Chico to find. Today is more celebration. Today, Che he march into Havana. The generals they try to make the coup d'etat, but the people they do not accept.'

I was picturing a plate of this *pata negra*, some crusty bread, perhaps a little chutney. It was a long time since I'd had something decent to eat. 'Are you sure that's wise?' I said, probably a little too abruptly.

'What?'

'I mean, allowing your offsider to take the glory.'

The welcoming smile slowly dissolved into a frown as the eyes narrowed. Fidel got to his feet and walked back around to the other side of the table. He picked up the cigar smouldering in the ashtray, bit on it impatiently and leaned over to me, both fists planted on the table. 'He is closer,' he said out of the side of his mouth. 'The glory is for all.'

In for a penny, I thought. 'Oh, yes, of course it is. But a leader knows ...' I stopped and gave it a little more consideration. 'Let me put it this way. Would Macarthur have allowed one of his generals to wade ashore in the Philippines?'

'What do you mean?'

'It's obvious, isn't it? He said he'd return, made a big deal out of it. Well, his whole damn army returned. But whose picture was on the front page?'

Fidel slowly sat down. 'Go on.'

'That photograph, that was staged. It was Hollywood. He really returned the day before, but there was no photographer there, or he ran out of film, or his camera got wet, I don't know. The point is, Macarthur went back to that beach the next day when there were no Japs to spoil proceedings, got all his generals lined up behind him, and note I say behind him, and they got that picture.' I drew an imaginary headline in the air. 'Macarthur returns,' I said solemnly. 'And they got that film, and they got their hero for the morning editions.'

'Macarthur, he did this?'

'His PR people did it. Don't get me wrong, Macarthur knew what he was doing. He had a whole squad of PR people following him about, getting shots of him with that corny corncob pipe. He knew how to win the battle. Audacity, do you know that word?'

Fidel shrugged. *'Audacia.'*

'*Audacia*, that's what it is in Spanish?'

'*Si. Audacia.* Like you are now.'

'Now you're getting the hang of it. Macarthur, you see, he had the *audacia*, not just how he won the battle, but how he told the story. You've won the battle. Now you have to control the story, tell it the way you want.' I drew another imaginary headline in the air. 'Castro takes Havana.'

Fidel chomped on his cigar and drummed the table with his fingers. 'You do not understand. I tell Che to occupy the barracks, not the city. Military installations, these are important to take the weapons for the revolution.'

'Ah, that's different. The weapons, of course. But occupying the city, that takes a triumphant march, tanks rolling in front of cheering crowds. People tell me it's a wonderful feeling.' I watched the irritation fade and imagined the eyes acquired just the hint of a faraway look. 'You need the Hollywood touch, a dash of *Ben-Hur*, a victorious staged entry into *your* city. In fact, you could have a victory march right through the whole country, all the way to Havana.'

'You think this will not be the way? Of course! The people they will make it be the way.'

'Well don't be in too much hurry to get there. Take your time. Let the people see you. Let the photographers take your picture. Let the reporters interview you.'

'Already they want to interview me. Already they come.'

'Well do it on your terms. Don't let them in here. You go out to them. Let them crowd around you, have a sort of press conference, but do it on the run. Don't let them pin you down. They'll only ask you questions you don't want to answer. I was given some good advice years ago, and I know I'm not in the same racket as you, but it's still good advice. Never meet the press unless you have something sexy to offer them along with the drinks.'

'What do you mean sexy?'

'Nah, that's just the way it was put to me, for my racket. In yours it just means you give them an interesting angle for their story, but it's the angle *you* want to give them. And don't let them ask a lot of questions. This is your parade, you can handle it the way you want. And let me give you the best piece of advice of all.' I paused for effect. What happened last night didn't matter now. This was the next round and I was fresh.

Fidel stared at me, but I made him wait. 'Go on,' he said finally.

'Learn to laugh at yourself.'

He bristled and grabbed the cigar from his mouth. He hadn't seen that one coming. 'Laugh at myself?'

'Look, for your people, you're the conquering hero. That's fine and good. For the foreign press, learn to smile, laugh, make jokes with them. They'll love it. Especially the Americans. You want to be on Huntley and Brinkley don't you?' I paused again for the answer, but Fidel just glowered at me with unwavering eyes. 'Put the cigar back in your mouth.'

Now he scowled, but did as he was told. I bent down low to the floor in front of the table, squinting up at *el Gigante* and making a frame with my fingers. 'That's the way,' I said. 'Never let them photograph you doing normal everyday things, like having breakfast, washing your underwear. You're no ordinary man.' I twisted my hands one way and another, studying his face all the while. 'I want to see you strutting your stage when the photographers are around. No sitting. And you're a tall guy, make them shoot low angles. Make them look up to you. You understand what I mean?'

'I know what it is to look up.'

'Good. What's that cigar?'

He took it from his mouth and looked at it. 'What do you mean?'

'Who made it? What's your brand?'

Fidel waved his hands and made a face. 'It does not matter.'

I got to my feet. 'Yes it does. What is it?' I took it from Fidel's hand – politely – and looked at it closely.

Fidel shrugged and said, 'This one is Upmann.'

'H Upmann? A magnum?'

'*Si*, H Upmann, a magnum,' Fidel said, losing patience.

'Good,' I said, handing back the cigar. 'Macarthur had his corn-cob pipe, from now on, whenever there's a photographer around, keep that in your mouth. What better symbol could there be of Cuba than a good H Upmann cigar hand-rolled on a virgin's thighs? Keep some in your pocket, hand them out to the foreign reporters. They'll love you.'

Fidel brandished the H Upmann magnum at my face. 'You tell me what I know. Already I do this. We all do this. *Puros*, we always smoke them. People know this.'

'Maybe in Cuba they do. Your stage isn't just Cuba anymore. Your stage is the world. In America they think big cigars go with big shots ... tycoons, chairmen of the board in their three-piece Brooks Brothers suits. Here you are in your beard and your rumpled rebel green. They've never seen anything like you. The photo that Herb Matthews took, the one that made the front page of the *New York Times*, did you have a cigar?'

'No, I had the rifle.'

'Ah well ... you can forget the rifle from now on. The revolution may be just beginning, but the war's over. A *puro*, that's what you need now.'

'It was the look up,' Fidel said.

'What was?'

'The photograph in the *New York Times*.'

He bent down to a row of battered briefcases under the table, opened one and shuffled through papers. He extracted a sheet, unfolded it and spread it on the table. It was a front page of the *New York Times*. There was Fidel looking apprehensively and, if not for the rifle with telescopic sight he was clutching, it could even be said innocently at the camera. Closer to Li'l Abner than Mr Murder Incorporated. *Castro Still Alive and Fighting in Mountains*, said the headline. *Cuban Rebel is Visited in Hideout.*

'See, the camera it has the look up,' he said. 'You, have you put the photograph on the front page of the *New York Times*?'

'I'm afraid so,' I said. 'And not always in the most positive circumstances.'

'Me also. This one the second time. First time they say I am dead. Ha! This time even they want my autograph for the proof.' He stabbed at the paper beneath the photo, and sure enough there was his flourish of a signature with the legend: *Sierra Maestra, Febrero 17 de 1957*. 'You, have you put the autograph on the front page of the *New York Times*?'

'*Companero*, my autographs have been many places . . . on bad cheques, bad contracts, even across certain bad parts of the female anatomy . . . but never, I have to admit, have they ever seen fit to print it on the front page of the *New York Times*.' And never, I thought, have I carried it around with me to trot out at any opportunity.

Fidel grinned and then laughed. It was a small victory. He took another cigar from his top pocket and offered it to me. 'The symbol of Cuba, *companero*.'

He lit it for me and I drew on it theatrically. I blew a great cloud of smoke into the air and raised my nostrils to it. 'Aah, smell that. Revolution is in the air.'

'Revolution is in the air,' Fidel cried, like he was on a balcony again, thrusting his cigar defiantly at the gods.

The door flew open and a nervous *barbudo* had his tommy gun levelled straight at our navels. Fidel laughed and dismissed him.

When the door was closed again, he strode over to it, leaned his head out and let fly with a torrent of abuse. He slammed the door shut and grinned at me. 'I keep them on the toe,' he said. 'Chico he take too long to find *la pata negra*. Before he find I not hungry anymore.'

'Look,' I said, 'you're a busy man. No need to entertain me. I only came because we need Woodsie for a scene we're shooting this morning.'

'Woodsie?'

'Beverly. Young Beverly. You know ... so high, shaped like a girl, blonde hair.'

'Ah ... *si* ... Beverly. She go for the helicopter this morning. I send you to her.' He opened the door again and delivered those outside another blast.

I had to wait for my plate of *pata negra*. I was driven across town with an armed escort to Moncada Barracks where I found Beverly the centre of attention, perched on a tank, blonde hair cascading under rebel cap and eager *barbudos* at her feet. On the return journey I asked her how she enjoyed her helicopter ride with Fidel. Fidel didn't go with her, she said. The helicopter was thrilling, soaring over rooftops, peering down at toy people on toy streets, but there was no Fidel. Tired of you by then I suppose, I said. I wasn't interested in toy people. I was interested in what happened between the two real people, but Beverly refused to hear me.

We shot the funeral scene in the chapel that afternoon, maintaining the dignified silence despite the boisterous revelry that persisted outside in the streets. That night I allowed Beverly the single bed and made do with the floor. I lay there for hours attempting to manoeuvre my back into a position that didn't cause pain, and listened to her steady breathing. Eventually I could stand neither the pain nor the suspense any longer and switched on the bedside lamp. Within a few minutes the steady breathing stopped and her eyes blinked into the light.

'So are you going to tell me what you got up to?' I said. I was fixing a cigarette into my holder, which allowed me to give the impression that my question was merely passing the time of night.

'Nothing,' she croaked, and so quickly did she respond that I knew she had been waiting for me to ask.

'It's been three days,' I said. 'Nothing happened for three days?'

'No, not much.'

'The whole country has been taken over and you did . . . not much.'

'Yeah . . . we ate oysters once.'

'Oysters? You can't stand oysters.'

'I didn't really eat them. Fidel ate mine as well as his. Wow, he can sure eat. All the while he was stuffing himself with oysters he was yakking about ham.'

'You know what they say about oysters . . . they're an aphrodisiac.'

'They say? That's what you say.'

'So all you did in three days was watch him eat oysters.'

'I didn't see him so much. He was busy with his army and all. Boy, he talks a lot, too. He could talk the hind leg off a junkyard dog.'

'Very colourful. So he eats a lot and he talks a lot. What else does he do?'

'His mom and dad weren't married, did you know that?'

'No, I haven't caught up with his memoirs yet.'

'That makes him illegitimate, doesn't it? That makes him a bastard, right?'

'The world is full of bastards, honey. You can never be sure who's one and who's not.'

'You oughta know.'

'That's my point. I don't know. I think I'm one myself. My mother's had so many affairs . . . you can never really be sure where you come from, can you?' She said nothing. 'So . . . oysters and talk. Nothing else? I find that hard to believe, Woodsie.'

'Not everyone's like you.'

'You just said he's a bastard, and I said I might be one, too.'

'That's not what I mean. He's not like you, that's all I'm saying.'

'There seems to be some divergence of opinion on that matter.'

'Is that why you're so darned curious all of a sudden?'

'It's not him I'm curious about,' I lied, 'it's you.'

'You never cared much before.'

'Well, now I'm curious about how you spent three days in the middle of a revolution not doing much.'

'Yeah . . . sure.'

'All right Woodsie, have it your way. I'm curious about both of you.'

The only sound in the room came from vehicles moving around the square. I looked at my watch. It was three in the morning and there seemed to be more activity outside at that strange hour than at any time since Fidel's balcony speech.

'Where were you when he made his speech?' I said.

'Here in the hotel,' she said. 'I hardly even heard it. Anyhow, he went on for so long I fell asleep.'

'You missed a great party.'

'I didn't miss all of it. I watched it later, and from a mighty fine position, too.' She yawned and stared blearily at the ceiling.

'All right, I'll bite,' I said when it was obvious she was not volunteering. 'What mighty fine position would that be?'

'After the speech, I don't know how long after, I was woken up and then taken out the back and around to that other place, where he was.'

'The town hall?'

'Suppose so. There were so many of those soldiers and all I could hardly tell where I was. Anyhow, he took me out onto that balcony.'

'The one where he made the speech?'

'Yeah, and we had to bend down real low, like crawling, so they couldn't see us down below. All the screaming people and all. And we sat on the floor there and listened to all the cheering and singing. He really liked that, I could tell. It was so dark I could hardly see him, but I could tell. He was like this little red glow from his cigar, that was all I could see. But he didn't stop talking. All excited, he was. He sat there and talked . . .'

The little red glow in the dark. Fidel hiding behind his little red glow. 'More talking?' I said.

'He likes to talk more than listen.'

'I get the feeling he likes to talk more than anything.'

'Well, he had to kinda shout really. He talked about living in the mountains and fighting and all. He said in the early days when they took over a village, the people used to come out to see them in the middle of the night, and they'd be holding candles and wanting to touch their beards. He said in those days they didn't cheer a lot, just looked and kept quiet. Then he got kinda sad and stopped being so loud.'

I was sure she was holding back. Fidel, the Don Juan of the university, the Casanova of Cuba, and all he did was . . . talk? 'He got you to touch his beard then, did he?' I said.

'No. He held my hand for a bit cause he was sad. I couldn't see his eyes, but I could tell he was sad from his voice. He was way away from me, had to reach over. He liked my hair. Stroked it with his hand. I guess he hasn't seen much hair like mine.'

'Gentlemen prefer blondes, honey,' I said with a click of the tongue. 'That's what they say.'

'Yeah...' she said like she had just come to a realisation. 'He was kinda like a gentleman. He never stopped talking. I felt like I oughta be taking notes or something. Like I was his secretary and we were working late. He was really sweet, you know.'

'Sweet?'

'And there were all these names. He'd talk about folks like I should've known who they were. But I had no way of knowing what he was talking about. Except Lucia. He talked a lot about her.'

'He talked about Lucia? To you?'

'Yeah. She was with us all the time. Whenever I was with him, so was she.'

'The mother hen. I guess that explains it.'

'Except on that balcony.'

'Ah, so you were alone with him on the balcony?'

'Well, she was kinda there, too. Not in person, but he talked about her so much. It was creepy, you know. In the dark, down low like that, with all that noise around, and guys with guns everywhere in the room behind. I mean, is that weird or what? And what about all that cheering? It was for him, but a lot of the time it was like he was just sad. Like he'd done what he set out to do and now he didn't know what to do next. Weird, huh?'

'Yeah...' I said. 'That's what it is, I guess. Weird. Maybe old Fidel's interests lie elsewhere, do you think?' She didn't answer. 'Or not up to it, perhaps.'

I could hear the steady breathing had resumed. It was better she didn't hear that last crack, what with my own record in recent times. Maybe she did hear it and was just sparing me the embarrassment. She had got the weirdness off her chest and slept the sleep of the innocent. I had got the curiosity off mine and reached for the lamp switch. Now doors were banging along the corridors inside the hotel and, with all the noise outside, I knew it was only the innocent who would get to sleep that night. I fixed myself another cigarette, got my back as comfortable as I could and stared into the blackness. It wasn't until the room was flooded with sunlight that I learned that the revolution had moved on. Fidel had finally worked out what to do next and began his victory march to Havana without me.

23
Castro takes Havana.
Havana, 8 January 1959

The *yanqui* film company caught up with the revolution that same day. It was a triumphal parade in the best Roman tradition, with tanks and jeeps and trucks replacing chariots, squeezing their way through a crush of excited citizens across Cuba's rich agricultural flatland. Buses, cars and bikes were appropriated for the revolution to transport the growing rebel army on its way to Havana. In the daylight they were showered with flowers, and at night lit by candles. No longer satisfied with merely touching the fabled beards, people kissed them. Everyone in Cuba had become a *candelada*. And I wasn't sure when it started, but I noticed that Fidel had taken to wearing a rosary around his neck. He seemed to know more about symbolism than he had been willing to let on.

Or perhaps he was just a quick learner. Reporters, photographers and cameramen joined the victorious caravan, jostling for angles, hustling for interviews. Even Herb Matthews returned to see what he had started. Fidel never let himself get pinned down, gave interviews on the run, standing in a jeep or high on a tank for the photographers below him, cigar in his mouth, a smile on his lips. He seemed to have picked one reporter from the mob, Jules Dubois of the *Chicago Tribune*, to allow close to him, perhaps because he was the only one wearing a suit and tie, or perhaps satisfied that he wouldn't be asked unwelcome questions. Other American reporters, starved for copy, hunted for angles. Even I was interviewed.

The interesting angle Fidel himself was fond of supplying day after day was a biblical one. He gave them the twelve apostles of the Sierra Maestra, the original dozen who had survived with him the first battles in the wilderness and had now delivered salvation to the people of Cuba. Just twelve warriors had beaten the thousands, brought down the dictator, changed the country forever. The inconvenient fact that there were actually considerably more survivors from those early days went unreported. All that was missing was the halo around Fidel the Redeemer, and as I said to Carlos we could expect any minute to see him delivering a blessing to the assembled flock. Whoever it was he had made president in Santiago, I said, what we were now witnessing was the making of the real one. No, said Carlos. What we were witnessing was the making of a god.

No longer was he being called *el Gigante* with a wink. Now he was *el Lider Maximo*, and it was said with adoring eyes. Whatever melancholy Beverly thought she sensed on the balcony was shrugged off in a tide of euphoria. Now, in every town he passed through he made time for a sermon on the mount, finding another balcony to deliver a speech that went on for hours, on occasion all night. There was no time for reflection when the ritual of deification was at hand. When it was quiet, when the caravan rested and the crowds briefly went home, Fidel relaxed with a pick-up game of basketball with his men, or took a jeep for a spin, stirring up more adulation in the back blocks, soaking up the intoxication like an old rummy suddenly handed the keys to the distillery. 'Viva Fidel!' they cried when he scored. 'Viva Fidel!' when he passed. In between, he hastily dealt with affairs of state — appointing ministers one day, sacking them the next. God's will.

All of this I witnessed at close quarters. Barry and the company left the parade to shoot secret arms shipments arriving in the darkness, gun battles on beaches, but they were just scenes in a movie. For once I was part of the real action. Carlos finally gave me a 26 JULIO armband. I wore it with pride and took my turn on a jeep and a tank. In Santa Clara a woman kissed the cuff of my pants and a boy held my shoe, running along beside the tank, screaming with joy at the top of his voice. Everywhere the faces — men, women and children, black, white and mulatto — were filled with exhilaration. And I was sure that not one recognised me, not one was doing this because I was a film star. They were doing it because I was part of the revolution, the salvation. I was even prepared to accept that Hemingway had a point about this liberation business.

Waiting for us up the road was Havana and a million *habaneros* suffering collective guilt. What had they done to help bring about this national epiphany? What were they doing while a hated dictator cowered and killed their neighbours, tortured their friends, stole their national treasure? How had a handful of bearded idealists brought deliverance from this devil while a country averted its eyes? When Fidel said in Santiago that the revolution begins now, it was the invitation for the entire nation to climb aboard a tank and wave a 26 JULIO flag, to claim their place in the victory. And they couldn't wait to do it.

January in Havana had always been the height of the tourist season, when the trumpet vine bloomed to herald the spin of the wheel, the roll of the dice, the liveliest of the live shows, the shortest of the short-time beds. January was cooler, the harsh sun softened by high cloud, and although dry over the rest of the island, it was the gentlest of Havana's wet season months. I liked January in Havana. For all the above reasons, of course, but also for the way the fog rolled over the Mallecon in the morning to conceal the retreat of anyone seeking the comfort of their own bed, and the freshening sea breezes in the afternoon that brought opportunity to a sailor seeking a challenge.

January 1959 was not like that. The yachts were tied fast to their moorings. The casinos were closed, the cabarets deserted, the bars shuttered. The action now was outdoors. Revellers, chanters, flag-wavers spilled into the streets; musicians played to the accompaniment of blaring horns of cars roaring aimlessly through the midst; 26 JULIO had become the date everyone wanted to keep. There were looters until a few were shot. After that they confined their activities to the abandoned mansions of Batista henchmen and the despised casinos, dragging slot machines into the street and helping themselves to the coins, taking to Batista's parking meters with baseball bats. Pigs were let loose in the Riviera Hotel, despoiling the Las Vegas vision of Meyer Lansky, Jewish-American. The tourists welcomed by the flowering of the trumpet vines that January were from the east not the north, arriving by road not chartered plane. From Oriente Province, and specifically the Sierra Maestra. From the cradle of *la Revolucion* to the feasting table – Havana.

Todo el mundo estaba de fiesta.

For the parade into the city Fidel shared his luminescence around, jumping from jeep to jeep to tank among his gun-waving, wide-eyed rebels. Chico was continually at his shoulder, his particular eyes peeled. As they inched their way through the swamp of delirious *habaneros* by the harbour, I was invited to share the moment's anointed vehicle. Above the acclamation I heard a lone trumpet play a piercing fanfare. Cubans and their music. *Adelante Cubanos* . . . Riding into Paris in '44, I thought, and doing it at the shoulder of de Gaulle.

That night the caravan moved on to Columbia Barracks, headquarters of Batista's defeated army. 'Fidel! Fidel! Fidel!' the masses cried at every pause in yet another long address. Three white doves of peace were released in front of the stage and to the amazement of everyone there, one settled on his shoulder. A hush descended as seasoned rebels solemnly removed their hats, men fingered their rosaries and women fell to their knees. Fidel himself was unmoved, continuing to plumb the depths of an unfathomable capacity to speak, but to everyone else on the vast parade ground it was the ultimate ordination, the divine acceptance.

In the hush I wondered how I could ever have presumed to lecture this man about symbolism. I turned to Barry who was attempting to capture the moment on film from the fringe of the assembly. 'Where does he go from here?' I said.

'Wherever it is,' said Barry, 'you can bet it'll be downhill.'

He went to the Havana Hilton. It was nearly daybreak when we followed the circus back into town. A tank was guarding the entrance to the hotel like a colourless sculpture under the shiny new spearmint high-rise. In the driveway, Cadillacs and Lincolns had been replaced by jeeps and military trucks, and in the lobby exhausted rebels sprawled over leather sofas, their machine guns and mortars placed like chess pieces across the chequered floor.

Chico escorted me up to the twenty-third floor and told me to wait. I watched the sun rise over the harbour. The only ships I could see in port were navy vessels, and the cruise liners were conspicuous by their absence. A door burst open and Fidel appeared, his arm around a *barbudo* who had one of his own arms in a sling. I was introduced to *companero* Che. 'Che is my finance minister,' Fidel said, before the two rebels involved themselves in a heated exchange in Spanish.

Eventually, Che shrugged and chewed on his cigar as he looked me up and down. 'Fidel thinks you are Errol Flynn, senor,' he said. 'Who are you really?'

'Why . . . Errol Flynn.'

'No, no, no, senor.' He moved in for a closer inspection of my face. 'I have seen this gringo, this Errol Flynn. You are not him.'

'I assure you, *companero*, I am the gringo.'

'*Companero* is it?' Che puffed on his cigar and blew the smoke from the side of his mouth. 'So if you are Errol Flynn, you are wounded. I know this because I read it in the *Los Angeles Times*. You do not look like you are wounded.'

'What do you mean?'

'Errol Flynn wounded in leg, fighter with Castro. They get this wrong?'

'Is that what they said? I wouldn't say . . .'

'Someone say, or why do they print?' Che put his arm around Fidel's shoulders. 'You tell them our *commandante* is the idealist. You say you know what makes him tick. I have known him for these years, stood beside him in the battle, but I do not know what makes him tick. How is it that you know such a thing?'

I examined the faces for a sign, but couldn't tell if I was in trouble. 'They, ah . . . they said that too, huh? Well, you know what reporters are like.'

'Maybe you do know what makes me tick,' Fidel said. He flicked a finger back and forth in front of his face like a metronome. 'Tick, tick, tick, tick . . . maybe *Los Angeles Times* it says the truth. *Los Angeles Times* it is the good paper, no?'

'Oh yes, a reputable paper,' said Che in the style of Bud Abbot, the straight man of the team.

'So it must be true!' laughed Fidel. He patted the new armband on my sleeve. '*Viva la revolucion, companero.* You tell them how Castro he take Havana. This is the truth also.'

He strode off with Chico close behind, leaving me standing in the middle of the room with Che still giving me the once-over.

'I am the medico, you know,' he said. 'The doctor. I can give you the treatment. We clean the wound with maggots and then we draw the infection with the leeches. Maggots and leeches, I save many lives with them. How about yours?'

'Oh, you're too kind,' I said, 'but I think it's okay now. The reporters, they exaggerate. You know how it is.'

Che shrugged and followed after Fidel. 'Not too kind,' he said over his shoulder. 'The true revolutionary he is always guided by kindness, *companero* . . . by love even.'

24
A revolutionary guided by love.

Havana, 9 January 1959

After a few hours of restless sleep I took breakfast in a quiet corner of the hotel coffee shop, protected from inquisitive eyes by a potted palm. It was already mid-morning, but every one of the widely spaced tables was occupied either by rebels in drab military green or tourists in bright tropical cotton. Their attitudes seemed to be the reverse of their wardrobes. I ordered vodka to be followed by coffee. From what I could see there wasn't much in the way of breakfast to be had even if I wanted it, which I didn't. Unless it was something out of the ordinary, something like acorn-fed ham fetched by a revolutionary gunman, I wasn't interested. Barry had taken everyone else off to pick up more Havana street scenes and I had a few hours to kill before my call. A lull had descended over the city after the week-long party. The revellers and even the victorious army seemed to be sleeping off their collective hangover. From all appearances in the coffee shop of the Hilton, the tourists didn't trust any of it and were staying off the streets. With the casinos closed as well, they looked at a loss.

The vodka arrived first: Zubrowka, as ordered. 'My sweet, sweet glass of grass,' I said to myself, inhaling its delicate scent, 'how I missed you all those weeks,' and allowed it to go straight to my head. A crew-cut young American soon followed it to the table, clean and pressed in pleated trousers and sober white shirt with buttoned-down collar and more buttons on the short sleeves that allowed the blond hair on his tanned arms to glisten. He gleamed like Tab Hunter, a serious Tab Hunter, with clear blue eyes and a Pepsodent smile, too self-assured to be an autograph hound, too conservative to be a tourist in Havana. He excused himself and asked if I would mind a few questions. A chance to unblot my copybook with Fidel and Che, I thought, perhaps even set the record straight about my sore leg. I invited the young man to pull up a chair. 'You look too clean-cut to be a reporter,' I said.

'I'll take that as a compliment,' the young man said, the smile apparently fixed.

'So you should. They're hard to come by.'

He reached his hand across the table. 'I'm Dwight Dodd,' he said with sincerity. 'I'm with the Economic Liaison Office.'

I took the firm handshake. The name was as uncomplicated as the man appeared to be. 'Dwight, like the president. You must be important.'

'Everything's important these days, Mr Flynn. My father served with the president in the Philippines. I'm named after him.'

I was curious. Stand-up young Americans were thin on the ground in Havana, especially serious young Americans who couldn't recognise when they were being ribbed. 'So I take it you're not a reporter. Economic whatever you said doesn't sound like a newspaper.'

'Economic Liaison Office. Sorry if I gave you the wrong impression. I didn't mean to.'

'No, my mistake. I jump to too many conclusions, but at least it's exercise. So you have an office here? You're not a front for

United Fruit are you? Is that what Economic Liaison means? United Fruit?' I grinned at him. It was only a joke after all, but still Dwight didn't seem to get it. He even looked surprised at such a suggestion.

'Oh no sir, I'm attached to the embassy,' he said, lowering his voice.

I had to lean forward to catch what he was saying. 'Ah, the embassy.' I took the cue and lowered my own voice. 'I understand.'

'What do you understand, sir?'

'Aren't you a little young for this?'

'I majored in Latin American studies, sir.'

'Well, shouldn't you be getting drunk with your fraternity buddies at Princeton?'

'Stanford, sir.'

'Sorry, Stanford. California, I should have known.' The waitress arrived with a cup and filled it with coffee. I asked him if he would like some.

'Thank you sir, but no thank you.'

'Something stronger? I can recommend the vodka.'

'No sir, thank you.'

'Come on, we're not in Kansas now, Tonto. They don't care about age limits here.'

'I believe that's Toto, sir. Tonto was the Lone Ranger's sidekick. Toto was the dog you're referring to in the *Wizard of Oz*.'

I took a cigarette from the packet on the table and fixed it to my holder. 'How did I know you'd know that? Help yourself to one, they're Egyptian. Rather good.'

'Thank you, but I don't smoke. You know sir, Castro, he's not much older than I.'

'I suppose you're right.'

'Yes, sir. And Einstein, he published his theory of relativity at twenty-five. That's my age.'

He was so primed with his validations that it seemed obvious he had been required to justify himself regularly. 'Is that so?' I said. 'And what theory have you got in you, Mr Dodd?'

'I have a theory, sir, that you are very close to Castro. About as close as any American I know.'

I sipped at my coffee and wished it were vodka. Already I could tell another would soon be required. 'I don't know about that,' I said.

'Well, it's only a theory, as you say. But I've seen you arm in arm with him, right here in this hotel.'

I called the waitress over and ordered another vodka.

'I suppose you know he's set up his headquarters in the penthouse,' said Dwight. 'He's very difficult to get to. You have to go through Chico Morales and Lucia Perez to speak to him. They guard him mighty fiercely. Do you know them?'

'Yes, I know them. What do you want to know? He gives press interviews all the time. Why don't you just ask him at one of those?'

'Oh no, sir. What my office needs to know is more personal than that.'

'Personal? Like what?'

'Well sir, as you know, the United States has significant investment in Cuba. Mining, sugar, oil refineries. My office is interested in protecting US investment, that's what we do.'

'You haven't mentioned casinos.'

'Oh, the casino people can take care of themselves.'

The waitress returned with my vodka. 'I've heard they've left the country,' I said.

'Not all of them.'

I swirled the lone ice cube around in the glass and watched the whirlpool form. 'Fidel's more interested in social issues,' I said. 'Health care, education, farmers' rights. I don't think he's too interested in economic issues.' I drank half the glass. Toto was observing me so intently I felt like a laboratory rat.

'If you don't mind me saying, sir, they're all economic issues. It's started already. The new government has taken over the warehouses of the United Fruit Company. There are enough cans of Del Monte and Libby's in them to feed a substantial proportion of the US for a year. You see what I mean?'

'Or all of Cuba for many years,' I said, finishing the glass.

'You know sir, Batista was once a young idealist just like Castro. He overthrew a dictator, too. Castro will be the same. The redeemer will become the tyrant, just like before.'

I wondered how someone so young could be so certain about such a thing. But of course, *only* someone so young, so buttoned-down, could be so sure of himself. 'Latin American studies major, eh?'

'Cubans have a saying, do you know it? *Antes era incendiero, ahora soy bombero.*' He looked at me expectantly.

'My Spanish is not that good.'

'Once I was an arsonist, now I am a fireman.' He waited for me to say something, to even indicate that I understood, but all I was thinking about was another drink.

'You must have heard what's being shouted in the streets,' Dwight continued. 'If you go outside now you'll hear it.'

'What will I hear?'

He leaned forward and lowered his voice even further. '*Paredon, paredon, paredon.*'

'Sorry . . . what's that mean?'

'To the wall. They'll be killing off the old regime any minute now. And I mean literally.'

I always liked to think I had unusual depths of patience, in Hollywood terms that is, but Dwight was now getting on my nerves. 'Look,' I said, 'I don't mean to be abrupt, but what do you want from me?'

He sat up again, holding himself erect in his chair, hands together on the table in front, the 'candid standard', as it was called in the trade, the indicator of honesty and openness, just like his namesake on TV telling lies to the nation. I almost expected him to say 'my fellow Americans', but he said, 'You're close to the man. You could be valuable to my office.'

'Why don't you speak to one of the reporters? Jules Dubois, he's close to him too, you know. Closer than me. More reliable than me, too, I suspect. Or even better, Herb Matthews. He's known him for years. Extremely reliable.'

Dwight nodded and grinned a knowing grin. 'You can't trust reporters, sir.'

'Well I don't know anything. I may have some experience with liaisons, so to speak, but I certainly don't know anything about economics.'

'No sir, I understand that. And I understand that it's probably because you don't know about economics that you are experiencing difficulties with the IRS. Like I say, that's perfectly understandable. But my office is in a position to help you with that.'

Suddenly I found myself short of breath. 'How?' was all that I managed to get out.

'My office is in a position to help, that's all I can say at this time.'

Now he was very much on my nerves, and I could feel them beginning to buckle. I took a deep breath, quietly and slowly. 'Just how are you attached to the embassy?'

'Your friend, Pedro Rodriguez, the sugar farmer . . . we helped him just last week. Got his whole family out of the country, to Florida. He could have found himself up against a wall.'

'I'm not that desperate.'

'Forgive me, Mr Flynn, but you could be. You never know with these things. And if and when that happens, we may not be in a position to help then. Citizenship is not guaranteed for folks born in a foreign country, you know. Tasmania . . . where is that exactly?'

'You still haven't told me what you mean by *attached* to the embassy. Are you some kind of . . . what, Central Intelligence? That's what it is, isn't it?'

'No, sir, not at all. Although our office is also attached to the State Department.'

'With strings attached, no doubt. Look . . . Dwight . . . I'm not trained for whatever it is you want me to do. You have to go to school to learn your cloak and dagger stuff. That's what you're talking about, isn't it?' Dwight offered nothing. 'I'm just an actor.'

'Precisely. You're good at being someone else.'

'Most people are other people, though, aren't they? Their lives a mimicry, as Oscar Wilde put it.'

'Oscar Wilde, he was an actor, too, wasn't he?'

'Not quite. Anyway, Fidel agrees with you. He thinks I spend my life trying to be someone else. Maybe you're more like him than you realise.'

He pulled a face and shook his head like the notion was absurd. 'I think I'll have that coffee after all, if you don't mind.'

'You're staying that long, are you?' I said, catching the eye of the waitress.

'As long as it takes,' Dwight said with a grin. 'I can really help you, you know. If you help us. You helped the British during the war, didn't you?'

I ordered the coffee and another vodka for myself. 'Make it a double this time,' I said to the waitress. When she had gone I said to him, 'Are you asking so you can check your information or just to let me know you have it?'

'We hear you've got a bit of a game going with old Fidel,' Dwight said, still grinning.

'He's only old to you, chum. What do you mean, game? Who told you this?'

'My office has had a word with some of your people. We've heard you two have this thing going, this latent homoerotic competitiveness.'

'Christ, I don't even understand what you just said.' But I could hear Chloe Mahon saying it.

'Have you noticed how it is with men and women and status?' Dwight said. 'Status, when it comes to someone it changes the whole game.'

'What game? You keep talking about games.'

'The battle of the sexes.'

'What do they teach you in Latin American studies at Stanford? And what would I know? I'm homoerotic.'

'With men, status attracts sex. With women, sex attracts status. Weird, huh?'

He was all wide eyes and shaking head, like a schoolboy who had just been told what 'fuck' really meant. 'Not that weird,' I said. 'I guess you just didn't have enough time to study the Chinese Imperial court. Anyway Toto, I think I've had enough weirdness for one day.' I pushed my chair back and stood up just as the waitress arrived with a tray holding cup, coffee and glass of vodka, and I nearly sent the lot crashing to the floor. My clumsiness embarrassed me and I sat straight back down again. The waitress quickly poured the coffee and left us alone.

Dwight blew gently over his cup and sipped carefully. 'No, I've never really had reason to look into the Chinese Imperial court. Or Tasmania either. Until now, of course. Where did you say it was?'

The way he could move so effortlessly between artlessness and menace was disarming. 'I'm American,' I said. 'I have been for sixteen years.'

'And how long were you a Nazi?'

'What are you talking about? You just said I helped the British. How could I do both? You seem to have a lot of half-cocked information at your fingertips.'

'How long are you going to be a communist?'

He was too bright and breezy to look like any of the beetle-browed inquisitors from the LA Attorney's office, and way too sociable, but the technique wasn't so far removed: jab with the left, and then tag you with the right cross just when you think you've dodged it.

I could feel sweat beading on my forehead and I considered which was the more obvious giveaway – leaving it there to glisten or wiping it off. I tossed the vodka down my throat, ice cube and all, throwing my head back and flicking a hand across my brow, all in the same unfortunately conspicuous movement. 'If that's some sort of threat,' I said, 'Senator McCarthy is no longer with us. You can't do that kind of thing anymore.'

Dwight slowly returned his cup to its saucer, taking care to position it exactly in the centre. 'Mr Flynn, my office is not interested in whether you have communist sympathies or not. We don't have an opinion on the matter. We're interested in whether Castro has.'

'Has what . . . the sympathies or an opinion?'

'The sympathies.'

'You want me to tell you? Is that all you want?'

'We want you to help us find out. He's a bit . . . how can I put it, undefined.'

'I'll tell you. He's not communist. He told me himself that only Batista thinks he is. It's just Batista's propaganda. Like he says, you don't see any red stars, do you?'

'Uh-huh, uh-huh,' Dwight said, nodding and weighing it up. 'All that may be so, but for someone who's not a communist he seems to have a lot of people around him who are.'

'Like who?'

He looked around the room. 'Ernesto Guevara for one,' he said quietly. 'His brother for another.'

'Raul?'

Dwight nodded and clicked his tongue. 'Paid up, card-carrying members of the party.'

It was the language of another time, the era of witch-hunts for un-American activities and reds under the bed. I leaned back from the table. I hoped it looked like I was finished. 'Well you know what it's like, Toto . . . everyone loves a party.'

'They say Raul looks Chinese,' he said. 'They say his real father was the family cook. He's a lot shorter than his brother, but I've never seen him up close. Does he look Chinese to you?'

Now I was certainly finished. 'Look,' I said, 'if Fidel is a commie then he's a better actor than I am. I've told you what I know.'

'That's not what my office wants from you,' Dwight said. 'We want your assistance.'

'To do what?' I said testily. 'I've asked you that half a dozen times already.'

'I'm sorry,' Dwight said, and he looked genuinely concerned to have caused any upset. He leaned in close again and spoke barely above a whisper. 'There is a cruise ship in the harbour, a German one.'

'There are no cruise ships in the harbour,' I said just as softly. 'Only the navy.'

'It arrived this morning. There's a girl on board. She's very good with languages. My office would appreciate it if you could take her to Castro and suggest that he should put her on as his interpreter . . . to help him with his dealings with foreign officials, the press, and so on.'

'Why would he do that?'

'Our information is that you have been quite successful in offering Mr Castro professional advice in this area.'

'A girl? How old?'

'Nineteen, I believe. Should be young enough for him, I think.'

'Young enough for him? Just what do you mean by interpreter?'

'Just get her close to him, Mr Flynn, she'll do the rest. Directly to him, not to any of the palace guards. Especially avoid that old flame of his, Lucia Perez. Our information is that she is still jealous of other women around Castro. You have an appointment with the girl at three this afternoon on the ship. She's expecting you. In fact, I hear she can't wait to meet you.'

'Sorry, chum. Can't do that. I'm shooting this afternoon. Have to be at the Hotel Comodoro at two. Sorry,' I repeated, like I meant it.

Dwight frowned and studied his coffee cup on the table. I could almost hear the gears of his mind engaging. 'Okay, change in plan. She'll be at the Comodoro at two as well. I'm sure she'd enjoy watching you work.'

'Listen . . .' I put my elbows on the table and buried my mouth in my hands. 'This isn't an assassination, is it? I'm not like you. I'm not a my country right or wrong kind of guy.'

'No sir. We just need to understand what he stands for. Our only interest is the protection of American economic assets.'

'Because I like him, you know,' I said. 'I wouldn't get involved in any dirty business, whatever way you threaten me.'

Dwight laughed his sunny Pepsodent laugh. 'We're not in any kind of business like that. Maybe you've read too many Hollywood scripts. Economic liaison, that's all we do. It's dull, but necessary.'

'What's her name?'

'Renate Spinoza. You can expect her at two.'

'Is that her real name?'

'Does it matter?'

'She's going to pass me a note written in lipstick, is she?'

'Pardon . . . I don't understand.'

I shrugged and sat up. 'You're right, it doesn't matter. Is this normal procedure for you people, getting outside help like this? Is this kind of thing covered in your manuals?'

'Unconventional times sometimes call for unconventional methods.'

'Sorry, maybe I'm just slow, but what's so unconventional about a revolution in Latin America? I haven't had the privilege of a Stanford education, but isn't it a rather common event?'

'There's no such thing as a common revolution, though, is there? They're all different. Even in Latin America.'

'I see . . . I see what's going on. This has all happened too fast for you, hasn't it? The house of cards tumbled a bit too quickly and you guys have been caught flat-footed. Am I right?'

Dwight sipped slowly at his coffee. 'Mr Flynn, would you say this Castro . . . would you say he's a capable man?'

'What does that mean?' I sighed. 'Capable of what? Winning a revolution? A month ago I wouldn't have said so, but look what's happened. Running a country? Well, obviously I have no competence to give you an answer. Thank goodness for that.'

'What I mean is, do you think, in your experience and from what you have seen, do you think he knows what he's doing?'

'I would say, Mr Dodd, that Fidel probably knows what he's doing about as well as you know what you're doing. And like you, he doesn't share such knowledge with me. Is that good enough?'

Dwight's eyes methodically roamed around the room as he finished his coffee. 'Raul is getting married, have you heard?' he said casually, like he was passing on a bit of neighbourhood gossip.

'Raul Castro you mean?'

'Yes, it's just been announced. Of course it could just be an arrangement, you know, to deflect attention from his partiality for . . .' His methodical gaze settled on me as his eyebrows slowly arched. I had no intention of finishing his sentence. 'We don't know much about his fiancé yet,' he finally added. 'Another rebel apparently. There were quite a few female rebels up in those hills, am I correct?'

'Yes,' I said, 'quite a few rebel girls.'

'Well, they're all down here with the rest of us now. I suspect things are going to return to normal sooner than everyone thinks. These Latin American countries are all the same. Nothing changes for long.'

Victor Malenkoff was waiting in the lobby of the Comodoro. It was several weeks since I had last laid eyes on him and the change was revolutionary. The Panama suit hung from his shoulders like a small white tent and his legs protruded from the short pants like the poles. He had lost perhaps one of his chins. The only items of apparel that seemed to still fit the diminished frame were the broad-brimmed hat and the open-toed sandals. The attitude had not changed a whit. 'Fleen!' he bellowed across the thinly inhabited lobby, raising his arms for a bear hug. 'What has happened to you? You look like you have not had a decent meal in months.'

Pot and kettle, I thought, but decided to allow Victor's opinion to pass uncontested. In fact, I was still feeling better than I had in some years. Yes, I had lost a little weight, but not so much that it made more than one notch difference to my belt, and I was the better for it. The disagreeable food had curbed my appetite, the unreliable supply had reduced my alcohol consumption, and the physical effort required to follow a mercurial army around a mountainous theatre of war had given my body a rare opportunity to detoxify, if only marginally. The leg was still giving me a twinge, but that was abating day by day, even without the generous offer of maggots and leeches from the medico with the truncated name. From Victor's appearance it was obvious that the stress of being in Havana, waiting for the inevitable tide of change and having no ability to influence events in even the smallest way, except to flee before it, was more taxing than riding on that tide, however bumpy the ride.

'Victor, you've always been a man of taste and discernment.' I freed myself from the welcome and gazed pointedly around the lobby. Among the new hotels that had sprung up in Havana since Batista came to his arrangement with Lansky, this was undoubtedly the most modest. 'Couldn't you do better than this?'

Victor shrugged and pulled a face. 'You do not have to stay here. It is a location, no? Through the camera one hotel is the same as another. And this one, it is out of the way of the revolution. Look around . . . do you see rebels to get in your hair? No.'

The Comodoro was on the edge of town on its own private stretch of Caribbean beach. 'Very thoughtful,' I said. 'How are you dealing with everything, old sport? The barbarians got to the gate a little sooner than expected, eh.'

Victor shrugged again, this time with more of a slump, his eyes raised to the heavens. 'Oh Fleen, what can I tell you? It is difficult. Perhaps I can buy a future, pay my tributes to the conqueror, but who knows how long.'

'Tributes? Are you being leaned on?'

He took my elbow and began steering me through the lobby. 'Come. Your friends are setting up around the pool.'

I freed my arm. 'I'm waiting for someone first. So . . . are you being leaned on?'

'It is the tradition, no? The Caribbean, it has always had its pirates.'

'Not these people. You might be surprised.'

'You think they are so different? They have you brainwashed, no? They are pirates like the rest. They even have the beards. The only difference is the nature of the tribute. These conquerors do not ask for gold, they ask for tractors, for pigs, cows, fertiliser.'

'They asked you for tractors?'

'They have not got around to me yet. I am a very small fry. When they do they will ask me for *la donativo* like everyone else, the donation for their new Cuba. Some chickens, perhaps. A chicken in every pot, they promise. But listen to us, talking about such things in public like this. You see how good this hotel is? We can discuss anything. Come. Your friend will find you by the pool.'

Apart from a handful of extras provided by the hotel, only Marie and I were required for the swimming pool scene. Barry said proudly he would get the whole sequence in just three shots, and puffed his chest a little as he said it, like it was some sort of cinematic breakthrough. He sat me down at a table under an umbrella and draped me in a sheet. The hotel's barber and manicurist went about their business with my head and my hand. 'Remind me what I'm supposed to be doing, sport,' I said to Barry.

'You're being pampered, enjoy yourself. You're playing a Hollywood character, remember? You're trying to be conspicuous, attract attention. You know, like you did in Santiago. Just be yourself.'

'I've never done this in my life.'

'Well, we've run out of cars for you to drive into the goddamn pool. Let's just get this.'

The first shot was a pan around the pool area with the obligatory dive off the high board by a bathing beauty. The camera found me sitting in the sun getting pampered, but not enjoying it.

'Can you try to not look so distracted,' Barry said. 'You look like you can't wait to be somewhere else.'

'Sorry, sport.' I *was* distracted. I didn't know what I was about to get myself into, what Dwight Dodd was getting me into. It was well past two. Perhaps the girl wasn't going to show. Perhaps the plan had changed again and I was off the hook. 'Do you want to do another?'

'Nah . . . I'll live with it. Just see if you can work up a little enthusiasm. You're a big time reporter on a secret mission. You're trying to make an important contact.'

If only he knew, I thought.

The second shot was Marie's entrance. Sheathed in slinky white like a Miami hostess, she strolled onto the pool deck, her hourglass figure rescued from the olive green uniform that had for so long restrained it.

'We can do this one better,' I said. I slipped an arm around Marie's waist and led her back to her first position. I suggested she swing her sexy white sunglasses by her side, stop by the edge of the pool, and make a show of putting them on while subtly swaying her hips. I showed her how to do it, giving my best impression of Lupe Velez. 'It's your entrance,' I said. 'One of the three golden rules. Make it count.'

The third shot followed her long walk around the pool to my table. She was no Lupe Velez, but the way she got her hips swaying had me thinking about what else I might be able to teach her. Just now, though, the script required me to give her the brush-off – another pesky autograph hound – and for her to insist on shaking my hand. When she did she slipped me a note written in lipstick. If only it had been so easy in Santiago.

'Okay, that's a wrap for here,' cried Barry.

'What about close-ups?' I said.

'Don't need 'em.'

'Faces . . . we need faces.'

Barry sat in the chair next to me for one of his heart-to-hearts. 'Marie we can do, sure. She's gorgeous. But if we do her then we have to do you and, buddy, frankly, after what we've been through for the past couple of months, and without make-up, your fans aren't ready to see that kisser like this.'

'Christ, thanks Barry.'

'Hey, at least I'm honest.'

'Yes, there's that. What about the note? A close-up of the note written in lipstick.'

Barry got to his feet and dismissed the idea with a disdainful flick of the hand. 'We're shooting black and white. What's it gonna look like? Nothing.'

I thought about having a swim. The water looked inviting and Victor had found a hotel pool free of rebels, as promised. Marie looked even more inviting. But then I saw Renate Spinoza. I knew it was her. And now I also knew that Dwight Dodd knew what he was doing and that Marie was free to leave with Barry as originally planned. I assumed she would be American, but now I realised I should have known – Renate Spinoza, a German cruise ship. If she were American she would be sashaying across the pool deck in tight three-quarter length pedal-pushers, chewing gum with disdain and preoccupied with Ricky Nelson. This teenager knew how to make an entrance in European style, and needed no coaching. She lingered in the sunlight exuding confidence, a casual glance and a finger to the corner of the mouth the only overt movement. She didn't force eyes to turn in her direction, she simply radiated a mute siren call and was patient while it swelled. It was the sort of entrance Kate Hepburn could pull off, but she was better looking than Kate Hepburn and wasn't wearing pants. And like Kate Hepburn she would not make the first move.

I went to her like I had known her for years. 'You're late,' I said, glancing at my wristwatch. 'I expected you a couple of hours ago. You missed all the fun.'

She blew a kiss over each of my cheeks. 'I've been watching,' she said with a smile. 'I didn't wish to interrupt.' There was only the most vague of accents, but it was difficult to tell what it was.

'Can I get you something? Coffee, a drink? What's the plan?'

Her eyes flashed at me. 'What plan?'

'Sorry, I mean what's your schedule, do we have time?'

'Fleen . . . you keep this one under wraps.' When Victor walked he still threw himself around like he was transporting bulk, even though much of it had been off-loaded. 'Such a delightful girl,' he said, taking Renate's hand and raising it to his lips. 'I entertained her while you worked. You should be careful where you leave her, you know.'

'So . . . you've met Renate.'

'She is from Hamburg. Such a wonderful city. We have had much to talk about.'

'That's the first time I've heard you say something positive about anywhere in Germany,' I said. 'Don't listen to him, Renate. He'll tell you anything.'

'I can look after myself,' Renate said.

'She is right, Fleen,' Victor said before turning to Renate. 'But you will have to be en garde. He is a great swordsman, you know.'

Renate smiled indulgently. 'Please don't assume because I am young I don't understand you.'

'Young?' said Victor with mock innocence. 'Oh, I never gave it a second thought.'

'No,' she said. 'You were too busy with the first one.'

He gave a low whistle and waved hot fingertips in front of his mouth before blowing them out. 'I like this girl, Fleen. Your taste has improved. I will give you a ride back to town so I can listen to her some more.'

Victor drove us back to the Hilton, although not quite all the way. He had to drop us on the street as the driveway was choked with military vehicles. I suggested to Renate that she wait in the bar while I tracked down Carlos. She said she would wait in the coffee shop. I looked around the lobby filled now with loitering diplomatic types in ties, on-the-make types in open-necked shirts, rebels with a glint in their eye. Good thinking, I said.

It took me twenty minutes to find Carlos. The ballroom had been set up as a temporary press centre with local and foreign reporters scattered around tables, ankle deep in old news. The atmosphere was thick with smoke, the clatter of typewriters and the raucous buzz of restless voices. In a far corner was *Revolucion*, the rebel newssheet, fast becoming the national newspaper. Carlos had to be torn away from a scrimmage of persistent cigar-chomping reporters, who continued to bark questions at him even as he found a quiet corner to give a private interview to the one 'correspondent' who had been with them in the final days of the battle.

I told him the story about Renate: how it was fortunate for them she happened to be in town, how proficient she was with so many languages, how well she could deal with the pushy members of the foreign press. Hers would be another agreeable face of the revolution, I said, a new dimension to men and beards and military drab. I must have been convincing because Carlos said he understood. It was not his decision anyway. Nobody made decisions about anything, he said. Just *el Lider Maximo*, who made decisions constantly, and just as constantly changed them. Had I heard – Havana was the capital again? Carlos was happy to pass this one to the penthouse.

He said there was a special elevator in the garage in the basement. He said we should only go down late, not before eleven, but not after twelve. After twelve we would be swamped by the traffic. There would be a guard. He would search us, but he wouldn't stop us. I was known, and I would be with a girl, so the guard would understand. The elevator would take us directly to the twenty-third floor. Chico would be there. Chico knew me, and he would do the rest. I asked if Lucia would also be there. Lucia could complicate matters with her mother hen act. Lucia wouldn't be there, Carlos said. At that hour, on that floor, Lucia knew better than to be there.

I went to the coffee shop to find Renate and tell her there was going to be a long wait. I saw Dwight Dodd first. The gleam that seemed to surround him simply attracted the eye. A few tables beyond was Renate, sitting over a coffee with, of all people in Havana, young Beverly. Obviously it was dangerous to leave Renate alone.

'Hey, Cap'n . . . Renate's been telling me what you're up to.'

'What I'm up to?' I sat down and laid on the nonchalance. My nerves were beginning to jangle again and I wondered what state they would be in by eleven o'clock.

'Yeah . . . sounds like a nifty job,' Beverly said. 'Wish I could speak some other languages. Did you know she can speak thirteen, as well as American?'

'Not all of them fluently,' Renate said. 'A few I am still working on.'

'So what's number thirteen?' Beverly said eagerly.

'Vietnamese. It is one I am still working on.'

'Well, you're young,' I said. 'You've got plenty of time.'

'Not as much as you might think,' she said.

'What about Italian?' said Beverly.

'Of course.'

'Say something in that. I love Italian.'

'What would you like me to say?'

'Something romantic. Those Eye-ties always sound so romantic.'

'*Nel mezzo del cammin do nostra vita, mi ritrovai per una selva oscura, che la diritta via era smarrita.*'

'You make it sound like opera,' Beverly said. 'What did you say?'

'It is a poem.'

'A very old poem, if I'm not mistaken,' I said.

'Is it romantic?'

'Not really,' Renate said. 'It is about a man who found himself lost in a dark wood.'

'Was he just by himself? That sure doesn't sound romantic.'

'Perhaps, Woodsie,' I said, 'if we had time to listen to the whole thing. It depends whether you find the notion of an afterlife romantic.'

'At our age we can afford that,' Renate said. 'Although Dante was not a young man when he wrote it.'

'Then perhaps I can enlighten you,' I said. 'One reaches an age when the afterlife is not at all romantic. It's a prosaic consideration that occupies far too much of one's time.'

Renate smiled and sipped her coffee.

Beverly suddenly grabbed my hand. 'Hey, we had a parade today, did Barry tell you? We had our own little victory parade, just for us, and I got to ride on a tank down the middle of the street. All the people were cheering. It was really great.'

'You too, huh?' I said. 'Euphoria seems to be the latest drug.'

'We filmed the whole thing,' she said. 'They stopped the parade so I could jump down off the tank and run into Johnny's arms. Now that's what I call romantic.'

'It certainly is,' I said. 'Beats an inferno for romance, that's for sure.'

Now Renate broke into a quiet chuckle. We ordered some food and found the kitchen had returned to normal: the entire menu was again available, hotel hamburgers, the works. The bar had not skipped a beat, revolution or not, and I had my supper served in a glass. At precisely eleven o'clock I said that it was time to make a move. We passed Dwight Dodd on our way out, still sitting with two other clean-cut Americans. Not so much as a glance was exchanged.

Beverly took the lobby elevator up to our room, Renate and I the back stairs down to the garage. The *barbudo* was sitting on a chair in front of the elevator doors, a tommy gun across his knees. As soon as he saw me he pressed the button. He then frisked us carefully, making sure he felt deep into both crotches, although he seemed to favour neither. We rode the elevator to the twenty-third floor where Chico was waiting. He searched us again. He told us to wait and disappeared behind the grand double-door entrance to the penthouse suite.

He was back within a minute or two with a plate of bread and ham, which he placed on the coffee table between us. '*La pata negra*,' he said, and returned to his position in front of the elevator. For half an hour we waited in a silence broken only by muffled raised voices coming from behind the double doors. Renate tried some of the ham and said it was good. I told her the pigs were fed on oak leaves or something. Eventually, without any apparent signal, Chico crossed to the other side of the room and ushered us into this latest inner sanctum of the revolution.

The sitting room was like a teenager's bedroom. Clothes and papers and trash littered the floor; plates of food, some half-finished, some untouched, were stacked on a table; guns were piled on a sofa; the television was on, the sound a low rumble. Three *barbudos* were huddled in conversation, which they stopped as we were led past. Their eyes followed us down a corridor to another closed double door. Chico knocked tentatively. A grunt came from the other side. He opened the door a few inches. '*Perdone, companero*,' he said, and then nodded brusquely to me.

Fidel was sitting up in a vast bed in striped pyjamas, puffing on a cigar. He offered no sign that he considered this scenario absurd, that a man in his position should receive visitors in any other manner. The room had a pink glow to it and the windows were wide open. There was quite a breeze that high up, whistling through the room and disturbing the heavy drapes.

'Ah, *companero*,' he said affably. It was the innocent Fidel, the one with the boyish grin, the appealing eyes, the soft voice. 'You are here to help me again. Carlos he tells me.'

'*Commandante*,' I said, 'permit me to introduce Senorita Renate Spinoza.' Mission accomplished, I said to myself, now for the strategic withdrawal.

'What did you think of the *pata negra*?' Fidel asked. 'Good, no?'

'Yes, very good,' I said, already inching backwards to the door.

'The *cerdo negro* is Spain's gift,' Renate said.

Fidel slowly removed the cigar from between his teeth and I stopped inching backwards. 'So you are the interpreter,' he said.

'*Si puedo ser de ayuda, senor, seria honorada,*' she said.

Fidel nodded with approval. 'Her accent very good, *viejo*. Cuanto tiempo ha sabida usted esta movie star?'

'*Desde que yo fui una nina, senor.*'

'A girl?' Fidel said with a chuckle. 'She say she know you since she was a girl, *companero*. What they say about you is true, no?'

'Errol, *es amigo de mi padre, senor,*' Renate said.

'Ah,' Fidel nodded, 'he knows your father. It is good I do not know your father.'

'Renate is a language student,' I said. 'Heidelberg, wasn't it?' Renate nodded. 'It's wonderful luck that she's here. As soon as I heard I thought it would be ...'

Fidel held up his hand. 'You no need to tell me,' he said. 'I understand. I do the interview and we see. You can leave her here, *companero*.'

They were the words I had been waiting to hear all day. I quickly took my leave, rode the elevator down to the garage and made my way up to the coffee shop. My side of the bargain was complete. Now it was up to Dwight Dodd and the Economic Liaison Office to fulfil theirs. But Dwight Dodd and his Economic Liaison buddies were now nowhere to be seen.

Beverly was sitting on the bed in her underwear painting her toenails, resting her chin on her knee and looking down her leg to her gorgeous slender ankle. 'That was quick,' she said.

'Not quick enough,' I said. I went into the bathroom and stripped to the waist. I splashed water over my face and found myself looking into a mirror half the size of a shop display window, a mirror that could not be avoided. Barry had been cruel, but honest. And he hadn't told me anything I didn't already know. Without preparation, without make-up, he had done the right thing refusing to expose this face to Errol Flynn fans. For Errol Flynn fans the face in the mirror would be a horror picture. For Errol Flynn himself it was a picture of Dorian Gray. 'Einstein's right, you know,' I called out. 'Time is relative.'

'What do you mean?' she called back.

'Did you know he was only twenty-five when he came up with that?'

'What?'

'I wonder if it would have been different if he didn't come up with it till he was forty-five or fifty-five. I wonder if science then would have been influenced by a little philosophy.'

'I can't hear you.'

'More Dante-esque, perhaps . . . influenced by the anticipation of a journey into the dark wood.' I splashed some more water and stared through puffy eyes at my puffy eyes. 'Or even the dark alley. When every year becomes a significantly higher proportion of the years you have left, what does that equal?'

'I told you, I can't hear you.'

I grabbed a towel and dried my face while standing in the bathroom doorway. 'The older you get the faster time flies. Why is that? Because perception of life equals time spent divided by time left. Or should that be the other way around? Where's Einstein when you need him? There's another relativity theory in that, don't you think?'

'You said you were going to live another fifty years,' she said, concentrating on the smallest of her toenails.

'When did I say that?'

'For your book. I heard you say it to Earl. And you said it to Chloe as well.'

'When?'

'At that place on the way to whatsitsname. You know, the one with the square where we heard all those gunshots the first time.'

'Santa Clara? That was, let's see, must be a couple of months ago.'

'So?'

'That's what I mean about the relativity of time. I don't suppose it's what Einstein meant, but he was only twenty-five, so he wouldn't understand. What proportion of my time left on earth might two months be? Two per cent? Twenty per cent? What if it's, say, fifty per cent? That means I'll be dead by May. I only have to recall our arrival in Havana to realise how long I have left. That seems like yesterday. In spite of all that we've been through since then, it seems like yesterday.'

'Yeah, but ... you said you were going to live for fifty years.'

'What if I'm wrong? I'm sure if I ask a hundred doctors I won't find a single one to tell me I'm right. Do you know when you start to realise you haven't that much time left? When you stop saying maybe one day. You know, like maybe one day I'll take a raft down the Amazon, or sail a balloon over the Himalayas. Or maybe one day I'll go back to where I was born, see what it's like, if it's the way I remember it. Tasmania ... do you know where that is?'

'No.'

'No, not many do, it would appear. Maybe one day . . . I stopped saying that a while back. It's memories, not dreams you think about when you stop saying that.'

'Don't be so morbid.'

'Morbid?' I threw my head back and laughed and felt better for it, almost a few minutes younger. 'Have you been spending time with Chloe?'

'I don't listen to Chloe anymore.'

'That's good. Life's too short to listen to Chloe. Einstein's other theory.'

'Are we gonna see Renate again? I like her.'

I went back into the bathroom. I didn't know whether I should be feeling guilty about Renate or about Fidel, but guilt is always better felt in private. 'Maybe one day,' I said, and nudged the door shut with my foot.

25
An odd sense of pointless prescience.
Havana, 10 January 1959

It was another Saturday in the good time capital of the world, except the times were changing. I lay in the shade of cabana number ten on the pool deck of the Havana Hilton, a bottle of vodka and a bucket of ice at my disposal. From there I could quietly observe the two shows that had been in performance all morning: the girls in cabana number one, and the *rebelde* in the pool. The girls seemed to have cornered the market in skimpy bikinis in Havana. They never sat still for long, parading up and down like they were on a catwalk and strutting the length of the diving board, but never getting wet. Word had got around that cabana number one and the diving tower were in direct line of sight from the suite of *el Gigante* on the twenty-third floor. Fidel may have told of his ascetic life in the mountains often enough to the press, but the female population of Havana wasn't buying it, and Dwight Dodd's hypothesis about status and sex was being demonstrated before my eyes.

The *rebelde* didn't seem to care who could see them. They had spent all morning making it clear that they could now have any swimming pool they wanted. They cavorted like schoolboys, jumping and diving on top of one another, laughing and splashing and racing to the other end. They were obviously trying to impress the girls, but the girls were after bigger fish. I fancied they were reluctant to go into the water themselves not because they didn't want to get their hair wet, but because the water had begun to carry an oil slick.

It may have been a different pool, but for the second time in twenty-four hours Renate found me relaxing on the deck. 'You sure have a hard life,' she said.

I shielded my eyes from the sun. Until that moment I wasn't sure I would ever see her again, but certainly did not expect to see her looking exactly like she did the day before — same confidence, same control, even the same wardrobe. 'Didn't we do this scene yesterday?' I said.

'Are you on your own? Where's your little friend?'

'She prefers the Nacional. It's more romantic.'

'Tired of romance, are you?'

'Oh, I like to let her spend time with people her own age. It helps both of us retain our perspective. Did you get the job? You look like you might have?'

She sat on the next sun lounge and put her feet up. She had a masculine self-assurance about her. 'I've handled my first assignment already.'

'Should I ask what, or would that be ... um, personal?'

The confidence extended to taking no notice of my jibes. 'Fidel went cane-cutting this morning with Che. Well, actually with Che and a small army of the press.'

I grinned and shook my head. 'The boy's a quick learner, I'll give him that.' I glanced at my watch. 'So has he given you time off? It's past midday. You must have been, ah ... on the job for twelve hours already.'

'Are you always so provocative? Your boss has given you time off, too, huh?'

'Do you mean Barry? He knows better than to work me in the morning unless completely necessary. I have to fuel up, you see. Would you care for a drink?'

She held out an empty glass. I filled it with ice and she tipped half of it back. 'Not so cold,' she said. 'I'm not American.'

I poured her a double. 'Where is *el Lider Stupendo* anyway? Still bending his back?'

'Only over a conference table. He's locked up tight with Raul and Che. Affairs of state.'

'Amazing, isn't it? They're all just boys.' I watched her drink half the glass, and the strange ways her lips moved. 'I'm shooting again this afternoon. Would you care to watch? It's an interior. Upstairs in one of the rooms. You'll be nice and close to the action. And we're even shooting sound, like a genuine movie.'

'You make it sound irresistible,' she said. 'Perhaps if I have nothing better to do.'

My father always reminded me that a straight line is the shortest distance between two points, and I decided to take the direct approach. 'Off the record,' I said, 'it'll go no further, scout's honour. Is the *commandante* all talk, or is he, you know, a man of action? I've had reports, off the record, as I say, that he says more than he does. What's your . . . educated guess?'

She smiled and slowly shook her head. 'I'm sorry. Professional confidentiality, you understand.'

'Of course. And just what is your profession?'

She considered me for a moment and then lifted her gaze across the pool. 'Well . . . it looks like I do have something better to do.'

Chico was marching purposefully around the pool deck. He ignored me and spoke briskly in Spanish to Renate. She nodded and agreed. 'I've been summoned to the twenty-third floor,' she said to me. She got to her feet and finished her drink before following Chico.

'Come if you can,' I called after her. 'Room . . .' I couldn't remember the number.

'I'll find you,' she called back. 'I'm good at that.'

'I'll just bet you are,' I said to myself. I watched her make her way through the parade of bikini babes at the end of the pool and shook my head. 'Sorry, girls, but you're out of your depth.'

I entered frame from camera left, holding some papers. I went to my bag on the sideboard by the window and did a double-take to the camera, like I had just noticed it there. 'Well, I guess this about winds up another stage in the fight to rid Latin America of tyrants . . . dictators. But the spirit started by this handful of wonderful rebels is spreading and growing stronger every day. And all you young men and women fighting for political freedom and your own beliefs, I wish you good luck.'

I packed the papers into the bag followed by some clothes. I looked wistfully at my 26 JULIO armband before packing that as well.

'Cut!' called Barry. 'Beautiful. We'll move downstairs for the balcony shot.'

'Do you think there was enough of the armband?' I asked him. 'I could have presented it better. Should we do another?'

'It's fine,' Barry said. 'You wait up here. We'll call out from below when we're set.'

'Loved the pause,' said Renate, stretched out on the bed. 'Tyrants . . . oh, um . . . dictators. Did you write that?'

'What are you now, a critic?'

'Fine sentiments you expressed there. In my country we'd call it naïve.'

I sat on the bed and lit a cigarette as I watched the crew pack up the gear. 'Now you've got me confused. You see, I always thought that word was French, and I was kind of led to believe that you were German.'

'Who told you that?'

'What, the French part or the German part?'

'The German part. The word comes from the Latin.'

'Of course. I was forgetting you're a languages major from Heidelberg.'

'We don't have *majors* at Heidelberg, we call them . . .'

'Oh, sorry. I thought all you people had majors in something or other. So you're not a kraut?'

'I didn't say I was, and I didn't say I wasn't.'

'You told Victor you were.'

'What I told him is unimportant. He is unimportant. So what's your picture called?'

'*Assault of the Rebel Girls,*' I said as the last of the crew left us alone on the bed. 'What we just did is the final scene. You know, the one before the credits roll. You are a kraut, aren't you? I can hear a . . .'

'Why do you care?'

'I'm just fishing to find out if I'm important. Now that I've served my function, that is.'

'How do you know we haven't got other functions for you to serve? You did so well with your first.'

I grinned and flicked the holder up and down in my teeth. It was the sort of thing you just couldn't do with a naked cigarette. 'You may be German, but sister, you're definitely not nineteen.'

'Don't I look nineteen?'

'Sure, but so what? You don't look German.'

She pulled the pillows out from under the bedspread and stacked them against the bedhead, fluffing them up and making herself comfortable.

'What was it you said that so impressed Fidel last night?' I said.

'Professional confidentiality, remember?'

'No, I mean what you said before I left. Something about his blessed ham.'

'Oh, *cerdo negro*. Black pig. It's where they get *la pata negra*, that's all.'

'That's all? Sister, you had him hooked from the moment you opened your mouth.'

'Of course. That's what I do.'

She winked at me. It was subtle, and if I hadn't been gaping at her I could have easily missed it, but I was sure it was a wink.

'I am an enigma to you, aren't I?' she said.

'One thing I do know, Heidelberg's not the only school you've been to.'

She chuckled and leaned toward me. 'May I have one of your Egyptian cigarettes?'

I offered her the pack and lit one for her. She held it between slender fingers by her face and blew smoke nonchalantly from the corner of her mouth. Her eyelids drooped a little, adding a world-weariness to her many other attractions, the sort of jaded detachment that was well beyond her years, however many there might have been. 'Now I do believe you're a kraut,' I said. 'I've only ever seen that look in one other woman, and she was a kraut.'

'Really,' she said indifferently.

'Not just *a* kraut, actually. *The* kraut. Marlene Dietrich.'

'Really,' she said again in exactly the same way.

'Yes, although looking at you lying there like that, perhaps there's more of the Greta Garbo about you. Maybe you're Swedish.'

'You flatter me by comparing me with lesbians? Really, Mr Flynn, I expected better from you.'

'Maybe I'm just fishing again.'

'And did your fishing work on Greta Garbo and Marlene Dietrich?'

'Oh, they were too old for me.'

'That sounds like you're trying to make excuses. Could it be that there are two women in Hollywood who have resisted your famous charm?'

'I've never really been much of a fisherman. I've always found it easier to buy my fish from a shop. You get better ones there, too. Caught by professionals.'

'You won't shock me, you know. If that's what you are trying to do.'

'No, I'm quite aware of that. Sounds like my call. Time for my Romeo number.' I went out onto the balcony and looked down at Barry and camera below.

'The papers,' Barry yelled. 'You'll need the papers for continuity.' I retrieved the papers from my bag and took my position again on the balcony. 'Okay,' called Barry, 'imagine we're the victory parade. Look down at us and then go inside.'

'What's my motivation?' I said.

'Your what?'

'Never mind. Just joking.'

'Okay . . . action!'

I gazed down, squared up my papers on the balcony rail and went back into the room. Renate hadn't budged. 'Cut!' came the call from below. 'That's a wrap for you today, chief.'

I dropped onto an armchair and looked at her, fixing myself a fresh cigarette. 'Well, that's it for me. What are you up to?'

'Did you find out what your motivation is?'

'Oh, I think it was to pack my bags and move on to the next revolution. That kind of thing.'

'They're going to have trials, you know.'

'Who are?'

'Your friends.'

'They're your friends too now.'

'You are an older friend. I will not be expected to attend.'

'Attend what?'

'Their trials. They will ask you to be a witness to their justice.'

'Me? Why me?'

'They will want it to be known that these people were given justice. They will want you to report that.'

'I'm not a reporter.'

'But you have been behaving like one.'

'Why don't they get a real reporter? Why not Matthews or Dubois?'

'They trust you. You can't trust real reporters.'

'Is that from your field guide?'

'What do you mean?'

'Your boss said the same thing.' I got up and paced around the room. I did not like the sound of this. 'Are you sure? It's not some new mission you people have come up with for me, is it? Dwight seems to have the idea I've done this sort of thing before.'

She dropped her half-finished cigarette in the ashtray and helped herself to another. 'It's something I overheard them say.'

'You heard Dwight say?' I said, offering her a light.

'No. Fidel and some of the others. They made sure I heard it.' She didn't want the light. She seemed happy just to have the cigarette show off her long fingers.

'Jesus Christ,' I said. 'Where's all this going?'

'I think you'll find at great speed along that road paved with good intentions. You know that one?'

I sighed and sat down again. 'If only . . .' I shook my head despairingly and lit myself a cigarette off the last one. 'Let me tell you a story.'

'I like to be told stories.' She worked her shoulders deeper into the pillows and smiled expectantly at me. For once she looked like a teenager.

'Good,' I said. 'When I was at boarding school I had this crystal radio. I bought it from one of the other boys, one of those boffin types, so at night I could listen to music in my dorm in the dark. My bed was next to a window, and directly above me was the housemaster's room. He had a regular radio, a wireless they used to call it, and I could hear what he was listening to. I discovered that if I tuned my little set into the same program I could hear what he heard, but for some reason I picked it up early. Something to do with the mysterious workings of crystals and vacuum tubes, I suppose. Anyway, I'd hear whatever it was, and then he'd hear it a few seconds later. It was a strange sensation, knowing precisely what was coming, like I was just ahead of the game. I could listen for hours and not care what I was listening to, just knowing that I was hearing it first. It was an odd sense of pointless prescience, but it's always fascinated me.'

'Such an interesting story,' she said, making it obvious it wasn't. 'Why are you telling me this?'

'I don't want to see too far ahead. Five minutes, that would be enough. Why couldn't Einstein have put his mind to something like that? Something practical. Five minutes . . . imagine what you could do with five minutes of genuine prescience.'

'Ah, now that's disappointing. I thought you were good for more. Here I was expecting a fine Swiss watch, and I find an egg timer.'

'A grandfather clock these days.'

'You surprise me. You are not above self-mockery. Not what I expected of a Hollywood legend with your reputation.'

'Self-awareness, I prefer to think.'

She sat opposite me on the edge of the bed and took my hand, drawing it to her mouth to light her cigarette from mine, fixing me the whole time with those sultry eyes. She placed her two hands on my knees. 'Let me help you with a little of your prescience. In five minutes, who knows what will happen here? But tomorrow or the next day, I can tell you that these people will begin to parade their old enemies in front of some sort of tribunal. They will accuse them, condemn them and shoot them, and probably all within the five minutes that intrigues you so much. And you . . . you will be required to witness this.'

I waited for the wink. I hoped for the wink. The sultry eyes didn't so much as blink. 'I can't tell with you people. You're professional liars.'

She rubbed my knees. 'Who is *you people*?'

'Did Dwight put you up to this? Am I your next assignment? Trying to scare me out of the country, is that it?' She didn't flinch, just kept on rubbing my knees and fixing me with her Marlene Dietrich eyes. 'Can you really speak thirteen languages?'

'So many questions. Where do you want me to start? Yes, thirteen languages, plus American of course, don't forget that. It's just a matter of learning how to get your tongue around them, don't you find?'

'Ah, yes, it's what you do. And Dwight?'

'He knows where I am. It's his job to know.'

'I thought his job was economic something-or-other.'

'But at the moment I'm not, as you so eloquently put it, on the job myself. Satisfied?'

I stilled her hands by covering them with my own. 'Is Dwight happy with you?'

'What do you mean?'

'Is your mission accomplished? Was one night enough to give him what he wanted? I'm talking about Dwight, of course.'

Her lips slowly spread into a grin. 'You don't believe me, do you? You were a means to an end, not an end in yourself.'

'Then why do I get the feeling you're still on assignment?'

'Sometimes, Mr Flynn, I like to work for myself.'

'Ah,' I said with an exaggerated nod of understanding. 'A bit of freelance.'

She slipped her hands along my thighs and, without taking her eyes from mine for a second, undid my belt and my trousers. 'So what's going to happen here?' she said. 'Where's that crystal ball of yours?'

'Who's doing the fishing now? It was a crystal *set*, anyway.'

'Not from where I'm sitting,' she said as her long fingers gently released me. 'Well, how about that . . . it's true what they say.'

'What do they say?'

'That you are a big star.'

'But it's not what they say, is it, honey? It's what they whisper.'

26
Castro, he doesn't like to lose.

Havana, 11 January 1959

This time the mojo really was back, whatever the mojo was. This time there would be no downhill slide on the rollercoaster ride. This time it was all up. I hadn't felt like this since before Africa, before the roots of hell. No, it wasn't Africa after all. It wasn't my back and it wasn't just in my head. All along, all it took was someone like Renate to remind me where it was. Now I was certain she had been to more schools than Heidelberg. If she was really nineteen then she must have started school early. I wished I'd known her when she was fifteen.

I squeezed lemon over my boiled shrimp and listened to Victor's latest theory about the future of Havana. Barry was listening too, politely. Barry was good at listening politely. I usually stopped the Russian with a joke or an argument or a red herring. But my mind was preoccupied – it hadn't really moved on from yesterday. Why would I want it to move on from yesterday? Let Victor occupy my ear while Renate lingered in my mind. I found a corner of it to think about the Olympiads, my old drinking buddies, John Barrymore, W C Fields, John Decker. How we would invite along a stiff stuffed shirt, and one of us was designated to listen to his boring life story for two minutes and then, with his soul in mid-pour, look him in the eye and blurt out 'Oh, shit!' and hurry off. The Oh Shit Club, that's what we really called ourselves. 'Oh, shit!' I said.

Victor stopped in the middle of a sentence, a forked shrimp hovering before his lips. 'Have you forgotten something?' he asked.

'No, remembered actually.'

Both men stared at me like I was a fool. 'Anyway,' Victor said, 'as I was saying . . .' And on he went.

I ate my shrimp. Victor had insisted we all have the shrimp in memory of Meyer Lansky. Dear departed Meyer Lansky, whose favourite meal was said to be the boiled shrimp at Monseigneur. Meyer Lansky obviously liked skulking in dark corners. Even at lunch the Monseigneur was dark. Even on a sunny day in the tropics. It was below street level with heavy drapes, dark wood, ornate furnishings and far too many gilt edges. In a town where the definition of 'classy' had to be given in French, this was the *haut de splendeur*, the *altesse* of Havana dining rooms. The shrimp came in cut crystal, the lemon wedges in a little net, and the daiquiris with a swizzle stick topped by a crown. I swizzled my vodka.

I wondered if Beverly knew. Women could smell it on a man, but if she did she hadn't let on. She had chatted about her day, painted her nails and gone to sleep. Before I left for the Monseigneur she even asked again when we might be seeing Renate. Have to do it soon, I said. I didn't say 'we'. I didn't say 'I'.

Victor kept droning on, happy to have the floor to himself, and I diverted myself by watching Snowball. *Bola de Nieve*, because he was round and black. When I first saw him in his white tie and tuxedo, I thought the man at the piano was Louis Armstrong. But Louis Armstrong didn't play the piano and certainly didn't have the voice Snowball had. Not for the first time I wished my Spanish was better so I could understand the words. I felt like listening to a romantic song. I wondered if there was a song about a Renate. Probably not, it wasn't a romantic name, like Sweet Lorraine, or Mona Lisa, or I'll Take You Home Again Kathleen. I'll Take You Home Again Renate. Renate with the Dietrich Eyes. I shook my head and took a drink to remind myself to act my age. I wondered if Renate was her real name anyway, or just her professional alias. I wondered what she was doing right now. I wondered when I could see her again. The Wonder of Renate. If I could see five minutes into the future, what I would like to see was Renate coming down the steps to the Monseigneur. 'Oh, shit!' I said again, looking Victor in the eye.

'What is wrong with you, Fleen?' he said impatiently.

'Have you ever fucked a lesbian? They're the best.'

Now they stared at me with dropped jaws. 'Come on, chief,' Barry said. 'We're in a high class joint here.'

'Oh, I just thought it was time we talked about something interesting for a change. So . . . have you?'

'Fleen, these revolutionaries, they turn your head,' Victor said. 'You spend too much time with them.'

'You're probably right, Maestro,' I said. 'That's always been my problem, though, hasn't it? I look for causes and they wind up with me in a romp. Makes you wonder about my . . . motivation, doesn't it?'

'If you want a more interesting subject, tell me about that new friend of yours,' Victor said. 'Have you finished with her yet?'

'Why? You interested?'

'Of course not. She is far too young.'

'Oh, that's right. You never gave it a second thought. She's out of your league, chum. In this country, as of last Friday, she's out of everyone's league. Except one, of course.'

'And by that you mean yourself. Fleen, you can be so selfish.'

'No, Maestro, I don't mean myself.'

'Pardonnez-moi, m'sieur.' A waiter was at my shoulder, bending slightly at the waist and speaking Spanish-accented French in my ear. 'There is the telephone for you, m'sieur.'

'Well bring it over,' I said.

'Pardon, m'sieur, but the gentleman he say for you to speak at the bar.'

'What gentleman?'

'He did not say, m'sieur.'

'Oh shit!' I said by way of excusing myself.

'Mr Flynn?' asked a familiar voice. 'This is the Economic Liaison Office. Your car is ready for you now.'

'My car? Is that you, Dwight?'

'Sir, if you take the rear exit you will see a brown Buick with our men waiting for you.'

'Dwight, it is you, isn't it?' It didn't actually sound like Dwight's voice, but it was certainly his manner of speaking.

'I suggest you do it right now. Don't hang up, just walk away from the phone and go directly to the rear exit.'

'What is all this? I'm having a nice leisurely Sunday lunch.'

'Yes, I'm sorry to interrupt you, sir, but this is important. We are ready for you now. Don't return to your table, don't speak to your friends. Don't hang up and go quickly. Do you understand?'

'No I don't. What . . .'

'I'm hanging up now. Go quickly.'

The line went dead. I stared at the handpiece waiting for an explanation. Was my romp not over yet? I looked at Victor still pontificating and Barry still politely listening. Snowball came to the end of his song, whatever it was. I decided to do what I was told, to go out the back to the car and sort out what on earth was going on. The others could a wait a few minutes while I did that.

The Buick was where I was told it would be, waiting in the alley behind the kitchens with the engine running and three men inside. A back door opened and I bent down to see who was behind it. 'Well, what a surprise, it's Toto.'

As I expected, Dwight Dodd was in the back seat. In front were two beefy marine types in civilian suits and regulation haircuts. 'Get in,' he said.

'Look, what's all this about, chum? Haven't you finished with me?'

'Get in.'

'I'm not getting anywhere. What do you want?'

The front passenger door opened and one of the marine types stepped out, took a grip on my arm and forced me into the car while the other hand protected my head. The door was closed, the marine resumed his seat and the car drew away.

'Embassy responsibilities extend to kidnapping citizens, do they?' I said. 'I am still a citizen, aren't I? You haven't cancelled me?'

Dwight's attention was fixed on the road ahead. 'Take route B,' he said to the driver.

'What's route B?' I said. 'Where are we going?'

'Slow down,' Dwight said. 'Take it nice and slow.'

'How long is this going to take, whatever it is? I was in the middle of my lunch. My friends will think I've run out on them.'

They pulled into the traffic moving briskly along La Rampa. 'Keep it under thirty,' said Dwight.

'Look here,' I said. 'Fuck your bloody directions. What the hell is going on?'

Finally Dwight turned to face me. 'The bloody directions are for your own good.' He looked through the back window at the traffic. 'Castro knows about Renate.'

'What does that mean? Is she in trouble?'

'It means *you* are in trouble.'

'Just a minute, what do you mean he knows? He knows she's working for you?'

'No. He knows about yesterday. About you.'

'About me? What about me?'

'About you . . . and her.'

I was suddenly swamped with pins and needles. I could feel my face tingling and my cheeks flush. It was a long time since I had felt this kind of discomfort. Embarrassment, that was what it seemed to be. And it wasn't because Fidel knew. After all, that was the idea. It was because good old stand-up Dwight knew. I felt I had broken some code of honour, let the boy scouts down.

'You can't go back to the hotel,' Dwight said. 'We're taking you to the embassy. You'll be safe there.'

'Safe from what?'

'I don't think you appreciate the position you're in.'

'Is this about what Renate said? That I'm supposed to be some sort of witness?'

It was the first time I had seen Dwight unsure of what would happen next. 'She told you that?'

'She said they expected me to report on their trials.'

Dwight frowned and stroked his chin. Once again I imagined I could hear the ticking of his mind. 'She shouldn't have told you that.'

'Broken her professional confidentiality, has she? Maybe she had her reasons. Maybe she cares about me, have you thought of that? Some folks do, you know.' Dwight didn't answer. 'Have they started? The trials, is that what this is about?'

'Partly.'

'Partly? What's the other part?'

'We can't afford to have a US citizen involved in their kangaroo court in any capacity. There's going to be a bloodbath.'

'No, I don't believe that.'

'It's started already.'

'And I don't believe that. I've spent time with these people. I don't think you understand them. I saw them hand all their prisoners over to the Red Cross. People like that don't have . . . *bloodbaths*.'

'If I could, Mr Flynn, I'd take you out to the sports stadium where it's all happening and show you the blood on the wall.'

'No, not Fidel. I still don't believe you.'

'He's leaving it to his brother. Castro himself, and Guevara, they are too smart. They've washed their hands of it. Your name will be on the list, I suspect.'

'What list?'

'Well, what would you call it? Enemies list . . . death list, I suppose.'

For the first time since my troubles with the IRS began I was truly glad to be a US citizen. To be safe inside a US car with two US marines who looked like they could handle anything that came along, on my way to the US embassy with its big metal gates and ironclad protection. I lit a cigarette and drew the comforting smoke deep into my lungs. Whatever damage that smoke was doing, and I'd been told it was doing much, it was worth it. I looked at Dwight, still casting his eye over the traffic on the Malecon. 'Jack Warner used to say with Flynn you forgive a lot. He used to tell everyone that. I'm really harmless, you know.'

'I guess you've never played your little games with people like these,' Dwight said. 'Would Jack Warner cut off your head with a machete?'

Such a violent image from the lips of a boy scout. It was as hard to accept as Fidel with a firing squad. 'How worried should we be about Renate?'

'She can handle herself. She's professional.'

'And I'm an amateur, is that what you mean?'

'Everyone's a professional at something, aren't they. We just have different jobs. Right now ours is to get you out of the country.'

'How, in a diplomatic bag?'

'Something like that,' Dwight said. 'You're lucky. You're getting out while you're ahead. A lot of people in this country won't be so fortunate.'

'What am I ahead of?'

'Ahead of the game, Mr Flynn. You're ahead of the game.'

'More games. You're always talking about games. This whole situation, this revolution, what is it to you guys? Just one of your war games?'

'No, the situation here is no game. It's deadly serious. You, on the other hand . . . I'm talking about the game where the old stag butts heads with the young buck. Have you ever seen that in your *National Geographic*? You've won. Congratulations to the old stag. But Castro, he doesn't like to lose. That's why we're getting you out of the country.'

'You've got it all wrong, chum. It's no game, Fidel and me. It's a scrap. And in a scrap the only way to clinch it is to go for the balls, don't you know.' I wound down the window to flick my cigarette. Dwight quickly leant over to stop me and wound it up again. He took the cigarette and stubbed it out in the ashtray.

'Cuba's no game either,' the boy scout said. 'And you want to know why? You only have to look at a map. You take a good look next time. Take a look at Cuba, and take a look at the US. This island is like a sword, a scimitar, with its point right up against our soft underbelly. We can't afford to have anything but a friendly hand in control of that sword, you know what I'm saying? There's a new hand on it now and we're not sure if that's a right hand or a left hand. You know what the left is in Latin, don't you? Sinister. That's the kind of hand we have to make sure doesn't take control of the sword. A left one. Cuba's had lots of coups and revolutions and wars, but on the whole, we've been happy with the way they've sorted themselves out. This one might be different, we don't know yet. That's why there's a Renate. You did the right thing by us there, and we'll do the right thing by you with the IRS and wherever else we can help out. As for what happened yesterday, it happened. You can't plan with absolute precision when there are human beings involved. We'll forget about it. I can't speak for Renate, of course. You can ask her yourself one day, when this is all over.'

'When what's all over?'

'The revolution. Haven't you heard? This is just the beginning. Castro said so himself.'

The young American had always been so matter-of-fact. Even when he was attempting to put the fear of God in me, the menace had an undeniable honesty to it. Now it was just propaganda. I felt like I was listening to a script reading from one of my flag-waving World War Two efforts – *Objective Burma*, or *Edge of Darkness*, or any of them.

'Yesterday was part of the plan, wasn't it?' I said. 'It was part of your game, not mine. I was just your pawn. You wanted to get Fidel jealous, was that the plan?'

'Are you talking about your own plan now?'

'Don't try and turn this on me,' I said, but I didn't think I was very convincing.

'Mr Flynn, you won. You had your ... what was it? Your scrap, and you won. If what you just said were true, that would be cheating, wouldn't it?'

There was not a trace of a smile on his lips, no note of irony in his voice. Cheating was for degenerates, for double-dealers, for persons who lacked moral fibre. Stanford men like Dwight could not abide cheating.

'You want there to be a bloodbath, don't you?' I said. 'That'd suit your purposes. Who's going to report it for you? Is that what Renate's doing? Is that what she's really up to? She's not American, that's convenient, isn't it?'

'You'll be in Miami tonight. Find yourself a good bar and get yourself drunk. Forget about Cuba for a while. We'll inform your colleagues and help them in any way we can. We'll see if we can't get Miss Aadland back to you quickly. I'm looking forward to seeing your movie. *Assault of the Rebel Girls*. Sounds like my kind of movie.'

27
Front page challenge.
Toronto, 13 January 1959

'Thank you and good evening everyone,' Fred Davis said as the applause of the studio audience died down. 'Well panel, I hope you have your thinking caps on. We've got, I would say, a difficult story for you to track down tonight on Front Page Challenge, and I would certainly say an intriguing one.'

I could hear the compere from behind the curtain that screened me from the stage and the audience. The production assistant smiled at me. 'Won't be long now,' she said. 'You must be used to this.' I was, of course. I had been on so many of these mystery guest panel shows in the past few years, in fact any TV show prepared to pay me, although this was my first in Canada. And never before at such short notice. Just two days ago I was enjoying a quiet Sunday lunch in balmy Havana, looking forward to a leisurely return to Port Antonio, and here I was in the middle of a bleak Toronto winter about to be put under the microscope. It was a pity – a crying financial shame – that our picture wasn't ready for release. I'd received so much publicity over my little Cuban escapade on both sides of the Atlantic that I probably could have settled my dispute with the IRS without the assistance of Dwight Dodd. Who was to know everyone would make such a song and dance over a lousy 'wounded' leg?

'Let's get right down to business now,' Fred said, 'and first of all have a look at our mystery headline, and then we'll all meet tonight's front page challenger.'

'Okay,' said the girl. She took me by the arm and led me through the curtain. 'They're just showing viewers at home the headlines and the story now.'

As I stepped onto the stage the audience buzzed and burst into applause. 'At least I've still got some fans in this part of the world,' I said, offering a modest wave.

'Oh, I should say so,' the girl said.

She led me up the steps to a seat behind a high bench, sat me down and adjusted my jacket. 'Knock 'em dead,' she said. Below me were the tops of four heads at a longer bench and, in front of us all, the audience maintaining their enthusiastic applause.

Fred welcomed me with a smile from the compere's desk. 'Okay panel, let's see what you can do with our story. Obviously our challenger is hidden behind you. I will tell you though that an international story is in the offing. Gordon, would you start us off, please?'

'The international story concerns a person, does it, in politics, sport or the entertainment field?' asked a balding head below.

I cleared my throat. I always disguised my voice in these shows. 'Well, yes,' I said in a campy falsetto.

'Well yes,' Gordon echoed. 'Is it entertainment?'

'No, it's work,' I squeaked.

'But you are in the entertainment field, are you?'

'Well . . .' I added a coy little giggle for effect. 'In a way.'

'In a way. Would I recognise you?'

'You might,' I giggled. The audience loved it.

'Are you an American?'

'Yes.'

'And did this event happen in the United States?'

'No.'

'Are you a man?'

Now the audience joined me in the giggle. 'Well, I have to think that over, but generally speaking, yes.'

'You are a man. And did this happen in New York City?'

'No.'

'Did it happen in Hollywood?'

'No.'

'Did it happen in any city?'

'Yes.'

'Pass to Toby,' said Gordon.

'Did it happen on land?' wondered a younger female voice below.

For the new panellist I thought I might mix things up a little. 'Well yes, I'd say it did,' I said in a broad Australian accent. 'I'd say it happened on land.' And I added a loud sniff, like a sheep shearer between beers.

'You do a very good English accent,' Toby said. 'Did this happen in England?'

'No, it didn't.'

'Did it happen in a continent beginning with A?'

'Nope.'

'Scott,' Toby said, passing the baton.

'Did it happen in Cuba?' asked the third panellist.

'Yep.'

'Are you Errol Flynn?'

'Oh God . . .' I said as the audience rushed to applaud. He had got me in one.

Eventually the compere appealed for calm. 'Yes, you've got it, Scott. So what would the headline be?'

'It would be Flynn takes Havana,' said Scott, and I hoped this would never be seen in Cuba, but the audience thought it a wonderful joke. 'Single-handed again, I bet,' added Scott, and he probably enjoyed my wince, too.

'Oh well, that war was going on too long,' I said. 'I just had to straighten it out.' It was one of my standard retorts to one of my many standard taunts.

'Castro's victory over Batista, of course was the headline,' Fred Davis said to camera. 'And as you well know our challenger is Mr Errol Flynn.'

The production assistant climbed up to me and showed the way down to a chair in front of a microphone. 'Can I smoke?' I asked her.

'You can do anything you want,' she said.

'I just need something for my hands to do,' I said, fixing a cigarette into my holder.

She smiled and gave me a little flutter of the eyelashes. 'We'll be taping again in just a moment.'

A camera was rolled into position in front of me and slowly moved in as the audience was encouraged to applaud once again. Not too close, I thought to myself. Wouldn't want to scare all my Canadian fans.

'Mr Flynn,' the fourth panellist began, 'we got conflicting reports here about your part in the revolution. The first reports said that you fought side by side with the rebels, and then we had a report quoting Mr Castro saying he never heard of you. What is the truth?'

We live, we die, and always sooner than we'd planned, that's the only truth. But of course I didn't say that. 'Ah, well the truth is as Mr Castro said the other night. He said he'd been asked this question himself many times, and that I was certainly with him. He said this on the late news on Sunday, I think it was. As for fighting with the rebels, I didn't pick up anything more dangerous than a ballpoint pen. I didn't consider myself a belligerent. On the contrary, an observer and a correspondent. I'm awfully sorry, by the way gentlemen, if there are any newspaper people here . . . if they'll stay out of my racket, I'll stay out of theirs.'

The audience chuckled and I started to relax. I sucked on my holder and waited for the next question. It came from Gordon.

'Errol, there was a fellow down there named George of the NBC and . . .'

'Not George Raft?' I said. I was feeling more comfortable by the minute.

'No, but this fellow went on the air to say that you were there, and he was with you, and he guaranteed everything you said. So he backed you up.'

Good old Gordon, I thought. Must send him a box of cigars. 'Well, I'm happy to hear that, because it's quite true.'

'Why exactly did you go to Cuba?' Toby asked.

For a romp. Chasing a cause and turning it all into a romp, my particular talent, don't you know. But I didn't say that, either. 'Well, first of all, it was very difficult to get there. And number two, I didn't know what to expect. But this man, Fidel Castro, exceeded every expectation I had. You see things in a man under duress, and this man will rank in history with some of the greats.'

Toby nodded and appeared to accept my complete avoidance of the question. 'I was just wondering,' she said, 'how you justify his executions without trial.'

Christ, such a sweet voice for a piranha! Dwight and his buddies had got to the Canadian press, no doubt about it. I thought it best to show no hesitation. 'No, I cannot justify that, because I've only read about it in the newspapers. I only know that he told me personally time and again that the people who had done such atrocious things to the Cuban people would be given justice that they did not really deserve. Now, there are radical elements in his movement, I suppose, and in the time of revolution you can't control wild people. I know that he himself, and his brother Raul, and his little old lady mother, who's a doll, she really is . . . they don't believe in summary retribution.'

How long was this Canadian Inquisition? I wanted to be back in the green room with the vodka that was waiting on ice. They'd got Zubrowka in just for me and I could smell that sweet, sweet grass. Perhaps I shouldn't have had quite so many before the show. Perhaps I should have expected their questions. It was all over the papers, after all. Perhaps I should have prepared my answers, and then perhaps I wouldn't sound like a blundering apologist. And to think I had presumed to lecture Fidel about dealing with the press.

'Mr Flynn, if I may interrupt you,' Scott said. 'You obviously have a very warm feeling for these people, and you were also in Spain during the civil war there. Do you notice any similarities between the spirit in Spain and the spirit in Cuba?'

If they were going to ask the commie question, they would have to ask it themselves. I wasn't volunteering anything on the commie question. This wasn't some Washington witch-hunt. Let everyone figure that one out for themselves.

'No, not at all. This is a popular movement. The people of Cuba were trodden underfoot. If you could just see for yourself the horrible things that regime did to its own people you would understand why they rose up with Fidel Castro, and why they fought for five and a half years. Nobody seems to realise that this has been going on for five and a half years.'

Fred Davis rescued me. 'Mr Flynn, thank you very much. We certainly appreciate your coming to our program tonight and hearing first hand your report on what has been going on in Cuba.'

I was led away and the audience, at least, was generous about my performance. 'You were great,' the production assistant said. I could get myself into more trouble here, I thought.

In the green room I was on to my second vodka before Fred Davis joined me. 'That wasn't so hard, was it?' he said.

'No,' I agreed. 'Kind of like *What's My Line* with tougher questions.'

'Not so tough, you did fine.'

'Yes, but . . . nobody ever believes me when I say I didn't really win the war single-handed. But it's true, I didn't.'

'Not even Burma?'

'No, I had a couple of pals help me out.'

'Tonight was so quick,' Fred said. 'Scott pinned you down with one question.' He hailed one of the panellists across the room. 'Hey, Scott, get over here. We had to stretch it out,' he said to me. 'That's why your Q and A went on a bit. You were about the shortest challenge we've had. Not even two minutes.'

'So, no sixty-four thousand dollars?'

'Not even a brass ring or a kewpie doll. You're too famous.' The panellist joined us. 'This is Scott Young. He calls sports.'

I shook his hand. 'Sports? You could've fooled me.'

'Well, I watch the regular news, too,' said Scott. 'Say, that late news story you were talking about, the Castro one. Is that the one I saw? That guy gives interviews from his bed in his striped pyjamas.'

'Fidel's no ordinary leader, I think that part's clear.'

'You bet. He looked like a convict.'

'Anyway, he made the CBS news at last.'

'I think it was on NBC,' Scott said. 'You know, you missed your calling, my friend. You beat everyone to that story.'

'Just a matter of being there, isn't it?'

'Tell me this,' said Fred. 'Now they're saying that hundreds of Cubans are fleeing to Miami. Is that true?'

'Well, from what I saw in Miami, I'd say it was thousands.'

'So what are they afraid of?' asked Scott. 'Some say this Castro, he's Attila the Hun, and others that he's Robin Hood. What do you think?'

'Hey, fellas . . . the show's over, isn't it?'

'No, I was just . . .'

'I'm biased,' I said. 'I guess I know Robin Hood a little better than I know Attila the Hun.'

Scott laughed and went to get himself another drink. His place was taken by Toby, the only woman on the panel, club soda in hand. She had fine features, bobbed dark hair and gleaming teeth, and looked like she was the one who had just arrived from Hollywood. Without the makeup she shone, lighting up the room of sober-suited middle-aged men. 'Are you a reporter, too?' I asked her. 'I suppose you've got your own column.'

'Gordon's the one with the column,' she said. 'I'm an actress, although only in television.'

'Only television? So am I these days. I should have known, with your looks.'

She covered her smile with a sip of club soda. 'Is this the notorious Errol Flynn charm?'

'No, I thought you must be a newspaper woman. You asked the probing questions.'

'In like Flynn, was I?' she said with an innocent face, causing Fred to splutter on his whisky.

'Yes, that's what I mean,' I said. As pleasant as she was, I wasn't going to let her get away with that. If she was an actress then I knew just how vulnerable she was. And if what she said during the show was anything to go by, she had as much idea about accents as Bette Davis. 'But just so you know I'm not trying to charm you, you'll have to work on your accents. That was no English accent I put on out there.'

'It wasn't?'

'No, it was Australian. I do a good one, being one myself. Anyway, you shouldn't be an actress. Don't you know actors are just trying to be someone else? You look happy in your own skin.'

'Might I say . . . so do you. Whatever your accent.'

'Oh . . .' I didn't know what to say to that. No one had ever said it to me before, and I hadn't thought it since I arrived in Hollywood all those years ago. Fred made his excuses and left us standing in the corner alone.

'So what is going on down there in Cuba?' she said.

'Just another revolution. You know what these banana republics are like.'

'Yes, it seems to never end. Is it dangerous?'

'In what sense? Why does everyone assume something sinister about these people?'

'I mean for us. Or for the States especially.'

'Well, I'm told it is, but what would I know? The more I think I know, the more I know I don't. If you know what I mean. I'm told they're jabbing us annoyingly in our soft underbelly. What do you say to something like that? Does every country have a soft underbelly? I seem to remember the British said that about the Turks way back, and then someone else said it about Italy in the next war. Or was it Greece? If every country has one, then that would make the US the soft underbelly of Canada. Does that make sense?'

'Not to me,' she said with a smile that suggested she appreciated the logic.

'You know what I really think . . . I think that everyone's getting hot under the collar about Cuba because what they've got down there is a new generation of young people who've told the old people they're fed up with the way they do things. I think that our own old people are scared that that sort of thing might be catching.'

'What, of a revolution in America? College boys taking up arms, or the beatniks, is that what you're suggesting is in the stars?'

'No, I'm just . . . but you know what . . . many of Castro's rebels are students. Perhaps as many as . . .' I caught her brow beginning to knot in a sceptical frown. 'But what do I know about politics? I'm just an actor. These revolutions, they're always from the bottom, have you noticed that? The have-nots want what the haves have. In Cuba now there are a lot of haves who've suddenly been made have-nots. The next one might be from the top, then we'll see what happens.'

'You sound like you know something no one else does.'

'Are you probing again? You sure you're not a reporter?'

'Definitely,' she said. 'And I'm happily married in this skin of mine, too.'

'Now, why did you say that?'

'Oh, you know . . . just wanted to avoid any confusion.'

That night I avoided any confusion and had dinner in my room in the hotel. I watched my performance on *Front Page Challenge* while polishing off the room bar, and then gazed out over the Toronto skyline. It was so disciplined, so hygienic, so cold. The hotel was quiet, the streets below calm. The television carried news of traffic snarls and Hollywood divorces. The prime minister spoke of taxation reviews and hospital building. How far it all was from the Sierra Maestra. I wondered what Beverly was doing in Havana and when Dwight might get around to spiriting her out. I wondered what Renate was doing. Was she on to her next mission, or was it still Fidel? Dwight said she could handle herself. I hoped that for once he knew what he was talking about. The Wonder of Renate. I knew I'd get over my wild infatuation. The wilder it burns the faster it burns out. There had been so many months of inactivity that when I fell into bed with her it was almost like falling for the first time, when the flush of new passion hoodwinks your brain into thinking it's something more. Like a callow schoolboy shown the ropes by a crafty domestic helper. Other than Beverly, Renate was my first for months and I was never in the habit of abstinence, unprepared for its effects. I reminded myself she was just one of those well-known means to an end.

I missed Beverly. Yet another unfamiliar sensation. It was her legs that first attracted me on the set when Gene Kelly introduced us – long lithe legs and slender ankles. Ankles and legs only last so long. Assets of any kind only last so long, as I knew myself only too well. Lili Damita was one of the most beautiful women in the world, but that didn't last. Beverly had more loyalty and integrity in one of her painted fingernails than Lili had in her whole once-gorgeous body. *Diligo ergo sum.*

I wondered if it were true what Toby said, that I looked happy. I didn't feel happy. Perhaps it was too soon to feel anything. I would have to weigh up these months, to put a little distance between Cuba and wherever else in the world I might go to put the whole episode into perspective. I had always hated looking in the mirror, but perhaps this year would be a year for reflection. I drew the curtain and didn't bother to change out of my clothes, just lay in the middle of the queen-size bed and, for a start, reflected on why I wasn't lying there with the production assistant with the twinkle in her eye. I turned out the lights. 'See Canada and die,' I said.

28
Tell him it was just a game.
New York, 23 April 1959

The gathering in Central Park was more carnival than political rally. This many people didn't go to political rallies in America. Only baseball attracted this sort of crowd. Thousands of rugged-up happy faces shone under racks of floodlights and trees yet untouched by spring. Cuban flags and 26 JULIO banners waved, and parents lifted their little *barbudos* – children in olive green *rebelde* fancy dress, complete with Castro beards – above the heads for the photographers. It was quieter and more controlled than Santiago or Havana or any of the dozens of other towns we had passed through on the triumphal march through Cuba, but I sensed the same blend of expectation and adoration, although dialled down for the American market. I stood on the edge of the crowd under a hat and behind my false nose and listened to a different Fidel than any that had delivered a balcony speech in that heady first week of victory. There was no haranguing, no fist thumping, no five hours of rambling improvisation – dialled down for the American market. The audience was full of Cubans as well as Dominicans, agitating for their own Caribbean revolution, but most of the speech was delivered in English for the benefit of the press. He spoke of 'the great American desire for a humanist democracy', and I imagined the eyes of the great American press glazing over. 'Freedom with bread, bread without terror,' he said, which got the crowd cheering. Expectations for a chicken in every pot had been scaled back. He found regular opportunities to repeat 'The Cuban revolution is not, never was and never will be communist', like a well-rehearsed mantra, and in perfect English amongst what was otherwise a rather engaging mangling of the language.

A scuffle broke out not far from the podium and he had to pause as police descended amid screams and shouts in a Babel of languages and dragged a man away. All in a night's work for Fidel and the fuss barely broke his stride. 'The Cuban revolution is not, never was and never will be communist.'

I left before he finished and took a cab down to the midtown hotel where they were staying. Seventh Avenue was a parking lot. People were spread right across the road from sidewalk to sidewalk and they didn't look like they were going anywhere. I asked the cabbie what was on at the Garden tonight. 'Nuttin,' he said. 'Ain't you heard? The Reds have invaded Manhattan.'

That's when I realised the centre of attention wasn't Madison Square Garden at all but the hotel across the street. There were so many protesters, police and reporters that I had to walk the last block. The sidewalk was littered with pamphlets. I picked one up: 'Cuba is the Hungary of America', it said next to a lurid cartoon. It was difficult to work out if it was pro or con Castro, but the cartoon of Fidel with devil horns left no doubt. It seemed like half of Miami's Cuban exiles had come to picket the Statler-Hilton. Castro was both a Commie and a Dictator, according to the more succinct of the signs, and they carried more lurid cartoons of bearded monsters, wailing babies and firing squads. All of Havana's cartoonists must have been chased out of Cuba.

The lobby bustled like the Havana Hilton after the victory. There were no machine guns or mortars, but there were armed rebels lounging around, officials rushing, reporters pushing and shoving and staff besieged behind their desks. I searched among the beards for the familiar face I was after and then took a position in the bar that gave me a view over the circus, and waited.

I was nursing my third vodka when the flashbulbs began popping out on the street. A surge of bodies and turmoil swept through the revolving doors and across the lobby. At its centre was a core of olive green caps, one of which must have been Fidel. All the lobby elevators were called and filled with olive green, and the doors closed and slowly the shouting subsided and the crowd drifted out onto the street and into the bar. Eventually, the rebel I was waiting to see came through the front door. It was the weary walk that I recognised rather than the face. He had shaved off his beard, a true revolutionary act. He looked exhausted and struggled with a briefcase stuffed so full it couldn't be closed and flapped open with his every heavy step. I reached him in front of the elevators. 'Well, look who it is,' I said jauntily. *'La voz de la revolucion.'*

Carlos' tired features stirred in stages into a happy smile. 'Senor Errol . . .'

I pumped him on the shoulder and cleared my throat. *'Aqui Radio Rebelde,'* I announced, cupping a hand over my ear. *'La voz de la Sierra Maestra.* I never could get the rest of it.'

Carlos placed his case carefully at his feet and shook both my hands. 'It is good to see you, senor.'

'I saw you at Central Park up on the podium. I thought I'd wait for you here.'

'He made the good speech, no?'

'Yes, the good speech. What was that disturbance?'

'They say a man with the bomb.' Carlos shrugged. 'Who knows, senor?'

'And look at you . . . a secret agent now.'

His hand went to his shaven chin as he smiled ruefully. 'Everyone in Cuba now wants the beard. To not have the beard, this is to be the rebel now.' He looked over his shoulder and then leaned into my ear. 'In the Sierra it was okay to be the saint. Now we are just men, no?' And then he arched his eyebrows and laughed like he was astonished at what he had just heard.

'Well, I'm glad to see you haven't lost your sense of humour. Listen, can we have a little talk? Have you got five minutes for an old *companero*?'

'*Si*, of course.'

I led him back to the bar. I ordered drinks and found a quiet booth in the corner. 'This is quite a show you chaps are putting on. New York seems to think Fidel is Elvis Presley.'

Carlos shook his head. 'Is crazy, senor. Two days ago we arrive on the train from Washington at the Penn Station. *Mi dios!* So many people. Police, they must make the special convoy to take us to the hotel. This hotel, senor. It is only . . .' He shook his head again. 'If I stand at the front door I can spit to the Penn Station. New York in April, it is like Havana in January.'

'You know, Fidel once asked me to help make him famous. Make him famous like me, is what he wanted. He left me behind long ago.'

'He has the help, you know. The American company, they tell him what to say, to smile, always to smile and to make big with the cigar.'

'Is that so?' I said. 'A PR company, is that what you mean?'

'PR, *si*. Propaganda, Fidel say. He is good, no? He eat the hot dog and the hamburger for the photographer, has the cigar for the reporter. He knows where to go, what to say. I say here in New York, he should see the Museum of Modern Art, he say no. He say zoo, Yankee Stadium.'

'I always said he was a quick learner. I saw a picture of him with Nixon.'

'Oh, Nixon, mayor, Secretary of State, Princeton, Harvard . . . he is busy, all the time they want him.'

'Eisenhower?'

Carlos grimaced and bobbed his head side to side. 'The president, no. They say he plays at the golf somewhere. But Fidel they put him on the television, *Meet the Press* and Ed Murrow and Ed Sullivan. You have seen him, no? He make the speech to meeting of women lawyers.' He grabbed my arm and lowered his voice. 'They love him, senor. The women, even the lawyer women, they swoon for him. That is the word, no? They say that in the *New York Times* . . . swoon. That one I had to look it up.'

The waiter arrived with the drinks. Carlos played with his swizzle stick for a moment. 'Everywhere we go, they ask about *communista*. The reporters they ask every day. Fidel he say it is not the red *revolucion*, it is the olive green *revolucion*. Still they ask. They ask about the cigar and they ask about the *communista*. These two things, always. The cigar, this is just the fun. But the *communista* . . . America has the obsession with this, no?'

'It's the red menace, sport. It's the longest running show in town.' I took a drink and looked Carlos in the eye. 'Look, I want to see him. Can you get me in to see him? I don't want long, just an opportunity to clear the air, you know what I mean? Could you do that for me?'

'Senor, not you also. You are not to ask him about the *communista* also?'

'No, nothing like that. I couldn't give a damn about that. I just want to . . . I think he's got the wrong idea about me.'

'You wish to tell him he is wrong? Fidel is never wrong. He will not see you to tell him he is wrong.'

'No, I don't want to tell him that . . . Look, I think when I left Havana there was a misunderstanding. I just want to clear it up. I like him, you know. I'd like to think he was a friend.'

'I think he is, senor. I never hear about this. He never say to me that you are not the friend.'

'You remember Renate Spinoza? You remember her? The interpreter, you got her an introduction to him, remember?'

Carlos' shoulders slumped and face descended again into the weariness he had displayed in the lobby. 'Oh . . . I think I understand why you think you are not the friend. I forget about you and her. You take her to him, no? I forget that.'

'Well, I'd like to forget it, too. But I can't. I feel responsible for what happened.'

'Senor, it happened after you are gone. Fidel never has . . .'

'Yes, but it started with me. All these rumours now, whenever I hear them . . . well, you know.'

'Senor, if that is what you wish to speak to Fidel, I suggest to you no. He has much anger for this. The newspapers in Miami, they print so many of the lies.'

'Carlos, if anyone understands that, it's me. I had to go through a long and costly trial once, headlines, whispering . . . well, I never really got over it. Rape is a terrible word, the shame it carries, it'll haunt you for life. But the newspapers love to print it. It sells ink. And it's so easy to start rumours. I don't know if Renate started it herself or someone else did it for her, Fidel's enemies, who knows? I have my own ideas. I know none of it's true, but it's all over the place, everyone's talking about it. Young German girl, rape, abortion. The papers love that word even more. They whisper that one, whisper it so softly it's worse than shouting it from the rooftops. I've got an idea where it's coming from, and I think Fidel should hear me out.'

Carlos shook his head slowly. 'Senor, Fidel, if he hears this, just say the first word, he will make them throw you from the door.'

'Listen, do you remember when the papers here in America started calling your trials down there a bloodbath? Do you remember that?'

'Oh, senor ...'

'I do. It was precisely twenty-four hours after I heard someone use that precise word in Havana. Bloodbath, rape and abortion ... these are words someone has been trying to pin on Fidel, and I think I know ...'

'Senor, it makes no use. Fidel he does not listen to me. I tell you, I say museum, he say Yankee Stadium. I say yes, he say no. I say black, he say white. Before if I say to him, see Senor Errol, he see you. No more. He listen to no one now he make himself the prime minister. You don't know, he has changed. Before he say no, he no want the power, now I see he want it all. Even Raul, his brother, when they talk they shout only. If Raul is not his brother I think Fidel he shoot him. Che he send away, do something else. He listen to someone one day, minister this, minister that, never listen to him next day. Only one he listen to one day and next day is Chico. He is the only one, I think.'

'Chico?'

'*Si*, his *pistolita*. Ever since that woman, that young woman ... I cannot say her name.'

'Renate?'

'*Si*, that one. Ever since all that trouble, Fidel, he go crazy. All the time he worry about assassination. Everyone want to kill him, he thinks. Chico he guard him night and day. He listen to Chico because Chico he tell him the cigar it will explode, the pineapple it will explode, the chicken it have the poison. Fidel now he burn the underwear. Chico tell him there is the powder in the underwear, so no laundry, he burn every day.'

'Are you saying Renate ...'

'Please, senor, we must not talk about this.' He picked up his drink, looked at it, and put it back down.

'Could Chico get me in to see him?' I said. 'Chico knows me. He knows I'm harmless. Could you ask Chico to do that? You still have influence with him at least, surely.'

Carlos sighed. 'Maybe senor, I do not know. Maybe. When do you want this?'

'Now. Now would be good.'

'Okay senor, I try. I think maybe no, but I try. You wait.'

Carlos was gone for half an hour, time enough for me to calm my nerves with two double vodkas. When he returned he was shrugging his shoulders, but smiling.

'Chico he try. I tell him, he say he try.'

'Ah, that's good, that's good. Trying for tonight, you mean?'

'*Si*, for tonight he try. We wait.'

Carlos' Bacardi had lost its ice and its fizz. I grabbed it and got to my feet. 'I'll get you a fresh one of these,' I said, and took it over to the bar. When I rejoined him at the table I was carrying two drinks, and swinging from one fist I had my 26 JULIO armband, red and black with strings attached. 'Look what I found the other day,' I said. 'I wore it around for weeks when I got back to Jamaica.'

'You wear it when you see Fidel. He like to see you wear it, I am sure.'

'So is he still as popular as ever? People still call his name out in the street, want to kiss his beard?'

'*Si*, Fidel, in Miami he is the dictator, in Havana they cheer. It is the way, no? In Miami they lose, in Havana they win. There are more in Havana. And you, *companero*, how are you?'

'Am I still your *companero*? If everything's changing day to day down there ...'

'If you are in Havana, maybe it change for you also. But you are *companero* in New York, eh.'

'So was I on the list?'

'What list?'

'The list of people to be put on trial in January.'

'I know no list. Why you? Why you put on the trial?'

'I was told that I was on the list. That's why I left so quickly.'

'Oh . . . I hear you leave for the film you make.'

I nodded and drank my vodka. 'Anyway . . . to answer your question, I'm okay. The doctors have given me a year to live, but they're always doing that.'

'You are here to see the doctor in New York?'

'No, the doctors are in LA. I'm just here doing a job for *Goodyear Theatre*. You know it? It's a TV show. And also some scenes for our Cuba movie. I go back to LA tomorrow.'

'Your Cuba movie, it is finished?'

'Not yet. It's coming along. Post-production is slow and boring, not like location shooting. Certainly not like location shooting in the middle of a revolution. They were good times, Carlos. I didn't think so at the time, mind you. And neither did my back.' I held it with both hands and stretched to make my point. 'I never thought I'd say this, but I hold a certain fondness for hammocks.'

Carlos stroked his shaven chin and said, 'We all have that, senor. We have our soft bed and we dream of our hammock in the Sierra.'

'It seems so long ago now . . . a lot of water under the bridge. We're using some of the footage to cut a documentary together as well. A documentary about the revolution. Do you know Victor Malenkoff?' Carlos shook his head. 'No? Well, he's left Havana now. But he got his hands on some good footage himself. He said he got it through your people, so I thought you may have met him, but Victor has his own way of doing things, I guess. We're thinking of calling it *The Truth About the Cuban Revolution*.'

'Ah ... and what truth will you tell?'

'Well, like I said, I hold great affection for those couple of months. I think you'll like what we're doing. I think Fidel will, too.'

'If that is so, you should tell him. It will be good for you when you see him. I think maybe you tell him you call it *The Truth About the Fidel Castro Revolution*, he like it even more, eh.'

'Good idea, chum, I'll tell him that.'

Carlos appeared to be relaxing under the gradual influence of the Bacardi. 'It will be good for him to see you,' he said with a comfortable smile. 'I show you something.' He heaved his stuffed briefcase up onto the seat beside him and reached inside to retrieve a thick hardcover book. He dropped it onto the table with a heavy thud. 'Jules Dubois, he write what he say is the truth also.' I turned it around to read the cover. *Fidel Castro: Liberator or Dictator?* 'Not all look at our revolution with the affection, senor,' said Carlos.

'Well, you know what they say, my friend, you can't trust a reporter.' I pushed the book aside. It was irrelevant. I looked around the bar, now jostling with newspaper men on stakeout. 'I used to come here to listen to Glenn Miller in the old days,' I said. 'It wasn't a Hilton then. It was the Hotel Pennsylvania. *Pennsylvania six five thousand*,' I sang. 'It's funny, you know. In some ways, those days don't seem as long ago as the Sierra Maestra. I don't mind saying, in fact I've told everyone, I had the time of my life in those couple of months. I haven't enjoyed myself so much since I was a young roustabout roaming the world, looking for adventure. I think I found something there, you know. I think I found that I was happy in my own skin. Someone said that to me after I came back, and I had to think about it for a while, but I think she's right. We all have our revolutions, don't we. It's never too late.'

Carlos stared wistfully at his glass. 'For us it was Havana,' he said. 'Havana it make the change. Who can say there would be such a change when we take Havana? In the Sierra, we know who we fight, we know the enemy. After Havana we must make the enemy. Without the enemy, no fight. Without the fight, no *revolucion*. Without the *revolucion* . . .' He shrugged. 'Some time I think the peace it is harder to win than the war, no? Some time it frighten the fighting man more. The hammock it can be easier to lie in than the soft bed.'

'So where does the *revolucion* go next? What's after New York?'

'We go to Texas, Canada, South America. Fidel he still make the victory parade. Maybe then he look for the new enemy. And you?'

'Back to LA, the old enemy. I've got a week in a sound booth to look forward to, doing voice-overs for our movie. It's boring, but necessary. And here comes my good friend, Chico.'

I jumped to my feet as the *pistolita* elbowed his way through the press of reporters. His olive green fatigues were clean and carried sharp creases, but otherwise he looked like he did at Maffo and Palma Soriano and Santiago – pistol on hip, knife on belt, and dark look on face. Carlos sat with his drink and barely looked up until Chico began speaking to him in Spanish. Their conversation went to and fro for a moment before Carlos sighed and nodded. 'It is unfortunate Fidel he say no.'

I looked to Chico for an explanation. 'But why . . . ah, *por que?*'

Carlos shrugged and answered for him. 'It is difficult, senor. I tell you so before. Maybe one day he . . .'

'*Digalo lo que companero Fidel dijo,*' Chico snapped at him.

'What did he say?' I asked.

'He say I must say to you what Fidel say to him.'

'What did Fidel say?'

'*Fidel asegurara que morira con sus botas en,*' Chico barked. He turned on his heel and strode back through the crowd.

'Well . . .?' I asked impatiently.

'He say he will make it so you die with your boots on.'

I turned to see Chico's back disappear. I sat down slowly and finished my drink. 'Fidel said that, did he? Not bloody Chico?'

'Fidel said that, senor. He say many things now he not mean. Today he say one thing, tomorrow the other. One day he forget all this.'

'Yes . . . well . . .' I picked up the 26 JULIO armband from the table, folded it and put it back in my pocket. 'One day maybe he will. You know, I never knew he was such a fan of my movies. Fancy that. He was probably just a teenager when he saw that one. Probably sat up the back of the Santiago picture palace with popcorn in one hand and some little senorita's tit in the other, dreaming that it was Olivia de Havilland's . . . and wishing he was me. He's not so different from an American after all, is he? Probably would have traded his best baseball bat and glove to be me up there on that screen with my tongue down sweet Olivia's throat. But what those kids never really understood about that was that my tongue never went down Olivia's throat. I never kissed her except for a cold hard cinema clinch or a happy birthday peck. Never fucked her. Just dressed up in my Colonel Custer outfit, or my Robin Hood, and played at fucking her. You tell that to Fidel when you see him. You tell him it was just a game.'

'I think senor, only you can tell him that. I cannot even remember what you mean.'

I had to laugh. I laughed and thumped the table. 'You're jolly well right, old chum. I'll tell him myself first chance I get. So . . . until then, should I spend the rest of my life looking over my shoulder, do you think?'

Carlos shrugged. 'All of us with Fidel, we all have the life looking over the shoulder. You, *companero*, I think maybe he never have the time for you.'

29
Last hurrah of the golden years.
Vancouver, 14 October 1959

I awoke early on that last day in the Hotel Georgia, my back so painful that I had been forced to spend a good part of the night on the hard floor. At least the nightmares were letting up. Beverly was still fast asleep, her long blonde hair straggling over her angel face. We had been in Vancouver for five days, had signed the deal for the sale of the yacht on the second day, and should have been gone by the third, but Vancouver wouldn't let me go. From the time we touched down from LA it had been one long party. The press met us at the airport and gushed when I gave them the scoop. I told them I would be playing Humbert Humbert to Beverly's Lolita, and it would be the most sensational movie of the year. Art imitating life, I said. So what if it was all a lie? You can't trust reporters anyway. They loved it when I clowned around with my friend George's bowler hat, their flashbulb's popping as I reprised the old 'That's What You Jolly Well Get' song and dance. With my back in the shape it was in the routine was stiffer than the 1943 original, but it was only Vancouver after all. I confirmed that it was from my cameo in *Thank Your Lucky Stars*, and added that the reason I was a lucky star was because while I was making that film I wasn't flying bombers over Germany or storming beaches in the Pacific. The same old lines, but Vancouver loved it. Familiarity hadn't bred contempt, not like LA. And not like New York since I had made a fool of myself on Jack Paar's TV show, draping myself in a Cuban flag, fencing with a walking stick, and showing off my famous revolutionary war wound. Too much vodka in the green room again that night.

On Saturday I signed over the *Zaca* to George, the biggest private sale of the biggest private yacht in the world. Signed over the last precious asset in my life. Putting pen to contract I said that it hurt, but it wouldn't kill me. George was an old pal and had some good ideas for the boat's future. He even wanted me to captain it on a sunken treasure expedition, which sounded like an idea for yet another bad movie, but what the heck, I was fifty now and adventures were hard to come by at that age.

We celebrated with a big night at the Cave Supper Club. Every woman in Vancouver, it seemed, wanted me to sign her menu card and kiss her hand, and every newsman wanted my picture with the young blonde on my arm. I had to dance, owed it to my public, but it made my back flare up so much we had to leave early. The Sunday papers were full of me.

We should have left that Sunday, I had commitments in New York, and by that time commitments were so few that I couldn't afford to ignore them. But George kept inviting people to his house, and the party just went on and on. It was the good old days all over again. The *candeladas* appeared from nowhere and I shone for them as brightly as I could manage. George's sprawling ranch house reminded me of my own up on Mulholland Drive, where I had spent the happiest, quietest time of my life, but Darling Lil had that now. She had just about everything except the *Zaca*, and at least now she would never get that. Darling Lil. I had always meant it to be an ironic handle, but now I could only say the words through gritted teeth. How had I ever fallen for her in the first place? A shipboard romance was all very well, but marriage? A few years of marriage, a lifetime of pain. She was the siren to my Ulysses and I should have tied myself to the mast, but I was starstruck, never been to Hollywood before, and she was . . . well, she just loved what she always called my biggest asset. In those days it was about my only asset, and now here I was, almost the full circle. Back to the unknown remembered gate. Darling Lil. She was older than me. I should have known. Should've known I wasn't made for marriage. Two more wives didn't teach me a thing. And how many *liaisons*? I loved that word, ever since meeting Dwight Dodd. Now I had my seventeen-year-old wood nymph with the heart as gold as her hair. I had tried to list all those liaisons for my new book, but it was impossible to remember them all, even an accurate attempt at their number. I told the publisher I would sit down with the LA phone book and make a list, but he said you could go too far, even in a tell-all memoir. A rough guess would do, he said. How about five thousand, I suggested, and he agreed that was a good round number. Even the LA Times would print that, and *Confidential* could knock it up to whatever they fancied. I wouldn't even sue them.

Five thousand women. Or perhaps four thousand women and a thousand girls, give or take. Beverly began to stir. If I worked backwards, which was certainly easier than starting from the beginning, she was probably only a couple of dozen or so from the end. I thought about calling her number 4976, but then thought better of it. I thought about saying she was one in a million, but I'd already heard what she had to say about that. Right there, right then, I wanted her to know that she was more than just one in five thousand. 'You are the greatest love of my life,' I said to her. As it slowly dawned on her, she smiled a droopy-eyed wood nymph smile. What can I tell you? Sure, a trifle exaggerated, but

I meant it when I said it. I had always meant it when I said it, my whole life. At least I always imagined I did. But what did I ever know about love? You learn about love in the cradle, don't you, so what would I know about it? All I knew then was that I had been making such a joke of myself that whole year and she had stuck by me through every embarrassing episode and, as much as I knew how, I loved her for it.

'That's sweet,' she said. 'But I don't believe you. How's your back today?'

'Awful. I'm glad we're going today. I'll get it looked at in New York. There's a good bone guy I know there.'

'Are you sure it's only your back?'

'Why honey, what else could it be?' I grinned. 'I'd like to swing by George's house, say goodbye. Say goodbye to his kids, too. They're great kids.'

'Good old Uncle Errol,' she said.

'That's one thing I regret, you know. Not spending enough time with my own. I've got four wonderful kids and I hardly see them.'

'Four that you know about, Cap'n. So is that all you regret? That's not bad, is it? Just that after fifty years.'

'No, there's two. I never learned to play piano.'

'Okay, two. Still not so much.'

'Well, Woodsie, there are many things, many many things I would do differently given my time again, but I won't be given my time again, once you're dead, you're dead, so what's the point of having a whole bunch of regrets? Maybe I haven't got time to learn the piano, but my kids I can still do something about, so regretting the past has a point, you see what I mean?'

'As long as you're happy, I'm happy.'

'Now you're the one being sweet.' Carefully I raised myself from the bed and straightened up. I had to hold my back with both hands. No chance of touching my toes this morning. Maybe after the bone guy put my spine into some sort of order. I noticed that the pain had moved around to my side as well. 'In spite of everything you may think,' I said, 'I find I actually like being myself these days. And if you ever think I'm saying that I'm not happy in my own skin, I'm acting. I'm not searching. Thirsting, of course. One has to have a good thirst.'

'I don't think you're unhappy in your skin,' she said. 'I think maybe your liver and all, they're unhappy, but I think you're having a ball.'

It was the funniest thing I ever heard her say. I laughed and it hurt to throw my head back like that. I opened the drapes and let the soft autumn light into the room. Autumn in Vancouver was like the depth of the deepest winter in LA, like nothing in Jamaica or Havana. Or the Sierra Maestra. I looked forward to my first drink of the day. This was a good time of day, wherever I was, because I always had that to look forward to. 'Vancouver,' I said, gazing over the bleak rooftops of the city and shaking my head in wonder. 'How did we ever get here?'

'By plane,' she said. 'Weren't you paying attention?'

I fixed myself a cigarette and filled my lungs. Lucky Strike, lucky streak, lucky to be alive at fifty. 'Sometimes I wonder if I've ever paid attention to where I'm going. You're right, I should be paying attention, because life's a journey, isn't it? That's what they say, don't they?'

'Who's they?'

'I don't know ... anyone worth listening to. They say it's a journey, the philosophers, the thinkers. But it's the poets who really nail it. It's like Ulysses trying to get home ... the journey is to arrive where you started, the unknown remembered gate, and find that you know it for the first time. That's what the thirst is really all about, isn't it? A thirst to understand where you come from, not where you're going. If you truly know where you come from, you can decide for yourself where you're going. Then you'd pay more attention to it. Do you think that's reasonable?'

She went into the bathroom and I heard the tinkle of water. 'Is that you, Tinkerbelle?' I said.

'That's the sound of me smiling,' she said.

'Sounds to me like the sound of you doing something else.'

'I'm smiling because I'm happy, and I'm happy because you're talking to me like I'm an adult, and not once this morning, not once in all what you just said, did you say anything about your mother.'

Funny and profound, both within a minute or two. 'Perhaps I'm closer to home than I realise,' I said, and poured myself my first drink of the day.

We had lunch with George and his wife at their ranch house on the other side of town, and I played tricks for the kids, making coins appear from their ears and crossing plastic swords with the adventures of Robin Hood around the living room chairs. George said he would drive us to the airport and we left in plenty of time. As we were crossing the Lions Gate Bridge the pain in my back became acute and I had to lie across the seat, sweat beading on my brow. Beverly said that maybe we should see a doctor, get some painkillers. It was a long flight to New York. Funny, profound, and now sensible. George said there was one nearby, a friend of his. His apartment was just on Burnaby Street and he was always there on Wednesday afternoons. They helped me into the elevator and stretched me out on a sofa. The doctor gave me a shot of Demerol and told me to lay off the drink on the plane. I thought it was a good joke and asked if there was any vodka in the house. The doctor thought *that* was the joke. He said I should stay on the couch and rest for half an hour, we had plenty of time to catch our plane, and then he said he had a couple of phone calls to make.

After he left the room I asked George to cut out the nonsense and find the vodka for me. George said he didn't think that was a good idea, but I said I would get up and stumble around for it myself if he wouldn't, and he relented. When the doctor returned I had finished my first drink. He didn't notice the bottle or the empty glass. He said a couple of friends were dropping by, Errol could say hello. Errol said that would be okay, but he would have to have a drink if they wanted him to be sociable, and that was how it all started, the famous final fling, the last hurrah of the golden years of Hollywood. The sailor's home stretch.

They came in twos and threes, arriving with eager smiles and the rustle of chiffon, and soon there were twenty people squeezed into the apartment. The doctor opened up his bar, emptied his refrigerator and put Lawrence Welk on the hi-fi, but I was obviously the feature attraction. Slowly and relentlessly I was backed into a corner of the room by a phalanx of overdressed inquisitors. I held them at bay with my Hollywood impressions of Bette Davis, WC Fields, Clark Gable. I amused them with my Hollywood stories, and of course their favourite was the John Barrymore, how some old pals had propped up his just-deceased body in my living room when I came home from the studio one night, and I had been talking to it for five minutes before sensing all was not well. 'It was only when I noticed he wasn't drinking that I realised he was dead,' I said, and they laughed and begged for the next one. Eventually, I had to stand against the wall to relieve the pain in my back. The Demerol seemed to have little effect, but as always the vodka helped. 'I don't think I'll be taking Burma single-handed again any time soon,' I said when they asked if I was all right.

They wanted to know why I had fallen out with Castro, because everyone had heard about that. '*Hush-Hush Magazine* ran a story that it was all over a girl,' said a woman wrapped in a fox fur.

'Really?' I said. 'Only one? That's not like *Hush-Hush* to play down a juicy bit of tittle-tattle. No, I'm afraid the rather dreary fact is Fidel blamed me for some bad press others gave him. He can be a touchy son-of-a-gun. Doesn't easily forgive.'

'If you ask me,' said a man with a pipe, 'all this hero worship you read in certain sections of the liberal press is just so much romantic muck. He's just another Red, am I right or am I right?'

'Well, our State Department doesn't seem to know the answer to that one,' I said, 'and I'm sure they've got people working on it all the time, so what would I know? All I know is I like him. That won't change, whether the smart young men in the State Department decide he's a Red or not. Or even their smart young women. They have some very smart young women too, you know.' And then I glanced around furtively. 'There's no FBI here, is there? Nobody's with the Economic Liaison Office, are they?'

They laughed and asked if I still saw Castro. 'Well,' I said, 'seeing as he has put a price on my head, I thought it a good idea to keep my distance.'

'Are you serious? He wants you dead?'

'That's what I'm told. I don't plan on asking him personally, if you know what I mean.'

They went a bit quiet then, until a woman in black organza said, 'Errol, would you give me an autograph for my daughter?'

'Yeah, autograph her tits,' said a loud baritone voice close to the bar, but the woman ignored him and pulled a chequebook from her handbag. She tore out the next number and offered me the back of it.

'Are you sure this is for your daughter?' I said. 'It can make a difference to what I say.'

'Oh yes ... she's fourteen.'

'Ah, you see, I can get myself into trouble there. I'd better just sign my name.'

'In that case,' the woman said shyly, 'it's for me.'

'I thought that might be the case,' I said and scribbled on her cheque. She looked at it and giggled and blushed.

'Tell us what it says,' called a man in a plaid jacket louder than the baritone.

The fellow with the pipe took hold of it and read it aloud. 'Darling, we'll always have last night, Errol Flynn,' he said, which had everyone doubled up.

'I've written that in anticipation, honey,' I said. 'You'll note I dated it tomorrow, so I've got something to look forward to.' And they howled. Beverly groaned at me – she'd heard it all too many times.

Organza woman scanned her cheque. 'He's right! Tomorrow's date!' She looked at me differently then.

They wanted to know how long I was staying in Vancouver, and I told them I was on my way to the airport. 'What's the rush?' they said.

'I've got a TV show to do in New York,' I said.

'Not *What's My Line* again,' the baritone said wearily. 'You normally get juiced up more for that one, don't you?'

'Yes, Errol,' the black organza said as she pawed my jacket. 'Why not stay a little longer?'

I considered breasting the baritone, but I didn't want to spoil the party so early. 'To tell you the truth,' I said, 'I was hoping to get a spot on the *$64,000 Question*. I could do with $64,000, then maybe I could afford to get juiced up more often. But I understand that one got cancelled, so I'm doing something called *The Big Party*, and Gypsy Rose Lee is going to be on it with me, so you'll understand when I say that, as good as this party is, I really would like to see, ah, more of Gypsy.'

When they stopped laughing a woman under a Liz Taylor bubble cut said, 'I heard you were doing a TV show about Captain Blood.'

'Yes, I heard that one, too. I don't believe it, of course. I can't see myself frigging around the rigging at my age.'

'What about movies?'

'*Assault of the Rebel Girls*,' I said. 'Watch out for it.'

'Errol's memoirs will be published soon,' Beverly said. 'He's written three books.'

'What's it called?'

'Well, I wanted to call it *In Like Me* . . .' I waited for the laughter to subside. 'But my publisher is more prosaic. *My Wicked Wicked Ways* is the latest idea.'

'Sounds like a headline in *Hush-Hush*.'

'I wouldn't know about that,' I said.

'Didn't you sue them once?'

'No, I sued *Confidential*.'

'For a small fortune, I heard.'

'Very small, unfortunately. Pyrrhic, even.'

'Say,' the baritone said loudly to Beverly, 'are you that girl, the blonde that *Hush-Hush* said he left behind in a Havana hotel?'

'Now, fellas,' I said, 'Woodsie is too young to be hearing about *Hush-Hush*. I'm told it's all homos, nymphos and negroes, and she doesn't know anything about that sort of thing, and neither do I. Now, I'm going to take a little lie down. My back is killing me. Something's killing me, anyway, and it feels right now like it might be my back. It's dark outside and we've obviously missed our plane, so I guess I'll be staying one more day after all. Don't go away . . . I'm taking you all out to dinner after I've had a rest. So . . .' I clicked my heels and saluted the room. 'Like Macarthur, I shall return.'

'How about your party trick?' the baritone called after me. 'The one where you play the piano with your John Thomas.'

'Errol regrets he can't play the piano,' Beverly said, which was good to hear, because I was told you should always leave them laughing.

I limped into my last bedroom, closed the door and lay down on the floor. Just days ago I had said that signing away the yacht wouldn't kill me, but how else would you explain what was now happening? There was a new pain in my chest and down my arm. I crawled up onto the bed and lay there in the full understanding that this would be the last bed I would ever lie in, and I was in it alone. *Alone!* For Errol Flynn it was like dying without my boots on, so I had the last laugh over Fidel after all. If only I *could* laugh. I thought about removing my shoes to make my final victory complete, but the effort was beyond me.

I wasn't hot, I wasn't cold, I wasn't shivering and shaking. It wasn't malaria this time. The pain seemed to be descending over my entire body like a shroud and my ears rang with the noise of the party in the other room. I just wanted to leave, to put the pain behind me, but I never could leave a party. I could hear Woodsie's tinkling laugh, the wise-guy's rumbling baritone, the black organza's excited babble – I could hear them all above Lawrence Welk and the muffled clink of glass and ice. Cue the music. Swell to finish. There was banging and thumping and I wondered if it was dancing or fighting. Dance to Lawrence Welk? A one and a two . . . that's not dancing. George was fighting. No, he was laughing. What was the joke now? Flynn takes Havana, that's what they were laughing at. That was the joke of the year. But Flynn takes Castro . . . that was a fact, ladies and gents. That was a $64,000 fact. I couldn't move my arms. It was all over, I was through. No more comebacks. The looks, the fame, the fortune . . . all gone. Where was the faith now I really needed it? You make your bed, you gotta lie in it, and I was lying in my last one now. Dissolve to end sequence, folks.

On the silver screen of my mind a close-up of my mother began to take shape, and then dissolve into the final montage of my life . . . oh mama, mama, mama, here I come, mother . . . out of the dark alley now, the dark wood, and in like me . . . here I am, the American correspondent . . . look out the porthole, Mama, see that moon? . . . The pain, the pain in Spain . . . don't bet on blondes, boys . . . oh no, that's my line, what's my line . . . where's the mojo, Woodsie . . . you'll never find mother that way . . . the diamonds, the diamonds, that was a close shave . . . watch out, Yulu, the croc, the croc . . . take my shoes off, please take them off, can't die with my boots on . . . ah, Renate, you're a pro, you're on the death list now, lost the game . . . all my ducks in a row . . . all in, I'm all in . . . Warner, you dead yet, Cyclops . . . tell me your life, Jack, oh shit! . . . too much too soon, Jack . . . thirsty, thirsty, thirsty, mama . . . it's fucking intoxicating, yes, it is . . . my shoes, please . . . choose a side, Fidel, you have to choose a side . . . look out for Don Juan, he's a man of good faith . . . God, what now, what now, mother . . . Flynn takes Havana . . . Flynn takes Castro . . . just five minutes, just give me five minutes, please . . . that's life, glamour boy, that's life . . . only a script . . . only a script . . . home at last . . .

And then in the blackness I saw a pinpoint of light that grew and grew. How could light be so beautiful? How could pain simply disappear? I heard the door open and saw Beverly poke her head into the room. 'How y'all doin' now, Cap'n? You been mighty hush-hush in here.'

I saw myself lying on the bed, my face blue. She looked at it and drew a sudden breath. She felt my hand. She squeezed and I wanted to squeeze her back, but I had no control over it now. She squealed like a seventeen-year-old girl. The door flew open and crashed against the wall. George, the doctor, the lot of them poured into the bedroom. The doctor felt for my pulse.

'He's dead.'

Beverly squealed again. 'No, he's sleeping . . . he's just sleeping, that's all!'

'Is he really dead?' the woman in black organza asked, and rifled through her handbag quickly to make sure her precious damned autograph was safe.

'I'm afraid so,' the doctor said.

'Hey, Doc,' the loud baritone said to him, 'your home'll be a shrine now.'

'Check the windows,' said George.

'What for?'

'For Castro's assassins. Didn't you hear what he said?'

'Don't be ridiculous. We're on the nineteenth floor.'

Beverly began to sob, squeezing my hand and stroking my blue cheek. I could see how puffy it was now. 'I think I'm pregnant, you know. I'm having his baby.'

Pregnant? I turned away from the light. I wanted to go back. She was just a kid.

'That's what they all say,' said a woman in a pencil skirt, but not so Beverly could hear.

The people up the back craned their necks for a better look. This was something, this was. This was just about the biggest thing ever in Vancouver.

Beverly's sobs grew louder and louder. George put his arm around her shoulder and I wanted it to be mine. 'He'd had enough,' he said.

'Enough?' she wailed. 'Of what?'

'Of everything. Of it all. Of all the . . .'

'Not me! Not enough of me. What do I do now? I'm gonna have his baby!'

'What do we do now?' said George. 'I'll tell you what we do now. We have a drink. That's what we do now. Get me a vodka.'

The doctor went outside and returned with a glass. George took my clammy hand and bent the fingers around it. It spilled all over the bed.

'Here, help me,' he said. 'We'll do a Barrymore. He always wanted to be Barrymore.' Two men helped him prop me up with pillows. 'Get him another drink.'

The doctor fetched the whole bottle this time. George wrapped my fingers around the glass again, steadied it, and filled it with vodka.

'How long before he's stiff?' asked someone up the back.

'The Swordsman? He's been stiff since the day he was born.'

And they laughed and they laughed and they laughed. Even Beverly, who knew the truth.

They raised their glasses. 'To the Swordsman,' George said. 'Jack Warner said he was all the heroes in one magnificent, sexy, animal package. And who are we to say otherwise?'

'The Swordsman,' they chorused. And they laughed and they drank and they partied around the bed, and they considered how they could tell this story for the rest of their lives. The party would become bigger for the newspapers, its wildness more explicit for the television, my exit more dramatic for their dinner parties. The twenty citizens of Vancouver would soon become hundreds, the hundreds who were there the day Errol Flynn played his final scene. The truth is that I simply made my exit to a soundtrack by Lawrence Welk. Exits are never as important as entrances.

George put the cigarette holder between my blue lips, but there was nothing to hold it and it tumbled down my chest and into my lap. 'Too soon, Errol,' he said. 'Too soon.'

Los Angeles, 27 December 1959

Beverly was glad it was raining. It wasn't much more than a drizzle, but it matched her mood and kept other people off the street, and when other people weren't on the street there was no one looking at her with her bloodshot eyes and his John Barrymore false nose. She hadn't slept all night and had to concentrate so she wouldn't stumble. She had just put her head down on the sofa that still smelled of him. The sofa that was all she had left of him apart from the clothes and some photos. And his survival kit. Flynn Enterprises. She doubled the coat across her chest, hunched her shoulders and slid her folded arms down to her tummy. If she had been right about the baby she'd be about four months by now and could have felt it. How wonderful that would be, to feel his child. She had cried all through his funeral. When Jack Warner said there would never be another like him, she smiled through the tears because she knew how right he was. When Dennis Morgan sang 'Home is the Sailor' she almost collapsed. Barry had to support her. Barry was good support these days.

She reached the newsstand and bought the Sunday edition of the LA Times. She wrapped the great bulk of it under her coat and trudged back home to read it on their sofa. She found the review tucked away in a corner.

CUBAN REBEL GIRLS

The producers of *Cuban Rebel Girls* cannot seem to make up their minds what to call this film.

The posters do indeed say *Cuban Rebel Girls*, but the title on the screen is *Assault of the Rebel Girls*.

One is left with the impression that perhaps the idea was to exploit the newsworthiness of the word 'Cuban'.

That is probably a good marketing ploy, because this offering needs all the help it can get.

This reviewer, however, had no such difficulty making up his mind. This film stinks.

There seems to be no point to it, except as an apology for Fidel Castro and his band of merry cutthroats who are currently painting Cuba a new shade of Red.

The credits open with the news that 'Errol Flynn presents' this strange confection, making it the dashing swashbuckler's final contribution to American cinema, and that is truly a Hollywood tragedy of . . .

The phone rang. She was going to ignore it, but it might be the press again.

'How you doing, Woodsie? We missed you last night, honey.'

'I'm sorry, Barry. I couldn't do it.'

'You're the star. A star should be at her opening night. Seen the paper yet?'

'Yes. It's not good.'

'We'll see what the others say. The politics are against us now, which is a shame. Castro's on the nose these days. Even with movie reviewers.' He waited. 'Hey, the book'll be out soon. They say it'll be a sensation.'

'Did you know he dedicated it to me? To his small companion, he . . .' She couldn't say the rest.

'That's all right, honey. You think about that. Remember what Jack Warner said . . . there'll never be another like him. That's the truth, isn't it, honey? That's the goddamn truth.'

She knew it was the truth, and that was the trouble. 'One in a million,' she said.

As she hung up, the tears came again and stung her eyes. She dragged herself up from the sofa and opened the survival kit. She poured herself a Zubrowka and passed the glass under her nose. Who said vodka had no smell? The herby aroma of bison grass and alcohol. What hurt most was not being allowed to bury him under his favourite almond tree in Jamaica, the tree with the sunlounges, where no one could see them or what they were doing. She shivered as the image of that green sea filled her head. She couldn't bury him where he always said he wanted to be buried because no one listened to her. No marriage certificate meant no rights, but she knew he loved her. He had told her so the day he died. He'd never said it before, but he said it then. Everyone has their revolution, he said. It's never too late.

Acknowledgements

This book borrowed on the talents of many people, principal among them being Jacinta di Mase and her faith, Rory McCourt and his counsel, Rebecca Sparrow and her enthusiasm, Madonna Duffy and her belief, Christina Pagliaro and her guidance, and Oola Anderson, who unstintingly gave of all the above.

And, of course, Errol Flynn. As a young boy, *My Wicked, Wicked Ways* was the first grown-up book I ever read, sneaking it from my mother's shelf whenever I had the chance. After watching all those movies on late night TV, I would have given my best cricket bat and glove to be like Errol then.

Gathering background for this story went by way of countless books, articles and scuttlebutt, some of which have been plundered, others disregarded. Certainly Fidel has been the subject of many books, even the odd wink and whisper out of Miami, but the one I found useful was *Family Portrait with Fidel* by Carlos Franqui, who was with him before and after the revolution, and was at different times both confidant and pariah of *el Gigante*. Errol's legacy is rather the reverse: his story comes to us mostly through scuttlebutt. However, two books were useful. His own, naturally – *My Wicked, Wicked Ways* – and *Errol Flynn: A Memoir* by his ghost writing accomplice, Earl Conrad. Some of the others weren't even worth reading.

Of Woodsie, the third protagonist, apart from the odd scurrilous tabloid article, not much has been written. More has been said, and perhaps, for the purposes of this story, the most eloquent is the statement by her husband of forty years as quoted in her January 2010 obituary in the *Los Angeles Times*: 'She never stopped loving Errol Flynn.'

w + Fri:
800 ov
Shrs. $180.00
70 Div

70.0 90.0
1075

Feet First:
8.00 =DB 160.00   SD=?
12.00